mystery that exposes the dark underbelly of undocumented workers in the United States and the multiple
indignities and dangers they face every day. Detective
Jimmy Vega does his best to walk the line between
being a good cop and a compassionate soul, his own
background giving him insights into the population of
Lake Holly, New York, that other officers don't—and
don't want to—have. Just when you think you know
where this powerful story is going, it takes another,
unexpected turn, bringing a conclusion that left me
stunned."
**—Maggie Barbieri**

"This timely and engrossing series opener from
Chazin introduces . . . the engaging, psychologically
complex Vega [who] must confront unwelcome
aspects of his past as his investigation builds to a
shocking conclusion."
**—*Publishers Weekly***

"Chazin's novel is one of the most genuinely phenom-
enal examples of storytelling. Full of twists and turns,
the narrative leaves readers guessing, but it also does
a brilliant job getting them invested in the characters.
The reader truly cares for them and wants them all to
avoid any kind of danger. In addition to that, the novel
also makes an affecting statement about hatred and
racism in a small town, and how the race lines drawn
in these settings can sometimes rip an entire population to pieces. It's a powerful read."
**—*RT Book Reviews***

"The intricate plot and the important social issues
combine in this strong debut of a promising series."
**—*Booklist***

Also by Suzanne Chazin

*The Fourth Angel*

*Flashover*

*Fireplay*

# Land of Careful Shadows

## SUZANNE CHAZIN

KENSINGTON BOOKS
http://www.kensingtonbooks.com

KENSINGTON BOOKS are published by

Kensington Publishing Corp.
119 West 40th Street
New York, NY 10018

All Kensington titles, imprints and distributed lines are available at
special quantity discounts for bulk purchases for sales promotion,
premiums, fund-raising, educational or institutional use. Special
book excerpts or customized printings can also be created to fit specific needs. For details, write or phone the office of the Kensington
Special Sales Manager. Attn.: Special Sales Department. Kensington Publishing Corp, 119 West 40th Street, New York, NY 10018.
Phone: 1-800-221-2647.

Kensington and the K logo Reg. U.S. Pat. & TM Off.

ISBN-13: 978-1-4967-0228-9
ISBN-10: 1-4967-0228-X
First Kensington Hardcover Edition: December 2014
First Kensington Mass Market Edition: August 2015

eISBN-13: 978-1-4967-0364-4
eISBN-10: 1-4967-0364-2
Kensington Electronic Edition: August 2015

10 9 8 7 6 5 4 3 2 1

Printed in the United States of America

*To my daughter Erica:*
*the best story of my life,*
*the one without an end.*

*They came without rancor, without thinking,*
*forming a large centipede of careful shadows,*
*surprised at being so numerous*
*at not discovering in so many faces*
*a kind smile, a pair of eyes*
*to look into, on passing, without mistrust.*

—From **Exodus**, *by Mexican poet Jaime Torres Bodet*

# Chapter 1

It was the Day-Glo orange basketball sneakers that nearly got him killed. Adidas adizeroes with EVA midsoles. A hundred dollars on sale. You could have picked him up on a satellite transmitter as he swung his legs out of the open door of his black Escalade to untie the laces.

"Stop right there, sir." The voice, full of sinew and muscle, didn't fit the freckle-faced altar boy in the police raincoat before him. "Step out of the car slowly and put your hands on the roof of your vehicle."

Jimmy Vega stopped untying the laces and pushed back his Yankees baseball cap. "Hey man, chill. I only pulled over because—"

"Sir? Get out of the car and put your hands on the roof of your vehicle."

It was the "sir" that got to him. The knife-thrust of the word. All that coiled aggression tricked out as politeness. And okay, maybe he looked suspicious in his dark hoodie, pulling up on the gravel shoulder of this wooded two-lane a few hundred yards from where the

Lake Holly cops had just found a body. But did this rookie really think he'd put it there?

"Just give me a minute to change out of my sneakers." Vega slid a hand toward his back pocket. "Hey, if it makes you feel any better—"

That's when he heard the familiar rattle of plastic. A cheesy claptrap sound, totally out of sync with the smooth piece of hardware that produced it or the fresh-from-the-academy holster that cocooned it. Vega's hand shot out of his pocket like his jeans were on fire. The cop had his Glock nine millimeter pointed inches from Vega's chest.

"Out of the car! Now! Hands on your head!"

All the blood drained from Vega's extremities. His throat constricted. His bladder muscles developed amnesia. He was almost more embarrassed at the prospect of pissing his pants than at the prospect of getting shot. How odd that this little man-made contraption could so completely unmake a man.

He laced his fingers behind his head and willed his voice to stay calm by pretending he was still undercover, still behaving like somebody he wasn't.

"Okay, officer. Relax. I'm getting out of the car. My hands are locked behind my head." He stated the obvious because he felt he needed to, felt this guy needed all his senses relaying the same information if Vega was going to walk out of this in one piece. Stupid what runs through your head at a time like this. He hadn't finished his paperwork on last night's job. He had a lottery ticket in his wallet worth twenty dollars that he hadn't collected on yet. He was no more than half a mile from his daughter's house and she had no idea he was in Lake Holly, though maybe under these circumstances, it was best she didn't know.

He tried to sidestep a puddle but it ran the length of the driver's-side door. Cold, gritty water sloshed between his toes the moment his feet hit the ground. Rain slipped under the sleeves of his hoodie when he locked his hands behind his head. A few hundred feet east, a circus of emergency vehicles beat out a blood-red rhythm against the bare trees that stood in mute witness on either side of the road.

"So you don't panic, I've got a nine millimeter in the waistband of my jeans. My badge and ID are in my back right pocket." He supposed the rookie had already surmised the first part and never considered the possibility of the second or he wouldn't be in this mess. Something burned slow and deep. He thought he was past the stage where people judged him by the color of his skin or the cast of his features. He thought his line of work insulated him from that. But now, spread-eagled across the Escalade, he wondered if all he'd really done was get better at navigating people's prejudices. When he steered himself within the bounds of their assumptions, he managed to avoid the shoals and reefs that used to cut him so unexpectedly. When he didn't—well, here was the result.

A vacuum cleaner of a voice suddenly boomed over his shoulder. "He isn't that detective the county was supposed to send by any chance? Vega? James Vega?"

The young cop's voice faltered, the testosterone wavering as it sank in. "I thought—he looked—he didn't show me any ID—"

"You wouldn't give me five freakin' minutes to change out of my sneakers," hissed Vega. He felt safe enough to turn around and face the kid now. The cop's eyes, so full of suspicion a minute ago, now looked wild with panic and bewilderment. Vega studied the wavy brown lines that ran along the sides of his orange high-tops and shook his head. Water squished out of the fabric when he shifted his feet.

"I'll take my stuff back."

The cop held out his gun, keys, and ID without meeting his gaze. Vega waited for an apology. It didn't come. Not that it would have changed anything. But still.

"I'll take it from here, Fitz." The man with the vacuum cleaner voice casually stepped into view. He was a head taller than Vega, broad as a side of beef, with the put-upon look of a cop near retirement who felt he was not near enough. He was dressed head-to-toe in white Tyvek coveralls that made him look like a giant marshmallow. He held out a fleshy hand.

"Detective Lou Greco, Lake Holly PD." The detective dropped his chin and peered at Vega over the black rims of his glasses, beaded with rain. "I see you came dressed for the occasion."

"I didn't get the part that said 'black tie.'" Vega shoved his badge and keys into his pockets and returned his gun to his waistband. "I was up all night doing a meet-and-greet between a couple of heroin dealers and a rookie undercover. I didn't have time to change." His skin still felt coated in sweat and nicotine.

Greco nodded to Vega's sneakers. "You got another pair of shoes?"

"I was trying to switch into them when your local representative from the Aryan Brotherhood stopped me."

"You should have been clearer that you were a cop. Fitzgerald sees a gun under your hoodie at a crime scene, he's going to think the worst."

"Not that he was profiling or anything."

Greco ignored the dig. In his mind at least, the situation was already behind them when in fact Vega was just feeling the recoil. His fingers were only beginning to get back sensation. His bowels and bladder still felt temperamental. The back of his head throbbed as if he'd been cold-cocked. It would be hours before the flutter in his chest died away, weeks before the memory lost its primal hold on his senses. Still, what choice did he have except to move on? He had to work with these guys. He'd had to work with guys like Fitzgerald and Greco his whole career.

It might have been easier if being a cop had been a lifelong ambition. But the truth was, it just happened. One minute, he was the reluctant holder of an accounting degree (his mother's idea), planning for the day when he'd chuck it all for the wide-open road and his steel-string guitar. The next, he was out of work and in debt with a baby on the way. The county was recruiting Spanish-speaking officers. Vega needed a steady job with medical benefits. So he traded in his six-string for a nine millimeter and told himself he was doing for his kid what his old man had never done for him. There were worse reasons to give up on your dreams.

He sat in the Escalade and peeled off his high-tops and socks, tossing them onto the floor of the passenger side where they immediately formed their own ecosystem. He shoved his bare feet into black leather work boots.

"You don't have another pair of socks?"

"Nope." He had a pair of white crime-scene coveralls and booties that would keep him dry enough, and a button-down shirt and pants for later. But he hadn't anticipated his run-in with Fitzgerald.

"Gonna have blisters tomorrow," said Greco.

"Better than bullet holes."

"True."

Vega suited up and followed Greco down a path slick with mossy rocks and acorns. Through the bare branches, Vega could see the tin-colored reservoir for which this town fifty miles north of New York City was named. Back when he was a boy, the only things you could find in Lake Holly were the fan-tailed sun perch you could catch with a cheap rod and a loaf of Wonder Bread, the snapping turtles that sunned themselves on the broad, weather-beaten rocks, and the flakes of shale that if you threw just right, you could skim halfway to Bud Point.

Now unfortunately, you could find much, much more.

She was lying in a soupy mix of dead leaves and branches that had gathered in a pocket along the shoreline. If not for the reams of yellow police tape strung like parade garland or the dozen or so officers milling about in white coveralls, Vega might have assumed he was staring at an old picnic blanket. Its pattern, once distinct, was now brackish and covered in algae.

"Dog-walker called it in around o-seven-hundred this morning," said Greco. "Female. Been in the water for at least a few weeks is my guess. No obvious trauma to the body."

"You've ruled out drowning?"

"Duh. Give us townie cops *some* credit." Greco snapped on a pair of blue latex gloves and squatted before the victim. He edged up one sleeve of her jacket. The underside of the material showed some sort of black-and-silver snowflake pattern. Beneath the sleeve, a frayed, algae-covered rope encircled her skeletal wrist.

"She's got three more just like it—one on each limb. Don't think it's a fashion statement."

"Any indications whether she was dead going into the water?"

"The medical examiner will have to rule on that. The ropes are pretty thick. Three-strand nylon. She was tied down to something. Whoever tied her wanted her to stay a spell."

"Find any ID?"

"On her? Negative," said Greco. "But we found a handbag about thirty feet up the hill with a photograph in a zippered pocket. Forensics is gonna have to figure out if it's related, but I've got a feeling it's her. She's Hispanic, in case you're wondering."

"How can you tell?" A bumpy, gray-white film covered the victim's face. Both eye sockets were empty. Only a long, thin tuft of black hair remained on the back of her head like some ancient Chinese scribe.

"We played Ricky Martin and she danced."

"Better Ricky than Dean. I'd have tied the ropes myself."

Greco grinned. Puerto Ricans versus Italians. Cops never tired of ethnic jokes.

Vega pulled on a pair of gloves and bent down to examine the victim. She was lying on her side; her body bloated to perhaps twice its normal size, yet her jaw had receded, exposing an overbite. Her clothes had begun to fall apart but the zipper on her jacket still worked. Vega opened it to reveal the remains of what appeared to be a pink buttoned-down polyester blouse over blue jeans. No jewelry, though that may have been stripped. Her ankles had decayed much faster than her sneakers. The contoured soles sported the brand name Reebok. Vega could still make out the red racing stripes along the sides.

"The sneakers made me think jogger when I first saw her," said Greco. "We had that freak warm spell early last month. But the clothes are all wrong for it."

Vega had to agree. He exercised in whatever old T-shirts and gym shorts happened to be lying around. But his ex-wife and teenage daughter seemed to have whole wardrobes devoted to getting sweaty and none of it looked like this.

Vega shielded his eyes from the rain and searched out a thirty-foot overhang on the far side of the lake. The steady April drizzle had turned the rock face black.

"Guess it's safe to say, given the time of year and the ropes on her limbs, she didn't Bud out, either."

"You know about Bud Point?" asked Greco.

"Jumped off it, actually. At seventeen." After a few cold ones, if you hit the water just right, you became a legend. If not, you became a statistic.

Greco's jaw set to one side. "So were you suicidal, shit-faced—or just plain stupid?"

"I did it to impress a girl. Though I think I inspired more pity than awe that night."

Vega could still see himself at the edge of that cliff, his hair in an embarrassing mullet, dressed in discount-store jeans his mother—the only parent at his school with an accent—bought in one of her many excursions back to their old neighborhood in the Bronx. He didn't fit in at Lake Holly High. Not with all those fair-haired kids in Top-Siders and polo shirts. So he decided to stand out in some way he'd chosen, some way that wasn't thrust on him without his consent. When that girl batted her blond lashes and told him she didn't think he was brave enough to jump, he proved her wrong. If adolescence were a permanent state, the species would die out.

Greco wiped the rain off his glasses slowly and deliberately. Vega felt the grind of gears as he did the math. "I thought the closest this town got to Hispanic culture back then was watching reruns of *I Love Lucy*."

"I guess we were what you'd call, 'the tokens.'"

"Different place now, that's for sure. Whole town's crawling with 'em."

*"Them?"*

"I'm talking illegals, Vega. Not *your* people."

He said it the way Anglos often did—like there was a chasm of difference between the two groups when to Vega, the distinctions sometimes felt as porous as the paper that divided them. Maybe that's why the words stung so much. The acid couldn't help but leak through.

"Come on, Vega. Don't get all PC on me. You drove through town this morning. You had to have seen them."

He saw them. Of course he saw them. They were huddled in groups in front of the Laundromat and under the deli awning where Vega went to fetch his coffee. Their eyes were wary beneath the soaked brims of their baseball caps. Their shoulders were hunched, whether from rain or cold or fear, he didn't know. He felt their collective intake of breath when he walked by, the way their adrenaline seemed to hitch up a notch and their voices turned soft as prayers. They were like soldiers in a war zone, bracing for everything and nothing, all in the same instant.

"Are we discussing the latest census figures? Or does this conversation have a point?"

"Got something you should take a look at on the hill."

Greco led Vega up an embankment slick with mud. On the other side of a downed tree, two county crime-scene techs Vega knew were on their hands and knees, poking around a thicket of thorny barberry bushes. Greco picked up an evidence pouch beside one of them and handed it to Vega. It contained a red shoulder bag with two buckles across identical outer pockets. The vinyl had flaked off in places, exposing a whitish backing beneath.

"You haven't found a wallet, I take it?"

"No wallet, driver's license, cash, or ID," said Greco.

"Sounds like a robbery."

"Could be. The photograph was zipped into a small pocket. I don't think the person who tossed the bag even knew it was there."

Greco handed Vega another evidence bag containing the snapshot. A square-shouldered young woman with almond-shaped eyes was sitting on a sagging beige couch with an infant girl on her lap. Both the woman and child appeared to be Hispanic. The resolution was fuzzier than Vega would have liked, as if the woman had been bouncing the child on her knee when the photographer snapped the picture. Still, Vega could make out enough details that he would have been able to identify the woman if he'd known her. Her smile revealed two prominent front teeth that were slightly bucked. Around her neck, she wore a silver-colored crucifix with tiny bird wings dangling beneath each of Christ's bound arms.

"Never saw a crucifix with wings on it before," said Greco.

Vega thought about his own much simpler crucifix that his mother had given him when he got confirmed at Our Lady of Sorrows. He'd stopped wearing it after he married Wendy. Not that she'd asked him to. It just seemed hypocritical to pretend to a faith he had no connection to anymore. Looking at this photograph, however, he felt a sudden urge to dig that crucifix out of his dresser drawer and wear it, if only for the joy it would bring his mother.

But it wouldn't. Not anymore. Funny what you remember and what you can make yourself forget.

"If the crucifix doesn't turn up in the lake, we should check the state pawn registry," said Vega. "It's distinctive enough that we might get a hit if someone tries to hock it."

"We'll have better luck tracing the crucifix than we will tracing the kid," said Greco. "Even if the photograph's only a few months old, she'll be tough to identify."

The little girl in the photo had to be no more than about five or six months old. From the tender, possessive way the young woman held the child and the comfortable ease of the baby, Vega felt certain he was staring at a mother and daughter. The little girl was wearing a bright red velvet dress with silk white bows across the front. Her crown of shiny black hair was carefully combed and held back from her face by a headband with an enormous red bow. Gold posts glimmered from her earlobes. She gave the photographer an unfocused smile that could have been the result of familiarity, or the bouncing gyrations of her mother.

The red velvet dress made Vega think the picture was taken around Christmas. He flipped the bag over to look for any markings on the photo.

"No date? No names? Nothing? This could have been taken anywhere."

"You got it," said Greco.

"At any time."

"Yep."

The baby could be a year old by now. Or she could be twenty. In the lake, two scuba divers bobbed and dove like overfed seals, looking for something no one wanted to find. If the woman in the photograph was the corpse on the shore, where was the baby?

"That's not the worst," said Greco. "There's one thing more." He picked up a third evidence bag and handed it to Vega. Inside was a single sheet of loose-leaf notebook paper that was beginning to disintegrate.

"This was found inside the main zippered compartment."

Vega brushed the rain off the bag and looked down at the handwriting. The words were printed in capital letters using black ballpoint ink that had blurred slightly from dampness and exposure to the elements. But the words—in English—were still easy enough to read:

*GO BACK TO YOUR COUNTRY. YOU DON'T
BELONG HERE.*

"Shit," said Vega.

"Shit is right. Walk with me," said Greco, handing the bagged envelope back to the techs. "We need to talk."

They walked in silence, their boots kicking up the slick leaves underfoot. Vega tugged the drawstring tighter around the hood of his coveralls to seal out the rain and fought the limp that was coming on from the blisters that were blooming, large and watery, at the back of each ankle. Voices and sounds came at him from every direction. He could hear the whoosh of water as divers broke the surface. He heard the rustle of a body bag being loaded and zipped by the lake. He listened to the static of walkie-talkies from different police agencies drowning each other out until even the occasional moment of radio silence seemed punctuated with feedback.

Greco removed his latex gloves, one inside the other, and shoved them into a bag. From a pants pocket beneath his coveralls, he produced a package of red licorice Twizzlers and held them out to Vega. Vega declined. Greco took one and shrugged.

"Used to smoke." The detective looked down at his gut. "Sometimes I think smoking was better for my health."

He yanked a piece of red licorice off with his teeth and stared out at the lake. The edges were indistinct this time of year. Runoff from the winter snows swelled the shore, drowning small saplings and birches that would normally rest on solid ground. Mud compressed around their heels, tugging at them like an insistent beggar. Above, a canopy of bare branches laced a lint-colored sky.

"Both our agencies need to sit on that letter," Greco said finally. "Far as I'm concerned, we're best off not calling this a homicide until we get a suspect. It'd be like putting a torch to gasoline, if you know what I'm saying."

"Because of Dawn and Katie Shipley," said Vega. It wasn't even a question. Everyone in the county knew about the mother and her four-year-old daughter who were struck and killed in Lake Holly on Valentine's Day by an illegal alien driving drunk without a license. For weeks now, there had been rallies and angry editorials in the local newspaper calling for more stringent laws against illegal aliens—though not, Vega noted curiously, for stricter penalties against drunk drivers, as if the man's immigration status was what killed the mother and child rather than his intoxication.

"They just set a court date for Lopez this week," said Greco. "It'll be months before he's tried—on the taxpayers' dime, no less. Who knows if they'll even deport him after he's served his sentence? Probably depends on who's hanging curtains in the White House."

"So I guess we'll blanket the media with that photo and hold back the rest."

"Yeah. If the press asks what happened to this chick, we'll just tell 'em it's under investigation."

"She's a mother," said Vega softly.

"Huh?"

"The woman. In the photograph. She's a mother. Same as Dawn Shipley." *Same as my mother,* Vega wanted to say. But he refused to offer up any more of his grief to police indifference.

"Yeah, okay, she's a mother. Whatever. I'm just saying we're best off doing this slowly and quietly, without all the ruckus you know will take place if we make this public."

"What about the baby?"

Greco surveyed the lake where the divers continued their grim search mission. One of them suddenly broke the surface, holding something over his head. It was a Velcro-strapped sneaker. Toddler-sized. The white leather had turned dark green from the water but Vega thought he could make out the round cartoon face and punchbowl haircut of Dora the Explorer on the side. Suddenly, everyone got a little quieter.

Greco cursed so softly, it sounded like a prayer. He swallowed the rest of his Twizzler and wiped a sticky hand down the side of his coveralls. Even the radios went silent. Vega saw one of the officers near the shore make the sign of the cross. Greco did the same. Vega kept his hands at his sides.

And he tried, as always, not to think about Desiree.

# Chapter 2

"You didn't tell me you were new to homicide."

Those were Greco's words of greeting as Vega settled himself at the borrowed desk of a Lake Holly detective on vacation. The town had maybe six detectives with at least two on leave at any given time. It simply wasn't equipped to handle a homicide without help from the county. That didn't mean, however, that every local cop liked having a dance partner.

"I'm not exactly a rookie, you know," said Vega. "I've been a detective for seven years and a patrol officer for eleven before that."

"Yeah, but a pal of mine over at county tells me you were working undercover until about eight months ago."

"Four commendations for doing it too. That's why they still haul my ass back on occasion like they did last night. Either way, this is hardly my first homicide."

Greco wedged himself into the only other chair in the cubicle. He had to step over a python-sized bundle of cables to do it. The Lake Holly police station was housed in an eighty-year-old building muscled out of Depression-era brick and full of half-hearted renovations that didn't quite work. There were new Andersen windows set into crumbling concrete sills, handicap-access ramps that led to areas only accessible by stairs, and enough computer wiring snaking across the perimeter of every cubicle to rival a den of hackers.

"I'm just, you know, feeling you out," said Greco. "We're gonna work together and all, I'd like to know how come the county sent you."

*Because I find kids,* Vega wanted to say. But he didn't want to talk about that case or the fact that finding them didn't always mean finding them alive. So he searched his borrowed desk for a pad and pen and scribbled a name that he handed to Greco. "That's Captain Frank Waring's direct number and e-mail. He's the commanding officer of the county detective division. You want to question his judgment, please feel free." If Greco really had a friend at county, he'd know that calling a decorated ex-Navy SEAL like Waring with such a punk question was likely to bounce a townie cop back to handing out parking tickets for the remainder of his career.

Greco folded the paper without looking at it and stuffed it into his shirt pocket. "So, what sorts of homicides have you handled?"

Vega crossed a bare ankle over the opposite thigh and picked at a blister. He was going to have to buy some socks and gauze pads if he hoped to get through the day.

"My last involved two gangbangers who got into a fight over a haircut one gave the other."

Greco chuckled. "And my barber gets mad when I don't tip enough. What'd the scumbag do? Take a little too much off the ears in retaliation?"

"I could've lived with that," said Vega. "No. He pulls out a Jennings .380 piece of crap and misses. Kills a grandmother in the next apartment, a woman who was the sole caretaker for her three grandkids who are now all in foster care."

"Figures."

"I had to convince the makeover king to cough up his dissatisfied customer in open court."

"Talk about a bad hair day."

There was a knock on the fabric partition. "Excuse me, Detectives?"

Vega broke into a sweat at the sound of that voice. A wave of shame and disgust fisted up in his chest that this freckle-faced kid could have such power over his senses. He told himself he was being ridiculous, but fear is such an unreasonable emotion. It makes you hate yourself almost more than the thing you feared.

"Do your mea culpas later, Fitz," said Greco. "We're busy here."

"I know. But I wanted to bring something to your attention." The kid kept his eyes on Greco. He seemed almost as nervous of Vega as Vega was of him. "I just took a call from a landlord in town who said his tenants skipped without paying their last month's rent."

"This is news?"

"No, sir. But I ran the tenant's name—José Ortiz— through our database to see if he had any outstanding warrants. I found a José Ortiz at that address who was cited about six weeks ago for harassment after an officer responded to a nine-one-one domestic violence call from his wife. The police report said the couple has a two-year-old daughter as well. The landlord hasn't seen any of them in several weeks. Plus, Ortiz missed his court date two weeks ago on the harassment charge."

Vega and Greco exchanged looks.

"Who was the officer on the call?" asked Greco.

"Bale. He's on vacation in Florida right now. But I pulled a copy of his report."

Fitzgerald handed Greco a copy. Greco scanned it and cursed. Then he handed it to Vega. According to Bale's notes, the complainant, a woman who gave her name as Vilma Ortiz, had bruising and swelling on the left side of her face. A man in the apartment, who said his name was José and that he was her husband, admitted to punching her in the face because he believed she had a boyfriend. On paper, it was a textbook case of domestic violence assault.

Except it wasn't—because the officer never made the arrest.

"Let me get this straight," said Vega. "Your patrol officer sees obvious evidence of physical assault, the perpetrator admits the assault, and your officer slaps him with the equivalent of a parking ticket—which he skips out on anyway? What do you have to do to get arrested for assault in Lake Holly? Put someone in intensive care?" He turned to Fitzgerald. "Or maybe it's just traffic stops that get you guys fired up."

Fitzgerald studied his feet. Greco spread his palms, all reason and beneficence. "These domestic situations usually work themselves out."

"*Work—themselves—out.*" Vega repeated the words slowly. "Far as I can see, the only workout going on here was a man using his wife as a punching bag. If Bale had arrested him like he should have, we'd have fingerprints and a positive ID. Now, we've got zip."

"Who's the landlord?" Greco asked Fitzgerald.

The officer checked his notes. "Salvatore Busta-mente."

Greco groaned. "Guy's got four broken-down build-ings in town and enough tenants packed into them to populate a small banana republic. If this county had any balls, we'd enforce the housing codes and put that asshole out of business."

"I gather you know this upstanding citizen," said Vega.

"I've been in his buildings on complaints numerous times. Even the roaches try to find other accommoda-tions."

"Sounds like you two have a history," said Vega. "Want me to talk to him?"

"Nah. He'll respond better to a fellow *paisan,* trust me. In the meantime, you should probably visit La Casa, the Latino community center, and see if anybody there can identify the photograph or tell us where Ortiz has disappeared to."

Vega grabbed his jacket to leave. Still, something about that police report bothered him. On his way out, he cornered Fitzgerald away from the detectives' bullpen. Fitzgerald tried to duck into a conference room but Vega blocked the door.

"About this morning," Fitzgerald stammered. "I didn't know—"

"Save it for the family of the guy you put in the morgue one day." He could see he was scaring the kid a little. Good. He needed scaring. "Look, you want to square things between us?"

"Yeah. Sure."

"Then tell me what happens when Lake Holly gets a domestic violence complaint."

"Nothing." Fitzgerald looked around nervously. "I mean, nothing out of the ordinary, Detective—"

"Vega's fine. Just call me Vega. How 'bout you walk me to my car?"

The kid got a panicked look in his eyes.

"You think I'd be stupid enough to assault a fellow cop in uniform?" asked Vega. "What you did to me this morning was a huge overreaction. But I'm willing to chalk it up to inexperience if you level with me now."

Outside, the rain had stopped, leaving serrated puddles that collected along the uneven blacktop. An American flag flapped crisply on the flagpole above them. Fitzgerald looked down at Vega's blistered ankles beneath his dark slacks. "You're limping."

"Gee, I wonder why."

At the Escalade, Vega turned to face Fitzgerald.

"So, you get a DV complaint. How do you determine whether or not to make an arrest?"

"Well, if the victim wants to press charges and all, we can arrest the assailant—"

"And do you? Normally?"

"Um, it depends—"

"On the victim's immigration status?"

Something in Fitzgerald's eyes retreated. "We're not allowed to ask about immigration status."

"I know that," said Vega. "But you've got an idea the moment you meet them—from their ethnicity, where they live, how willing they are to give you their full names—"

"That's profiling. We're not allowed—"

"Cut the police academy bullshit, Fitzgerald. What

do you think you did to me? You know as well as I do that every cop sizes up the people he comes into contact with even if he doesn't admit it. All I want to know is why Bale didn't arrest José Ortiz for beating the crap out of his wife. Was Bale lazy? Does he believe domestic violence is a personal matter? Or is there some unwritten rule in town that frowns on making DV arrests when the parties involved are suspected illegals?"

*Bingo.* Vega read his hunch in the young man's eyes.

"It's—it's sort of discouraged. With complainants we suspect are—undocumented. On account of—then the victims have like, you know—special victim status—"

"They're eligible for U visas," said Vega.

"Yeah." Fitzgerald kicked at a puddle. "I mean, I personally don't have a problem with a crime victim petitioning the government for permission to stay in this country legally. And maybe it really would be dangerous for a woman like Vilma Ortiz to go back with her husband to her own country. But there's a feeling in Lake Holly that letting undocumented women file for U visas because their husbands or boyfriends hit them is—sort of—"

"A way to con the system into supplying green cards to illegals."

"Yeah."

Better black and blue than green seemed to be the sentiment in Lake Holly. Vega sighed. "Okay, Fitz. We're even now."

The rookie didn't seem so sure. He looked back at the building. "I hope I didn't just screw myself out of a job. How's it going to look if Vilma Ortiz ends up being the body in the reservoir and I just drew a big fat bull's-eye on the department for allowing her husband to put her there?"

"Could've been the boyfriend, don't forget."

"Fat chance of him ever coming forward."

"Oh, he'll come forward," said Vega. "I'm going to find him and send him an invitation."

# Chapter 3

The man sat with his back against the cinder-block wall, feeling the clammy embrace of his rain-soaked hoodie. It was freezing in the center. He blew on his hands and rubbed them together. Today of all days, he needed his fingers to work. He couldn't go on much longer like this.

He tried to open the brown paper bag from the hardware store without disturbing the English class going on in the middle of the room. Ten men in baggy dungarees and well-worn baseball caps were wedged into student desks in a semicircle. A gray-haired white lady in a long, shapeless sweater stood before them, drawing something on a chalkboard. A scaffold and a noose. The man wondered what aspect of North American customs she could possibly be illustrating. Not exactly *Welcome to the United States!* But then, he knew that already.

He had traveled under a name that wasn't his to a land where he didn't speak the language. This was his second trip across the border and each time had altered some fundamental aspect of his character, changed just a little the limits of what he was capable of—for better or for worse. It was a necessary part of the journey. The first rule. To get here, every person had to be willing to break a law of man or God, to abandon the notion that he was above reproach. Some would do it only once. But once broken, it was easier to sin again. Rodrigo wished that wasn't true. But he knew only too well, it was.

He asked his friend Enrique what the noose on the chalkboard was for.

"It's hangman, *güey*. Haven't you seen them play hangman here before?"

Rodrigo shook his head. Enrique explained the game while Rodrigo pulled out his purchase from the hardware store. A package of glue. The glue had cost $2.32— more, he was sure, than it would have cost in a big store on the highway. But he had no way to get to the highway. He didn't even own a bicycle. And his right work boot needed fixing. The leather had separated from the rubber sole. When he walked, it flopped about like a dying fish. He suspected the glue wouldn't fix the boot but he saw no alternative. Without the boot, he couldn't work. Without work, he couldn't buy new boots.

He was pressing the leather upper hard against the glue on the rubber sole when Enrique's cousin Anibal walked up to them. Anibal stared at the shoe a moment, then pulled a piece of string from one of his pockets and handed it to Rodrigo.

"Here. Tie this around your boot. Maybe this will hold it together until the glue dries."

"Many thanks." Rodrigo was glad of Anibal's and Enrique's company today. Both men were from his hometown in Guatemala and he knew them well. Anibal was a year older than Rodrigo, dark and quiet with a broad mustache that hid his mouth and eyes that turned into slits when he smiled.

Enrique was five years younger than Rodrigo and the opposite of his cousin in every way. As a boy, he could never sit still. He used to tape mirrors to the tops of his feet so he could look up girls' dresses. He put chili powder in the priest's wine during communion. People used to say he moved like he had crickets in his underwear. He had a little sister, Sucely, who once fell into the river when Enrique was supposed to be watching her. Rodrigo swam out and rescued her in the swift-moving current. It was one of many bonds that tied them together and made them look out for one another.

Anibal smoothed his thumb and forefinger down each side of his mustache, something he always did before he delivered bad news.

"The heat won't be fixed for a while, unfortunately. The repairman won't be here for at least another hour."

"*Ay, chimado!*" Enrique cursed. Anibal gave his younger cousin a disapproving look. He was a deeply religious man who didn't use bad language when there were women present—whether they understood or not. Rodrigo respected him for it—wished he could retain so much of his honor. He'd vowed many things before he left Esperanza seven months ago and he'd already broken the most important one.

"I put our names in the job lottery at least," said Anibal.

Rodrigo looked over at the front entrance. On a wobbly card table sat a canister full of numbered Ping-Pong balls. Above the canister, a dry-erase board noted the numbers and corresponding first names of the men hoping their number might get pulled if someone came in looking for day laborers.

"Have any employers come in today?" asked Rodrigo.

Anibal shook his head. "Not yesterday, either. The economy is still not good." Rodrigo finished knotting the string firmly around his work boot. It pained him that he'd had to borrow from Anibal to buy the glue. On his first journey to the United States, he'd been able to earn enough to build his family a house in Guatemala with concrete walls, a sturdy tile roof, and an indoor toilet. He'd done nothing he was proud of on this journey—and a whole lot he wasn't.

Anibal read the worry in Rodrigo's eyes. He patted his friend on the shoulder.

"Things will get better once the weather warms up. It's still only early April." The top joints of the last three fingers on Anibal's left hand were missing, the result of a printing factory accident in Guatemala. When potential employers came around, Anibal always kept his hands in gloves lest they cost him a job.

The men were quietly talking among themselves when they suddenly noticed a palpable buzzing in the room, a nervous rush of energy Rodrigo hadn't felt so strongly since Arizona where every *cholero* in a uniform made him go cold inside, made his knees shake and his throat turn to sand. And then he understood: there was a police officer in the community center. He wasn't dressed in a police uniform and he was Spanish-looking. But the consensus seemed to be that he was one just the same, mainly because he carried himself with the sort of stiff authority they all seemed to have, from Central America, to Mexico, to the United States. Plus, there was a bulge underneath his jacket. A gun.

He was standing near the front door, just outside the glassed-in front office where the director of the center and two other employees were. There was no room for a fourth person in the tiny office so he stood in the doorway with an air of impatience, rattling a big envelope in his hands.

"What do you think he wants?" Rodrigo asked Enrique softly.

"What does every police officer want? To arrest somebody. Relax, *güey*. It has nothing to do with us."

"It's about a woman," said Anibal, who had managed to overhear a little of the conversation.

"It's always about a woman," said Enrique. "All of life is—when you come right down to it." He tapped his foot restlessly and slid his eyes in the direction of the center's director, Adele Figueroa. *Cajeta,* the men at the center called her, after a type of Mexican caramel sauce. Enrique had a crush on her. They all did. But Enrique especially. Sometimes he came to the center just to watch the soft swing of her hips, the roundness of her buttocks, the way her blouses cleaved like question marks to the contours of her body. Rodrigo could never understand why Anglos seemed to prefer women whose bodies were all sinew and gristle and sharp edges. Maybe deep down, they were afraid of sex. Maybe that's why women dressed like men here.

The officer slapped a stack of flyers on the wobbly card table by the front entrance and followed Adele Figueroa to her office at the back of the building. Rodrigo wanted to watch the graceful slide of her hips, but his gaze was transfixed on the table, at the flyer with a photograph of a mother and child. The mother wore a silver crucifix around her neck. It was partially obscured by the baby's red bow but Rodrigo knew it well. He had brushed his hand against it many times. On each side of Christ's outstretched arms, small bird wings dangled. *Milagros*. Catholics in his homeland put *milagros* next to statues of patron saints or crosses to plead for divine intervention. He had seen symbols of body parts—hands and legs. He had seen animals and wings and likenesses of saints. All pleas for God to mend an ailment, alter a fate, answer a prayer. The words across the flyer were written in Spanish and English: DO YOU KNOW THIS WOMAN OR CHILD? At the bottom was a phone number to contact with information.

Rodrigo's heart compressed against his ribs. He knew what the flyer meant. He didn't have to be told. So much for her prayers and *milagros*. Why was it that God seemed to favor least the ones who counted on him most?

They would come after him. He was sure of it. He was trapped as surely as he had been at the Arizona border when the helicopters hovered overhead and he'd had to throw himself under cactuses and mesquites to escape. Run and hide. Run and hide. That's all he knew anymore.

"Are you okay?" asked Anibal. "You don't look well."

"I need to leave."

"But the glue on your boot hasn't dried."

"It's good enough. I have to go." Maybe they didn't know yet, but at some point they would. There weren't enough *milagros* in the world that could save him from that. He was going to have to pay for his mistakes. In the end, God makes everyone pay for his mistakes.

# Chapter 4

Adele Figueroa traced a finger across the face of the woman on the missing person's flyer. A sweet face, absent of guile, with something pleasing and expectant in the pucker of flesh beneath her eyes, the way her full lips revealed her gums when she smiled. Adele wished she could have identified the woman or the baby for the detective, but she didn't recognize them. Neither did her two volunteers who were also sitting in this cramped, freezing office, trying to hold down the fort until the heating repairman arrived.

"I'll be sure to put up the flyer and let you know if anyone comes forward," Adele told the detective.

"Thanks." James Vega was his name. His business card said he was with the county police. His dark good looks gave him away as Latino but he seemed nervously out of place standing in the doorway of the front office. His large moody eyes scanned the room like he was half-expecting to find someone from the FBI's Most Wanted list playing a game of hangman. He was about as far removed from Adele's sense of Latino as a Taco Bell burrito. She was anxious for him to leave so her clients could calm down. His presence was like a yellow jacket in a bus full of preschoolers.

He stayed in the doorway, rattling his manila envelope of flyers. "How about José Ortiz? Have you seen him recently? He's got a wife, Vilma, and a two-year-old daughter."

"No."

" 'No,' you haven't seen him? Or 'no' you don't know him?" He spoke like a man who was used to getting his questions answered. She refused to be cowed.

"I know who he is. I haven't seen him in awhile. And I've never met his wife or daughter." She stood up, hoping he would take the cue to leave. But cops were like bad houseguests. Once you invited them in, they never left of their own accord.

"He have friends or family in town? Someone who'd know where he's disappeared to? He skipped out on his last known address."

"Can I ask what this is concerning?"

"I'm following up on a domestic violence complaint."

She resisted the urge to roll her eyes. "Come now, Detective. You're not here for that."

He looked taken aback. "So you think domestic violence is no big deal?"

"I think it's a very big deal," said Adele evenly. "My center runs a support group for victims and a hotline in Spanish. But the Lake Holly Police Department doesn't seem to share my sentiment—at least not when it comes to my clients. So let's not pretend that's why you want to speak to José Ortiz."

"Huh." He rubbed the back of his hand along his chin, weighing the situation, weighing her.

"I'm not being coy, Detective. I honestly don't know where he is. But I will ask around."

"Okay then."

Adele moved toward the doorway, hoping to encourage him to leave. But instead, he turned away from her and scanned the big room beyond the glass cubicle as if he were sizing it up for a stakeout.

"You've got a lot of security cameras on this building. Front and back exits and the parking lot as well. Had a problem?"

"An incident last month. Someone set a fire in our Dumpster and spray-painted some disparaging language across our parking lot."

A muscle twitched in the folds of those moody eyes. "Did the Lake Holly PD do an investigation?"

"We didn't have the cameras up at the time. We got them as a result of the incident so there was no video footage. No witnesses have come forward. No arrests have been made."

"You said, 'disparaging language.' What did they spray-paint?"

Adele glanced at the two dozen or so men in the room beyond the cubicle. "Is this necessary?"

"I'm afraid it is."

Not here. Not within spitting distance of all these terrified immigrants. "My office. In back." She turned to one of her volunteers sitting at the computer. "Kay, do me a favor? When the repairman comes, get me?"

"Sure thing, Adele."

She tied a wool shawl around her that a client from Peru had given her and led Vega through a back room with bright yellow cinder-block walls and a scattering of pool tables. There were men everywhere—playing pool, talking in groups. All of them had their jackets and hoodies on. Adele hoped the repairman would hurry up and get here so she could go home and warm up. She was supposed to be off on Sundays. She had to help Sophia with her diorama. Her third-grade class was studying Native Americans and Sophia's teacher insisted the children make their Indian longhouses using only natural materials. Sophia ended up in tears last night because Adele had constructed the frame out of cardboard instead of twigs from the garden. Where her clients were concerned, Adele could do no wrong. Where her daughter was concerned, she could do no right.

"Your heating system's broken?" asked Vega.

"Thermostat's acting up."

He scanned the room. "You'd think they'd all go home. It's cold enough."

"Home is a corner of a crowded attic or basement. No matter how cold it gets here, this is better."

She opened the door of her office, another glassed-in fishbowl, this one containing just one battered gun-metal gray desk. Behind it was a colorful display of Latin American folk art. There was a weaving of women balancing baskets of corn on their heads beside an acid-green mountain and a painting of a sunny marketplace overflowing with tropical fruit. Vega nodded to the art-work.

"I'll bet it doesn't look like that or they wouldn't all be here."

"In their dreams it does. Doesn't Puerto Rico look like that to you?"

She caught something defensive in the set of his jaw. He didn't like being sized up, even if he did it all the time to others.

"How do you know I'm Puerto Rican?"

Actually, Nuyorican if she had to guess. The Bronx accent in English, probably in Spanish as well. That streak of arrogance. There was something about the way he carried himself that told her he didn't really comprehend her clients' fear or desperation. There was no history there—at least not in the same way.

"I was under the impression most Spanish-speaking police officers in New York were. Though usually Puerto Ricans are like Texans. They have to tell you they are right away."

"Do most Harvard lawyers generalize as much as you do? Or only the Ecuadorian ones?"

That stopped her. "How—?"

"—Your degree's on the wall behind you, and I figured you wouldn't have the Ecuadorian flag on your desk if you weren't."

"The flag is in memory of my parents," said Adele. "They were from Ecuador and I feel a strong connection. However, I was born here."

"Well I was born in the Bronx."

"So you don't think of yourself as Puerto Rican?"

He hesitated. "We're not talking about me, Ms. Figueroa."

She'd hit a nerve. Why, she wondered? She thought all Latinos felt a connection to their heritage. A flower cannot survive long when cut from its stem.

She closed her office door and took a seat behind her desk. Vega settled himself in the only other chair in the room. She steepled her fingers under her chin and willed her voice to stay cool and professional.

"Go home fucking beaners. You don't belong here."

"Excuse me?"

"That's what was spray-painted on the parking lot."

"Oh. Gotcha." He took a pen and notebook out of a pocket in his dark blue Windbreaker. "Those were the exact words?"

"You think I'd forget them?"

"How many people saw it?"

"Hard to say. Maybe upward of a hundred people including all the sanitation workers and auto body mechanics who work on the street. Not to mention all the contractors and volunteers and clients at the center. It took maybe three or four days before we were able to scrub off most of it. We've since repaved because it never came off entirely. May I ask why this interests you so much?"

"I'm curious, is all." He smiled and held it a moment too long, like he was posing for a picture with someone he tolerated rather than liked. One of his eyeteeth was crooked. She hadn't noticed that when his smile was genuine.

"You had a hate crime at your center," said Vega. "And yet, far as I know, it never made the news. Seems to me you'd be screaming for blood, if not with the local PD, then with some immigrant rights group. It's not like you don't know your way around a courtroom. So what gives, Ms. Figueroa? What aren't you telling me?"

*Stuff a lot worse than a few spray-painted words in a parking lot,* thought Adele. But what was the point of opening up to a cop? This guy wasn't her clients' friend. Both sides knew that. The fastest way to lose the good will—and funding—she'd built up in the community was to turn La Casa into a lightning rod for suburban intolerance. She could kiss off her roving medical and dental clinic after that. And her after-school tutoring program and a host of other needed social services. Besides, this cop wouldn't even be here if he weren't fishing for something. And then it hit her.

"That woman on the flyer—she didn't just *die,* did she, Detective? She was murdered. And for some reason you're not sharing, you think it might be a hate crime that José Ortiz is mixed up in, in some way."

Vega's face lost all expression and his eyes turned dark and flat. "The case is still under investigation."

"Right. And you wonder why the Latino community doesn't trust the police."

"Oh, so *you're* the Latino community and *I'm* the police?" He got a bemused expression. "I hate to break this to you, but you've probably got about as much in common with these people as I do."

"You're not trying to help them," said Adele. "I am."

"I *am* trying to help them. I'm trying to find the identity of a dead mother so her family can put her to rest in her own country. I'm trying to find a coward who used his wife as a punching bag. What are you doing? Giving them a place to shoot pool?"

That did it. Her temper was up. "You spend five minutes at La Casa, you think you understand the Latino community in Lake Holly? You don't have a clue. Things get reported. Police investigations get done. We just handle it differently. That's how come we're still here. After everything that's happened, we're still here."

Vega sat up a little straighter. "Everything? What *everything?*"

"We've had some—incidents. I see no point in stirring the pot right now."

"I see." Vega rose and walked over to her bookshelf. He picked up a trophy, dusty with age, the gold plating chipped in places.

"You fenced?"

"When I was a teenager."

"I thought fencing was for the country-club set. Right up there with polo and crashing Daddy's Mercedes into the swimming pool."

He had a poor boy's longing disguised as contempt. "There was a YMCA near our apartment," Adele explained. "I showed talent, I guess. My parents certainly couldn't have afforded it otherwise."

He returned the trophy to the shelf and bit back a grin. "A Latina lawyer who's good with a sword. Now that's a combination every man's gotta fear." His liquid eyes settled on hers a beat too long. "Except me. I like a challenge."

He had her. He knew it, too. That was the worst part about Latino men: they knew how to seduce. In college, she'd stayed clear of all that heat and heartbreak. Married a safe, sensible Anglo. Divorced him too. Maybe there was a connection.

She turned away from Vega and offered up a slow exhale she hadn't even known she'd been holding in. She opened a file on her computer and printed out two names. Then she handed him the sheet of paper as if nothing had passed between them.

"What's this?"

"Scott and Linda Porter. Two people you should speak

to. Scott's an immigration and criminal defense attorney in town. He's also chairman of the board here at La Casa."

"His name's *Scott Porter,* and he chairs La Casa?"

"He's not Latino, no," Adele admitted. "But no one's more committed to helping the undocumented. You should speak to his wife, Linda, as well. She handles most of our initial interviews with clients. If the woman you're trying to identify ever set foot in Lake Holly, chances are, Scott or Linda knew her. They might know where José Ortiz is too. If he's had run-ins with the police, he's probably spoken to Scott at some point. "

Kay knocked on Adele's door to tell her the heating repairman had arrived.

"I've got to handle this," said Adele, rising from her seat.

"Sure thing." Vega shook her hand.

"I'm sure your intentions are well placed, Detective. But I have a center full of living, breathing clients to worry about and you have only one dead woman and a child who may or may not be missing. Do your investigation, by all means. But please keep in mind that the needs of the living must trump the dead."

"I don't see why one should affect the other."

"You will. Trust me."

# Chapter 5

Vega didn't call the Porters to tell them he was dropping by. He always found people to be more candid when he caught them off-guard.

It was only a ten-minute drive from La Casa to their house, but the scenery changed rapidly. In town, the houses were bunched together like cereal boxes, delineated only by their rickrack rooflines and chain-link fences. Out of town, the houses became more affluent and the land turned pastoral, rising sharply until all that surrounded Vega were vistas of skeletal trees and the remnants of old stone walls. In a couple of weeks, the magnolias and dogwoods would leaf out and soften the landscape; the forsythia would unfold its yellow tendrils like a blonde letting down her hair. But for now, everything had a washed-out and sorry feel from too much rain and salt and snow.

Vega drove along Lake Holly Road, past the reservoir. Yellow crime-scene tape still blocked the entrance. He tapped his horn and raised a hand to a Lake Holly patrolman in a town cruiser who'd been stationed there. The divers hadn't found any evidence of a child in the water so far, though that toddler's sneaker gave them all pause. Greco said no news was good news. Vega hoped he was right.

Farther up on the left, Vega saw the familiar field-stone pillars of The Farms. He almost turned in, he was so used to driving there, rolling up his ex-wife Wendy's long, Belgian-block-lined driveway, rapping on the side door of the big white Georgian colonial, chatting up Rosa, the maid, in Spanish like he was the gardener asking for a glass of water, then waiting awkwardly outside for his daughter, Joy, to come sauntering out. He and Wendy were two completely different people now, if they had ever indeed been the same to begin with.

A quarter mile east, Vega came to a wooded road of homes made of cedar shingles and walls of glass. The area felt more natural than The Farms, though no less lavish. He matched Scott Porter's address to the number on a rusted green mailbox, then snaked his way up a steep driveway. He was thankful he wasn't doing this in January. Even now, with no chance of frost, he felt a certain give to the tires as they hugged the edges of the uneven blacktop that crumbled into dust and ravines on either side. It constantly amazed Vega that people who lived in expensive houses often had the most sorry-looking mailboxes on the most inaccessible roads. It was some sort of reverse snobbery he couldn't quite figure out.

At the top of the driveway, the land leveled out before a large white house with shutters the color of guava paste. It was supposed to be a colonial, but the dimensions were all wrong. The front porch was too narrow, the windows too large with too many partitions. There was a cupola on the roof that looked added and the siding was some sort of recycled material that didn't hold paint well. Still, it was huge and clearly expensive.

In the backyard, there was a giant redwood swing set and an enclosed trampoline. On the driveway, there was a freestanding backboard and hoop. A regulation-sized soccer net leaned against the stacked outdoor furniture on the patio. The Porters had kids—indulged kids. He wondered if the family was home. Both bays of the garage were open. One car was missing but the other had a black Acura RL parked in it. Vega felt a thud of longing for his own black Acura TSX, the purr of the engine, the way it zipped around corners. Not since his old Firebird had he loved a car that much. But he was tempting fate to even think about that car. Not when Joy was safe. Cars could be replaced.

Vega grabbed a flyer from a stack in his car and got out. When he turned around, he saw right away why the Porters had bought this house. The view was amazing. From their driveway, Vega could see all the way down into Lake Holly to the gray granite spires of Our Lady of Sorrows. He could hear the lonely peal of a train whistle as it left the station, the spray of wet tires on Lake Holly Road, and the muted airlock hiss of a car door slamming in some driveway far below. All the noises that fought for attention down there were distilled into something pure and harmonious up here.

He dodged puddles on the driveway and trudged up the steep risers of the front porch that he suspected were never used. He rang the doorbell. A dog barked from within. It sounded like a friendly enough bark, but just in case, he stepped back as the door opened. A woman pulled on the collar of an eager golden retriever.

"Down, Mango. Down, girl." The woman was crouched with the force of the dog but she lifted her chin to take in the stranger at her door. Vega's eyes met hers and he felt like an M-80 had exploded in the doorway, throwing him backward, nearly knocking him off that too-narrow front porch. In those few seconds, he took the whole of her in: the comma shape of her jaw unaltered by age, the fluid way she tossed her ponytail, once blond, now faded to the color of fresh-cut lumber, the dancer's legs that still managed to go from crouching to standing in the time it took him to catch his breath.

*Linda. Not that Linda.*

"Jimmy?" A small crease appeared in the center of her forehead as if she couldn't decide whether she was glad to see him. He stuffed the flyer into his back pocket and stood there awkwardly, trying to summon the words that would have flowed so effortlessly all those years ago. She was supposed to be living in the Midwest somewhere—an alternate universe alive only in his dreams. Not here.

Not here.

The dog lost interest in the encounter and scampered off behind the door, her tags jingling until they faded away into another room, tinkling against her water dish. Linda stuffed her long fingers into the back pockets of her jeans the way she used to at seventeen as if they were scarf ends she might lose if she left them hanging. *Linda Porter. Linda Kendall Porter.* He wished he'd known the "Kendall" part before he found himself on her front doorstep. He couldn't talk to her as a cop. He couldn't talk to her at all.

"It's so amazing to see you." She stepped forward and hugged him, planting a kiss on his cheek.

A kindness, he knew. Much nicer than "what are you doing here?"

"I'm sorry, Linda. I didn't mean to barge in like this. I came to talk to you and your husband, Scott. Except, I didn't know it was you. I mean—I was looking for Linda Porter. Adele Figueroa sent me." He was stumbling all over his words. He wished someone could have warned him. Just standing in her doorway, taking her in gave him the same sensation as eating ice cream too fast—that burst of something foreign and physical on the brain, that sense that your body can betray you when you least expect it. If she dared him to jump off Bud Point again, at this moment, he just might do it.

He took in her features the way he couldn't at first. She had always had an aristocratic face—not beautiful by traditional standards. Too much nose. Her eyes too small and pale a blue to stand out. Yet she had aged well, not like many natural blondes who grow pinched and waxy when the rosiness of youth begins to fade. Age had stripped her to her essentials and made her striking. Even in the simple V-neck sweater she was wearing, she would turn heads.

She hooked an arm in his and led him inside her front hallway as if his coming were something she'd been looking forward to all day. She had always possessed the casual ease of the privileged. It's what drew Vega to her and scared him at the same time. He could never be that comfortable in his skin.

The house looked much better inside than out. From the double-height entryway, Vega could see a living room off to his right with a Persian rug and leather couches, and a formal dining room to his left with a pot of pink orchids on the center of the table. His boots were still muddy from the lake this morning and he felt embarrassed standing on her high-gloss red oak floors.

"This is sort of a shock for both of us," he said. "I'm here on the job." He fumbled for his badge. "I'm a detective with the county PD."

"Really?"

"Really really. I'm here on an investigation."

"Wow. I never thought *you'd* become a cop."

Her words pricked some delicate membrane inside of him. He felt himself deflate with the slow unalterable physics of a balloon.

"I'm sorry, Jimmy. That came out wrong. I just assumed after—"

"Hey, if you can't beat 'em, join 'em, right?" He said the words too brightly, hoping to put a period on that chapter in his life, to close it once and for all.

"Come, let me hang up your jacket. Scott took our daughter to get new soccer cleats. They should be back any moment. You want something to drink?"

"Coffee, if you have it, would be fine. Black with sugar."

"Let me make a fresh pot."

Vega followed Linda through the dining room into a large family room and kitchen all rolled into one. The kitchen was done in high-end cherrywood. The countertops were granite, the appliances, Sub-Zero. The Porters were doing well. He took a seat at the counter. The dog rubbed up against Vega's leg and he gave her a pat, wishing he had more time for a dog in his own life. Joy had always wanted a dog. Wendy was allergic to them.

"So you want to tell me why you're here? Or are you just going to handcuff us when Scott gets back? Not that I mind the handcuff part." She grinned and her smile was better than ever on her raw-boned face, full of shadows and planes that caught and swallowed the light.

Vega laughed. "I don't even keep cuffs on me. They're in the car. But don't worry. You're safe. All I want to do is ask you some questions."

"That's how it always starts, doesn't it? In the TV shows."

"It's a lot more tedious and full of paperwork in real life."

Linda undid her ponytail and refastened the rubber band twice around her hair to put it back exactly as it had been before. Vega always marveled at women and their hair, how they could play with it, restyle it, brush it, all without missing a beat in their conversations. If he talked while he shaved, he cut himself.

She went over to her kitchen cabinets and began opening them with the manic force of a TV chef, all the time keeping up a running commentary about how messy the house was when it wasn't messy at all. He'd forgotten that when she was nervous, she babbled. When he was nervous, he clammed up, instead studying the photographs on some bookshelves that flanked the flat-screen television. Between clay turtles and uneven pinch pots sat a row of photographs. Linda in various sundresses and tank tops standing next to a wiry man with thinning blond hair and gold-rimmed glasses. Scott, no doubt. Vega wanted to feel the neutral emotions he would have felt if he were looking at a photo of a friend and his wife. He knew it was childish to feel anything after so many years.

"You stay in touch with anyone from the old days?" asked Linda.

"Not a period in my life I'm dying to relive."

"Oh, right." There was an awkward pause. Even Linda seemed at a loss for words.

"You?"

"A few. Megan Cartwright and Ann McKinley— who was Ann Lesser and then Ann Rothstein and then went back to her maiden name after her second divorce—"

"You see Bobby at all?" Vega wanted the question to flow, but Bobby Rowland's name could never flow between them.

"On occasion," Linda said slowly. "He still owns his dad's old hardware store downtown. I'm in there quite a bit. He's also the chief of our volunteer fire department." Linda stopped pulling out dishes and looked at him. "You know about his younger son, right?"

"I went to the funeral Mass." Vega nodded sadly. "When was it? Three years ago?"

"Just about."

Vega wondered if she'd been there too. He hadn't seen her but there were so many people and he was in and out quickly, cowed by the cavernous space that was filled with so much memory and grief. Before that, it had been more than twenty years since he and Bobby had spoken.

"I gather you've forgiven him," said Linda.

"Water under the bridge. Sorta pales beside losing your fourteen-year-old to cancer, you know?"

"And how about me? Do you forgive me?"

He turned to the bookcase and scanned the shelves. "Where are your kids' pictures?"

"You're looking straight at my one and only."

The only photograph Vega could see was a school picture of a caramel-skinned girl with onyx eyes. Her sleek black hair was long and parted on the side and her gaze had a sort of womanly awareness to it. Vega guessed her age to be nine or ten.

"This is your daughter?" He lifted the frame.

"Our Olivia, yes," said Linda. "She's Guatemalan." The loveliness of her daughter's face leeched all the nervous energy out of her. She seemed to finally exhale. "Scott and I spent two years with the Peace Corps there. That's how we met. We'd planned on having a big family but it didn't work out so we adopted Olivia instead."

"Is that where you picked up your Spanish?" She didn't study it in high school. Her family had insisted she take French. Ironically, that's where they met—in Madame Driscoll's French class. Vega bet neither of them could so much as order a meal in a French restaurant anymore.

"I learned more than Spanish in Guatemala," said Linda. "Being with the people—it changed our lives, gave us a calling of sorts. Not that Scott doesn't do standard criminal defense work as well. That's what pays the bills. But Latin-American issues are our passion."

"Huh. I thought I was the beginning and end of your Latin-American issues."

"You never thought of yourself as Latin-American."

"*You* did."

"That was my parents, Jimmy. That was never me.

And they've changed, like everyone else. They love Olivia so much, how could they not?"

The coffee was finally ready and she poured him a mug at the counter. She rustled up some Oreos, apologizing for not having anything better. She was about to launch into a conversation about the weather or some other inane drivel, when Vega reached over and touched her hand.

"Linda, it's fine. Relax. It's only me, okay?"

She sighed. "I'm sorry. It was just—such a surprise."

"Bad surprise?"

She stirred her coffee. Vega thought he saw some color come to her cheeks. "No. Good. All good." Her eyes, pale as dawn, registered approval. Twenty-five years later, and he still sought her approval.

"What about you, Jimmy?"

"What about me, what?"

"Are you married? Do you have kids?"

"Divorced. One daughter." He put the mug to his lips and took a sip. "She'll be graduating high school in two months. She's starting at Amherst in the fall on a pre-med scholarship." He wasn't sure why he added the stuff about Amherst and the pre-med scholarship. He supposed it was because Linda's family always looked down on him. He couldn't help feeling like his daughter's achievements were a vindication of sorts.

"You must be so proud."

He was. Sometimes he had to catch himself. He could become a bore about his daughter, telling everyone he knew about how she'd been selected to assist on a research project at Lake Holly Hospital, studying the efficacy of dietary education on low-income pregnant women. He didn't think he'd ever used the word "efficacy" in his life before Joy began working with Dr. Feldman. Now, he trotted out the phrase at least once a day.

"And your mom?" asked Linda. "How's she doing?"

He raised his mug to his lips but it just hung there. He felt the steam rising off of it, condensing on his face, as if even the coffee was crying for her.

"She died last April."

"Oh Jimmy, I'm so sorry. Was she sick?"

"No. She was murdered. In a botched robbery." His voice felt rubbed raw. He struggled with the pitch.

"Oh my God. Here?"

"In the Bronx. She moved back several years ago. She said she was happier down there near all her friends." He blamed himself for the move. If only he'd managed to hold his marriage together. Maybe he could have stayed in Lake Holly instead of having to move farther upstate. Maybe she'd have stayed nearby. So many maybes.

"You were close to her, I remember."

"Yeah." Talking about family had always been a sore point for him. Growing up, there was always the "what happened to your father?" And how do you answer that? How do you say he just up and left and not get those pitying, judgmental gazes?

It wasn't like his father really went anywhere. He wasn't in jail, wasn't a drunk or on drugs, despite what Anglos always assumed. He was a bass guitarist for a Dominican meringue band that played the Latin bars in the Bronx and Washington Heights in Manhattan. Sometimes, when Vega was little, he'd see him at Manny's Bodega on East Tremont Avenue, a ropy, good-looking man whom everyone seemed to like. His dad would even slip him a dollar or two and tell him a joke or roughhouse with him. It always made Vega wish for more and it was the wishing that hurt the most, the sense that his father's presence was little more than a fog that came without warning and left with the slightest change in temperature.

The dog lifted her head and ran suddenly out of the kitchen. Dogs always know everything before humans, it seemed. She came back a moment later, doing a little jig to herald the return of her master. Vega slipped off the kitchen stool, feeling self-conscious and guilty though he reminded himself that he was only here because of his job.

Olivia skipped into the kitchen first, brandishing an open shoebox to reveal two bright blue soccer cleats with lime green Nike swooshes running along their sides. Vega expected her to go all shy in his presence. Joy would have at that age. But the girl simply walked up to him as if he were an uncle she'd been expecting.

"Want to see my new cleats?" she asked. Her long, black hair had been tied back into two ponytails, and a baseball shirt—red sleeves, tan body—hung loosely over a pair of red sweatpants with the word "Justice" running down the side. Not a concept. A brand name. Shockingly expensive. Wendy used to buy their clothing for Joy.

Olivia was stockier than her parents. She had that Indian blood that tended toward a thick, square torso. But her eyes were large and full of energy. She looked like a happy child, like Linda and Scott were giving her a life she never could have hoped for in Guatemala.

"Those are pretty cool cleats," said Vega. He heard

Linda's voice in the mudroom off the garage, filling her husband in on the visit. Vega was sweating. He wondered what Scott Porter already knew about him.

"Detective? Good to meet you." Porter stepped forward, his handshake one psi short of a combat hold. Vega wondered if there was a little alpha marking going on, but what the hell? They were in his house. Linda was his wife. He was entitled to claim his territory.

Vega normally disliked criminal defense attorneys. A lot of them patronized cops, treated them as stupid and racist—little more than meter maids with guns. Vega had gone on one too many witness stands where some abrasive lawyer in a suit tried to twist his words or turn him into the bad guy for doing his job. But Scott Porter seemed more personable than that. Maybe it was his smile, the way it curved up a little too much on one side, gave him a goofiness that made him seem more sincere and amiable than most of his colleagues. Or perhaps it was because they weren't in a courtroom. Nobody's integrity was on the line here.

"Linda tells me Adele sent you."

"Uh, yeah." Vega waited for more, some mention of the past. But Porter just smiled his goofy smile. Linda sent Olivia up to her room to play. She poured her husband a cup of coffee and he sat down at the counter.

"What can we do for you?" Porter's eyes were blank. No one's that good an actor. Vega shot a look at Linda. She looked away and Vega felt a stab of something sharp and unexpected in his gut. Linda Kendall was his first love. He was hers. They'd lost their virginity to each other. He'd jumped off a goddamned cliff and nearly died to win her over. And Vega didn't even merit a mention to her husband? It never came up? Not even that terrible last time they were together? All these years, she'd never entirely left his thoughts. All these years it seemed, he hadn't even registered in hers.

Vega tried to brush the hurt from his mind and keep his thoughts on the job at hand. He found the flyer he'd stuffed into his back pocket and flattened it out across the kitchen counter.

"I'm here about a woman. Do either of you recognize her?"

Porter put down his coffee cup and stared at the picture. "Is she dead?"

"She was found in the reservoir this morning. I won't have a time frame for the death until the medical examiner looks at the body."

"Do you know what happened to her?"

"It's still under investigation."

"Where's the baby?" asked Linda.

"That's one of the things we're trying to find out."

Porter pushed his coffee aside. He stared at the picture a long time, as if searching his memory banks for a name. "I don't recognize her," he said finally.

"Let me see," said Linda, taking the flyer. "Hmmm. The picture's a little blurry. I don't recognize her offhand. I'd have to go back through my client files."

"Would she be in those files if she came into La Casa?" asked Vega.

"Not necessarily," said Linda. "A lot of people don't want their names or information in our system. They're afraid, even of us."

"How about the name José Ortiz? Do either of you know him?"

"Guatemalan from Quetzaltenango?" asked Linda. "Late twenties? Has a small scar on his cheek?"

"That's probably the guy. Do you know where I can find him?"

"I haven't seen him in several weeks."

"How about his wife, Vilma, or his two-year-old daughter?"

"I didn't even know he had a wife and daughter."

"Would you have a photograph of him in your files?"

Linda shook her head. "I'm afraid we don't take pictures of clients. It's a breach of confidentiality."

"Since when?" Hell, Vega had five pieces of picture ID in his wallet right now.

"Why do you want to find him?" she asked.

"I just need to ask him a few questions." Vega turned to Porter. "Maybe you've had some dealings with him? He was cited for harassment on a DV complaint from his wife about six weeks ago."

"Name's not familiar," said Porter. "Had he been arrested, I'd probably know him. But in case you haven't noticed, Detective, Latinos in Lake Holly tend to get arrested only if their victims are legal or their crimes make them deportable. Undocumented women—as I'm assuming Vilma is—are more or less on their own in Lake Holly."

"Has this always been the case?" asked Vega. "Or has the situation gotten worse since the Shipleys were run over?"

Linda looked at her husband. Vega sensed they'd had this conversation before. "We need to tell, Scott. This can't go on."

"Let's just say," said Porter, "that since Valentine's Day, the sentiment in Lake Holly among cops and locals seems to be that the only good illegal is a dead or deported one, and no one seems that picky which of those it comes down to."

"That's a pretty serious allegation," said Vega. "Got any proof?"

Porter cradled his coffee mug and scrutinized Vega as if seeing him for the very first time. "What's your interest in all this, Detective?"

"I can't ask what goes on in town?"

"In my experience, cops are never idly curious." Porter leaned forward. "What happened to that woman at the reservoir?"

"I told you, it's under investigation."

"Quit with the party line, Detective. We both know she's a homicide or the county wouldn't even be mixed up in the case. So let me take a wild guess: you want to find José Ortiz because you think he's involved. Maybe you saw that DV complaint and you're wondering if, while the cops were playing, 'see no evil, get no U visa' with Vilma, José went a little over the edge. But you're not entirely convinced you're on the right track. That's why you're fishing here. Because you already believe there's a pattern of hate crimes going on in town, and you want to know if the dead woman's part of that."

"I never said any of that."

"You didn't have to."

Silence. The men stared at each other. Vega wondered if he'd feel such a desire for one-upmanship if Porter weren't Linda's husband.

"Scott," Linda said, putting a hand on her husband's arm. "Show him the report."

"What good will that do?"

"More good than if you don't show him."

Porter shoved the flyer to one side of the kitchen

counter and left. Vega wasn't sure if he was following his wife's directive or disengaging entirely. His absence sucked all the purpose out of the room. Vega played with a pen on the counter. His head thrummed with silent accusations.

"I never told Scott about us," Linda said finally.

"No shit. Nice to see I counted for so much. I guess I should have figured as much when I never heard from you after that cop spread-eagled me across Bobby's old Plymouth and Bobby spread-eagled you soon after."

She pursed her lips. She'd never been one for crude language and Vega's life as a cop meant he lived on a steady diet of it.

"You never came back to school," she said softly. "Your mother never left a forwarding address."

"How could I come back to school? Everybody assumed I was a drug dealer after that. Bobby never copped to it. I was on probation. My music scholarship was history. We couldn't very well keep living with Bobby's dad as our landlord. We only moved to an apartment in Granville. You coulda called me if you'd wanted to."

"So could you," said Linda.

"You don't think I tried? Your parents hung up on me. They threatened to take out a restraining order if I got near you. I didn't need any more legal problems. And then I found out about you and Bobby." Twenty-five years later, and the memory still stung. "What the fuck was I supposed to do?"

"Don't curse, Jimmy. My daughter's upstairs."

"Sorry." He dropped his eyes to his coffee cup. He told himself it shouldn't matter anymore. He wished he could feel that.

Porter returned to the kitchen brandishing what

looked like a police report. Not Lake Holly's. This one said METRO-NORTH. That was the problem with the county. Too many police agencies: FBI, DEA, DEC, ICE. It was a dyslexic's nightmare every time someone dialed 911.

Porter slapped the report on the counter in front of Vega. "I don't know what I'm doing showing you this or why it will help anything." Then he took a deep breath as if he were about to plunge into very cold water.

"After Dawn and Katie Shipley were killed in February, there were a number of incidents in town, most of them small. A couple of fistfights at the high school. Some graffiti in back of the supermarket. A fender bender between two middle-aged guys that ended up in punches and epithets being exchanged.

"But then," said Porter. "Things started to escalate. In early March, someone set that fire in the community center's Dumpster. No witnesses. No leads. Personally, I thought they needed to look at the kids who were suspended for those fights at the high school. One of them was Bob Rowland's older boy—the one who works with him at the hardware store?"

"Matt," Linda offered.

"Matt Rowland, yeah," said Porter. "The kid's had a few minor brushes with the law. But the cops said they spoke to Matt and his friends and they all had alibis. Then, about a week later, two Latino males were beaten and robbed in Michael Park. They were very drunk and couldn't identify their assailants, so once again, we had nothing."

Porter opened the police report. "Then, two weeks ago, this."

Vega flipped through a stack of glossy 8 x 10s. All he could tell from the photos was that someone had found their way in front of a northbound train near Lake Holly station. The victim had been pureed as a result, the mother of all roadkills. Muscle, bone, and tissue lined the tracks in striations and puddles. The only part of the person that was preserved was a backpack that had been tossed to one side. It lay there, completely unblemished, mocking the grisly remains of its owner.

"His name was Ernesto Reyes-Cardona," said Porter. "He was a Honduran busboy, age twenty-one, a resident of Lake Holly. He was last seen at two a.m. on March twenty-seventh, walking home from his job at the Lake Holly Diner. The ME says the cause of death was electrocution. His foot touched the third rail and he collapsed before he could get out of the way of the train. His sister—my client—believes he wouldn't have been crossing the tracks if he weren't being chased. But once again, we have no witnesses."

"What about the video cameras at the train station?" asked Vega. "Didn't they pick up anything?"

"Reyes was too far away from the platform. The cameras close to the station show a figure running and then collapsing across the tracks. But they didn't pick up images of anyone in pursuit. Either no one was chasing him or they were far enough behind that they never got on camera."

"Did the engineer give a statement?"

"He says it was too dark to see anything. All he saw was a bundle of something on the tracks. By then, it was too late to stop."

Vega scanned the report. It looked thorough enough. No whitewash. No leads, either. He slid the report back to Porter.

"My wife wanted me to show you, so I'm showing you," said Porter. "Is there a pattern of violence against Latinos in Lake Holly since Edgar Lopez ran over Dawn and Katie Shipley? Absolutely. But it has been next to impossible to build any of it into a case that would stand up in court. My clients are afraid to come forward as victims or witnesses because they fear getting deported."

Vega opened his mouth to argue, but Porter beat him to the punch. "And don't tell me about U visas, Detective. Or any of the other things that are supposed to protect innocent people from capricious prosecutorial misconduct. None of them is a magic bullet. People get deported if a federal judge decides they should. And that decision has a whole hell of a lot to do with which way the wind is blowing on any given day in Washington. Believe me, I've been doing this a long time. First, in the Midwest, and for the last seven years, here. I've seen too many people get deported over nonsense to risk a client that way."

"So you're not from around here?" asked Vega.

"I'm a farm boy," said Porter. "Frankly, I prefer the Midwest. But my wife is from Lake Holly. Born and raised here. She wanted to move back to be closer to her folks."

Porter rose. He looked exhausted. Vega took his cue and rose as well.

"Thanks for your time." He handed Porter his business card. Porter stared at it a moment, then cocked his head.

"You don't happen to have a daughter named Joy, do you?"

"Yeah. She's a senior at Lake Holly High."

"I play tennis with an obstetrician named Marc Feldman."

Vega puffed out his chest a little, ready to deliver his "efficacy" speech. But something in Porter's face threw him off balance. The goofy smile. It was gone, replaced by a look of concern.

"How's she doing?" asked Porter.

"She's—doing great," said Vega. "Just ask Dr. Feldman."

"Marc hasn't seen her since the accident."

"Your daughter had an accident?" asked Linda.

"Nothing serious," said Vega. "She stalled out my car about a month ago on the train tracks north of town. The car got totaled, but she walked away. She's probably just been busy at school." Joy loved working for Dr. Feldman. It seemed inconceivable to Vega that she'd just stop. It seemed even more inconceivable that neither Wendy nor Joy would have thought to tell him.

"Have her call Marc," said Porter. "He's been worried."

He wasn't the only one.

# Chapter 6

The cops in town referred to Vega's old neighborhood as *La Frontera*—"the border" in Spanish. It was just a short walk from the station house. Vega was dying to grab some dinner, take a hot shower, and put some new gauze pads over his blisters. But the residents of *La Frontera* were working-class people. The only time he was likely to find them home was in the evenings.

He left the Escalade at the station because it was easier to walk than to find parking at this hour. He trudged up the hill, past the fortress-like doors of Our Lady of Sorrows that took all of Vega's strength to open as a boy. He turned onto Magnolia. All the streets in this part of town were named after trees. Until he moved from the Bronx to Lake Holly when he was eleven, Vega had no idea there were oaks and pines and sycamores and magnolias. To him, a tree was a stick in the ground with a necklace of dog feces around it and a plant was a factory that you hoped you were lucky enough to get a job at when you finished school.

A landscaper's truck rumbled past and a man in

muddy jeans hopped out of the cab, a backpack slung over one shoulder. Two other Latino men rode by on bikes. Lights flicked on behind closed curtains. The smell of fried onions and chilies called out to his stomach. It was a different place than Vega remembered. The lawns were sparser. Some were paved over entirely to make room for more cars. Clusters of cable dishes sprouted like mushrooms from rooftops and mailboxes were stacked atop one another along doorways. Everything seemed more crowded. Noisier and grittier. But it was full of families, full of life. There were toy bins and faded Little Tikes playhouses in the front yards and pots of geraniums along windowsills. There were work boots and tools being aired out on front porches and bicycles padlocked to chain-link fences. In some ways, Vega thought, he might have been happier growing up in the neighborhood now than when he stood out as the only dark-skinned kid on the block, the only child without a father—there, solely because John Rowland could get more rent from an overworked Puerto Rican nurse than he could a white family. Not every idealized neighborhood is ideal for every child.

He started on one side of the street, at a stucco house with six mailboxes and, armed with a copy of the dead woman's picture, talked to every man or woman who opened the door. He spoke in his most respectful Spanish. He stressed that he was only here to find out if they could identify the woman in the photograph or knew the whereabouts of José or Vilma Ortiz. He didn't show his badge unless they asked for ID to keep the encounters as low-key as possible.

Some residents tried hard to help, staring at the photo, calling on other household members to see if they knew her or the Ortiz family. Others—probably the most recent arrivals—opened their doors only a crack and shook their heads without giving the photo more than a passing glance. After two streets, Vega couldn't say for sure whether no one knew his subjects or whether people were too scared to get involved.

It was past eight p.m. by the time Vega limped down Maple Road. His ankles hurt. His head throbbed like there was a mariachi band inside. He was about to call it quits for the night when a silver Mercedes SUV with tinted windows turned the far corner and slowly cruised down the street, then double-parked about twenty feet in front of him. This wasn't a street where silver Mercedes normally traveled.

The driver flicked on an interior light. Vega saw two figures inside, a male and a female. Vega watched the male in the front passenger seat power down the window and thrust out a lanky brown arm. He was wearing a green-and-beige checked shirt that Vega recognized as the uniform of a cashier at the local supermarket. He had the build of a teenager, but there was no slouch to his posture, none of the nervous energy so common in puberty. He seemed to have an adult air about him, a wariness of overstretching his boundaries. And in that moment, Vega recognized his daughter's boyfriend, Kenny Cardenas. He recognized the SUV, too. His ex-wife had one just like it. Which meant he had no doubt who was in the driver's seat.

She was sitting very still, head bowed like a child caught doing something she shouldn't have. Her long, black hair fell across her face. She made no attempt to tuck it behind her ears. Kenny had his head turned toward the window. Vega suspected they were in the throes of an argument, though it lacked the passion and drama he'd expect from two teenagers. Maybe they were breaking up.

If so, Vega could hardly say he was disappointed. Not that Kenny Cardenas was a bad kid. He was a straight-A student like Joy and, from what Vega could surmise, a popular and likable boy at Lake Holly High. But it was an open secret that Kenny and his family were undocumented. His father, Cesar, mowed lawns for a living. His mother, Hilda, cleaned houses. Kenny and his three younger sisters crossed the border from Mexico when they were in elementary school. And sure, things were getting better for young people in Kenny's situation. If his father could marshal the time and resources, he might be able to apply for temporary legal status for Kenny that would allow him to get a driver's license like all his friends and to apply for jobs without resorting to fake ID. But that didn't change the fact that nothing in the boy's future was guaranteed. Not a college degree or a job with benefits or a chance to put down real roots in this country. Vega wanted better for his daughter. Maybe she couldn't understand that now, but she would someday.

He told himself to back away. Pretend he was never here. That was the right thing to do, to respect their privacy. But he couldn't leave until he was certain she was all right. He squinted through the windshield. The two teenagers were talking now. Joy was shaking her head vigorously back and forth. Kenny had his hands raised in a gesture of frustration. Vega watched her duck her head for a moment—to open the car door? To retrieve something from her purse? He wasn't sure. But there was no mistake in his mind about what happened next.

As Joy lifted her head, Kenny reached across her seat and brought his fist down. His daughter's head bobbed and jerked in response.

In seconds, Vega had the passenger door open and Kenny Cardenas splayed across the hood. A stream of Spanish invectives flew from his lips. Joy wouldn't understand them. She only knew the stilted Spanish she got from textbooks at school. But Kenny would.

"You think you can hit my daughter, *pendejo?* You think that makes you a big man? Hitting a girl half your size?" Vega wished he could have gotten his hands on José Ortiz after he punched his wife. Maybe this town wouldn't be in the mess it was now.

"Dad!" cried Joy. "What are you doing?"

Vega didn't answer. He kicked the boy's legs apart and shoved him hard against the SUV. Kenny went to protest. Vega yanked the boy by the back of his shirt. "How does it feel when someone threatens you? Huh, *cabrón?*"

"Dad! Stop it!" Joy tugged on her father's jacket. "He didn't hit me."

Vega kept a tight hold on Kenny's shirt as he turned and looked at his daughter. Her eyes were slightly swollen, her black mascara smeared enough to resemble one of those pouty ingénues on MTV. But that could have been from crying. She wasn't bruised or bleeding. There were no markings on her face.

"I saw him," Vega insisted. "Through the car window. I saw him bring his fist down."

"I was trying to recline my seat. It wouldn't budge so he had to bang on the headrest."

"It's true, Mr. Vega," Kenny gasped. "I didn't hit her."

Vega released Kenny's shirt and stepped back. His

heart was pounding at the thought of what he might have done to the boy. He felt no better than that rookie Fitzgerald. He braced for Kenny's anger but saw something shrunken and defeated instead. Whatever Vega had interrupted this evening, it had already been going badly before he'd finished it off.

Joy paced the sidewalk, her black high-heel boots clicking on the pavement, her silver bangles jangling as she pushed her bangs out of her face. She'd always been one for drama.

"What are you doing here, embarrassing me like this?" she demanded. "I'm not five years old anymore. You can't spy on me like this."

"I wasn't spying. I'm working a case with the Lake Holly PD. I was interviewing people in the neighborhood. I didn't know you'd be here."

"It's okay, Mr. Vega." Kenny looked pretty shaken up but he muscled the quiver out of his voice and tucked his shirt back into his jeans. "No harm done."

"No harm?" asked Joy. "He could have killed you."

"Joy"—Kenny patted the air and gave her a reproving look—"It's okay."

She folded her arms across her chest and bit down hard on her lip. She was still a child with her emotions, Vega noticed, trying them on like a flashy pair of shoes whether they fit the occasion or not. Kenny, he suspected, had no such luxury. There were some emotions—anger, jealousy, regret—that he simply couldn't afford.

"I have to go now," said the boy. "I have to finish my homework." He nodded over his shoulder to a wood-frame colonial. The front porch sagged. Paint peeled in ribbons from the siding. The house had originally been a one-family. Judging from the number of mailboxes by the front door, Kenny, his parents, and three sisters now shared it with three other families.

Kenny shot a quick glance at Joy. Vega caught something pained in the gaze. "See you," the boy said softly. Then he hustled up the front porch steps.

"Call me," Joy shouted after him. Vega heard the desperation in her voice. He felt the hurt as if it were his own. Kenny didn't answer as he opened the front door and disappeared inside.

Joy stood next to her mother's Mercedes, bobbing up and down in her black boots. The temperature had dropped and the skimpy Pepto-Bismol pink jacket she was wearing wasn't nearly enough. Vega sloughed off his navy blue police Windbreaker and draped it over her shoulders. The shoulders of the Windbreaker sloped down her tiny frame and the sleeves dipped below her fingers. Vega zipped it up for her like she was still in preschool.

"I can do that myself," she said with a trace of embarrassment.

"I know. Sorry." He stuffed his hands in his pants pockets. He could feel the cold bite right through his shirt.

"Now *you* don't have a jacket."

"I'm okay. Maybe you could drive me down to the police station? My car's in their parking lot."

"Sure."

Vega eased himself into the passenger side of Wendy's silver Mercedes. He wished Joy was driving him all the way north to his house tonight instead of six blocks to his borrowed county car. The seats had those automatic warmers in them. The car's engine purred like a contented tiger. He could have closed his eyes and stayed in that Mercedes all night.

Joy checked her rearview mirrors and pulled back onto the street.

"Are you still sore at me?" asked Vega.

"You never told Kenny you were sorry."

"It was an accident."

"You still could have said you were sorry."

"I'm sorry, all right? I made a mistake. You make mistakes too, you know."

He was referring to his Acura that she'd totaled. She looked ready to dissolve into tears.

"Hey," he said softly. "That was a stupid thing for me to say. I'm just tired and cranky. You forgive me?"

"Sure." Silence. She was like a complicated machine that he'd lost the instructions to. He could watch the gears turning but he had no idea what was going on inside. Which reminded him.

"I was talking to a man today who plays tennis with Dr. Feldman." He waited for a reaction. It was his cop training. He always let the other person fill in the blanks. But Joy said nothing so he was forced to continue.

"He said Dr. Feldman hasn't seen you in a month."

Still no response.

"I thought you liked working at the hospital."

"I've just—been busy."

"With what?"

She chewed on a fingernail. All her nails were bitten, he noticed. She never used to bite her nails. Even the skin around the cuticles looked red and inflamed.

"He's not worth this kind of heartache, Joy. You're better off without him."

"You don't know the first thing about Kenny."

"I know you've got big opportunities coming up and he doesn't."

"For your information, Kenny was accepted to Binghamton University for the fall. Pre-med, just like me. La Casa just awarded him a scholarship."

"I hope for his sake, things work out. But even so, the kid's got a tough road ahead of him. I don't want his limitations to hold you back."

Joy made a face.

"What?"

"Didn't Grandma and Grandpa say the same about you?"

Not in his presence. In his presence, Dr. Kaplan and his wife were unfailingly polite. Stilted, but polite. They were Democrats, after all. They marched for civil rights. They gave generously to PBS and the Anti-Defamation League. But in private, Vega knew, they breathed a sigh of relief when Wendy left him for her nice Jewish investment-banker second husband, Alan, and a house in The Farms. Upward mobility, Vega supposed. Wendy moved upward. He got the mobility.

"That was prejudice, Joy. This is different."

"Why? Because you're on the other side now?"

"I'm not on anyone's side."

"Oh come on, Dad. As soon as you got the chance, you got as far away from your Puerto Rican roots as possible. You never spoke Spanish to me—"

"Because I didn't want to embarrass you. Do you have any idea what it felt like to be the only kid in Lake Holly whose mother had an accent?"

"I liked Abuelita's accent. I would've liked to have

known that side of my culture better. Now she's dead, I never will."

Something parched and painful settled in the back of Vega's throat. Regret. He'd never expected it to have such physical weight. God, he missed his mother. Every minute of every day. And where was he when it all could have been different? Going through the divorce, he supposed. Moving to cheaper digs farther upstate. Taking on more overtime to pay for child support.

Never once did his mother berate his choices, even if some of his visits were hurried between work shifts, even if he rarely brought Joy because Wendy considered the Bronx too dangerous, too dirty—too Spanish. His mother cooked things like *alcapurrias* and *piñon*—fried meat fritters and beef-and-plantain casserole that Vega loved but sometimes upset his daughter's stomach. The neighborhood wasn't safe for an innocent like Joy to wander in so they stayed in his mother's stuffy apartment where his daughter sat, pale and mute on the slipcovered couch, the blue of the television drifting across her face until Vega took her home. He wanted their worlds to mesh. He wanted the two people he loved most to get to know each other better. But it required the conviction that his world—his life—was *worth* getting to know and Vega, always trying to fit in elsewhere, never had that sort of confidence. And now, as Joy said, it was too late. The concrete had set. It would never be other than what it was.

"Dad? Are you okay?"

"I should've tried harder," he said softly. "I guess I didn't want to force a world on you that you weren't interested in."

"But I *am* interested."

"You say that now, Joy. Now, when it's cool, or whatever, to be ethnic or different. When you were a kid, it was the last thing you would have wanted. You remember how you used to complain that Abuelita's apartment was always too hot—even in winter? And you were never comfortable sitting on her furniture because of those plastic slipcovers. Remember?"

Joy giggled. "My legs used to stick to them. Every time I moved, they made like, farting noises. How did you deal with that growing up?"

"I never sat on the living-room furniture. It was always for company."

She got a sudden dreamy-eyed look on her face. "You know what I did like? That little doll she crocheted on the back of the toilet. The one whose pink skirt hid the extra roll of toilet paper. What happened to that doll, Dad?"

Vega closed his eyes and leaned back on the headrest. He tried to blot out the image that stuck in his head. The crocheted doll lying on the black-and-white ceramic floor tiles of his mother's bathroom, one eye open, one closed, her cotton-candy pink yarn skirt soaked red with his mother's blood.

"I don't know what happened to it," he said finally.

They both were silent after that, listening to the soft hum of warm air percolating through the vents.

"I'm sorry, Dad. I didn't mean to bring up Abuelita. I know you're still hurting a lot."

"I'm glad you brought her up. She'd be glad too. As a matter of fact, there's something I've been meaning to give you."

"What?"

"I came across her favorite pearl earrings a couple of weeks ago. I took them out of her apartment after . . ." Vega's voice dropped off. To say it was to imagine it and he was still wrestling with that. "Anyway, I know she'd want you to have them."

"I'd like that."

They were at the police station now. Vega gestured to the parking lot. "If you can turn in here, my car's right there in the lot." He pointed to the black Escalade.

"Wow Dad, nice car."

"It's not mine. It belongs to the county."

"They let cops tool around in Escalades?"

"It was impounded from a heroin dealer. Last night I needed to look the part. I won't get it again, trust me."

"I thought you weren't working undercover anymore."

"I'm not. I just had to help another cop make a few connections."

"In Lake Holly?"

"Nah. South of here. I'm in Lake Holly to help the local guys track down the identity of a dead woman."

"Dead? As in murdered?" Vega forgot that violent death wasn't an everyday occurrence for most people. Plus, Joy had always been impressionable. When she was little, movies had to be prescreened, nightlights left on throughout the house. Before bed, Vega used to have to make an elaborate show of rendering her room monster-free by dabbing witch hazel on the doorknobs. So he lied.

"She drowned. That's all. These things happen." Vega undid his seatbelt and put his arm around her. It felt good to feel her loose and willing for once in his embrace. "This Kenny stuff—you'll see—it's not going to matter once you're up at Amherst."

He caught a shadow of something cross her face and wondered what secret fear or insecurity he'd blindly trampled now. Her moods changed like quicksilver these days. She could seem so brash and independent one moment, so childlike the next.

"I'm sorry, Daddy," she said thickly.

"About what?"

"About totaling your car."

"I don't care about the car, *Chispita*. You're the only thing that matters."

*Chispita*: "Little Spark." He used to call her that after the plucky young heroine in a Mexican telenovela his mother used to watch when he was a kid. The last time he called her *Chispita*, she cringed. This time she seemed almost grateful that someone could still see the little girl inside the skimpy pink jacket and black leather boots.

She shrugged off his jacket and handed it back to him. Vega kissed her cheek, feeling the dampness from her earlier tears with Kenny, the way they made her skin smell all yeasty like she was a little girl again, riding on his shoulders, burying her face in his chest when something frightened her or turned her shy. He would have to get comfortable with saying good-bye to her in a couple of months. It felt too soon.

He stepped out of the car. "Drive safely, *Mija*." It's what he always said. His stand-in for "I love you," when I love you was too hard to say. He slapped the window of the passenger's side and stood shivering in the cold as he watched her red taillights fade down the street, braking at a traffic light before turning into the darkness beyond.

# Chapter 7

"**O**ur Juanita Doe didn't go into that lake under the influence, that's for sure. The average five-year-old in this country's got more pharmaceuticals in him than she had."

At least Greco wasn't calling her a "chick" anymore. Vega supposed he had to be thankful for small favors. Like the bad coffee Greco was handing him now as he walked into the detectives' bullpen on Monday morning. Neither of them had gotten much sleep the night before.

Vega leaned against the side of Greco's cubicle. "I gather the autopsy results are in?"

"Nah. I just figured I'd make something up. Keep it interesting." Greco pushed the report into Vega's hands. Vega pulled up a chair and set down his coffee. He could smell the remains of an Egg McMuffin in Greco's trash. There was still a smudge of bacon grease next to his computer. Greco's workspace was demarcated by a fabric partition and a file cabinet with a two-year-old calendar of Florida travel scenes taped to one side. It had been up there so long, the edges had curled and the

Gulf waters had faded to the color of urine. Vega knew Greco had three or four grown kids and a wife up north somewhere but there were no pictures in sight. He wondered what that said about the man.

"You've looked through the report already?" asked Vega.

"Enough to give you the highlights." Greco pulled a red Twizzler from an open package on his desk and offered one to Vega. Vega declined.

"I don't know why you eat that sugar-coated wire insulation."

"This, from a Puerto Rican who's probably never met a food he hasn't deep-fried and smothered in Tabasco sauce." Greco tore off a piece of the red licorice between his teeth and adjusted his black glasses. They were too big for his face and gave his eyes a perpetually startled expression.

"Cause of death is a skull fracture," said Greco. "Manner, undetermined. Estimated time of death was four to six weeks ago. So she died in late February or early March. Any earlier, and Gupta says she would've just been fish food."

"No water in the lungs," Vega noted. "So whoever tied her down didn't do it to drown her. She was already dead."

"I ran a check on those ropes this morning," said Greco. "They had a green tracer line running through them. I thought that might make them easy to pin down. But it turns out everybody carries that rope, including Rowland's Ace Hardware downtown. All the landscapers use it."

"Yeah, but Rowland's has like nineteen different kinds

of rope with any number of different-colored tracers running through them," said Vega.

"You shop there?"

"Nah. I just remember all the ropes from when I was a kid. Bobby Rowland and I used to hang out in the store a lot. We were friends. His dad was our landlord." Vega thumbed the report some more. "Dr. Gupta has no idea how her skull got cracked?"

"She says it could have been the result of an assault with a weapon like a baseball bat. There were fractures to her ribs consistent with an assault. But she says the cracked skull also could have been the result of falling backward against a hard surface."

"Like being thrown off Bud Point?"

"I asked. Gupta said she'd have sustained more broken bones and compression injuries. And don't tell me about your little swan dive at seventeen, Vega. You were the luckiest bastard in the world."

"Then how does Gupta explain the rib fractures, if not from assault?"

"She said it also could have been bad CPR."

"Bad CPR?" Vega made a face. "That's like killing someone by taking their pulse."

"Gupta says she's seen similar rib fractures in people who have heart attacks and get CPR from someone who doesn't know what they're doing."

"Welcome to the future of managed health care," said Vega. Greco gave a throaty chuckle. It sounded like a car backfiring. Vega took a sip of coffee. Next time he'd bring his own. Anglos didn't have a clue how to make coffee. "Did Gupta manage to lift any fingerprints?"

"The tissue was too damaged from being in the water so long," said Greco. "But the lab did manage to match her DNA to a bloodstain on the shoulder bag so we can be pretty confident the bag was hers and she's probably the face in the photograph. The lab also lifted a fingerprint from that letter. I ran it through the database. No matches. Whoever wrote that letter has no police or immigration record."

"Anything come up on the Dora sneaker?"

"The model was manufactured within the last five years. Sold in Target and Walmart. No DNA or prints. No way to tie it to a particular child."

Vega had already combed the missing persons databases. Nothing matched. Even the pawn registry came up cold for that crucifix. He could see how a woman could end up unreported. But a little girl? How does someone not miss a child?

But he knew the answer to that already. With his own eyes, he had seen how a child could become forever lost. Desiree was two. She never saw three. He would always blame himself no matter what the official report said.

"What gets me," said Vega, "is the media. Not one newspaper or television station has picked up on the flyers we sent. I figured, with a child involved—"

"Technically, we don't know for a fact that the child *is* involved," Greco reminded him.

"Her mother's dead. Little kids don't stray far from their mothers."

"Could be a father or grandparent is raising her," said Greco. "As for the woman—well," Greco spread his hands apologetically. "Comes with the territory." They both knew that a dead Latina, especially one who might be undocumented, was unlikely to garner the same sort of media coverage as a white American woman.

"We'd get all the media attention we needed if we broadcast our suspicions," said Vega.

"That'd be like using a fire hose to extinguish a candle. No thank you," said Greco. "I don't want to be the guy cleaning up *that* mess."

"Is that what you told Adele Figueroa after someone torched the community center's Dumpster last month?"

Greco drummed his fingers on his desktop. "What, Sherlock? So now you think a bunch of dumb-ass kids decided to move from vandalism to murder?"

"How do you know the fire was started by kids?"

"I don't. But in my book, if it walks like a dog and shits like a dog, it's not a camel with a personality disorder. That fire had all the earmarks of a few punks fired up on their own rage and bravado."

"The words that were spray-painted across La Casa's parking lot seem a little close for comfort, don't you think?"

"Easily a hundred people saw those words, Vega. They weren't poetic. Or original. That situation is nothing like what we found at the lake."

"How about Ernesto Reyes-Cardona? Is he a dog or a camel in your analogy?"

Greco blew out a long breath of air as if Vega had been sent as a personal test from God. Job's final burden. "That's not a Lake Holly police matter."

"I know. It's Metro-North jurisdiction. But it happened *here,* Grec. All of these crimes happened *here.* Scott Porter told me about two other Latino men who were beaten in Michael Park. Don't all these potential bias incidents make you wonder what's going on in town?"

"So now you're taking your cues from a guy who wants to hand out green cards like they're grocery coupons?"

"Is Porter right about what's happening in town or not?"

"That shit happens? That people sometimes behave badly? Of course. But I don't like your insinuation that we're not doing our jobs. Hell, you know the drill as well as I do. You try to interview an illegal, he won't talk to you. Or he gives you a fake name. Or a fake address. Even if these people give you a real address, they move every fucking week. They don't have steady jobs. How the hell can I catch a criminal if the witnesses and victims scatter like cockroaches every time I step into a room? Never mind all the shit I have to do when I finally *do* talk to them. I can't ask them the same things I'd ask my own kids if I caught them messing around. I see a white guy pissing on the sidewalk, I can bust his ass and no one's gonna do anything but applaud me for doing my job. I do the same thing to an illegal, and in two minutes flat, I've got Scott Porter and every Hispanic group in the county breathing down my neck and calling me a racist."

Greco's view of the world, 101. Vega leaned an elbow on the corner of Greco's desk and rested his cheek against his fist. "I see the county-mandated sensitivity training had a big impact on you."

"Yeah? Fuck you. You can't decide if you're for them or against them. That's your problem. Least I know where I stand."

Vega's view of the world, 101: wherever you are, you don't belong.

Neither man spoke for an instant. Then Greco turned away from Vega and punched a number into his phone. He told the person on the other end to wait around another ten minutes. He hung up and turned back to Vega.

"Ever meet a guy named Tim Anderson?"

"No. Should I have?"

"Depends," said Greco. "He's an accident reconstruction specialist for Metro-North Railway. He's down by the station now. You want to know about this Reyes guy, you can ask him yourself."

It took Vega a moment to process what Greco was saying. "So you mean to say that Lake Holly is working with Metro-North on the Reyes case—as we speak— and it didn't occur to you to tell me?"

"It occurred to me," said Greco. "But like I've said from the beginning—we want this situation at the lake to remain under the radar. There's no proof right now that Reyes was chased to his death, much less that his case has anything to do with any other. Is Lake Holly looking at the particulars? Hell, yeah. But are we broadcasting it from the rooftops? Not if we want this town in one piece, we're not."

"Not even to me?"

"Your jurisdiction is the reservoir. Not Metro-North or anything else that goes on in my backyard. You asked, so I'm telling you. But when you're not on lake property, we play things my way." He put his palms on his desk and pushed himself out of his chair. "Want to talk to Anderson or not?"

\* \* \*

They found Tim Anderson on the northbound side
of the tracks, about fifty feet from the Lake Holly station platform. He had an ex-military bearing about
him—rigid posture, buzz-cut blond hair, hundred-yard
stare. He was wearing a hard hat, insulated boots, and a
fluorescent vest that made him look like a maintenance
employee, but he was taking photographs and notes.
Vega assumed, given his radio and credentials with
Metro-North, that he knew how to stop the trains from
whipping through here when he was on the tracks. But
the vest gave Vega pause. He never liked trusting his
fate to anyone who relied on procedure—or the attention span of a civil servant during baseball season.

Greco made the introductions. A small crease gathered
between Anderson's eyebrows at the mention of Vega's
name. He ran a finger across his hedge-clipper-perfect
blond mustache.

"Do you have a teenage daughter?"

"Yeah." Everybody in town seemed to know Joy.
But this time, Vega wasn't so quick to trot out his efficacy speech. He felt suddenly protective. "Why?"

Then it hit him. If Tim Anderson did accident recon-
structions for Metro-North, he was probably involved
in Joy's stall-out on the tracks. Vega wasn't there when
it happened. He was working in the southern part of
the county that evening, handling a shooting outside a
bar. By the time he'd learned about the accident, it was
all over. Joy was back home; his Acura was history.

"You're a lucky man," said Anderson, shaking his
head at the memory. "Never seen a stranger situation.
But she walked away, so that's what matters."

"It was my car," said Vega. "I loaned it to her, so you
can imagine how I feel. It never stalled on me before."

Anderson held Vega's gaze for a moment.

"Your daughter," he said. "She's what? Five-three?"

"Five-two. Why?"

"Her driver's seat was pushed all the way back."

"So?"

"Strange—don't you think?" Tim Anderson had the arctic eyes of an Alaskan husky. Cold and humorless. If they worked together ten years, they'd never become friends.

"What's strange about it?"

"Hard to believe she was driving."

"If she said she was driving, she was. My daughter doesn't lie. Or drink. She passed the Breathalyzer the police administered on the scene."

"That she did." The words came out flat—almost sarcastic. Vega wondered if Anderson would be so free with his insinuations if Vega were a white detective. He could never be sure and it was the not knowing that always put him on the defensive, made him feel like a punk if he didn't react, a prick if he did.

Vega went to argue, but Greco hollowed a fist to his lips and cleared his throat. He didn't care about Joy's close call on the tracks. He was only curious when he was paid to be.

"Wanna tell Detective Vega here about our boy Reyes?" asked Greco.

Anderson pulled out his radio and presumably relayed a command to temporarily halt the trains coming from both directions into the station. Then he cautioned Greco and Vega to stay on the gravel along the outer side of the tracks. "Don't want to have happen to you what happened to Reyes."

Vega ran his eyes over the rails. There were two parallel steel tracks lying flat to the gravel with pressure-treated wood slats in between. Beyond them, set off to the side, was the third rail. It was elevated about six inches off the ground and covered—except for the underside—in a black, shock-resistant casing. During the day, it was easy to see, easy to stay away from. But at night, in the dark, running, Vega could see how easy it would be to cross the first two tracks and think you're in the clear, only to trip on the third rail. A moment of contact, that's all it would take. There were 625 volts of direct current running through that rail. Reyes would have fried from within long before he was pulverized from without.

"That's the camera that caught Reyes's image," said Anderson, pointing it out on the overhead walkway. "Detective Greco's seen the footage. Reyes is running at a forty-five degree angle from where I'm standing. At two-eighteen a.m. on March twenty-seventh, he crosses the tracks, looking over his left shoulder while he's running. He's pitched slightly forward. He must have not seen the third rail because three seconds later the footage shows him collapsed across the northbound tracks. The medical examiner said he died of cardiac arrest from electrocution, which is probably just as well because at two twenty-two a.m. a northbound Harlem Line four-car turned him into hamburger meat."

"He's looking over his left shoulder?" asked Vega. "Wouldn't that suggest someone was chasing him?"

"It would," said Anderson. "The question I keep coming back to is, why aren't we picking up the chasers?" He led Vega and Greco away from the tracks and gave an "all clear" on his radio. Then he pulled out a hand-drawn map from a pocket in his jacket and unfolded it. *Definitely ex-military*, thought Vega. It could have been an attack plan.

"This is the route from the Lake Holly Diner to Reyes's apartment," said Anderson. His finger drew an upside down L, beginning at the diner and ending on Elm Street in *La Frontera*. Vega saw right away what the problem was. The train station wasn't on his route home. Vega frowned at the drawing, then bounced a look from Anderson to Greco.

"So, if Reyes was headed straight home, why was he running in the direction of the train station? Is that what you're wondering?" asked Vega.

"I was thinking maybe he had a señorita he liked to see after work," said Greco. "But Reyes's sister said he always came straight home after his shift. He was too tired for anything else."

"Here's the real problem, no matter how you slice it," said Anderson. "Greco and I have been pulling video footage from that time and date at the banks around town. They're the only ones with cameras that operate twenty-four-seven. Nothing is coming up. We've got footage of three people using three different ATMs during that time period and we've interviewed them all. None of them saw anything and none of them fits as a suspect."

"Maybe Reyes's attackers weren't on foot," Vega suggested.

"We've considered that," said Greco. "The cameras don't pick up license-plate numbers, unfortunately. But even if you consider that option, we only had a few cars in town at that hour, and that includes one of our own cruisers and a couple of emergency vehicles."

"Emergency vehicles?"

"There was a call-out for chest pains that night to our ambulance," Greco explained. "Bob Rowland, our volunteer fire chief, was out and about in his SUV, probably for the chest pains call. And one of our officers was in his cruiser. Everybody's been interviewed and no one saw anything."

"So what does this mean, exactly?" asked Vega. "That Reyes was hallucinating and just decided to wander across the tracks? 'Cause from what you're saying, it sure as hell looks like he was being chased."

"We think he may have been pulled into a car and beaten," said Anderson. "We think he may have managed to escape somewhere near the train station and run across the tracks. But we need a witness. No witness, no case."

"That—" Greco told Vega, "is where you come in."

"Me?" This wasn't his case. Greco had made that amply clear at the station.

"See, I went back over the particulars of the Reyes case this morning," said Greco. "And there was one person we never got to talk to after Reyes died: the other busboy who worked the same shift with him at the diner."

"So you want me to talk to him?"

"We want you to *find* him," said Greco.

"Okay. What's his name?"

"José Ortiz."

# Chapter 8

A busboy at the Lake Holly Diner told Vega that
José Ortiz had a cousin in town, a woman named
Claudia, who might know where Ortiz had disappeared
to. The busboy didn't know the cousin's last name but
he knew she had a son who attended the Head Start
preschool that was part of La Casa.

Vega was both reassured and discomforted by this
information. Reassured, because now Adele Figueroa
could provide a path to Ortiz through his cousin Claudia. Discomforted, because he had to wonder if that
hadn't *always* been the case. Wasn't it possible Adele
*knew* Claudia was Ortiz's cousin all along? And, if she
could withhold information about Ortiz, wasn't it possible she was also withholding information about the
woman at the lake?

Adele was impossible to get hold of. She was in
meetings every time Vega called. She didn't return
messages. Not that Vega's ex-wife was any better. In
between calling Adele, Vega put in a call to Wendy at
Granville Middle School where she worked part-time
as the school's psychologist. He wanted to know why

Joy wasn't working with Dr. Feldman anymore or whether Wendy was aware of her and Kenny's breakup. Both women were unreachable. Story of his life.

He gave up reaching Adele by phone and tracked her down physically to La Casa's preschool around the corner from the main building. The preschool was housed in an aging Victorian with a bowed front porch. The backyard was enclosed in chain-link fencing and scattered with sandboxes, swings, and toys. A couple of dozen preschoolers, all Latino, ran about the yard, their voices filled with the hard exuberance that was the same in any language. Vega felt a sudden pang thinking about the baby in the flyer. He hoped she was in some playground like this somewhere. He didn't want to think she was another Desiree and he was already too late.

Vega watched two boys spinning a tire swing, wrestling with it and each other as they tried to hurl their bodies onto the rim. That's when he caught sight of a figure crouched over a small girl, tying her shoelaces. She was turned away from him so he had time to study the long curve of her neck and the smooth pink-white of her skin that reminded him of the inside of a seashell. Her blond hair mirrored the sun.

He felt such tenderness for Linda at that moment as he watched her brush dirt off the little girl's knees and zip up her jacket. She was a natural mother. He could see that. It radiated off her skin like pollen, infusing everything she touched. He could only imagine how hard it must have been for her to discover that she couldn't have any children of her own.

She rose to her feet and Vega felt a sudden panic that

she might see him spying on her. He quickly ducked into the building.

He found Adele on the second floor, in what had once been a bedroom of the house and had now been converted into a makeshift office of the preschool. The room was oddly shaped to accommodate the flue of a fireplace that had been boarded up on the first floor. Plaster fissures ran up the walls like geothermal fault lines. The floors creaked when he walked across them, announcing his presence.

Adele was seated behind a desk overflowing with folders of papers in no discernable order. Across from her sat a young mother with a toddler on her lap. The young mother's long, black hair was pulled back tightly into a ponytail. A small fringe of stray hairs framed her round, high-cheekboned face. The toddler sucked on a lollipop, her dark eyes staring up at Vega as if she half-expected him to break into song. A new preschool candidate, Vega supposed. He knocked on the doorframe.

"Ms. Figueroa? Sorry to bother you but we really need to talk."

"Perfect timing. I got your messages. Have a seat." Adele gestured to an empty chair across from the young mother. Then she turned to the woman and spoke in Spanish to tell her Vega's name and title. He didn't see why all this was necessary. The woman was going to be leaving anyway. The mother started telling Adele in Spanish that she needed to catch the three o'clock bus. But Adele looked at her watch and replied that the woman had plenty of time and motioned for her to stay seated.

"Uh, Ms. Figueroa?" said Vega. "I need a few minutes of your time in *private*." He spoke in English. He had a sense the mother didn't speak much English.

"I think she should stay for what you have to say."

That's when it hit him. "Is this Claudia?"

"Claudia?" Adele laced her fingers under her chin. She had a way of making Vega feel a step behind in all their encounters, like he was always walking in on the punch line without hearing the joke.

"A busboy at the Lake Holly Diner told me José Ortiz has a cousin in town named Claudia."

"Claudia Acevedo, yes," said Adele. "She has a three-year-old son, Damian, who attends preschool here."

Vega felt a cinch at the back of his neck, a tightening in his jaw. He'd been as honest as he could yesterday. And for what? So she could play games with him until she could tip off Ortiz? He braced a fist on one thigh and leaned forward.

"Do you mean to tell me that you knew *all along* that I could find Ortiz through his cousin?"

"Detective—"

"This is not some moot court at Harvard, you know, Ms. Figueroa. I found out this morning that Ortiz worked with Ernesto Reyes. He was the last person to see him alive. He may be the *only* person who can help the police find out whether Reyes was chased to his death. Don't you care about that? Or about the fact that his wife, Vilma, could be the body we found in the lake?"

"She's not. I can assure you."

"What are you, Ortiz's lawyer all of a sudden?"

"No, Detective. But this"—she gestured to the woman in the chair—"is Vilma Ortiz. And her daughter, Bettina."

The young mother, who clearly didn't understand a word of their conversation in English, bowed her head slightly at the sound of her name. Vega regarded her warily. He'd been blindsided by Adele on one too many occasions to look pleased that his supposed victim was sitting right beside him.

"I already know how your suspicious cop mind works," said Adele.

She turned to the mother and asked in Spanish for ID. The woman rummaged through her purse and produced a Lake Holly library card and a bottle of prescription eye medicine, both in the name of Vilma Ortiz. She handed them to Adele who turned them over to Vega. That was about as good an ID as Vega was likely to get from an undocumented woman in the state of New York. He handed them back to Vilma with a quick *gracias*. Then he pulled out a pad and pen from a jacket pocket.

"Can I have your current address and phone number, señora?" He asked in Spanish.

Vilma shot a hesitant look at Adele who nodded. In a soft, childlike voice, Vilma gave Vega her cell phone number and an address in Granville. Vega was able to verify the cell number on the spot by dialing it and having Vilma answer. The address was more problematic. He tapped his pen on his notebook. Adele seemed to read his mind.

"You're not here to hunt down José Ortiz for a missed court date, Detective," she said in English. "You're here to ask for his cooperation as a witness in a potential homicide. You start playing heavy-handed, you'll likely just scare the Ortizes off."

"Are you the appointed spokesperson for the family

now?" he shot back. "I should arrest *you* for obstruction of justice."

"On what grounds? I knew as little as you did yesterday. I'm just better at talking to people than you are."

"And when were you going to tell me about these talks? When the Ortizes sent a postcard from Miami?"

"As soon as I knew why they ran. You know it too, apparently."

"Reyes."

Adele nodded. "Vilma tells me José knows the police want to speak to him about Reyes but he's afraid because of the harassment charge. He feels he's in enough trouble with the police already."

"So he skips out on his court date? On his rent? He doesn't think that's going to get him into *more* trouble?"

Adele sighed. "You're asking a man who's had to run from authority figures his whole life to suddenly trust them. It doesn't work that way. I already told Vilma that her husband's best defense is to follow the law. But even I'm not always persuasive."

Vega thought about Vilma's beating six weeks ago and wondered whether a man like Ortiz could be persuaded of anything by a woman. He handed Vilma his business card and issued his own plea in Spanish. "Please, señora—tell the señor to call me. The police might be able to work something out with the missed court date. But he needs to come forward. Ernesto Reyes-Cardona has a family too. A sister right here in Lake Holly who believes he was chased to his death. Your husband is the only one who might know what happened."

"But my husband says he didn't see anything."

"There may be some small thing he has forgotten

that might be important. The police will never know unless they interview him."

The young mother tucked Vega's business card in her bag and rose, clutching her daughter tightly in her arms. She bowed her head. "Thank you very much, señor, señora. You have been very kind to speak to me today. I will talk to my husband. I will tell him to speak to you." Vilma sounded willing and compliant but Vega knew from experience that poor Latinos always showed deference to authority. It did not necessarily mean they would follow through. Vilma looked at Adele. "May I leave?"

"The detective has no legal right to detain you." Adele shot Vega a look that dared him to contradict her. She could feel his fury even before she'd finished seeing Vilma and Bettina to the door. He had his legs stretched out in front of him until they reached halfway under her desk. He'd taken over the room.

"Look, Ms. Figueroa," he said as soon as Vilma was out of earshot. "I don't like the way you do business here. You should've called me as soon as you got a lead on Ortiz."

Adele calmly took a seat behind her desk. She sat very straight in her chair and looked Vega in the eye. She was not the sort of woman who crumbled when a man berated her. This center would never have come into being if she were so easily cowed by men with power.

"You said, as I recall, Detective, that you wanted to *talk* to Mr. Ortiz. Which implies you needed his cooperation. If I'd simply turned over his whereabouts to you, he would have run, or developed amnesia, and you'd have nothing."

"You think anything's different after our little sit-down today?"

"I think Vilma will try to persuade her husband to come forward."

"Like she persuaded him not to beat the crap out of her six weeks ago—huh?" Vega took her silence for affirmation. "Take it from me, Ms. Figueroa, he'll never come forward. People like him always say one thing and do another."

*"People—like—him."* She repeated Vega's words slowly. "Are you referring to lawbreakers or immigrants without papers?"

"Technically, they're one and the same."

Adele felt something cold and hard settle in her gut. A vestigial response she could never entirely suppress. She would always be fourteen around cops.

"My mother and father had no papers, Detective Vega. They were hard-working, law-abiding people. Their sole crime was to want a better life for their children. In my book, they were heroes. So don't talk to me about your *technicalities.*"

Vega ran the back of his hand across his lips and regarded her for a long moment. He wore no rings—wedding or otherwise. She had a sense he was divorced.

"The police give your parents a hard time when you were growing up?"

"My parents never gave them cause."

"Doesn't mean it didn't happen." He leaned forward, chin resting on tented fingers. His eyes changed color in different lights, she noticed. Yesterday, they were the color of bittersweet chocolate. Today, with the sunlight streaming through the office, there were flecks of dark honey in the irises. She realized he was looking for an honest answer.

"My mother and father were teachers in Ecuador. Here, they scrubbed office toilets. They dreamed of owning their own business—just a little immigrant phone service center—nothing fancy. But that's impossible if you're undocumented. So they found a neighbor who was legal. She agreed to put her name on all the paperwork in exchange for a share of the profits. My parents worked for five years to get that business off the ground. Eighteen hours a day, every day. My sister and I had to raise ourselves. We didn't even see them except at work. When they finally started to turn a profit, the neighbor stole it all. Changed the locks on the doors. Took everything. All the phone cubicles my father had built by hand. The computers. The bank account. I went with my father to the police to help him file a complaint and the officers laughed at him. *Laughed.* They called him a wetback and said he got what he deserved. He never got over it. Two years later, he died of a heart attack. He was only forty-eight."

"I'm sorry," Vega said softly. "That must have been hard."

Adele nodded. She couldn't remember telling that story to anybody.

"The cops in Lake Holly—they give you a lotta grief?"

"Comes with the territory. But it's not just them. Grants and donations have been down since the Shipley incident. Our preschool director just left because she could get twice the money elsewhere. And in June, our lease at the community center is up. The landlord's not sure he wants to renew."

"Commercial property should be a cinch to rent in this economy," said Vega. "I'll bet you can get your pick."

"If I was opening up a Starbucks, you'd be right," said Adele. "But La Casa doesn't serve lattes and espressos. We're sort of at the bottom of the food chain. Nobody wants day laborers hanging around their neighborhood."

Downstairs, little feet pounded across the floorboards. Children's voices filled the house like water coursing through a shallow streambed. The children were coming in from play. Vega rose. "I should leave you to your work. I've gotta let Metro-North and the Lake Holly PD know about Ortiz."

"I'm headed back to La Casa anyway. I'll walk you out."

In the big room on the first floor, the children were putting away their coats in their cubbyholes and gathering around a long table where Linda and two teachers were pouring juice into Dixie cups and setting out oatmeal cookies on paper napkins. Adele grinned, watching Vega pick his way past the low tables full of tiny three- and four-year-olds as if he thought he might crush one. Adele nodded to Linda.

"Thanks for helping out here today. I'll be over at La Casa. Call me if you need me."

Linda put down the carton of juice and gestured—not to Adele, to Vega.

"Wait up, Jimmy. I want to talk to you a moment."

*Jimmy?* Adele looked at Vega and noticed a blush creep into his toffee-colored cheeks. He was attracted to this *rubia,* this blond Anglo-Saxon. Adele could feel it. And for some reason, it stung.

Linda must have caught the look that crossed Adele's

face because she quickly added: "Jimmy and I were friends in high school."

"Oh." The word had a glacial edge to it. Adele was behaving childishly. She couldn't explain why.

Linda called back over her shoulder, asking the two teachers to hold down the fort while she stepped outside a moment. She grabbed an Ann Taylor peacoat in the front hallway. Vega helped her into it. Adele managed to get into her own lumpy fleece jacket with no one's help, thank you very much.

Outside, the wind had picked up. The three of them walked along the outer edge of the chain-link fence to Adele's car. Linda turned to Vega.

"I was going to call you," she said. "But they needed me here this morning and I got busy."

Vega toyed with the fence, pulling on the links so they puckered and rattled. Adele noticed that he seemed nervous and tongue-tied in Linda's presence. He hadn't been that way at all upstairs. What was it about Latin men and their obsession with blondes? It's not like Linda was beautiful or anything. Her face resembled those pale likenesses in Old Dutch paintings: skin the color of just-cut apples, eyes that took on the ambient shade of the sky. She was skinny rather than svelte, bony rather than sculpted. When she turned her wrists, blue veins snaked along the undersides like she'd drawn them on in pen.

"I'm pretty sure I remember the woman in that photograph you showed me," said Linda. "I'm also pretty sure I filled out a client profile sheet on her but I can't seem to find it. She came in only once or twice to see if anyone wanted to hire her as a cleaning lady. I remem-

ber her because I had a job for a nanny. Most clients
will take anything you find for them. But she wouldn't
work in a home with little kids. 'No young children.' I
remember her saying that. I may have set up an interview for her. It would be on the intake sheet if I could
find it but I can't."

"Do you remember her name?" asked Vega.

"I think it was Maria. I don't remember her last
name."

"Well," Vega laughed. "That only narrows the list
down to like a third of the Latinas in the county."

"I know. Sorry," said Linda. "But even if I remembered a last name, sometimes clients give me fake ones
and change them periodically so that may not help you
as much as you think. But I do remember that she was
with a man when she came in. I see him at the center
from time to time. He never did an intake sheet. I've
asked a few times but he's always refused. I know he
usually comes in with Enrique Sandoval."

"I know Enrique," said Adele. Enrique had a crush
on her. She could feel it. The way he'd hop from one
foot to the other, like he was walking on fire in her
presence. Kind of the way Vega was behaving with
Linda now. "Enrique comes in with his older cousin a
lot. Anibal—"

"This isn't Anibal," said Linda. "Anibal has a mustache. And his fingers—" Linda held up her left hand
and made a slicing motion across the digits. Anibal
was so good with his hands, you'd have to look closely
to know that some of his fingers were partially ampu-
tated. "This other man—I saw him this morning before
I came over to the preschool. He and Enrique and Ani-

bal got picked for a job clearing brush over in Wick-ford. His shoe was falling apart."

"You mean Rodrigo." Adele had seen the boot. Tied together with string. They had some castoffs in a closet and she tried to find him a pair that fit but they were all too small. Adele felt bad for Rodrigo. He had so much dignity when he was trying to stuff his feet into the castoffs. He was so unfailingly gracious, thanking her for her efforts. It would have been easy to drive to Tar-get, buy a pair of cheap work boots out of her own pocket, and come back. But then she'd have to do it for every client. And they all had sad stories. So she helped Rodrigo get thicker string to keep the sole tied to the boot and hoped he'd either earn enough to get a new pair or someone would donate the right size.

"This guy's name is Rodrigo?" asked Vega. He bounced a look from Adele to Linda. "Rodrigo what?"

"I don't know," Adele admitted. "Unless a client does an intake sheet, we don't know anything about them."

"But you know what he looks like. You know who he's working for today."

Adele looked at Linda. She didn't normally get in-volved with the nitty-gritty of hiring the way Linda did. And beyond that, she wasn't sure if this was a con-versation they should be having.

Linda must have picked up on the same sense of foreboding. She folded her arms across her chest and gave Vega a wary look. "If I tell you where Rodrigo's working, what will happen to him?"

"Nothing." Vega shrugged. "I just want to talk to him."

"Like you just wanted to *talk* to José Ortiz?" asked Adele.

Vega gave her a dark look.

"I don't want to get Rodrigo in trouble," said Linda.

"This guy could turn out to be a material witness to a homicide investigation—"

"Oh, so now it's a homicide investigation," said Adele. "What happened to, 'I have no further information'?"

She'd caught him. She could see it in his face. If Rodrigo really did know this Maria and she was anything other than an accidental drowning, he was looking at all sorts of legal problems. Maybe Linda didn't know what the stakes were here, but Adele did.

Vega's Bronx accent became edgier and more pronounced. "You are impeding a police investigation, Ms. Figueroa."

"Not impeding," Adele corrected. "Just making sure all the safeguards are in place. You put together a solid case for probable cause and Rodrigo will come to La Casa, represented by Scott Porter, to answer your questions."

Inside the school, one of the teachers pounded out three chords on an out-of-tune piano someone had donated. The children began to sing "Itsy Bitsy Spider"— even the ones who didn't yet speak a word of English.

"I don't believe you two," said Vega. He punched the side of the fence. It made a sharp twanging sound. The fence was on its last legs. It needed replacing, like everything else at La Casa. "Here you make it sound like the police aren't doing their jobs—and the moment you can actually help—you lawyer up. That dead woman is Latino too, you know. And probably just as undocumented. *Dios mío,* she's a mother! She's got a baby somewheres. Doesn't she matter as much as your precious day laborers?"

Linda went to speak but Adele motioned for her to stay silent. This was lawyer-to-cop right now. "We are happy to cooperate, Detective. But you and I both know that you're not looking for an ID on a drowning. You're looking for a suspect in a possible homicide. And you're salivating because you think you've got one in your crosshairs."

"You wanna play games? Go ahead," said Vega, backing away. "Play all the games you want. But I'll get this guy. With or without your help."

"I'm just doing my job," Adele shot back.

"Yeah?" he stomped off. "Well so am I."

# Chapter 9

Work. Rodrigo finally had work. It had been two weeks since he'd gotten hired for anything. The last had been thirty dollars to move a treadmill and exercise bike from the basement of a house to the newly renovated master bedroom suite on the second floor. The exercise bike wasn't too bad. But the treadmill was sheer hell. It weighed 350 pounds and couldn't be disassembled. He, Enrique, and Anibal had all lifted it together and carted it up two flights of stairs. By the top of the second floor, they were all dripping with sweat. They got more exercise moving the equipment, he suspected, than the woman who paid them would ever get using it.

But no matter. Today was better. Today, he would get a hundred dollars for ten hours of work clearing brush and branches from a field, plus a sandwich for lunch. And there was more work tomorrow. And the day after that. The boss, a tall, thickset Paraguayan who came here thirty years ago when immigration was a matter of a plane ticket and a willingness to work, said he might need them for the whole week. That meant five hundred dollars. A chance to buy new work boots that didn't need to be held together with string. Enough money to phone home and wire some back. After his first trip to the United States five years ago, Rodrigo had been able to save enough to build his family a small cinderblock house in Esperanza with running water and electricity and to pay for his two older children's schooling. But they'd had to mortgage the house to pay for this second border crossing. Forty thousand quetzals, the equivalent of 5,200 American dollars. If he didn't send money home soon, Beatriz could lose the house. Juliza and Lorenzo would be kicked out of school. His little Stephany wouldn't even get to start on an education. Then where would his family be?

He refused to think that way. *Be positive.* It was early April, after all. Landscaping jobs were picking up. The men at La Casa said the U.S. economy was getting better. Tighter borders meant fewer immigrants. Less competition. Things were bound to turn around. He hoped so. *Dios mío,* he hoped so.

A lot of the Latin-American men Rodrigo knew hated the geography of suburban New York. Such cold winters. All those bare trees and gray skies and icy winds that whipped through your clothes like you weren't wearing any. But Rodrigo liked the landscape, liked the way the hills rose and fell in little puckers and swells, soft like a quilt on an unmade bed. He loved walking by the wood-frame houses in the evenings, seeing the golden glow from the windows, smelling wood smoke from chimneys in the crisp evening air.

His dream was to make enough money to go back to his hometown in Guatemala and live there with his family in comfort for the rest of their lives. If he could

*Suzanne Chazin*

achieve that, he would not think unkindly about his time here in the North. His *adventure.* That's how he liked to think of it. The two terrible journeys across Mexico and the border, two times nearly dying in the desert. That stretch in prison and then a detention center. The fear. The crushing loneliness—they would all fade in time. If things worked out, he would sit one day in the sunny, dusty square in Esperanza where the stray dogs roamed, playing dominoes with Enrique and Anibal, eating mangoes so ripe the juice ran down their faces, and they would speak of those hills. And their battle scars. And they would laugh.

It had been clear and mild most of the day, but it was late afternoon now and the heat of the sun had started to fade. Their boss, Señor Silva, was a gray-haired man with grizzled, leathery skin. Even when he spoke English to the *Norte Americanos,* his voice seemed laced with a strong Spanish accent. He had hired Rodrigo, Enrique, and Anibal to clear out a three-acre field behind a huge shingled house that looked big enough to be a hotel. Silva said the family lived in New York City and only came up on the weekends. The back three acres had been used as sort of a dumping ground for brush and vines and now the owner planned to landscape it. The land needed to be cleared right down to the dirt. Branches had to be removed, vines hacked, thorny bushes dug up.

When they got to the field that morning, the land was wet from days of rain. Beneath the brambles and weeds, there were sinkholes of mud. Anibal, always resourceful, helped Rodrigo wrap his sock in two plastic supermarket shopping bags before he stuck it in his tied-up shoe so his foot would stay dry. A good idea, but it didn't work. As the day wore on, the bags gave out and by lunchtime, Rodrigo's sock was soaked through and covered with mud as if he hadn't been wearing any boots at all. It reminded him of his barefoot boyhood in Guatemala where he didn't own a pair of shoes until he was sixteen. The difference was, Guatemala was warm, the ground mostly soft. Here, it was cold and wet and hard. The bag just added to the mess so all day, Rodrigo felt like he was walking on a dead fish.

Silva had two Weedwackers in his truck with his company's name, Green Acres Landscaping, on the side. But he said it was too dangerous for the men to use the Weedwackers until they had cleared the worst of the brush by hand. He had assumed the men would have their own work gloves and seemed annoyed when they didn't. But he handed them each a pair of thin ones from the truck. The gloves didn't entirely stop the blackberry thorns from piercing their skin but Rodrigo found that if you grabbed them hard, you often got less pricked than if you tried to be delicate about it.

They started with the large branches, carrying them over to the boss's wood chipper and feeding them into the machine. Rodrigo was thankful that Silva at least supplied goggles. He'd known a man on his first trip to the States who'd lost an eye from a piece of wood that shot out of a chipper.

Rodrigo and the men worked well together. Even though he wasn't related to Enrique and Anibal, here in the States, they treated him like a brother. Anibal had even started calling him that. *Hermano,* this, and *hermano* that. They all missed their families so they needed to invent connections wherever possible.

The work was hard. Bending. Cutting. Carrying. All

the thorns that stuck to your clothes and cut right through your hoodie and jeans. All the different plants you didn't want to get on your skin or you'd itch for a week. The insects you had to worry about. Ticks that could give you a fever and make your joints ache. Underground wasps' nests that could swarm if you disturbed them. But it was a million times better that they were all together. Together, they developed a rhythm. And always, they talked. What they would do first when they got back to Esperanza. (Enrique would find his young wife, Zulma, and stay in bed with her for twenty-four hours—only Enrique didn't use such polite language to explain it.) What they missed most. (Rodrigo: having little Stephany on his shoulders when he walked to church.) The funniest thing that happened since they arrived. (Anibal needed to buy some sheets for his mattress. He walked up to a saleswoman in a store and asked for "shits." She pointed to the restroom.) They worked hard but they laughed too and the laughing made Rodrigo forget how much he ached or how cold and wet his toes were. For a moment—just a moment—he actually forgot how very far he was from home.

Señor Silva never smiled, but as the day wore on, he seemed to grow a grudging respect for how hard his three employees worked and he left them on their own for several hours while he drove off to check up on other jobs. Enrique joked that they could slack off a bit now that the boss man wasn't here, but Anibal frowned.

"We have a chance to work with him for a week, maybe longer. If anything, he should come back and be surprised at how much we have accomplished."

Rodrigo agreed with Anibal. They had to give the

work their best effort. But even as he said this, he knew it would be hard to impress a man like Benito Silva no matter what they did. Rodrigo suspected Silva was more like them than he pretended, a man who had come here with nothing and clawed his way up. The American Dream, these *Norte Americanos* call it. Except it really was a dream now. Benito Silva came before Latinos had to worry about getting deported and starting all over again.

Rodrigo hoped Silva would be fair with them at least—pay them what he'd promised. Some employers start out with the amount that they are going to pay and they whittle it down over the course of the day. They deduct for a sandwich at lunch, for the use of safety equipment, for breaks to eat or piss, for transportation—for just about everything.

*Norte Americanos,* in Rodrigo's experience, were the best employers. Especially the wealthy ones. They were polite. They paid what they promised. They talked like you understood what they were saying and that was hard because you had to do a lot of nodding and guessing. But they seemed to want you to like them. The people who cheated him the most were other Latinos—the legal ones—and other immigrants in general, especially the ones who'd once been on the bottom themselves. They seemed to divide the world into cheaters and losers and they walked around with a held breath in them, waiting to see which one you'd turn out to be. Rodrigo would have thought that coming up the hard way would make a person more sympathetic to the suffering of others. But in his experience the opposite was true. To weather life at its sharp, remorseless margins, you needed thick calluses and an indifference to pain.

People didn't seem to shed those defenses easily, not even when they didn't need them anymore.

The men had gotten about half of the three acres free of vines, thorns, and branches by about four-thirty in the afternoon. Rodrigo removed his baseball cap and raked a hand through his sweat-soaked hair. He was dying for some water. Silva kept water in his truck but he had not returned for about two hours.

"He should be back soon," said Enrique, wiping his face with his sleeve. "He promised we'd quit at six."

The area had nothing around it. "Wickford," Silva called it, though if the men had had to walk back to Lake Holly from here, they wouldn't have had a clue what direction to start in. The house was on a winding road, narrow as a cow path. This time of year, with the trees not yet leafed out, Rodrigo could see a patchwork of other enormous houses on neighboring streets. Nobody seemed to be home. The entire area looked as if no one really lived here. Every now and then, he'd hear a dog bark from somewhere far off or the soft brakes of a delivery truck. Sometimes a plane would fly overhead and Rodrigo would stop for just a moment and watch the scarf of white tail smoke in the sky. He'd been on a plane once, a couple of years ago, but it wasn't a happy experience. It was the time they deported him back to Guatemala. The deportees were shackled together in a van with mesh windows until they reached the tarmac. Then they were frisked and escorted by armed immigration agents onto the plane. He would have liked to have enjoyed the experience, this coming home by airplane and seeing his family again. But it felt heavy with failure, especially after five months in prison, five months where he couldn't send a penny home.

The field they were working in felt hemmed in and isolated at the same time. To the left of the field was a small street that presumably wound toward some of these other houses Rodrigo could see. To the right was a wooded area, thick enough that even with all the leaves down, it felt dense and claustrophobic. Rodrigo hoped they wouldn't get stranded here when it got dark.

He turned back to helping Enrique dig up the roots of a barberry bush when he heard the slow creep of a car down the road. He wanted to believe it was Silva, but Silva's rusted-out Dodge pickup truck announced itself with the wheeze of an old man's lungs. This car was quiet. And slow. A neighbor's, perhaps.

Rodrigo straightened and leaned on his shovel. Enrique stopped shoveling and did the same. Both men were hoping for water. Rodrigo's throat was starting to burn. It was a panic reaction, he knew, a vestige of that first border crossing. He'd had to cut his four gallons of water—all thirty-three pounds—off his back to outrun *la migra*, even climbing a razor-wire fence barehanded. He'd spent the next twenty-eight hours in the desert, his hands swollen to the size of baseball mitts, drinking his own urine and praying that he wouldn't die nameless under some bush, his family never knowing his fate. Five years had gone by and still he couldn't shake that sense of panic he got when he went too long without water.

Anibal, hacking at the branches of a vine, grunted to Rodrigo and Enrique that the señor would be back soon and wishing it wouldn't make it come faster. But Rodrigo was now transfixed by the car.

It was an American car. Dark blue. Not an SUV or fancy sports car like the ones the Anglos drove around here. A maid service perhaps. A pizza delivery. But there was no company name on the side. This car was traveling like it didn't know where it was going. It pulled beyond the driveway of the house and turned onto the adjoining street. Rodrigo went back to his digging. Then he caught the movement from the corner of his eye. The car had made a U-turn. It was creeping alongside the house again.

"Ay, you two. This is no time to stop working," Anibal chided.

Enrique squinted at the car. His eyesight wasn't great. And besides, it was hard to see inside the sedan in daylight. Like looking in a pond caught in the glare of the sun. But Rodrigo's eyesight was much better. On his second journey across the border he'd earned the nickname *Ojos*—"eyes." Whenever the border patrol helicopters flew overhead, their rotors beating close enough to part the hairs on a man's head, the people scattered and threw themselves under mesquite bushes. It was what you had to do or the men in the helicopters would radio your location and *la migra* would ride up in their trucks and arrest you.

But the shade beneath the bushes was also the place where rattlesnakes curled up. Twice Rodrigo's eyes had saved another traveler's life by spotting the snake and redirecting the panicked person to another bush. It wasn't *things* he could see so much as *movement*. In the case of the snakes, the way the light pearled on their bodies in the sand, the way the dust seemed to shimmer around them. It was the movement he saw now again. A reach of a hand near the dashboard. Across something. A light bar. Only cops had light bars.

The car turned in the driveway. Only a couple of acres of field separated the car's occupants from the men. Rodrigo froze, hand on the shovel, watching as a man got out of the driver's side of the car. Dark blue police jacket. Mirrored sunglasses, even though the sun had traveled to the other side of the woods and the sky was bleached rather than bright. They couldn't hide his face completely. He was the Spanish-looking cop Rodrigo had seen yesterday at La Casa, the officer who was showing Maria's picture around. Another man got out of the passenger's side of the car—a big, heavy-set Anglo who looked less than thrilled that he might have to walk across a couple of acres of swampy brush.

Even at this distance, Rodrigo knew. He saw it in the way the Spanish-looking cop took off his sunglasses and chucked them in the car, his eyes never once losing focus on Rodrigo. He was the one they wanted. Not Anibal or Enrique. Rodrigo knew why, too. It was bad luck for him, no matter what he did from this point forward.

Rodrigo willed himself to shut down. To become a stone. To have no needs, no wants, no desires, no capacity for pain or fear or remorse. But he could not stop the thrumming in his chest, the wild panic he felt as the Spanish cop started walking toward them, picking his way across the puddles and brush in the field. He felt trapped like a cow off to slaughter, hemmed in by a terrain he didn't know. Fields in back. Streets and houses in front and to the left. Only a dark woods to the right. A chance to get away. *Run and hide. Run and hide.*

They would deport him if they caught him. Back in detention with all those big men and guards who punched and kicked you if you were too slow or didn't understand something. Back on that plane. To what sort of future? They would lose the house if he got deported. Lorenzo and Juliza would have to leave school. Stephany wouldn't even get to start. *Ay, chimado!* He wouldn't even get paid for today.

He broke out in a cold sweat. His breath turned ragged and shallow. His hands throbbed like they hadn't since he'd cut them up on that border fence. *Run,* a voice inside told him. *It's your only chance.* He'd run from so many people these past five years: the Mexican police, gangsters, border patrol agents, Arizona cops. He'd had machetes held to his throat and pistols to his head. He'd wandered the desert half-dead of thirst and seen things done to men and women in the name of greed and lust and ignorance that no man should ever have to see.

And so he ran.

It was all he knew how to do anymore. As a boy, he wasn't fast. Other boys always beat him in races. But you run differently when your life depends on it. You run pitched forward. You run without worrying about what you might crash up against. You can't feel the stitch in your side or the branch that scrapes your face or the stump that bangs your toe. You don't run to win; you run to survive and that makes all the difference.

He heard voices behind him. The cop's voice, cursing in a mixture of Spanish and English. And Anibal's voice, calm and reasonable as always. "*Mi hermano!* Why are you running? It will only make matters worse. We can talk to them. Please."

By the time he reached the woods, the string had fallen off his right work boot and the rubber sole flopped open. He ran with the foolish hop-step of a comic-book character, his boot so useless that it would have almost been better to kick it off. He scrabbled over a fallen log and his sole caught a snag, tossing him chest first into the mud. He started to claw himself to his feet when he heard a crash through the leaves and felt the thud of a bigger man's body landing full-force against him, the man cursing in a rough, guttural-sounding Spanish as he shoved a knee into the small of Rodrigo's back and cuffed his arms behind him. The man hoisted Rodrigo roughly out of the mud. Rodrigo's baseball cap fell off his head and tumbled to his feet.

The Spanish cop was muddy now too, and not too happy about it. He let out a stream of invectives, mostly having to do with Rodrigo's mother and the worthless life she gave birth to, namely him. Rodrigo looked through the woods and saw Silva's truck parked behind the cops. He'd never get his money or even a glass of water now. He could see Enrique gesturing wildly to the other police officer who looked bored and uncomprehending. Anibal had a hand on Enrique's shoulder. He knew what the limits of their power were here.

*Be a stone. Be a stone. Nothing can hurt a stone.* He had told himself the same thing that time the Mexican police had forced him and about thirty other people from that truck in Veracruz and stripped them of their money and valuables. They had grabbed Maria then. They had started to drag her off—Rodrigo and Maria both knew for what. Rodrigo stepped up. Foolishly, perhaps. He lied and said she was his wife. One of the *cerotes* punched him in the face, blackened both eyes, and threw him to the ground. But they spared Maria. She was grateful—too grateful. At this moment, Rodrigo almost wished he'd have let fate have its way. Then perhaps none of this would be happening.

The cop tugged on Rodrigo's handcuffs and told him to walk. It was difficult. The bracelets pinched his shoulders back uncomfortably. Without the benefit of hands, Rodrigo had nothing to break his fall. He hesitated for a moment, staring at his baseball cap in the mud, its frayed brim soaked and misshapen. The cop did not pick it up. Rodrigo offered it one last longing glance. He knew it would remain in the woods to molder and disintegrate—his little marker that he was here, that for one bright shining moment, he existed on this landscape of gray hills and gray trees and men with gray faces. He already knew he'd never be back.

Rodrigo took a step forward and fell. The cop yanked him to his feet and pushed him along. It happened again. The second time, Rodrigo fell face-first onto a decaying tree stump. It smacked against his lower lip with the force of a rifle butt. His vision went blank for a second and a white-hot pain shot through him the way it had when he'd taken those blows from the Mexican police. He could taste blood in his mouth along with pulpy sour bits of wood. He spit the wood out but he felt like a baby with drool running down his chin. Except it wasn't drool. It was warmer than that. And red. Bright red. His blood. The officer yanked him to his feet again and cursed. Rodrigo could feel his lip starting to swell as he mumbled an explanation and nodded his chin to his feet. The cop looked down at his useless right boot flapping open, his soggy, muddy sock beneath, and mistook the damage for being the result of the chase.

"Serves you right, *pendejo,* for running like that." The cop pushed Rodrigo forward, though this time at least, he held him erect, a hard grip on one shoulder. Rodrigo did not fall again.

On the driveway, handcuffed, his clothes covered in mud, his lip swollen and bleeding, his work boot falling apart, Rodrigo felt ashamed. Broken. Silva didn't even look at them—any of them. He was talking to the fat cop, a mixture of annoyance and resignation in the way he folded his arms across his chest, the way he gestured to all of them as if they were cattle that had broken through a stockade and needed to be rounded up and contained better in the future.

Enrique was talking at fever pitch to the Spanish cop, saying that the men were being hassled for no reason. Anibal, calm and resigned as always, asked the cop if he could go over to Rodrigo and wipe the blood from his friend's face. The cop relented and Anibal produced a rag from his pocket and gently brought it across Rodrigo's lower lip and chin as if Rodrigo weren't just a friend or even a brother. It was as if Rodrigo were his son.

"You will be okay, *mi hermano,*" Anibal said softly. He dabbed at Rodrigo's lip as gently as if he were wiping the skin of a newborn baby. Then he folded the rag to a clean section and worked up from Rodrigo's chin, all the time murmuring words of comfort. "God is with you. He will not desert you."

Rodrigo felt something thick and cottony well up in

his throat. His friend's tenderness, more than anything else that had happened, brought Rodrigo close to tears. He tried harder than he could ever recall to hold back his emotions. He would not break down in front of all these despicable, indifferent men. These *choleros*. He swallowed hard and looked up. A flock of geese crossed the sky in V formation. They were perfectly attuned to one another. They were together. As it should be. He wondered if he'd ever see Anibal and Enrique again.

Anibal spoke calmly and respectfully to the police officer. He asked why the officer had handcuffed his friend.

"Rodrigo knows. He wouldn't have run if he didn't."

Anibal said nothing, only gave Rodrigo a searching look. *Is it true?* his eyes asked.

Rodrigo turned away from his friend. He couldn't bear to look at anyone anymore. The police were going to ask him about Maria, if he knew she was missing. They would ask if he was innocent. And was he? Truly? He had broken one of God's sacred commandments. He had become no better than the *cabrones* he swore he would never turn into. He had let his family down. His wife. His children, too. And now they would all pay for his sins. How could he claim innocence in the face of all their misery?

"Let my friends go," Rodrigo mumbled to the officer through swollen lips. He was thirsty. So thirsty he'd have licked the puddles off the ground if they'd let him. "Do whatever you are going to do with me. But please— let them go."

# Chapter 10

Jimmy Vega and Louie Greco were supposed to be veteran detectives, experienced enough to talk a short, uneducated illegal alien into their car without him ending up looking like he'd gone through an MS-13 gang initiation ceremony. Instead, Rodrigo was sitting in the Lake Holly station house with a busted lip, a muddy, blood-soaked hoodie, a work boot he couldn't walk in, and the quiet, doomed demeanor of a man who knew he wasn't walking out of here tonight, if ever. Vega and Greco were in the shit now. Up to their eyeballs. No amount of TLC was going to make Rodrigo look like a poster child for Latino-Anglo relations in the community.

And now Scott Porter was coming by the station, no doubt to demand Rodrigo's release, having gotten wind of the situation from those other two men at the job site. (Vega and Greco should have detained them as well, but on what grounds?) Most immigrants have to beg for decent legal representation. It was just Vega's luck that this guy was getting it delivered to his door after being in police custody less than an hour. They'd barely had time to get his full name and feed it into the computer, let alone interview him.

They sat Rodrigo in a windowless conference room and offered him a Coke. He asked for water instead and drank half a quart in one swallow—not an easy feat for a man with a badly swollen lip.

There was nothing in the conference room but a couple of chairs and a big wall clock that ticked off the seconds and kept reminding Vega how little time he was going to have with Rodrigo before Scott Porter got a hold of him. The room was hot and stuffy. The fluorescent light fixtures buzzed. Down the hall, Vega could hear two cops talking about the Yankees' batting lineup for the season.

Vega scanned what the database at Immigration and Customs Enforcement—ICE—had kicked back on the man. Full name: Rodrigo Eliseo Morales-Aguirre. Age: thirty-three. Born in Esperanza, Guatemala. One arrest, two years ago, when ICE agents raided a food processing plant in Rhode Island. Morales's employer got a small fine for hiring illegal aliens. Morales—who bought a stolen Social Security card for three hundred dollars so he could work at the food processing plant—got charged with identity theft. He was jailed and deported, which made him an automatic felon the moment he reentered the United States.

"Why did you run today, man?" Vega asked him in Spanish. "All we wanted to do was ask you a few questions. You ruined my shirt." Vega gestured to his striped oxford, covered in a patchwork of drying mud. He was hoping to warm things up a bit, make it seem as if they'd both gotten off on the wrong foot. But Morales remained hunched and beaten, picking at a thorn that

had gotten wedged in his right palm. Vega hadn't noticed his hands before this. The knuckles were abraded,
the fingernails ragged and torn, the palms deeply callused. His hands told the tale of his life and it looked as
if none of it had been easy.

Morales kept his eyes on his hands. "I was supposed
to be paid a hundred dollars today," he mumbled softly.

"Maybe your friends will get it for you." But Vega
already knew the contractor would never pay. He'd
argue that the men hadn't worked a full day, that they'd
brought cops to the site. Vega had been stiffed by a few
contractors when he worked for them in college and he
was an American with a native's command of invectives
and a Bronx attitude. Rodrigo Morales didn't stand a
chance. Not that Vega was about to feel sorry for the
guy. He was in this country illegally after being convicted and imprisoned for identity theft. He ran from
the police and cost Vega a nice set of clothes. And besides that, what if he turned out to be the killer of the
mother at the lake? Sympathy had no place in a police
interrogation room.

"You got a local address, Rodrigo?"

Morales hesitated.

"I'm not ICE, man. We're not gonna raid the place,
okay?"

"It's just—I have friends there."

"Your friends aren't going to get deported." Vega
held up his notebook. "See? I'm not faxing it to ICE or
anything. I'm just putting it in my notes."

Morales mumbled an address. Vega was already betting it wasn't the right address. Right street, wrong house
number. Right house number, wrong street. He probably
shared a room with three or four other men for three

hundred dollars a month cash. Hot plate on the floor, mattresses or bunk beds against the walls. One bathroom for fifteen tenants. All his possessions could probably fit in one backpack if he had to leave in a hurry. That's why he was being detained in the first place.

"Cell number?" All these immigrants had prepaid wireless phones. The entire industry was founded on people without papers or credit.

"It's not working."

"What do you mean, 'it's not working'?"

"I haven't had enough money to pay for minutes in four weeks." There was a catch in Morales's voice. Vega suspected he had kids back in Guatemala. Before cell phones, some of these guys went months without talking to their families. Now, four weeks probably felt like an eternity.

"You've still got a number, right? For when you can buy minutes again."

Morales nodded and gave the number. This time, Vega was pretty sure he was telling the truth. He wouldn't fear offering up a cell number the way he'd fear offering up an address. In all likelihood, he didn't give his name when he bought his phone and he recharged up the minutes in cash.

Vega wrote down all the information and then slid a copy of the flyer across the table.

"Who is she, Rodrigo?"

Morales slowly traced a hand across the photo, then shook his head. "I can't go back to Guatemala. My family will lose everything." Vega heard the tight pull of his vocal cords, the barely suppressed panic. He may have closed down on the outside, but the adrenaline was pumping beneath.

"I told you, man. I don't care about your immigration status. All I want is for you to answer my questions."

Morales lifted his gaze and Vega saw his eyes for the first time. They were red at the rims, dark and deep as caves at their centers. Sad eyes. Old eyes. Too old for a man of thirty-three. Rodrigo Eliseo Morales-Aguirre already knew that he'd never see his hundred dollars. He already knew that no matter what Vega said, his criminal conviction pretty much guaranteed he'd be deported. Vega was a good liar but Morales had seen too much of the world to be easily lied to. Vega would have to try some other tack with him. Guilt maybe. He pointed to the photograph again.

"She's dead, man. And her daughter? We can't find her. Nobody's come forward to tell us where she is. She could be dead too for all we know. You want that on your conscience? A woman you knew buried in an unmarked grave thousands of miles from her home? No priest or anything to say a prayer for her? Her family never knowing what happened?"

There was no surprise in Morales's eyes when Vega told him she was dead. Then again, police officers don't chase people down and cuff them over a missing illegal. Even Morales knew that.

"How did she die?"

Vega thought he heard something tender in the man's voice. "First tell me her name."

Morales took a deep breath. "Maria Elena. I don't know anything about the child. I never saw her."

"What's Maria's last name?"

"Vasquez. But it wasn't real."

"You gave yourselves fake names?"

"Not us. The coyotes." Morales shuffled his feet on the floor beneath the table. His right work boot flapped open in front. Vega couldn't imagine how he'd managed to run in that boot, let alone work in it. Morales pulled a twig that had gotten lodged in his hair and dropped it to the floor. The police had let him wash his hands and face after they brought him to the station, but there were no facilities for detainees to do more than that.

"When you cross from Guatemala to Mexico," Morales explained, tapping his feet nervously, "the coyotes give you a Mexican passport. You have to memorize the information. That way, if the police stop you, you can say you are Mexican. Otherwise, they deport you back to Guatemala."

Vega thought deportations only happened if you made it to the U.S. It had never occurred to him that the whole process could stop before it began. "So her name on her Mexican passport was Maria Elena Vasquez?"

Morales shook his head. "Margarita Vasquez-Herrera. But I knew her real name was Maria Elena. I just never told her my last name and she never told me hers—in case we got caught."

"I see. And out of curiosity," said Vega, "what was *your* fake name?"

"Gonzalo Rivera-Jimenez. I was a thirty-one-year-old bricklayer from San Luis Potosi."

"You remember all that?"

Morales touched the back of his hand to his swollen

lip, crusted with dried blood. "I remember everything." For a moment, the weight of those memories seemed to settle on his broad shoulders. He massaged his temples like a man trying to rub out a stain that refused to disappear.

Vega pressed on. "Did Maria talk about her daughter at all? The one in the picture?"

"We didn't talk much about our lives."

"Did she say her daughter's name? Her age? Whether she had other children?"

Morales shook his head and took another gulp of water. He couldn't seem to get enough. Maybe it was a nervous reaction. "She only said she was coming North for her daughter."

"You mean, to provide a better life for her?"

He shrugged. "What other reason is there?"

This was good news at least, thought Vega. It was possible the little girl was back in Guatemala with a grandmother or other relative.

"Did Maria Elena come from your hometown?"

"No. I think she came from Aguas Calientes," said Morales. "About thirty kilometers away."

"Know anyone else from Aguas Calientes?"

"No."

That may or may not have been true, Vega realized. Morales wasn't about to give out the names of friends to a cop. "You met Maria where?"

"We were in the same group coming North. We both planned to come to Lake Holly."

"She have family here?"

"Not that I know of. I think she just heard it's safe." Morales shook his head sadly. Even Vega had to admit the irony of his words. *Safe, sure. Maria Elena is dead and Morales is likely to be imprisoned and/or deported.*

"So you and she came to Lake Holly together."

"We came together. But not—not in that way."

Vega noted a slight coloring in Morales's cheeks.

"What way was it then?" Vega smiled but it was a cop's smile. He was already a step ahead of Morales. Men all cut the same way when you come right down to it.

"We didn't—I have a wife and children in Guatemala."

"Yes," said Vega. "I gathered that part."

"Once we came here, I didn't—" Morales fingered a loose piece of veneer on the tabletop. "I promised my wife I would be faithful." He looked more upset than at any time during their conversation. Vega had to smile. Rodrigo Morales could survive anything; endure anything—except the reproach of his wife.

"Look man," Vega assured him. "You wouldn't be the first guy bearing up under difficult circumstances who forgot your vows for a while. Seems to me, a lot of the men who cross the border do that." Vega knew plenty who had abandoned their families entirely and made new ones here. But he had a sense Morales was not that kind of man. He seemed genuinely distressed by his infidelity. The question was, could he have been distressed enough to kill Maria Elena if, say, she wanted to keep the relationship going and he didn't?

"I stopped it," said Morales. "Soon after we came."

"So you were having sexual relations with Maria Elena and you decided to stop?"

"Yes." Morales looked down at his hands, embarrassed. "I stopped."

"When?"

"I don't remember. Sometime in October maybe?"

"I have a witness who saw you come into La Casa with Maria."

"That would have been in the fall. To help her find a job."

"Did she find one?"

"Not right away. But eventually, yes. She worked as a live-in housekeeper."

"Where?"

"I don't know the house. Somewhere on the hill away from town. Where the houses and lawns are very big and the trees very small. I've cut lawns there."

"The Farms?"

"Maybe." He jiggled his feet nervously again. "You never told me how she died."

"How about you tell me?"

Morales blinked. "I don't know."

"Sure you do. You ran, didn't you?"

"Because you were going to arrest me."

Vega leaned back in his chair and put his hands behind his head as if they were just chatting over a beer. "I haven't arrested you, Rodrigo. Like I said, we're just talking here. So tell me how she died."

"I don't know how she died."

Vega decided to offer up a few details to help Rodrigo's memory along. "She was found in the lake. Maybe she couldn't swim?"

"No. She could swim. We both can." Morales looked confused. "Did she drown?"

*Kind of hard not to, with four ropes holding you down.*

"So if Maria went into the lake," said Vega, ignoring Morales's question, "she'd be able to swim out?"

"I—I think so. We never swam there. What happened to her?"

"I think you know."

Morales frowned. "I don't." And then it hit him. "Are you saying she was murdered?" He was so focused on his lost hundred dollars and the likelihood of getting deported, he'd completely missed the reason they'd brought him in in the first place. He touched his chest like Vega had just planted a fist in it. "You think I killed her?"

"You busted your ass to come North to provide for your family. And all of a sudden when you try to break it off, she wants to call ICE to get you deported. She wants to tell your wife—"

"She never did those things."

"Okay, *threatened* to do them. And everything you've worked for is about to go down the toilet, Rodrigo. Everything. On account of some jealous woman. Come on—who could blame you?" In Vega's experience, people confessed much more readily to even the most heinous of crimes if he tapped into their desire to come off as reasonable and justified.

Morales moved his swollen lips but no sound came out. He seemed unable to mount so much as a "no" in his defense. If Vega could get fifteen more minutes with the guy before Porter showed up, he might make some progress. Of course the physical evidence—what there was of it anyway—still had to match up. And there was the matter of that hate letter. But Vega had to go where the circumstances took him and worry about making all the pieces fit later.

"Don't you want to tell your side?" he prodded.

Something burst inside Rodrigo Morales, some door he could no longer keep shut. He'd been able to hide his fear but not his anger. He kept his voice low, but there was a hard edge to it when he spoke.

"You have no idea what we went through to come here. None. They would have raped her in Veracruz."

"Who? Bandits?"

"The police *are* bandits," said Morales. "I passed out in a boxcar with a hundred people stuffed in like sardines just south of Monterrey. I would have died if she hadn't gotten me near a crack in the undercarriage to get some air. You think I would kill her after all we went through?"

"You cared about her. I can see that," said Vega. "You weren't just some cold-blooded killer who wanted her dead."

Silence. Morales stared at him. "You will never understand." He said the words like they were a curse, like he was wishing on Vega one tenth of what had been heaped on him. Vega felt a shudder travel down his spine trying to imagine what it would be like to be trapped in a boxcar under the blazing Mexican sun with a hundred other people crammed into it. And he wondered, for all he'd seen in his eighteen years as a police officer, in his years growing up in the Bronx, if he hadn't seen anything at all.

The door to the conference room burst open and Scott Porter stood in it, paperwork and pen in hand. The goofy smile was gone. He took one glance at Morales's face and gave Vega a look of utter contempt.

"I am Mr. Morales's attorney. I will be representing him in all future proceedings, Detective. I am instructing him forthwith to cease and desist all conversation or co-operation with the police." Porter turned to Morales and gave a synopsis in Spanish of what he'd just said. Then he handed Morales some paperwork to sign.

"You don't have to sign that paperwork, Rodrigo," Vega said. "You're not under arrest. All we're doing is talking."

"Talking, huh?" Porter switched to English and gave an exaggerated shrug. "So? Talk is over. Let him go."

"We need to detain him."

"To ID a dead body? C'mon, Detective. Stop bull-shitting Morales. Stop bullshitting me."

"All right," said Vega. He tried to smooth down his mud-stained shirt. He didn't look or feel very profes-sional right now. "She's a little more than a dead body."

Greco joined them in the doorway, cursing quietly under his breath.

"Ah. I see, gentlemen," said Porter, all courtroom theatrics now. "So to the Latino community, she's being presented as an accidental death. But between your-selves, she's a homicide you're trying to sweep under the carpet."

"Now hold on," said Greco. "We haven't ruled it a homicide. We're still exploring all the angles."

"By coercing and threatening a defenseless immi-grant into a confession, no doubt."

"We're not coercing anyone into anything," said Vega. Though in his experience, the only way you ever got ketchup out of a bottle was with a little pressure. "He's simply being detained."

"You have probable cause to detain him?"

"Mr. Morales has ID'd the victim and indicated that

he had a consensual sexual relationship with her," said Vega.

Porter turned to Morales and asked in Spanish if what Vega had said was true. Morales hung his head and nodded. Score one for the police. Porter bounced a look from Greco to Vega.

"Is my client a witness? Or a suspect you're too lazy to handle in a constitutional manner?"

"Careful, Scott," Greco growled. "You piss us off enough and I'd be happy to charge him right now. He's got a criminal record and a prior deportation order so we both know it's *adiós, Estados Unidos* as soon as that happens. ICE will put a hold on him faster than a drunk to a whore's tit. The charge doesn't even have to stick. The results will be the same either way and you know it."

Porter tossed off a small laugh followed by a look of disbelief. It was as if he were mugging for an imaginary judge. Vega sensed this was exactly how he behaved in a courtroom. Vega took back every nice thing he thought about him at Linda's.

"Are you two detectives blind? Or just incredibly stupid?" He gestured to Morales. "Have you looked at my client's face?"

Vega shrugged. "So? He tripped."

"Got a witness to that effect?"

Vega looked at Greco who widened his eyes behind Porter's back. The only person who could say for sure whether Vega was telling the truth was the very man he was trying to detain, maybe even charge with murder. Porter must have known that already or he wouldn't have asked. Defense attorneys always have a second act up their sleeve.

"You send my client to county lockup on some sloppy, poorly executed charge and I will make sure that his bruised and bloodied face is on the cover of the *New York Times* tomorrow morning and all over the Internet by ten a.m. And don't expect me to hold back the way I've been doing. I will tell them about the arson at La Casa last month and the Reyes matter and all the other bias incidents that have been happening in town. By the time I'm finished, Maricopa County, Arizona, will look like a bastion of brotherly love compared to Lake Holly and Detective Vega here will be fielding his very own redneck fan club."

"I didn't rough him up," Vega insisted. "He tripped on his boots. We were in the woods."

Porter smiled viciously. "Looks like you've got even less proof of that than you've got to hold my client."

Vega curled his fists at his sides and tried to remind himself that he had eighteen unblemished years with the county police. Scott Porter couldn't undo all that— could he? Would Joy be opening the newspaper tomorrow morning to see her father's departmental photo plastered alongside Morales's swollen face? Would Captain Waring, Vega's boss, be doing the same? Vega could kiss off a future in homicide if that happened. For that matter, he could kiss off *any* future. Waring had no patience for brutes and bullies. He'd not only fire Vega, he'd personally see to it that he never worked in law enforcement again.

Vega turned to Greco. He tried to quell the rising panic in his chest. "Got another room we can talk in, away from Mr. Porter's client?"

"Yeah." Greco frowned. Even he looked scared and subdued. "This way."

Porter told Morales to sit tight; he'd be back. In the hallway, Vega saw Adele. Not good. Not good at all.

"Aw, damn it to hell," said Greco. "Why don't you just call in the ACLU while you're at it?" Greco jabbed a finger in Adele's direction. "Is she Morales's attorney too?"

"No," said Porter. "But I think you *gentlemen*"—he put a sarcastic emphasis on the word—"would be wise to listen to us. Things would have gone a lot better if you had."

# Chapter 11

Adele Figueroa sat in a stuffy, overheated conference room at the Lake Holly police station watching Scott Porter, Detective Greco, and Jimmy Vega mark their turf like a bunch of pit bulls eyeing each other's jugulars.

"—He's a material witness if we say he's a material witness." *Vega*.

"—Do the words, 'civil rights violations' mean anything to you?" *Porter*.

"—We charge Morales with even one misdemeanor and he's history. *Adiós amigo.*" *Greco*. Apparently, Rodrigo had a prior conviction and deportation in his immigration records so Greco's words weren't idle threats. The man really didn't have a prayer of staying in this country.

Adele herself had no idea what Rodrigo's background was. She hadn't had time to question Enrique or Anibal about their friend after they burst into La Casa this afternoon just as she was ducking out a little early to get her nails done. She couldn't remember the last time she'd had a reason to get a manicure but she immediately canceled as soon as the men breathlessly spilled out the story of Rodrigo's arrest. Or rather, Enrique did. Anibal just stood there, baseball cap in hand, and asked whether Señora Adele could please find their friend an attorney.

Adele liked Anibal. She trusted his judgment. She was furious that Vega had gone behind her back and plucked Rodrigo off his work site like Vega was picking up a bag of laundry from the dry cleaners. She couldn't imagine how he'd found Rodrigo so quickly. But now that she was here, her afternoon plans shot, her evening plans headed in the same direction, she realized how little she knew about the man.

He'd been coming to the center for only about six or seven months, mostly in the company of Enrique and Anibal. He sat in a corner, hoodie zipped around him, frayed baseball cap down low across his brow, his eyes always on the door for a job to come in. He didn't take English classes. He never filled out a client intake form. He was polite and quiet but distant and reserved. The only time she'd really spoken to him was when she tried to find him a pair of work boots to replace his worn-out ones. And now the police were detaining him in what appeared to be a homicide investigation. She wanted to help the man if he was innocent. Certainly Enrique and Anibal believed he was. But what if they were wrong? She didn't want to put La Casa on the line for a criminal.

The men in the room continued to argue. Adele put a hand up. No one noticed. Finally, she slammed two fists on the table. All three jumped.

"This," she said, "is a pissing match and it's getting us nowhere. You two," she said, gesturing to Vega and

Greco. "You say Rodrigo is a material witness. But it sounds to me like you're trying to turn him into a suspect and you're frustrated that you can't browbeat some sort of confession out of him. And you"—she turned to Porter—"With all due respect, Scott, you've been waiting for a chance to air the town's dirty laundry for some time. Maybe Rodrigo is your man. But what if he's a legitimate witness to a murder? Or—God forbid—a suspect?"

"That gives the police the right to rough him up?" asked Porter.

"*Puñeta!*" Vega slammed a fist on the table. "I didn't rough him up!" Vega ran two hands down his face. He looked exhausted. He rolled up his shirtsleeves, which were spattered with mud. There were flecks of mud on the dark hair of his arms. He turned to Adele and spread his arms, all sweetness and charm. A former altar boy, she was sure of it. "I didn't touch him, Adele. On my mother's grave, I swear." *Adele.* He'd called her *Adele.* She wondered if the switch was accidental or calculated. She felt a pull and swallowed it back. He had played her before—gone behind her back this afternoon to get Rodrigo over her objections. How had he managed that so quickly?

"You need to be honest with us, Detectives," said Adele. "It will go no further than this room, I can assure you. But we need to know why Rodrigo is so important to you."

Greco and Vega exchanged wary glances. Cops were so distrusting, maybe because they did so much lying themselves.

It was Greco who finally spoke. "We have evidence that the victim was put into the water against her will."

"Against her will how?" asked Porter.

"Against her will. Enough said."

"What makes you think Rodrigo's involved?" asked Adele.

"For starters," said Vega, "he's admitted to a sexual relationship with the victim. Plus, he's married and has indicated that he's upset about his infidelity."

"So he moves from adultery to murder?"

"Happens all the time." Vega shrugged. "We don't know if it happened here or not. That's why we need to interview him some more."

"Oh, no siree," said Porter. "You don't get to keep my client while you try to build a case against him."

"We cut him loose and he'll jackrabbit," said Greco. "By tomorrow, he could be in Chicago."

"Oh, please," said Porter. "You know how often the police hand me that excuse?"

"Maybe because it's true." Greco fixed his eyes on Adele. "What time today did you meet with Vilma Ortiz and Detective Vega to discuss the whereabouts of her husband?"

Adele felt put on the spot. The lawyer in her never liked answering a question without knowing where it was headed. She looked at Vega, but he gave her a slight shrug of the shoulders as if to suggest he didn't know either.

"I spoke to them around two, two-thirty. Something like that," said Adele. Vega nodded in agreement.

"Detective Anderson of the Metro-North PD went to interview José Ortiz at five p.m. today at the address Vilma supplied," said Greco. "That address led to an auto parts warehouse in Granville. No one there knew anyone by the name of José Ortiz."

Vega felt embarrassed. And taken. Not that he could have done anything about it. "Her cell phone worked," he insisted. "I called her myself."

"Yeah? Well it's not working any longer," said Greco. "She ditched it. They're cheap enough. She'll buy another. Which means our only potential witness in the Reyes case skipped less than three hours after we had a bead on him." Greco turned to Porter. "So don't tell me, Scott, about how your boy Morales is gonna act like a tree and grow roots if we spring him."

Vega tried to brush Ortiz to the back of his mind. He had more pressing concerns. "We're just asking for twenty-four hours," he told Porter. "The more Morales cooperates, the faster it will go."

"I see what you're doing, Detective." Porter wagged a finger at him. "Don't try to bullshit Adele and me. You want to keep Morales here until the swelling goes down on his face. So that when you release him you don't have any explaining to do."

"I *don't* have any explaining to do." Vega rose partway out of his chair. "You want to be a prick about this? Fine. I'll charge him with resisting arrest and run his prints through the computer right now. That should trigger a deportation detainer from ICE and a nice one-way ticket back to Guatemala before the week's out. Hell, I couldn't book a *cruise* any faster."

"Stop it, both of you," said Adele. "This is a man's life you're playing with here. His friends tell me he mortgaged his house to make this journey. It cost him the equivalent of over five thousand American dollars. If you send him back, his family will lose their home. His children will have to leave school."

"What are we?" asked Greco. "A freakin' social services agency?"

"His personal situation is beside the point," said Vega. "He stays until we can clear him."

"Or yourself more likely," said Porter.

Vega was out of his seat. Adele leaned back from the table. She thought he and Porter might actually come to blows. But then Greco put a firm grip on Vega's shoulder and eased him back into his chair. He nodded to Porter and Adele. "I think we all need a short break."

The two detectives left the room, their voices peppered with curses that faded down the hallway. Adele looked at Porter.

"I don't really have a problem with the police detaining Rodrigo for a short period if they're only checking out his story."

Porter rolled his eyes. "The police are never just *checking out* someone's story, Adele. The longer Morales sits in this station, the greater his chances are of getting charged or, at the very least, deported."

"What if he's guilty of harming that woman?"

"It's the police's job to make that case in a constitutionally protected manner—not turn the station house into Guantanamo Bay."

Beyond the conference room, Adele could hear the staccato bursts of calls in progress from a dispatch radio and the beeps and percussive noises of various police scanners and equipment. Voices punctured the white noise, hard and nasal, and then died away, often in a chase of throaty laughter. It was the sound of men with power. She was so used to dealing with men who had none that the experience felt jarring—threatening. She could only imagine what it felt like to Rodrigo.

"Maybe it would be better if we stopped seeing everything as *us* and *them,*" said Adele.

"There has to be an *us,*" he shot back. "How else can we keep *them* in line? Look at Morales's face and ask yourself: Would they have picked up an American citizen and questioned him in such a cavalier and reckless manner?"

"I'm just saying perhaps we should try to find common ground."

Porter's lips thinned. He leaned forward. "What happened, Adele? Are you losing your nerve? When you started La Casa, you had so much fire. You wanted to take on the entire Lake Holly community. Lately it seems you just want to make sure there's enough coffee at the snack bar."

"Is that what the board has been saying behind my back? Do you want me to resign?"

"I want you to have a bigger agenda."

"A bigger agenda? What do you think the medical clinic and dental van are? Or the after-school enrichment program? Or our domestic violence support group?"

"I'm talking about addressing the fundamental inequities in this town."

"And I'm talking about what clients really need: jobs and housing and access to education and medical care. You want demonstrations and lawsuits and media coverage. All that will do is invite ICE to draw a big fat bull's-eye on Lake Holly." Porter probably thought he was the opposite of the men on the other side of the door. But Adele thought they were quite similar, so certain of their worldview, so contemptuous of others.

Vega and Greco came back in the room now and took their seats. Vega looked tired and chastened. Adele had to assume that even though he and Greco were partners, the fact that the case was in Lake Holly's backyard meant Vega was ultimately a guest in another police authority's jurisdiction. She suspected Greco had reminded him of that, though with Greco, you could never be sure what he was thinking. He gave no hint. Instead, he slowly unwrapped a package of Twizzlers. The cellophane sounded like small firecrackers detonating in the room.

"So here's the situation." Greco leaned against the conference table, his belly taking the brunt of the impact. "Pardon my French, Adele, but I don't give a flying fuck about Rodrigo Morales. He took a chance and came here illegally. He threw the dice and lost. I didn't tell him to come and I'm not gonna lose any sleep over sending him back."

He held out the package of Twizzlers to the room with a mumbled grunt and shrugged when everyone declined. He took one for himself and bit off the end, chewing it thoughtfully. Scott Porter wasn't the only one who could hold an audience.

"Now my partner? Jimmy Vega here?" Greco nodded. "He's Hispanic and all, so he's got a bit of a soft spot for these lawbreakers. So for his sake—and *only* his sake—I don't mind detaining Morales at the station without charges or an ICE hold while we check his statement against our evidence. But I want to be crystal clear: we're not doing this because Porter here thinks he's got anything on my partner. Excuse my French again, but Scott? You don't have a limp dick to bat with here. However, if you back off any grandstanding against Detective Vega or this department and you don't get into bed with the media, we will do our best to clear Morales or find probable cause for an arrest within twenty-four hours."

"I want him released now," said Porter.

"Not gonna happen, Scott," said Greco. "Twenty-four hours with no charges and no ICE hold. Take it or leave it."

"And if you can't clear him in that time?" asked Adele.

Vega gave a dark nod to Porter. "Then I guess your chairman of the board over there will call up the *New York Times* and fry my *culo.*"

Outside, the air felt cool and fragrant, brushing against Adele's skin like freshly laundered sheets. Something green and earthy lingered in the scent. She checked her watch. Sophia was already at her dad's for the night. Adele had her dress in the car—a red sleeveless chiffon she hadn't worn in perhaps two years. She hoped it still fit. She couldn't recall the last time she'd gone to a party. Since the divorce, all she did was work and take care of Sophia. She fished her car keys out of her pocketbook.

"Hey Adele, wait up. I need to talk to you a moment."

Jimmy Vega hustled across the parking lot. He wasn't wearing a jacket so he had to hunch his shoulders against the cool night air.

"Please make this quick," said Adele. "I have plans for tonight."

"Can you break them?"

"Excuse me?"

"Or just delay them. For an hour. An hour and a half. That's all I'm asking."

"I don't think you're in a position to ask anything of me. Not after going behind my back today."

"Look, I'm sorry about that. I really am." He gave her a pained look. "But you saw what went on in there just now. Porter's gunning for me. I've got a daughter almost ready to graduate high school. She lives in town with my ex-wife. I don't want her to see her old man make the papers this way."

"What was it you said about Rodrigo earlier?" She snapped her fingers with the courtroom theatrics of Scott Porter. "Oh yes, I remember: His personal situation is beside the point."

Vega winced. "I had that coming, I guess." He played with a scab on one of his knuckles. He had scrapes on both hands and a bruise along the inside of his left wrist. There were ghostly outlines of mud that had flaked off his shirt and droplets of something rust-colored that did not brush off so easily. Blood. Rodrigo's blood. Vega caught her looking at it now.

"I know what it looks like. But for what it's worth, I swear: I didn't beat him up."

She held his gaze and watched his Adam's apple rise and fall like he was standing before a judge, awaiting his sentence. "I believe you," she said finally.

"You do?" He brightened. "Then you'll help me?"

"Help you how?"

"Let me look through your client files."

"*What?* Are you out of your mind?"

"I need to find the intake sheet Linda did on Maria. Without that sheet I'm sunk. I've got no way to nail down her identity, no way to clear or charge Morales. Twenty-four hours rolls around, I'm a dead man. I'll never work as a cop again if Porter makes that police brutality charge stick."

"Do you understand what you're asking? You're asking as an officer of the law to search the files of people who may be in this country illegally. Do you realize what would happen to my center—to *me?*—if my clients knew I'd turned over their personal information to the police?"

"I'm not going to look at anything that doesn't pertain to Maria."

"Get a subpoena if it's that important to you."

"You really want your clients seeing a whole bunch of cops carting their private records out of La Casa? You think *that's* not going to create panic?"

He was bluffing, she suspected. He already knew he'd never be able to convince a judge to order the sort of blanket subpoena he'd need to find Maria's intake sheet. Still—with cops, you never know.

"Linda already said she couldn't find Maria's intake sheet," Adele reminded him.

"She didn't have all the information I now have from Morales. She didn't know her full first name was Maria Elena. Or that she'd crossed the border under the surname Vasquez. Or that she was from Aguas Calientes, Guatemala. Who knows? We might find someone else from Aguas Calientes—someone who knew Maria."

"I can ask around La Casa and see if anybody is from Aguas Calientes. But I can't give you wholesale access to client files. I'm sorry."

Adele put her key in her car door. Vega straight-armed it shut. He was close enough for Adele to see the sheen of sweat on his upper lip, the smudge of dirt he'd failed to wash off on the underside of his chin.

"Adele—please." He touched her elbow. "No one has to know but you and me." The phosphorous lights of the parking lot picked up the tiny crow's feet in the corners of his eyes. "I won't mess with your clients. I give you my word—which, as it turns out, is a hell of a lot more reliable than Vilma Ortiz's."

Vega had been right about the Ortizes. Adele sighed. Maybe she owed him something after all.

He saw her wavering. He offered up enticements like a game-show host. "I'll throw in dinner for you and your date. A movie too, if you want it."

"It's not a date. One of my former clients' daughters is having her *quinceañera*."

"Then you should thank me for sparing you."

"I like *quinceañeras*. Didn't your daughter have a big birthday celebration when she turned fifteen?"

Vega shook his head. "Joy's not really—she's only half—and I never—" Something dark crossed his features. Adele had the feeling she was treading on sensitive territory again. He stamped his feet against the cold. "I'm only asking for an hour, Adele. *One hour.* It's not just me you'd be helping either. If Morales is innocent, this might speed things along for him, too. He's in a holding cell in the basement of the station house. A closet, basically. No way to change his clothes or get clean. Nothing. If the guy's innocent, don't you want to help get him out?"

She didn't really know Rodrigo. But she knew Enrique and Anibal. They'd been coming to La Casa for about four years now, ever since they first arrived in Lake Holly. She didn't want to have to tell them that their friend was still locked up knowing she might have done more to help get him out.

"We go right now," she said, ticking off her list of demands. "We go in my car so no one knows you were ever there. You look only in the drawers that contain intake files since last September. And you can't remove anything. Do we have a deal? I open my drawers, you don't make me regret it."

Vega laughed. Adele suddenly caught the double meaning of her words. She blushed.

"Hey," he teased. "The night is young."

# Chapter 12

Adele's car was a Prius. Somehow it figured. All that good earnest Anglo training at Harvard. She probably gave to the Sierra Club and Amnesty International as well. Just like Wendy—Wendy who, when they were dating, took one look at Vega's red Pontiac Firebird with its magnesium alloy wheels, tinted windows, and subwoofers and asked him where he kept his fuzzy dice. His next car was a powder blue Honda Civic where the radio was preset to NPR. Welcome to the world of Anglo sensibilities. Parties without dancing. Food without spice. Women who dressed nearly the same as their men. It was like living with a coffee filter over your senses.

Then again, Adele wasn't Wendy. She had a candy-apple red dress under dry cleaner's plastic hanging from a hook in the backseat.

Adele unlocked her passenger-side door. Vega tried to brush the mud off his clothes before he climbed in.

"It's okay. The car's not that clean anyway."

It looked pretty clean to him. There was a booster seat in back along with a girl's backpack covered in pink and purple peace signs. Vega had already noted the lack of a wedding band. He'd bet the store at this moment that her ex wasn't Ecuadorian or even Latino. Vega and Adele were more alike than she'd probably care to admit.

"Thanks." He got in.

"You owe me big time, Vega."

"Agreed."

She pulled away from the curb. "You can start paying me back now."

"Okay. How?"

"Tell me how you found Rodrigo so quickly today."

He reached for a CD that was lying on the floor. On the front was a picture of a good-looking dark-haired guy in tight jeans and a T-shirt.

"You like Chayanne, huh?" asked Vega. His mother used to love listening to his songs. Love songs, all of them. They filled a void for her, gave her a safe place to tuck her passion. She kept the real men who flittered briefly through her life at arm's length from Vega when he was growing up. Better no man, she reasoned, than the wrong one.

"Chayanne's Puerto Rican, you know," said Vega.

"You're changing the subject."

He rubbed his palms along the thighs of his dark blue mud-stained trousers. He'd lied to find Rodrigo, of course. Called up La Casa ten minutes after he left Linda and Adele at the preschool and pretended to be a contractor. He told Kay, the woman in the front office, that he needed to deliver some compost to the landscaper who'd hired three of La Casa's clients for a job in Wickford that morning but he didn't have the contractor's contact information on him. Kay innocently gave up the name and phone number of the company: Green Acres Landscaping. He then dialed Green Acres and gave them the same line about needing a delivery address. He had a GPS location on Rodrigo in under ten minutes.

"How come you're so reluctant to tell me?" Adele pressed.

Because he knew she'd never understand his job and what it entailed. Some lies for the greater truth. Some pain for the greater salvation. If he told her he'd lied— played her own people against her—she'd think less of him, and for some reason that had nothing to do with the case, he didn't want that to happen. Do you stop being a good person when good people stop judging you as one?

"I got lucky," he said, forcing a smile. "Somebody at the station knew a couple of contractors in town and one of them knew where Rodrigo and his friends were working."

Adele's eyes settled on Vega's face for only a moment before turning sad and defeated. Something in his smile—he didn't know what—had given him away. It made him wish he'd told her the truth. But the moment was gone. He couldn't call it back.

There were no cars on the street when they rolled up to La Casa. The town dump was closed, as were the two auto-body shops. The security lights blazed brightly in the parking lot, pushing back the darkness. There was no moon tonight, only a gauzy wash of clouds that muffled the stars and reflected the man-made light back on itself. It was the sort of darkness Vega had known as a boy in the Bronx where day and night were relative measures, never pure or complete.

Adele pulled a key out of her bag and undid three locks on the front door, then opened it and flicked on the overhead light. Devoid of people, the rooms looked small, almost staged. Like a kindergarten during off-hours. The blackboards had been washed down. The computer keyboards rested above their monitors. The molded plastic chairs were upended onto a long table in the center. Adele explained that some of the immigrants who couldn't find work on a given day were offered a few dollars to mop and clean the center at closing. It's what kept some men at La Casa long after there was any chance a contractor was going to offer them a job. Five or ten dollars was the world to many of them.

Adele walked over to the glassed-in front office and unlocked it. The neatness did not extend to this room. There were still towers of folders and papers on every surface. A red light blinked on a phone. Adele punched in a code and listened to the message, then scribbled something on a Post-it note and stuck it to the front of one of the computers. How the person was likely to notice it in this chaos was beyond Vega.

Another key on her ring unlocked a file cabinet in the corner. The cabinet itself lay buried under a carton labeled CHRISTMAS DECORATIONS. There was no rhyme or reason to this office. No wonder Linda hadn't been able to find Maria's intake sheet.

Vega and Adele sloughed off their jackets and threw them over one of the two chairs in the room. Vega caught Adele eyeing his nine-millimeter service weapon in his hip holster.

"What?"

"Ever shoot anyone?"

"Only before I deport them."

"Smartass."

She fished a pair of glasses out of her handbag and began to thumb through folders in the top drawer, keeping her back to him. Vega leaned against the doorway, not sure what he should do or touch. She would probably think he was snooping even if all he did was move a pile of papers, so he kept his hands where she could see them. His eyes drifted lazily to the round firmness of her backside, the soft hourglass curve of her hips, the way her bob of shiny black hair reflected a halo of light. He'd always been attracted to skinny gringas, women who were all stretched sinew and pencil limbs. His last girlfriend was like that. So was Wendy. A vegetarian, lean as a matchstick. Clothes looked great on her. She looked great on him. But at night in bed, when he reached for her, it was like grabbing a chest of drawers—all sharp angles and edges that never quite wore down. Or maybe he wasn't talking about the physical Wendy at all. Maybe he was talking about something else.

She'd never called him back today. She could be like that sometimes, as if she forgot that Joy was his child too, not simply an extension of her life with Alan. It didn't help that her world had the gravitational pull of family, home, and faith that his so sorely lacked. There was no comparison. So he deferred. Again and again until he himself had to admit that he'd become a ghost in his daughter's life.

The funny thing was, he and Wendy had started out being charmed by each other's differences: Wendy, the Jewish, Barnard-educated psychologist, five years his senior; Vega, the fatherless, Puerto Rican working-class musician. Romance is built on such differences. Marriage and parenthood—they soon discovered—was not. When they first made love, it turned her on when he spoke Spanish to her. After Joy was born, she got annoyed if he blasted his salsa in the house. She considered everything brightly colored or sexy as "too Puerto Rican." Anything boisterous or playful made her stiffen and sulk. His friends thought she was a snob. Her friends treated him like a simpleton.

Their home didn't even feel like it belonged to him. Their shelves were lined with dreary tomes about the Holocaust and self-help books full of complaints disguised as advice. Her mother got upset every year when Vega put up a Christmas tree and made sure that by age six, Joy knew there was no Santa Claus. Wendy left him because she'd been fooling around with Alan and had gotten pregnant with twins—a devastating blow to Vega on so many levels. But on their divorce decree they cited "irreconcilable differences" as the reason for their split. Vega thought in many ways it was closer to the truth.

"There are so many stories here," said Adele, stacking folders on every surface that would take them. "Every life has a story, I suppose."

"In most cases, more than one." Vega felt like he'd lived about a dozen already.

Adele closed the drawer and handed some of the folders to Vega. They began carting them into the front room where Adele piled them on one side of the table. At first she wouldn't let Vega look through the folders. He just sat there balancing his chair on two back legs like a kid in detention. But finally, faced with the over-whelming amount of material she had to look through and her desire to make the *quinceañera,* she relented and handed him part of the pile.

Vega was struck right away by the variety of people who came through the center: a social worker from Colombia with a college degree, a stone mason from Guatemala taking basic literacy classes, a preacher from Honduras, a car mechanic from Mexico. He noted the less appealing aspects in some files too: the addict who crossed the border to break his drug habit, the alcoholic trying to get sober, the manic depressive who needed medications he couldn't afford. Adele snatched one file he was reading right out of Vega's hands.

"I thought this was about finding Maria Elena."

"It is. I'm not going to do anything with the infor-mation. I told you."

"You appear a bit too interested."

"I'll make a point to look bored."

She gave him an exasperated look. "You don't get it, do you? This isn't a game, Vega. These people have given up everything to be here and one arrest could take it all away. You have no idea what it feels like to be on the other end of your job."

She went back to reading a file. He went back to balancing on two legs of his chair.

"I've been on the other end," he said softly.

"For what? A DWI after some cop's stag party?"

His eyes got hooded. The irises turned inky. She didn't know he wounded so easily.

"I'm sorry," she said. "I just assumed—"

"I've never been like that." Not as a teenager, not

even after Wendy left him. He was tempted, mightily tempted. He put a few fists through a few walls, but he kept his dignity. And most of all, he obeyed the law.

"What happened?"

"I borrowed a friend's car when I was seventeen and accidentally ran a red light. A cop stopped me, searched the trunk, and found a pretty sizable stash of marijuana and cocaine my friend was keeping in there."

"Did you tell them it wasn't yours?"

"Oh, right. Of course." He smacked himself on the head. "Why didn't I think of that? The police are always sooo trusting of minorities, especially considering my friend was white and his dad owned the hardware store here in Lake Holly."

"You mean Rowland's Ace Hardware?"

"That's the one."

"Your friend was Bob Rowland?"

He seemed to realize belatedly where this was headed. "This is ancient history, you understand."

"You mean the drug use? Or the friendship?"

"Both."

"You didn't do jail time, did you?"

"Almost. The cop started calling me the usual names so I took a swing at him and got assault added to the charge. I did a night in jail but I had no priors so I got probation." Vega could still see himself, a skinny kid sweating through a borrowed sports coat before an in- different and patronizing judge. "It was a juvenile of- fense, fortunately, so it got expunged from my record when I turned eighteen. Still, it cost me a scholarship to study music. And not that it matters now, but it cost me my girl."

"Linda." It wasn't even a question.

Vega closed a folder without answering and slapped it on the finished stack. Maria Elena wasn't here. There were plenty of Marias, all right. But they were from El Salvador or Mexico or Peru. They were too young or too old or had come over at the wrong time. If anybody was from Aguas Calientes, Guatemala, they hadn't mentioned it on their intake sheet.

"Anybody else have access to these files?" asked Vega.

"All my front office staff," said Adele. "Kay and Linda and Rafael and Ramona. Plus, the board members, but they'd really have no reason to remove an individual sheet."

"You keep any records on people who hire your clients?"

"Some." Adele answered slowly. Vega caught her checking her watch. He was conscious of becoming that last party guest who wouldn't take the cue to leave. But he had to explore every option.

"Morales said he brought Maria to La Casa to find a job," said Vega. "If she found a job, wouldn't you have some sort of contact information for the employer?"

"Not necessarily. Look, Vega—" She pointed to her watch. "I've got to go."

"But if you have that information—"

"No—"

"No, you don't have it?"

She sighed. "Even if I had such a file, there wouldn't be that much personal information about a client in it."

"That doesn't matter. If I can track down the employer, I might be able to fill in the blanks from there."

"It's possible Maria never even got a job through La Casa. Or she did, but she didn't give us enough infor-

mation to verify that the person in our files is her."
Adele began to gather the files to put away. Vega took
out his wallet and slapped a fifty-dollar bill on the
table.

"Twenty minutes and fifty bucks says you're wrong."

Adele frowned. "What? You think you can buy me?"

"Buy you? Never. Bet you? Absolutely. You're a
lawyer and a fencer. My guess is, you hate to lose at
anything."

"So do you, apparently."

"I wouldn't know," he grinned. "I don't get much
practice."

She sighed. "Twenty minutes—if only to wipe that
smug look off your face."

"Deal."

The employer files were in Adele's back office in a
locked cabinet. A red light blinked on her answering
machine and she listened to her messages, scribbling
notes on a pad.

"Do you need to call someone? Let them know
you'll be late to the *quinceañera?*"

"I don't think I'll get Gabby's father. The whole
Martinez family's probably still at the church."

"I mean—" he stumbled about "—a date."

"It's not that sort of event."

"You could've fooled me with that pretty red dress
you've got in the car."

Adele blushed. He hadn't meant to embarrass her.
He wondered whether she had many opportunities to
wear such a dress if she was wasting it on the fifteenth
birthday party of a former client's daughter. He never
cared much for *quinceañeras*. All the frills and formal-

ity. All the rampant materialism dressed up in the guise of faith and culture. Just like Joy's bat mitzvah.

"Diego Martinez was one of my first clients at the center," Adele explained. "He was one of the plaintiffs in my suit against the town. I'm very close to his family."

"Sure. Okay."

Adele pulled four files out of the middle drawer and laid them on her desk. "These are the records we have of people who hired clients from the center between September and December of last year. I'm not sure what good it will do you. Like the clients, a lot of employers won't give us any information because they don't want to get in trouble for hiring someone without papers. So these files are mostly homeowners who hire clients sporadically."

She handed Vega a stack of folders and he began to thumb through the contents. Most of the individuals who hired La Casa's clients were from surrounding towns or The Farms. The board members themselves hired a lot of people. The jobs were what Vega expected: nanny, cook, groundskeeper, handyman, stonemason, housepainter.

Adele was right that the files were sketchy. Most offered a more telling glimpse of the employers than of the immigrants. One lady hired Rodrigo and his friends to move her exercise equipment—presumably because moving it required too much exercise. Another lady hired a woman to do nothing but clean out her twelve-year-old son's room. Still another, to babysit her three dogs while she went skiing in Aspen. There were outrageous requests as well: for a cook who could fix vegan, gluten-free meals. For a housekeeper who could care for three kids, two dogs, a four-thousand-square-foot house and also tutor the children in Spanish for their Regents Exams every evening. Vega wondered how these Anglos managed before they had a steady source of cheap labor. He supposed they actually had to raise their own kids, walk their own dogs, cook their own meals, clean their own homes, and mow their own lawns. The immigrants had allowed upper-middle-class Americans to live like pampered adolescents. No wonder the country was getting soft.

He even found a page from Wendy in the files. She had hired a man named Pablo to weed her flower garden. Kenny Cardenas's father Cesar was a gardener. He would have probably welcomed the work. Vega was surprised Wendy didn't hire him. Maybe it made Joy uncomfortable to have her boyfriend's father working like a field hand for her mother. Vega could understand that.

Adele slid a sheet in front of him. "I think I may owe you fifty bucks."

The sheet was dated September thirtieth of last year. Cindy Klein of 43 Apple Ridge Drive, Lake Holly, had hired a live-in housekeeper from La Casa. Name: Maria Elena Vasquez. Age: thirty. From Aguas Calientes, Guatemala. Apple Ridge Drive, Vega knew, was in The Farms. About four streets over from Wendy.

"If it's her, you can use the fifty to buy Gabby Martinez a *quinceañera* present from me for keeping you all this time," said Vega.

"You said Vasquez wasn't Maria's real name."

"That's what Morales said. I'll just have to see what I can get from Cindy Klein." He copied down the particulars in his notebook and dialed Klein's number. No answer. He was in the process of leaving a message with all his contact information when Adele got a call on her cell. He could hear her speaking to the caller in Spanish, assuring him that she'd be on her way soon.

Vega finished his call and stuffed his notepad in his jacket. "I'm real sorry I kept you, Adele. This helped a lot. I won't involve you or La Casa in any of this. You don't even have to drive me back to the station. I'll walk." He headed for the door.

"Come."

He turned. "Pardon?"

"You could come." Her words had the weightless quality of a child's soap bubbles. Vega felt like if he examined them too closely, they'd burst and disappear.

"You mean—to the *quinceañera?*"

She ran a finger absentmindedly across the dented edge of her desktop. "You want the Latino community in Lake Holly to open up to you and trust you." She shrugged. "A *quinceañera's* a good place to start."

"But I don't know Diego Martinez or his daughter Gabby."

"I was invited along with a date. You can be my date."

"Huh." Vega rubbed the back of his hand along the stubble on his chin. He was surprised and more than a little flattered. Adele fascinated him. That sharp intellect. That fiery streak. But she scared him a little too. Either way though, it was out of the question. "I can't, Adele."

She turned away. "Okay, never mind. Bad idea."

She thought he was rejecting her. It wasn't that at

all. He glanced down at his muddy, blood-stained shirt and trousers. "Look at me. I can't go to a *quinceañera* dressed like this. Not with you in that pretty red dress."

"You can just say 'no,' you know. You don't have to let me down easy."

"I'm not letting you down easy. Honest. I'd go if I had clean clothes."

"Really?"

"Really."

A smile slowly curved the corners of her lips. "Okay. Wait here."

She went into the front room and came back moments later with something on a hanger wrapped in a dry cleaning bag. Vega frowned. He wasn't wearing some castoffs she had lying around for the day laborers.

"Adele—"

"A couple of my clients have a little cumbia band going on on the side. I do them a favor and keep their clothes and instruments here so they don't have to worry about them getting stolen. The clothes are clean, I assure you. I get them dry-cleaned in exchange for the band playing at some of our events. I picked the shirt and pants of the tallest band member."

"I'm not wearing some mariachi getup—"

"It's not. It's just a black cotton shirt and tan pants. Would you at least look before you say no?"

The shirt was a hand-stitched *guayabera*, a traditional Mexican wedding shirt with four patch pockets across the front and tiny rows of tailored pleats running along the front and back. Vega had a shirt just like this before he married Wendy, also in black. He loved that shirt. It was comfortable, lightweight, and you never had to tuck it in. Wendy teased him that he looked like he was auditioning for the movie *Scarface*—all that was missing was the Cuban cigar. She gave the shirt to Goodwill a couple of years after they were married. He always said he'd buy another but he couldn't figure out when he'd wear it so he never did.

"Come on," Adele coaxed. "It'll be fun. Good music. Good food."

"My presence might make them uncomfortable."

"*Their* presence might loosen you up."

# Chapter 13

The *quinceañera* was in full swing by the time Vega and Adele showed up. They had missed the Mass at the church and the opening waltz but to Vega's mind that was better. All the formalities had been dispensed with. Men were already loosening their shirts and taking off their jackets and some of the women were kicking off their high heels so they could dance more comfortably to the cumbia and salsa tunes being rolled out at fever pitch by the live band. The smell of chili-and-garlic-spiced beef filled the air. Colored lights twinkled from strands that crisscrossed the ceiling of the assembly hall and gave the whole place a Christmas-like feel. In the middle of the dance floor, Gabby Martinez whirled around a sea of girls in poufy pastel-colored ball gowns. She was easy to spot because she was the one in pink ruffles wearing a rhinestone tiara and carrying a matching scepter that one of the teenage boys was stroking rather obscenely at the moment to all the teenagers' delight.

There were easily a hundred guests inside what had once been some sort of warehouse and now constituted the banquet space of the church next door: Iglesia La Luz del Mundo. In English: Light of the World Church. The immigrants didn't attend Our Lady of Sorrows, which probably explained why Vega never saw more than a handful of old-timers and bored children coming out of there these days.

"I don't know any of these people," he said nervously. "Maybe they wouldn't like me being here."

"Relax, Vega. You're my guest."

"Well if I'm your guest," he flashed her his best smile—"maybe you should start calling me Jimmy."

She blushed until she was practically the color of her dress. He wanted to tell her how beautiful she looked, the way the seams hugged her curves in all the right places, the way every man turned his head as she walked across the floor. But he knew he couldn't. Greco would have a fit if he found out Vega was here. It wasn't bad enough that he might be charged with police brutality. Now he was skating dangerously close to a departmental reprimand for conflict of interest. Being off-duty didn't change that. So he took a seat next to Adele and smiled and nodded at conversations in Spanish he could barely hear from wave after wave of people who gushed at Adele like she was royalty, which, in this world, Vega supposed she was.

A lot of these people owed their jobs and their sense of security in this town to her, including Diego and Inez Martinez who came running off the dance floor to embrace her like she was a long-lost relative. Vega had wondered before this why someone with a Harvard law degree would choose to spend her days running a struggling community center when she could have been a player on Wall Street or in some other glitzy and

powerful venue. But seeing the outpouring of affection
these people had for Adele, he could sort of understand. If he'd learned anything in his four miserable
years as an accounting major, it was that most things
worth having couldn't be totaled up on a balance sheet.

Adele caught Vega fiddling with a tin of mints on
his plate. The tin had Gabby's name and the date of her
*quinceañera* embossed on the front. "Hope you like the
party favors," said Adele. "I was the *madrina* who supplied them."

"You play godmother for the *quinces* of all your
clients?"

"Diego has long stopped being a client," Adele explained. "He's got a green card now and he's studying
for his citizenship test. He owns his own landscaping
business and a small house in town that was a wreck
when he bought it and is now the best-kept house on
the block. He grows beautiful tomatoes in his backyard
and always brings them to me in season."

"So he's a friend," said Vega.

"And a success story," said Adele. "A lot of these
people are. They're not all undocumented, you know."

"How do you know who is and who isn't?"

"I don't. Nor do I care one way or the other. Look at
them, Jimmy." Adele gestured around the room to men
and women laughing, dancing, eating, bouncing children on their shoulders to the music. "This is who they
really are. Not what you see at La Casa. Or when someone in a uniform steps in front of them. They want the
same things as you and I: a home, education for their
children, security. Is that really such a crime?"

Adele led Vega to the food table where they helped
themselves to plates of chicken with mole sauce and

tamales stuffed with spicy beef and tomatoes. Vega eyed the seven-tier meringue-frosted cake on a side table with Barbie dolls flanking each of the alternating pink and purple tiers. Gabby may have been turning fifteen, but she was still a little girl at heart. Just like his Joy.

"Did you have a *quinceañera* when you turned fifteen?" he asked Adele as they walked back to their seats.

She shook her head. "My mother baked a cake and I got to pick out a dress at AJ Newberry's, a discount store in my neighborhood. My parents said a party was a waste of money. They put everything to my education."

"Sounds like a wise choice," said Vega.

"It was. But at fifteen, I wanted a party. So I'm a soft touch when a struggling family approaches me to be a *madrina* now."

More people came over and Adele introduced Vega. She didn't say he was a police officer and no one asked so Vega kept that to himself. It's not like he was on duty, a fact he reminded himself of when he walked up to the bar to get a glass of white wine for Adele and a second beer for himself. He didn't pay attention to the stocky, broad-shouldered man in front of him until the man turned. It took Vega a moment to place the face out of context. But the man had no trouble placing him.

"Señor Vega. I didn't know you knew the Martinez family," the man said in Spanish.

It was Kenny's father, Cesar Cardenas. He was wearing a starched white shirt and a dark suit that looked more somber than festive. His hair was wet-combed into place. Vega had never seen him out of work clothes.

"I'm here with a friend," said Vega. He motioned to

Adele at the table. Of course Cardenas would have known Adele. Kenny just got awarded that scholarship from La Casa. Vega would have expected Cardenas to be bursting with pride over his son's achievement. But he realized after a moment that it wasn't just the suit that was somber. The man was too. Maybe Cardenas had heard about how Vega had treated Kenny yesterday. Vega fetched the wine and beer from the bar and nodded sheepishly.

"I guess you heard? About last night?" Vega took a sip of beer. He tried to be lighthearted about the whole thing. "Teenagers and breakups," he shrugged. "What are you going to do?"

"They are failing their classes," said Cardenas.

*"What?"*

"My son and your daughter. They are failing chemistry. And math."

Maybe Kenny was. But not Joy.

"That's impossible," Vega insisted. "I'd have heard about it. The school would have called."

Cardenas was far too traditionally Mexican to contradict another man about his family in public. Instead, he fixed his dark, sad eyes on Vega until Vega understood that perhaps the school had called and his ex-wife hadn't relayed the message.

"Joy would have told me," Vega argued. He would have said it with more conviction if he hadn't just found out yesterday about her blowing off Dr. Feldman for a whole month. Already, Vega felt the weight of Cardenas's words taking up residence in some dark corner of his heart.

"I don't understand," said Vega. "What's going on?"

Cesar Cardenas shook his head very slowly. Vega

could see in his lined and leathery face that he had asked that same question of his son. Shouted it. Begged it. And from the slump of the man's shoulders, Vega understood: Kenny hadn't told him anything either.

To hell with Wendy. This time, Vega was going straight to Joy and demanding that she answer him. She was no better than her mother at returning phone calls but he knew from experience, she'd return a text. He put Adele's white wine on the table and felt relieved when he saw her talking to a group of people on the other side of the room. He sat down, took a gulp of beer to fortify himself and pulled out his phone. Hunching over the screen, he texted two simple questions:

*RU failing schl? Whts goin on???*

Back came: *Out tonite. Talk tomrw.*

*Tomrw when?* he texted back. But he received no reply. He looked up to see Adele beckoning him from the other side of the room. He pretended not to notice as he stared at his phone, willing Joy to answer. He had no idea how long he'd sat like that, oblivious to the voices and thumping music around him. All of a sudden he felt Adele's hand on his sleeve. He looked up from his phone to see her standing there with Gabby Martinez, all decked out in her pink frills with a look of nervous expectation in her chestnut eyes.

"Gabby wants you to dance with her."

"Adele, I can't. Not now—"

"—Come on, Jimmy. You know the custom. Every man has to dance one song with the *quince*. Don't tell me a musician like you can't dance."

Vega looked at Gabby. Gabby looked at the floor. She still had those baby cheeks that he pictured showing up on all her elementary school photos. Her bed probably overflowed with stuffed animals, her back-pack with strawberry lip-gloss and packages of bubble-gum. She was standing on that threshold between childhood and womanhood. So fragile. So easily un-done by a look, a word, a gesture. Like Joy—Joy, who was unraveling faster than Vega could pick up the pieces. His daughter was not going to text him back tonight. All he'd be doing by refusing to dance would be to make another girl feel bad. He didn't want that.

He slipped his phone into his pocket and offered Gabby his arm. "I would love to dance with you."

They went out onto the center of the floor. The girl was nervous and timid when the music started. Her hands were sweaty. She apologized when she turned the wrong way. But it was a salsa and it was hard to re-sist the pull of the beat for long. Vega had forgotten how much he loved to dance. His grandmother had taught him how to salsa and, after all these years, it was still in his blood. He gave himself over to the music, moving his hips and twirling the girl this way and that until she was giggling with delight. The floor was crowded and a boy soon took her off Vega's hands. Vega turned to leave but a hand grabbed his. Not a child's this time. The confident grip of a woman.

"Don't quit yet," she whispered into his ear. "You're good."

His heart raced unexpectedly. He felt the heat in his cheeks. "You're only saying that because you don't know me yet."

He put his hand around the cinched red chiffon of her waist, feeling the gyration of her hips, the way they moved in perfect timing to his own. The music trans-ported him, shut down all that nervous energy thrumming inside his chest and redirected it to his legs, his hips, his hands. Made it into something pure and beautiful.

Adele moved effortlessly beneath his touch, spinning and dipping, her body flexing and relaxing at just the right moments. Having her in his arms felt so natural, so instinctive. It had been years since Vega had held a woman who had real breasts and a backside that didn't look like it belonged on a thirteen-year-old boy. He had no words for the pleasure and sensuality it stirred within him so he just laughed. She laughed too, her red lips parting just enough for him to feel her hot breath on his neck, soft as kisses. He rested his sweaty palms on her hips and swallowed back the fantasy of what it would be like to make love to such a woman. She made him feel whole, made him forget for just a moment all the pain and worry he was feeling: for his job, for this case, and most of all, for Joy.

A sound brought him back to earth. A woman's scream.

It came from the front steps of the assembly hall where some of the partygoers had gathered to smoke. Vega broke from Adele's grasp, grabbed his jacket, and ran to the front doors. Outside, the darkness felt flat and unyielding. It took Vega's eyes a moment to adjust. The screamer was being hugged by two other female partygoers. They were all talking feverishly.

"I'm a police officer," he said in Spanish. "What's the matter?" All three women started speaking at once.

"There's a man—"

"In the bushes in the lot across the street—"

"I think he's dead—"

"Or maybe he's just drunk."

"All right. Stay here," said Vega. "I'll go check it out. "

The church was on a side street that housed a plumbing manufacturer and two tire distributors. The lot was on Main Street, diagonally across from the church and tucked between two three-story stucco apartment buildings with mismatching front steps and filmy windows covered over in bed sheets. A mile or so north of here was the Main Street Anglos frequented, the one with organic grocery stores, sushi bars, Realtors, and nail spas. This part of Main was mostly warehouses, auto body shops, and cheap rental units. It was a part of town Anglos drove through rather than to. But it was not dangerous.

Not normally.

Vega heard a gurgle in the bushes.

"Police," he called out in English. "Do you need assistance?" No answer. He tried again in Spanish. The Spanish produced a moan. He removed a small flashlight from a pocket of his jacket and raked it along the brush. An overturned shopping cart—part silver, part rust—played hide and seek behind a tangle of thorny brambles. A pile of soggy insulation lay beneath a mound of dead leaves left over from last fall. The bright pink was still visible, poking through the leaves like cotton candy. Vega stepped closer and zeroed his flashlight on a bundle of bright red rags next to the insulation. The rags twitched. *A man*. The red had a slickness to it. *Blood*.

Vega took him for Latino but he'd been beaten so badly, it was hard to tell. His face was swollen and bruised. Blood congealed in his hair and stained his sweatshirt and jeans. Vega scanned the lot and road for a fleeing suspect. He saw no one. A crowd gathered on the steps of the assembly hall. Adele ran over.

"Keep everyone back and don't let them leave," he told her. "Call nine-one-one and tell them we have a man in need of medical assistance and ask them to get the Lake Holly cops on the scene." Vega had no authority here—as Greco would so quickly remind him if he could. Adele pulled out her phone and called in the information.

Vega picked his way closer to the man and crouched next to him. He managed to locate a pair of latex gloves in his jacket and slipped them on. He checked the man's pulse and the response of his pupils to light. His pulse was slow. His pupils were dilated. They didn't respond evenly. He probably had a concussion.

"Have you been shot? Stabbed?" Vega asked the man in Spanish. He searched for obvious wounds but didn't see any knife or gunshot penetrations. The man tried to get to his feet. Vega eased him back down. He could smell liquor on the man's breath. It was possible he was too drunk to know the full extent of his injuries. Most likely, the cops wouldn't know until he was assessed at the hospital. "An ambulance is coming. Relax, man. Who did this?"

The man's lips moved. His voice was a rasp.

*"Nadie."* ("No one.")

"C'mon, man. Somebody messed you up. Did they do it here? Or did they just dump you here?"

The man clutched his stomach and doubled over. He vomited blood. Vega wondered if his spleen had ruptured.

"You're hurt bad, brother," said Vega. "C'mon. Put the finger on those *pendejos*."

Vega heard the sirens. Ambulance, police, he couldn't tell. Some of the guests at the *quinceañera* were going to give the police the slip—that was certain. They didn't *all* have green cards like Diego Martinez. He spoke to the man again. "C'mon, brother. This is your chance to tell what happened. You don't tell now, later, everyone will say you made it up."

The man fell backward on the dirt and wiped a bloody hand across his face. *"Espero que lo hagan."* ("I hope they do.")

# Chapter 14

"Please tell me you haven't been drinking." Greco's first words when Vega met up with him at Lake Holly Hospital. Adele had driven Vega to the hospital—a decision that, upon reflection, Vega realized hadn't been the wisest of choices. It didn't help that Adele was still in her red chiffon dress, getting looks from every male doctor who passed by. Even Greco shot a sideways glance at her backside when he thought no one was looking. Beneath the armor plating, the man apparently still had a heartbeat—and a few other working parts besides.

"I was off-duty, Grec. I had two beers. *Two*. Do a Breathalyzer on me if you want."

Greco ran his eyes down Vega's black *guayabera* shirt. "You going native on me?"

"I was trying to get some leads."

Greco shot another glance at Adele who was at the nurses' station, getting an update on the beaten man. "I'll just bet you were."

"If I hadn't been at that *quinceañera* this evening, you'd be doing another homicide investigation instead of an assault." Vega tried to explain the chain of events that started with finding Maria's potential employer, Cindy Klein, but Greco cut him off.

"Get some coffee in you and jeez—hide that shirt. You look like you just stepped off a cruise from Cancún. And tell your *girlfriend* to get lost. Happy hour's over. You're working now."

"She's not my girlfriend."

"Keep it that way, you hear? For your sake and mine."

Greco had snagged a small, windowless conference room down the hall from radiology. Vega grabbed a coffee from the vending machine and followed Greco inside. The man did not look happy. He started talking before Vega sat down.

"We've got a situation on our hands that's going to blow this town out of the water and I can't keep a lid on it the way I did that chick up at the lake."

"You mean Maria Elena," Vega corrected. That "chick" had a name now. He wanted it used. Greco gave Vega a sour look.

"You can call her Carmen Miranda for all I care right now. We've got more immediate concerns." Greco slipped a black-and-white photo of the beaten man's face in front of Vega. The man's nose appeared to be broken, both eyes were swelled shut, and blood crusted his hair. "We've identified the victim as Luis Guzman," said Greco. "He's a regular in town. Been picked up before for drinking and urinating in public—that sort of thing. No papers, of course. He's in the ICU right now with a concussion, a ruptured spleen, and numerous fractures."

"You get a statement from him?" asked Vega. "He wouldn't tell me anything."

"He can't tell anyone anything right now," said Greco. "He's unconscious. But I don't need him to tell me what happened. Because I've got this."

Greco pulled out his smartphone and brought up a Facebook page. He scrolled down to a photograph of a pale bicep with an American flag and eagle tattooed across it. The words 100 PERCENT AMERICAN, were tattooed beneath. The picture was posted on Facebook at nine-thirty this evening. Beneath it was a caption: GOT A NEW TAT WITH BRENDAN AND EDDIE. THINK WE'LL CELEBRATE WITH A LITTLE BEANER HOPPING TONITE. Vega looked at the name of the holder of the page: Matthew Rowland.

"Bobby Rowland's teenage son? This is the guy who beat up Guzman?"

"It gets worse," said Greco. "I *got* the post because forty minutes before you called in the Guzman assault, Matt Rowland's two friends brought him into the emergency room with a knife wound to his abdomen. It's a superficial wound, but it matches a penknife one of my officers recovered near Guzman's body. Which means, depending on how you look at it, we've got Matt Rowland and his friends Brendan Delaney and Eddie Giordano for a hate-crime gang assault. And/or we've got Guzman for assault with a deadly weapon."

"Sounds to me like Guzman was defending himself."

"Maybe," said Greco. "But I'm screwed no matter what I do here. If Lake Holly lets Guzman walk on the ADW charge, we'll be called out for being soft on crime and illegals. Plus, you and I both know a guy like Guzman ain't gonna stick around to testify against Rowland and his pals. He'll jackrabbit faster than José Ortiz. No victim? No case."

"But if you charge Guzman on the ADW," said Vega, "the same thing's going to happen."

"Yep," said Greco. "Soon as I put his fingerprints through the system along with an ADW charge, the Feds are gonna slap an ICE hold on him. Even if he's found innocent, he'll be deported on immigration violations. Which once again leaves us without a victim to testify against those punks."

"You could file for a U visa for Guzman," Vega suggested.

"And what's the likelihood a judge is going to grant that sort of privilege to a drunk with a knife?"

"None," Vega agreed. "Which leaves only one option: charge Guzman with ADW and see if the DA's office can keep him locked up until *after* he testifies against Rowland and his pals." Which meant Guzman could look forward to a lengthy stay in the county jail followed by a one-way ticket out of the country. Meanwhile, Rowland, Delaney, and Giordano would remain free on bail until their trials. Nobody but another cop could understand how tough it could be to do the right thing and still end up looking like a creep.

"That's not going to solve all my problems." Greco took off his glasses and palmed his tired eyes. "I think these three punks might be behind the rash of hate crimes we've been seeing in town since the Shipley incident." Greco ticked them off on his sausage-like fingers: "The fire at La Casa, the assaults in Michael Park, maybe even Reyes and your Maria Elena."

"I don't buy Rowland and his pals for Maria's murder," said Vega. "You said so yourself, Grec. It takes time to tie ropes around four limbs, time to weight someone down in a lake. It takes a cool head to walk away from that when it's over. That's not the work of three adrenaline-filled teenagers looking for kicks on a Saturday night."

"That's why you need to talk to Bob Rowland, get him to convince his son to come clean."

The room felt suddenly airless and hot. "You've got the wrong idea about our relationship," said Vega.

"You were friends growing up, right?"

"Lotta history there."

"History's good. History makes people say things they shouldn't."

Vega ran his sweaty palms along the edge of the table. He didn't speak. There was nothing to say.

"Look, we've got no choice," said Greco. "Those three teenagers are already lawyered-up tight. If Rowland doesn't get his kid to come forward, Lake Holly is going to look like it's orchestrating a cover-up. Porter will definitely go to the media with this."

"But he agreed—"

"Our little deal with him only applies to Morales and only for twenty-four hours," said Greco. "You know as well as I do that once this shit storm hits, all bets are off." Greco laid out the particulars like he was going to roll the cameras himself. "Porter's got three white teenagers, all ex-football players over six feet tall, walking out of a gang assault charge and possible involvement in a string of hate crimes up to and including murder. He's got their five-foot, two-inch immigrant victim unconscious and under arrest on what's bound to look like a trumped-up charge. You don't think every Twitter feed and blog and news outlet in the country's gonna eat this up? Porter will drive a wedge through Lake Holly that no one will ever be able to repair, not even your vixen in red."

Vega tried to bite back the heat in his cheeks. He knew Greco saw it, which only made him more embarrassed. "Maybe the thing to do is to talk to Porter," he suggested.

Greco offered up a vicious smile. "He's already got you on the unemployment lines, my friend. He called your boss after our meeting this evening and told him he was considering pursuing a police brutality lawsuit against you and the county. And that was *before* the Guzman situation."

Vega felt like someone had landed a hard right when he wasn't looking. "Who told you that?"

"Your boss, Waring."

"Captain Waring called *you?*"

Greco gave Vega a moment to let that sink in. Guzman or no Guzman, Porter was out for his blood. Vega wondered if it would have made a difference if Porter had known about his long-ago relationship with Linda. Or maybe that was the problem. Maybe on some level, he already did.

"Why did *my* boss call *you?* Why not me?"

"What? So he can hear you say you didn't hit Morales? Save that for the department lawyers if it comes to that, Vega. Waring wanted to know what I'd seen and get my opinion off the record."

"But you couldn't see me in the woods."

"No," Greco agreed. "But I told him I thought you were a stand-up guy. I told him about how you could've fed Fitzgerald back his face in pieces after what he pulled the other day at the lake and you didn't." Greco leaned back in his chair and folded his arms across his belly. "And he told me about Desiree Soto."

*Desiree.* Vega hung his head. "I failed that child, Greco. She's why I moved to homicide and I'm still failing."

"From what Waring tells me, you did everything you could to save her. You pulled her stepfather off her. You threatened to kill the son of a bitch if he touched her again. You called Child Services as soon as you could. But you were undercover. You had a multimillion-dollar narcotics deal going down and you couldn't do more without jeopardizing months of police work. How could you have known what would happen?"

It was a hollow victory. To Vega, it would always be a hollow victory. Sure, he'd stayed in character. And yeah, the sting went off without a hitch. Desiree's stepfather got twenty years for racketeering, narcotics trafficking, and assault, bargained down to eleven because he ratted out some associates. The mother got five years, bargained down to two because she turned in her own sister. But the child just disappeared. And by the time Vega found her, she'd been buried for so long, nobody could prove Vega's suspicions that she'd been beaten to death, much less who did it or when. It was too little, too late. Nobody paid for what happened to Desiree. Nobody.

"Took me six months to find her body," Vega said softly. "*Six months,* mostly on my own time. Every little girl I looked at—on the street, in the supermarket, on a playground—I just kept thinking I'd find her. I keep thinking about Maria Elena's baby now and wondering whether we're already too late."

"Then talk to Rowland, man. Play on his conscience, his guilt, your friendship—I don't care. But we've got to know what his son did and didn't do before Porter drags this whole town through the mud and makes us look like a bunch of crackers and mall cops who can't shoot straight."

# Chapter 15

Vega's cell phone rang at seven a.m. Tuesday morning.

"Yeah?" He wasn't in a relationship right now. He didn't have to be nice to anyone first thing in the morning.

"Waring here. I wake you?"

*Coño!* Vega pinched the sleep out of his eyes and caught himself before he cursed his boss's early intrusion out loud. Vega hadn't gotten back to his house until after midnight. He lived an entire county north of his job in a two-bedroom summer cottage he was still in the process of rendering habitable five years after his divorce. It was the only thing he could afford on a cop's salary.

"No, Captain. I'm awake." The hoarseness of his voice gave him away. He sat up in bed and immediately felt a dull ache between his shoulder blades—a delayed reaction, he suspected, from his arrest of Rodrigo Morales in the woods yesterday. He wished he'd never met the guy.

"This situation in Lake Holly is snowballing, Vega."

"I realize that, sir." He swung his legs over the edge of the bed and tried to sound professional despite being dressed in nothing but a pair of undershorts. He kicked at a pile of dirty clothes on the floor, hoping for something to wrap himself in. The room was freezing, the upstairs insulation still on his "to do" list. He'd have to get that *guayabera* shirt cleaned and back to Adele soon. He didn't want to cost a fellow musician a gig for want of a shirt. "We're trying our best—"

"Your best wouldn't have resulted in a potential lawsuit against this department."

"No, sir." There was no point wasting his breath defending himself. Cops were inured to claims of innocence. It was like white noise to them.

"Get a damn good—and I mean *damn* good—reason to charge that immigrant or release him ASAP. And I'll tell you now, my strong preference is that you find a damn good reason to charge him. Because if he turns into some freakin' Boy Scout, we don't have a prayer of convincing a judge you didn't rough him up."

"Yessir, Captain." Vega's twenty-four hours with Morales were up at six p.m. He had eleven hours to find something strong enough to convince a judge—and Porter—that Morales was guilty. He hoped like hell that he could get hold of Cindy Klein. She was his only prayer at this point. He started telling Waring about his potential lead, but the captain cut him off.

"I didn't call for a status update. I called because I want you to put some pressure on Bob Rowland to confess."

"Uh—I think you mean Matt Rowland, his son," Vega suggested.

"I mean Bob Rowland." Waring gave Vega a moment to let that sink in. "Tim Anderson at Metro-North thinks Rowland is lying about his whereabouts the night Ernesto Reyes died. He went back over the available video footage. Rowland's fire department SUV was in the vicinity of the train station at the time Reyes died, yet Rowland never responded to the engineer's nine-one-one call."

"Greco said Rowland was responding to a call for chest pains."

"Anderson checked the records. The chest pain call was an hour and a half earlier."

"You think the chief of the Lake Holly Fire Department had something to do with Reyes's death?"

"More likely he's covering for his son who took his vehicle out that night," said Waring. "But either way, we need to know. Detective Greco tells me you and Rowland go way back so I want you to handle this."

Silence. Vega had never told Waring about his arrest at seventeen or the fallout that followed. There was a handwritten explanation somewhere in his personnel file in answer to the question: *Have you ever been arrested?* But it was not something a commanding officer was likely to look at without cause. Vega didn't want to dredge it up now, not when he was already in so much trouble.

"I think you should know," said Vega. "Bob Rowland and I haven't seen each other in years. I doubt I have any special leverage."

"Then find some, Vega. Today it's Rowland at the center of this shit storm. Tomorrow, Morales goes free and we've made no further progress in the case, it could be you. You get my drift?"

"Yes, Captain."

\* \* \*

There were two news vans camped out across from Rowland's Ace Hardware by the time Vega arrived. Outside the doors, there was the usual assortment of flowerpots, seed spreaders, and doormats, along with a sign: PLEASE RESPECT OUR PRIVACY. People came and left the store on a regular basis, all of them white, all with bowed heads and tight lips and hands ready to wave away reporters looking for comment. Vega suspected a lot of these people probably shared some of the same sentiments about the immigrants as Matt Rowland, albeit in more law-abiding and polite terms. But they weren't about to say it on camera.

Vega sat in his black pickup truck trying to psyche himself up to confront Rowland about his troubled teenage son. A day ago, he might have been able to do this from a safe distance, smug in the knowledge that his own daughter had leapfrogged the hurdles of adolescence. But he couldn't shake the roller-coaster sensation now burbling in the pit of his stomach whenever he thought about Joy. Neither Joy nor Wendy had returned his calls this morning. If he weren't under so much pressure with this case, he'd have camped out on their doorstep. Wendy would have hated him for it, but at least he'd have some answers.

He got out of his truck and forced himself to walk into the store.

He knew every inch of the place, from the gouges in the pine-plank floor, to the shelves that always smelled like sawdust and mineral oil. He and Bobby used to park their bikes in front and buy balsa planes his dad used to sell for twenty-five cents apiece. Then they'd bike up to the old water tower and launch them off. Afterward, they'd head back to the Lake Holly Grill where they'd order ice cream and play songs on the accordion-sized jukeboxes bolted to the walls of every booth.

The Lake Holly Grill was a Starbucks now. The water tower was a cell tower. No one played with balsa planes or listened to jukeboxes anymore. Everything was Hi-def and virtual.

He felt old.

Rowland was at the back of the store when Vega walked in, helping a customer choose between two different varieties of paint. He'd put on weight since Vega had last seen him. He'd taken to shaving his already balding head. His skin looked puffy and yellowish, like old Polaroids. But he still had those long, fair lashes that reminded Vega of a newborn calf. They hadn't seen each other since his son Charlie's funeral three years ago, a mere press of the flesh that Vega was sure Rowland would barely recall. He had to go back more than twenty years to remember anything of substance between them.

Rowland kept his focus on the customer but Vega had a sense he'd already been spotted. There was no surprise in Rowland's eyes when he finally looked up. He waited until the customer was headed to the register with his gallon of paint before he spoke.

"Matt's not here, Jimmy. He's recuperating from being attacked and not offering any comment at this time." Vega had a sense those were his lawyer's words. *Make sure you stress your son was attacked.*

"I didn't come to talk to Matt. I came to talk to you."

"I can't talk either." Rowland turned and vanished into the stockroom. Vega followed. It was a maze of eight-foot-high rows of metal shelving stacked with

dusty cardboard boxes. He and Bobby used to play as-
sassin in here. Vega leaned a hand on the doorway and
spoke to the dust motes floating under the sickly fluorescent light.

"C'mon Bobby, talk to me."

Silence.

"This is bullshit, man. The boy who stood up to Dar-
ren Hovey with me wouldn't run away like this."

There was a scrape of cardboard, a tinny sound of a
nail skittering across the concrete floor. Rowland
stepped out from the end of one of the rows of
shelves. He had his arms folded across his chest. The
fluorescent lights reflected off his shaved head. "That
was different, Jimmy."

"Why? Why was it different? Biggest, meanest kid
in the sixth grade calls me a spic. Challenges me to a
fight. You and me—we weren't even friends back then.
I'd just moved here. And I'm thinking, I've gotta face
that tub of lard after school by myself. Nobody's got
my back. And suddenly, there you are." Vega's eyes
locked on Rowland's. There was gratitude in Vega's
gaze. Always would be.

"You handled yourself pretty well as I recall," said
Rowland. "You'd have kicked his ass with or without me."

Vega shrugged. "That's beside the point. You stood
up for me, Bobby. We weren't even friends yet and you
stood up. How could the son of that boy do something
like this?"

Rowland grabbed a carton off a shelf and hefted it
over to a scuffed Formica table where the employees
took their lunches. The table sat next to a battered desk
and file cabinet, the closest thing Rowland had to an

office. Vega swore it was the same furniture he remembered his dad having twenty-five years ago.

"It was just a fight, Jimmy. A fight that got out of hand. That's all." The words sounded weak and threadbare, like an old pair of jeans that used to fit but didn't any longer.

"You believe that?"

Rowland opened the carton. Inside were smaller boxes of assorted screws in various sizes, along with an inventory list. He thumbed the contents and tried to match it against the list but Vega could tell his heart wasn't in it.

"Bobby." Vega put a hand on the box. Rowland looked at him. "What about the night Ernesto Reyes died? Was that just a fight, too?"

Rowland's eyes slid away from Vega's. And in that moment, Vega saw the truth like some slaughtered animal at their feet, all bloody entrails and feces, nothing clean or dainty about it. When it came to truth, there never was.

"You *knew*, didn't you? Goddamnit, Bobby." Vega slapped the table. "All of it. You *knew*."

"It wasn't . . . They didn't mean for it . . ." Rowland sank into the chair behind the desk and put his head in his hands. Vega took a seat across from him on a chrome chair with a seat patched in duct tape that he recalled from his youth. There were swivel casters on the bottom but one of the four casters only swiveled in one direction. He remembered that too.

"What about the other things that have been happening in town? The fire in the Dumpster at the community center, the beatings in Michael Park, that woman's body at the lake—"

The mention of the woman caused Rowland to shake his hands violently in front of him, like he was trying to stop a bus from running him over. "—No. *No!* Matt's no angel, Jimmy. But Jesus, you're wrong if you think he'd do something like that."

"Then have him come in and talk to us. Have him own up to what he did."

Rowland kicked at flecks of paint on the scuffed concrete floor. His voice was husky when he spoke. "I can't destroy my only surviving son."

"But that's just it, man. You *are* destroying him. Everybody's got to be able to look themselves in the mirror. Down the road, will you be able to? Will Matt?"

"I can only deal with the present."

"And how did that work for you back in high school?"

Rowland glared at Vega. "Getting some pleasure out of this, aren't you?"

"None," Vega answered honestly.

"I messed up bad for a while with drugs and drinking," said Rowland. "I never meant for you to get caught up in that and I'm sorry. But I'm not the reason you lost Linda even though you'll always blame me. She was about to break it off anyway. And if you didn't realize that, then you were lying to yourself."

"You didn't know her like I did."

"Believe me, Jimmy, I did." Rowland held his gaze. "Before you, in fact."

Something snapped inside of Vega. A vestigial bone he didn't know he'd had until he felt the splintered pieces probing the soft casing of his heart. "You sorry son of a bitch."

"You're right. I was." Rowland smiled sadly. "If it

makes you feel any better, I think she wished she'd lost it to you."

"It doesn't matter anymore." He tried to make himself believe that but he felt like he'd been carrying around a box of precious china only to discover there was nothing left but broken shards. "What's done is done. But Matt? You've got a chance to make that situation right, Bobby. Set both your hearts at ease."

"You think, huh?" Rowland fingered a framed photograph on his desk. A long-ago snapshot of him and his two sons before cancer snatched Charlie and hate snatched Matt. The boys were in the limbs of an apple tree. Vega could read something on Rowland's face in the picture, the way he hovered at the trunk while the boys found their footing, the forward thrust in his stance as if he could shoot out at any moment and catch them if they fell. In the end, he hadn't been able to catch either one.

"You've never lost a child, Jimmy. You have no idea what that does to you. You'd do anything after that to protect the ones you have left. Believe me, in my shoes, you'd do the same thing."

"I couldn't square it with my conscience."

"You'd be surprised what you can do when you have to." Rowland rose. "I have work to do. Let's just remember the friendship as it used to be, huh?"

# Chapter 16

Vega felt hollowed out from the morning, his allegiances blurred, his sense of his own history shattered. He'd gone into Bobby Rowland's store to convince his old friend to stop deceiving himself about his son. He'd come out wondering if the ultimate prize for self-deception didn't belong to Vega himself. When it came to women at least, he didn't have a clue.

He called Greco and updated him on his interview with Rowland.

"Sounds like we're on the right track thinking those punks are behind this string of bias attacks," said Greco.

"Yeah," Vega agreed. "But without Bobby coming forward, we're no closer to proving any of that. Too bad we can't find Ortiz."

"We did find him. Your friend Adele convinced Ortiz to turn himself in this morning."

Vega decided to let the "your friend" remark pass.

"Unfortunately, he turned out to be a waste of time," Greco added. "He saw nothing. He knows nothing. I've had dementia patients who give better testimony. And meanwhile, the clock is ticking on Morales. Porter's already putting on pancake and eyeliner in time for the six o'clock news."

Vega checked his watch. Eleven a.m. He had seven hours.

"Did you try Cindy Klein again?" asked Greco.

"Yeah. Still no word. I'm heading up to Apple Ridge Drive now. I'm going to camp on her doorstep if I have to."

"Just don't be obvious about it. That's The Farms, Vega. The neighbors see a Hispanic man without a lawn mower or a leaf blower in his hands, we're gonna have the switchboard lighting up with suspicious person calls."

There was something coldly antiseptic about The Farms in Vega's opinion, and it wasn't just because his ex-wife lived there. It called itself a neighborhood and yet repelled the notion at the same time. The houses—Georgians, Colonials, and Tudors, none under five thousand square feet—were lined up like sentries along broad swaths of perfect lawns. The driveways all emptied onto streets wide and untraveled enough to kick a ball around on.

And yet it always felt to Vega as if aliens from another planet had designed it. Every house had huge windows but most were covered over in multiple layers of drapes and shades. Lights and sprinklers flicked on and off from automatic timers. There were imposing front doors but it appeared no one ever went through them. There were multiple chimneys but he never smelled a fire burning. There was patio furniture and the occasional in-ground pool. And yet Vega could never recall seeing anyone outside when he drove by save for gardeners and handymen. SUVs and minivans shot in and out of three-car garages like their occupants were mole rats, always going somewhere else, forever in a hurry.

He missed The Farms of his teenage years—the real farm—where vines grew thick through hundred-year-old stone walls and the oaks and maples were so broad it took two people, arms linked, to encircle their trunks. He missed the rows of gnarled apple trees that, even after the real farm closed down, continued to produce their Macintoshes and Galas and Empires, mute and stalwart against the din of buzz saws and excavation equipment. When Wendy was three months pregnant, Vega carved their initials in a hundred-year-old oak on that farm. She told him their love would last as long as that tree. Now, the only trees Vega saw flanking those gabled Tudors and white-columned Georgians were the ones the developers planted, none of them wider than a teenage girl's calves. He supposed Wendy was right after all.

Forty-three Apple Ridge Drive was the style and size of a small Normandy castle. It couldn't have been more than about ten or twelve years old, yet the brick was milky with a lime coating that made the home look as if it had survived since Napoleon's time. There was a turret at the entrance and a huge stained-glass window with eagles and dragons across it. There were two enormous fieldstone chimneys running up opposite sides of the house and a three-car garage with elaborate wood-paneled doors across each bay.

Vega rang the doorbell. He expected no one to be home. You can never tell whether anyone is home or not with a house in The Farms. He was heartened when a woman in her late fifties answered the door. She was thin to the point of emaciated, with perfect white teeth and long, black hair that she blow-dried straight like she was still in high school. She wore high-school girls' clothes, too—tight designer jeans and a dark sweater that she accentuated with a leather-and-brass belt like something the conquistadores might have worn, slung low across her waist. Her slivers of hips could barely hold the thing up. A heavy gold bracelet encircled a bony wrist and her manicured fingers sported several rings that looked as if they were real, not costume.

"Ms. Klein? Cindy Klein?"

"Yes?"

Vega flashed his badge. "James Vega. I'm a detective with the county PD. I left a message on your phone?"

There was a momentary question on her feather-lined lips, a slight arch to her plucked eyebrows before she remembered.

"I'm so sorry, Detective. I didn't have a chance to return your call. And now I'm getting ready to host a luncheon. Can I call you later?"

"I won't take up too much of your time, ma'am. But this is important. May I come in?"

She hesitated. "Can I ask what this is about?"

He pulled out the flyer. "Do you recognize this woman?"

"Why—that's Maria."

"Maria what?"

"Maria—" She offered up a look of embarrassment and then remembered. "Vasquez. Maria Vasquez. She used to work for me. Is she all right?"

"No ma'am, she's not. She's dead."

"Oh my God. What happened?"

"That's what I'd like to come in and talk to you about."

Cindy nodded and beckoned Vega into an enormous central hallway where the light fell like syrup through the windows. A large pot of daffodils filled up a brass table in the middle of the hall. Off to the right was a living room with a dark-beamed ceiling. A black lacquer baby grand took up the far corner of the room. Vega eyed the piano wistfully. His mother used to have an old upright with missing keys when they lived in the Bronx. They'd had to leave it behind when they moved to Lake Holly. If he'd had more time and money, he would have loved to own another.

Cindy led him away from the living room to another big room with leather couches and Persian rugs that adjoined an open kitchen with hand-painted tiles. A wall of glass overlooked a rolling green stretch of backyard and the rear of another Farms mansion that looked as if it had been built out of sugar cubes.

"Would you like some coffee?"

"Sure, thanks."

Cindy called out to a stocky Latina cutting cubes of melon, presumably for the luncheon. "Carmen? Can you get us some coffee?"

"Yes, missus. How the mister like?"

*"Café sólo con azúcar, por favor,"* said Vega. *Black with sugar, please.* He exchanged a quick smile with Carmen, the recognition between them a bond that always caught him by surprise. He supposed he would always feel Latino around Anglos, always search out that comfort zone.

Cindy motioned for him to have a seat on the leather couch.

"Are you comfortable talking here?" he asked.

"Oh, it's fine." She moved a vase of orchids to one side of the coffee table along with a book of reprints from the Metropolitan Museum of Art. "Carmen is going to be vacuuming the living room for our guests and fixing the spread. She speaks very little English. She won't know or care what we're talking about."

In Vega's experience, that was never the case but he let it pass. "How long did Maria work for you?"

"About five months. What happened to her?"

"Her body was found in the reservoir. Her death is still under investigation."

"You mean she drowned?"

"We don't know yet, ma'am." Vega set the flyer of Maria on the coffee table and pulled out his notebook. "When did she stop working for you?"

"About a month ago. Sometime in early March, I believe." Cindy fiddled with her watch. Vega noted a starburst pattern of diamonds on the face.

"She leave of her own accord?"

"Not exactly—I sort of fired her."

"Why?"

"Well, see, actually, I didn't *tell* her I was firing her. I just sort of told her I didn't need a live-in anymore. Because I didn't want her to, you know, get spiteful or anything." She fiddled some more with her watch. "I can't believe she died. Right here in Lake Holly."

"Why did you want to fire her?"

"Well—is this all, um—necessary?"

Vega put on his best cop voice: lots of Bronx in the

accent. "This is a police investigation, ma'am. It's necessary."

Cindy picked up the flyer. "Is that her little girl?"

"What do you know about the child?"

"Very little. I made the mistake once of asking if she had any children. She started to cry. I don't speak Spanish, Detective. I knew there was so much I should ask but I didn't know how to and she didn't seem to want to talk about it. I figured the child was staying with a grandmother in Guatemala or something and she missed her. I respected her privacy."

"But you fired her. Why?"

Cindy fiddled with the coffee Carmen had brought over and waited until the housekeeper had left the room.

"Maria was a very hard worker. Very sweet and conscientious. But one day, I noticed one of my bracelets missing. This wasn't just some sentimental trinket, you understand. It was insured for three thousand."

"Did you ask her about it?"

"Well—no." Cindy dabbed at her lipstick. There were no wrinkles on her face. She'd had work done. A lot of it, judging from how tight her forehead looked. She couldn't have frowned if she'd wanted to.

"I didn't want to accuse her," Cindy explained. "But then several hundred dollars went missing from my husband's billfold. So I told her I was thinking of going without a live-in for a while. I figured I'd get her out and then a month or two later, hire someone else. But she went out one day and never returned."

Vega straightened. "You mean, she just disappeared?"

"I didn't know that at first. I mean, I'd already given her notice so I thought perhaps she was sort of deciding what she wanted to do. Maybe staying with a friend or something. I called her cell phone and left messages but she never called back."

"So you mean to tell me"—Vega leaned forward—"the woman took a three-thousand-dollar bracelet and several hundred in cash and you just let her walk out of your life?"

"It's—complicated, Detective."

Vega would never understand rich people. "Do you still have her cell number?"

"Somewhere, I'm sure." Cindy pushed herself up from the sofa and walked over to a drawer in her kitchen where she rummaged around. Vega heard keys and paperclips jangling against one another.

"Here it is." She rattled off the phone number. Vega suspected the number was the prepaid wireless variety that didn't require a name or credit check. Still, the police could trace the number and match it to the device and place of purchase. They could also trace any calls and text messages she'd made from her phone and when they'd stopped. It was the best lead he'd gotten so far. But something was still troubling him.

"I guess I'm not clear why you didn't report her missing. It's been over a month."

"I didn't know whom to report her missing to," said Cindy. "Her mother was in Guatemala. I have no phone number for her. I don't speak Spanish and I don't think she had any family in the U.S."

"And you didn't think the little girl in the picture would want to know where her mother was?"

"I thought perhaps they already knew. Maria had her cell phone with her when she left. She'd taken all her money, even her final week's pay—like she knew on some level she was leaving. I was afraid that if I went to the police, I would have to tell them about the missing money and jewelry and then I could actually get her deported."

"But if she stole from you," said Vega, unable to mask the frustration in his voice, "she *should* be prosecuted and deported. Otherwise, she could do it again to others."

"Well—the thing is . . ." Cindy played with one of her rings, a large speckled stone. It looked like a robin's egg to Vega. It probably cost more than he made in a month. "The bracelet turned up in one of my handbags about two weeks after she disappeared. I'd forgotten I'd put it there because the clasp had broken. As for the money—well, my stepson eventually admitted . . ." Her voice trailed off. "We've got him in substance counseling now. But you have to understand, Detective. I didn't know any of this until later. I just thought perhaps she'd moved on. Or gotten caught in a deportation raid or something." She waved a hand in front of her face. "I mean, anything was possible. You know how these people are."

Wendy's mother had said the same about him. When Wendy decided to ask for a divorce. He didn't know it until later, but it was Wendy's mother who insisted she break the news to him in a restaurant. Some place public. In case he became violent. He had never raised a hand to Wendy or Joy in thirteen years of marriage. But because he was Latino, Wendy's mother assumed he'd behave violently and impulsively like some wild animal instead of a deeply wounded, grief-stricken man.

He choked back the memory. "What date did Maria leave?"

"Hmmm. I don't remember the date. It was during that unseasonably warm period in early March. She had Sundays off so it must have been a Sunday."

"What time?"

"That, I don't know. I have a regular tennis match on Sundays. My husband tries to get in a round of golf if it's warm enough. We usually grab lunch and dinner out. We probably weren't even home when she left. The property is alarmed. She could have come and gone with just a punch of the alarm code."

"Did she give you any idea where she was going?"

"Sundays, when it was warm enough, she usually met up with her boyfriend."

"Do you know his name?"

"Only his first name: Rodrigo."

Vega felt a pulse of electricity surge through his body.

"And she was seeing this Rodrigo—in March?"

"To my knowledge. I think they were apart for a while, but then they got back together."

Another pulse of current. Morales had lied. He hadn't broken off the relationship after they arrived. It was still going strong right up until she disappeared. That lie and the time frame had just ratcheted him up from a person of interest to a suspect. "If I brought you a picture of Rodrigo, do you think you could identify him?"

"I think so," said Cindy. "He mowed my lawn here a few times but it's not like he had a car and picked her up here on a regular basis. I think they walked to some central point to meet each other."

"Did you see Rodrigo the day she disappeared?"

"No. I just remember Maria saying she was going to meet up with him."

"Do you know where they went? What they planned to do?"

"I didn't ask." She seemed to feel the heat of Vega's gaze upon her. "You think I should have reported her missing, don't you?"

"I think somebody should have. You could have told the cops what you're telling me right now—even left out the theft part if you'd wanted."

"I just—I didn't know enough about her situation to get involved. If it helps at all, I boxed up all her things. I kept thinking I should give them to La Casa but I never got around to it."

"Her things?" *Jackpot.*

"They're in the basement. You're welcome to take the whole box if you want."

Vega followed Cindy to a door on the other side of the pantry. She flicked on a light and led him down an unpainted set of wooden stairs. In a corner, next to a broken skateboard, sat a large cardboard box that had already developed a fine layer of dust along the top. She looked at her watch.

"Do you mind if I leave you down here? My luncheon is starting in a few minutes."

"That's fine. I'll probably be back at some point later today and have you ID a photo of Rodrigo." Vega would have to use Morales's arrest shot in Rhode Island. Nobody could ID him the way he looked right now.

Cindy went upstairs and left Vega in the basement. He could have taken the box back to the station house and gone through it there. But Vega wanted to see the contents first. He found a set of latex gloves in his pocket and slipped into them so he didn't contaminate anything with prints. Then he opened the box.

Maria's possessions didn't amount to much. A few modest shirts and jeans. Some underwear and socks. A sweatshirt with I LOVE NY written across it. A pair of cheap silver-colored sling-back sandals. Vega had to remind himself that she probably crossed the border with only the clothes on her back.

Everything in the box smelled musty. But even after weeks in the basement, Vega could still smell something of the woman on her clothes—a whiff of lavender from her shampoo. The vanilla moisturizer she rubbed on her skin. She was here—more alive in this box than she had ever seemed when Vega read the autopsy reports. For a moment, he could almost picture her with Morales—the way he'd stood up to the police for her, the way she'd dragged him to that pocket of air in that sweltering boxcar to save his life. Could all that have ended in one brutal moment? Vega would have liked to think not, but he had only to look at the love and hate he felt for Wendy to know that those two emotions were too closely linked to easily uncouple.

Overhead, Vega could hear a rumble of heels on the polished floors, the over-animated chatter of overindulged women. He didn't feel like walking the gauntlet past them with a dusty box from the basement. They'd probably assume he was here to fix the boiler.

He dug through the box a little more until he came to a plastic bag. Inside he found a stuffed pink rabbit holding an Easter egg along with a silver-colored bracelet with three charms clipped to it: a lollipop, ballet slippers, and a teddy bear. Both were clearly presents for a child. Vega was beginning to believe Maria's daughter was in Guatemala. He pictured a little girl in some rural backwater village waiting for word from her mother that would never come while her presents grew musty and old sitting in this rich white woman's basement.

There were no sales receipts, no way to know exactly when the items were purchased or how old the recipient was. Hell, with girls, you never knew. Vega remembered Joy loving her stuffed animals to death when she was three or four. But she was almost eighteen now and she still had two or three she kept on her bed. Last year, when Vega took her to a local carnival, she'd begged him to win her a stuffed bear by knocking down a stack of weighted bottles. Twenty bucks later, he'd managed to secure that five-dollar bear.

He was about to close up the contents for the police station when something at the bottom of the box caught his eye. It was sticking out of one of the pockets of a yellow hoodie. An envelope. He teased it out of the pocket. It was addressed to *Maria Elena c/o Cindy Klein, 43 Apple Ridge Dr., Lake Holy, NY, USA.*

Vega noticed that the town was misspelled "Lake Holy," not "Lake Holly." The return address was from a woman in Aguas Calientes, Guatemala: Irma Alvarez-Santos. The print was uneven and each letter looked as if it had been painstakingly scrawled. The top of the envelope had been ripped open. The letter inside was just a few short lines that looked as if they'd been scribbled in a third-grader's handwriting. Vega was not used to translating written Spanish, but if he went slowly, he could make out the meaning:

*My dear Maria,*

   *My heart is glad you are safe and have found
a good place to work. I pray to God every night
that He keeps you well and that your heart isn't
heavy with longing anymore. Here is your crucifix. May God keep you safe in His love.*

   *Your Mami*

Vega went through the translation in his head three
times. He was sure he had the words right. Irma Alvarez-
Santos had signed the letter "Mami." She was Maria
Elena's mother. That meant, in all likelihood, some part
of Maria Elena's name, even if she was married, was
Santos. They had a possible last name now. They had a
cell phone number. And they had an address of the next
of kin. A simple cross-check of ICE's database
might be able to fill in the blanks on her identity. At
least they'd be able to contact her mother and let her
know what had happened to her daughter. It was sad
news and, unfortunately, Vega was the one who was
going to have to deliver it. But at least the family would
have some closure.

   But a question now haunted him: What longing was
Maria's mother referring to? Unless Vega had screwed
up the translation, it sounded as if Maria hadn't come to
Lake Holly, as Morales had said, just because she
thought it was "safe." She'd come to ease some longing.
   *For what?*
   Vega was sweating by the time he lugged the box up
the basement stairs, out the garage, and toward his

truck on the street. There were cars parked along Cindy Klein's driveway and a gaggle of women walking up to her front door armed with flowers and small, delicate bags of gifts that seemed like a waste of time for a woman who clearly had everything. Vega avoided making eye contact with the women and they did the same. He was invisible to them. A workman. But he could not escape the three women walking straight toward him on the driveway. Skinny jeans. Large, dark sunglasses. Long, keratin-treated hair blow-dried to perfection and the sort of understated but expensive jewelry that would rival the GDP of a developing nation.

The woman in the middle was Wendy.

Vega put the carton down on the driveway and wiped his hands down his dark blue trousers. Normally he tried to avoid such encounters. But not today.

She was like the others of course. Well read. Well bred. Underfed. But there had always been something a little different about Wendy. The way her eyes crinkled with genuine warmth when she smiled. The way she pushed her lip out, little-girl-like, when something troubled her. She could freeze you out faster than a nor'easter in January. But when you were in Wendy's good graces, there was something almost celestial about the experience. You felt lit from within, warm and glowing. You felt like a better person somehow, like she set the benchmark and all you had to do was rise to the occasion.

She didn't look at him that way anymore and though he accepted it, he could never say it stopped hurting.

Wendy told the other two women she'd meet them inside and walked up to Vega, the heels of her leather boots clicking on the driveway. She lifted her sunglasses and looked him up and down. She sighed as if his plan had always been to screw up her day.

"What are you doing here, Jimmy?"

"My job."

"Moving boxes?"

"It's part of a police investigation."

"You're investigating Cindy Klein?" She waited for more but he didn't offer it. He wouldn't have even if they'd still been married. It was one of the first things he'd learned as a cop, not to talk about cases in progress. So he changed the subject.

"I thought you worked on Tuesdays," he said.

"Not since the school budget cuts." Up close, she looked tired, the skin beneath her hazel eyes bruised from lack of sleep. Makeup only hid so much. "I know you've been calling me," she said finally.

"Then how about you answer for a change?"

"Because it's not a conversation I want to have over the phone."

"Hey." He spread his hands. "I'm not *on* the phone."

Wendy made a face. "Not here. I'm late enough as it is."

"All right. How about in an hour or two?"

"Benjy has a doctor's appointment at one forty-five."

"How about after?"

"Sammy has karate at three-thirty."

*"Qué coño, Wendy?"* Vega kicked the Belgian-block curb of the driveway. He couldn't contain himself. "Joy has blown off her internship with Dr. Feldman. She's failing school. I caught her crying in front of Kenny's house the other night. You mean to tell me little Benjy's fucking karate lesson is more important?"

Wendy flared her eyes at him. "It's Sammy—"

"Whatever—" He couldn't tell the twins apart and didn't want to.

"And you don't have to curse, Jimmy. In English *or* Spanish. I'm not one of your foul-mouthed colleagues."

Vega shoved his hands in his pockets. He wasn't just embarrassing her. He was embarrassing himself, playing to all the class distinctions he'd always railed against. "I'm just worried is all."

"We are addressing the situation already."

"*We?* Who's *we?*"

"Joy. Myself—Alan."

"Alan doesn't get any say in this. She's my kid."

"Then maybe you should get to know her better. If you did, you'd know this has nothing to do with Kenny who, by the way, she's still seeing."

"Then order her to break it off. He's a bad influence on her if they're both failing school."

"Her therapist says—"

"Ah Christ, Wendy!" Vega kicked the curb again. "You sent her to a therapist?" *Therapy:* his ex-wife's answer to everything, except, oddly enough, their marriage. That she just ended without consulting any touchy-feely authorities on the subject.

"I didn't ask you to foot the bill," she countered.

"You didn't ask me *anything.*"

"Joy was having nightmares. I thought it might help her. Adolescents are very egocentric at this age. The developing frontal lobes of the brain aren't mature enough to—"

Vega cut her off. He wasn't in the mood to hear his

daughter dissected like a science project. "—She doesn't need to talk to a therapist. She needs to talk to *us*. Amherst is going to take away her scholarship if she keeps this up. Hell, things get bad enough she may not even graduate high school. If this is over some boy—"

"I'm pretty sure it's not."

"Then what is it? I'll do anything, Wendy. Just tell me how to make her better and I'll do it."

"I don't know." A sudden gust of wind coursed down the driveway and Wendy turned away from it. Her long, chestnut hair flew across her face and she raked it back. She folded her arms across her chest to fight off the cold but she was so narrow and her arms so long, that there just didn't seem to be enough of her to grab on to. She looked lost and frightened and for a moment Vega had the urge to take her in his arms, brush aside that hair, and comfort her even if he had no words of comfort.

"I have to go, Jimmy," she said, not unkindly. "They're waiting for me inside."

"Yeah. I know."

"Alan and I are taking the kids to dinner tomorrow night at that hibachi steak house in town. You know the one."

Yep, Vega knew it. It had been a five and dime when he was a boy. He checked out the restaurant menu once when he and Joy were looking for a place to eat. Their cheapest entrée was twenty-five bucks. He took Joy for pizza instead. She sulked through the entire meal, which really irked him considering how often she made Kenny's impoverished state sound almost heroic. It was one thing to deal with your boyfriend's economic limitations he supposed, and quite another when they were your dad's.

"How about I call you when dinner's over?" Wendy suggested. "Alan can take the boys back home and you, Joy, and I can sit down somewhere for coffee."

"All right." He picked up his carton and turned to leave. Then he thought of something. "Hey, Wendy? The nightmares—when did they start?"

"I don't remember. Maybe a month ago?"

"Before or after the accident?"

"After, I think. I'm not sure. She was shaken up that night and all. But I think that was more because your car got totaled. I mean, physically, she was fine."

"Yeah. Of course. Call me tomorrow."

# Chapter 17

Vega found Greco in the basement of the Lake Holly police station, down the hall from the holding cells. He was sprawled before a projection screen in a darkened room. Across the screen, two teenagers, a boy and a girl, were staggering down a dirt path in the woods at night. The girl's shirt was unbuttoned and the white of her breasts shone like two half-moons against the darkness. The lower right-hand corner of the screen was stamped with the time, date, and for some odd reason, the moon phase. It was taken last October fifteenth.

"Little early in the day for porn tapes, don't you think?" Vega dropped the carton of Maria's belongings on a table.

Greco gave a throaty chuckle and stuck a Twizzler in his mouth. "Not this porn, believe me."

"Is that the reservoir?"

"Yep. A hunter brought it in this morning. Seems he rigged up an infrared camera at the lake last October to track deer movement. He forgot all about it until yesterday. He thought we might find the footage useful."

"Find anything yet?"

"Yeah." Greco gestured to the screen. "That lake sees more action after dark than your average congressman's bedroom. It's a regular lovers' lane for the Lake Holly High crowd. Tell ya one thing—our boys are gonna have to do a better sweep of the area. Usually, we only do it in summer. But it looks like every time the temperature hits at least fifty-five, that place goes from *Bambi* to bimbo in under five minutes. Our buddy down the hall, Morales, is on here with Maria by the way."

"Do you have any footage of them last month?"

"I've only gotten up to mid-October so far. Why?"

Vega told Greco about his interview with Cindy Klein.

"If we've got him on camera for a Sunday in March, we may have the whole case right there," said Greco. "Take a seat."

Vega pulled up an uncomfortable metal folding chair—the kind they used for suspects when they were interrogating them. Greco nodded to the carton on the table.

"What else did you get?"

"Maria's cell-phone number. Maybe her last name. And what looks like her mother's address in Guatemala. I've already run a check on the number. It's a prepaid wireless account from Verizon."

"You request a subpoena for her phone records yet?"

"Just put the paperwork in now. I asked them to speed it up given our deadline with Morales. We've already got his cell number so we can do a cross-check there, see when they last communicated." Vega gave a quick overview of the rest of the contents of the carton.

"Still falls short of probable cause to charge Morales,"

said Greco darkly. It was almost three p.m. They both knew they were running out of time.

"I know," said Vega. "I'm going to go back to Cindy Klein and at least get her to ID Morales. But before I do, let's see if the video gives us anything."

They sped up the rest of the October footage. Greco was right about the teenagers. Most of them came loaded down with six-packs and fifths and probably a lot more besides. Vega called for Greco to hit the pause button on several occasions. Matt Rowland was on two segments of the tape, both times toting six-packs. Once, with two other boys that Vega suspected were Brendan Delaney and Eddie Giordano. Another time with a girl.

"How come we keep getting footage of people walking in and we don't always have corresponding footage of them walking out?" asked Vega.

"There are other ways to get to and from the lake," said Greco. "Hell, you probably used one yourself to get to Bud Point when you were a teenager. So if you're thinking that traffic in without a corresponding out means anything, forget it. There's no way to track anything about their movements except what you see on the screen."

Vega flipped through more images until one brought him up short. He hit the pause button. Another teenage boy. A lanky, good-looking Hispanic with a walk much older than his years. A teenage girl with long, dark hair, tight jeans, and bangs that hid her eyes. Vega could feel the heat between them radiating off the screen, the hormonal thrumming and anticipation of release. The boy held out his hand and the girl grasped it as she stepped over a log. She threw back her head

and laughed. It was how Vega used to feel with Linda
at that age. Light. Reborn. Like every sensation was
new and fresh and no one had ever felt this way before.
It all counted. It all mattered.

"You recognize them?" Greco frowned at the screen.

"No." Sometimes the only way to preserve something fragile is to leave it alone.

Vega started up the video again. They went through
all the November footage. By the end of November, the
temperature brought a halt to the nighttime revelries.
There were only dog-walkers and hikers after that.

The couples and drinkers didn't start up again until
that first week in March when a burst of unseasonably
warm temperatures brought everyone out of hiding.
There were plenty of people on the tape again. Joy and
Kenny, but no shots of Matt Rowland and only one of
Maria and Morales. The date stamp in the corner read
*Sunday March 8th, 4:23 p.m.* The film footage showed
the two of them walking down the footpath to the lake
with a six-pack of beer. Morales was holding Maria's
hand. At one point, she tripped and he grabbed her before she fell. Then he stroked the side of her face and
kissed her on her forehead, his lips lingering a second
too long before he pulled them away. She offered
Morales a weary smile that seemed to carry the weight
of the world in it. Vega felt sympathy for them at that
moment. The tenderness of Morales's gestures, the lan-
guid pace of their movements as if they both already
sensed something slipping through their fingers.

Was this the day Maria disappeared? If so, something about their time together already registered a
good-bye in it. Vega looked at his watch: three-thirty
p.m. He had two and a half hours to assemble enough

evidence to justify charging Morales in Maria's death. The tape was a good start. It proved that Rodrigo was lying about when he last saw Maria. If Vega could get Cindy Klein to testify that Maria disappeared on March eighth that would nail things down as well. There was just one thing troubling Vega: that hate letter. He mentioned it to Greco now.

"How do you know it had anything to do with the crime?" asked Greco. "It could've been sent to Maria by someone else before she got killed. It could have been sent to Morales and he just stuck it in her purse. The letter writer doesn't even have to be an American. Some immigrant from another country could've had a beef with her—or him."

All possible. Still, without a confession, the evidence felt incomplete. "Let me take another crack at Rodrigo," said Vega.

"You think he'll break?"

"He's been in that cell for nearly twenty-two hours. I think if he was ever going to break, he'll break now."

# Chapter 18

Rodrigo watched the minutes and hours tick by on the big clock across from his holding cell. He had been in this cell since six p.m. last night.

*Four paces one way, six paces the other.*

No windows. Fluorescent lights that blazed day and night and sucked the life out of every surface they touched. A thin, ripped, vinyl pad on top of a block of cement for a bed, a stainless-steel toilet. Not even a place to wash up. There was a television high overhead but they were having trouble with the cable so it worked only sporadically. Not that he wanted to watch it anyway. The officer had tuned it to an English language station that seemed to show nothing but rich *Norte Americanos* having parties with each other and fighting.

*Four paces one way, six paces the other.*

He was the only one in a bank of three holding cells. There was a constant thrum from the heating ducts. His lip hurt. His clothes were covered in dried blood and mud and stank of sweat. His nerves had gotten the better of his digestive system and he was cramping up with diarrhea. Every time he thought the worst of his life in the United States was behind him, he'd come up against some new hurdle to jump over, some new despair that threatened to overwhelm him.

*Four paces one way, six paces the other.*

He stopped walking and tried to close his eyes, but the moment he nodded off, his thoughts drifted to that boxcar in Monterrey, to the smell of unwashed bodies and super-heated air, to that feeling of being buried alive. He had never been afraid of small spaces before that, but he often awoke at night now with the sense that someone had just stuck a plastic bag over his head and he couldn't breathe. That's what he felt at this minute. He was choking to death in this concrete tomb. It was worse than that time he jumped into the river in Esperanza to save Enrique's little sister, Sucely. The water sucked them down to a dark place where they couldn't tell rock from sky. It felt like *La Llorona*, the spirit who drowned her children, was holding tight to their legs. Sucely grabbed his neck, nearly sealing off his windpipe. But he managed to claw his way back to shore. He was thirteen at the time. So young. So strong. He wasn't that strong anymore.

*Four paces one way, six paces the other.*

He thought of all the stupid shit he'd had to endure to get to this point. How the Mexican police boarded their buses and tried to trick people by saying, "*amárrate las cintas*"—the way Guatemalans say, "tie your shoelaces," instead of the Mexican, "*amárrate las agujetas.*" It was like a kid's game. If you moved, you were gone. If you forgot your fake birth date or the pretend place you were born, you were gone. If you were too bold or too scared, if you didn't have enough bribe money on you, if you complained, if you allowed even a shred of common decency to invade your veins, it was over.

And that was just to get to the border. Then it was the brutal desert crossing, the way you had to become an animal, always dodging helicopters, outrunning the big men in their uniforms with their gun belts and ATVs. The burning sun that boiled you from the inside out. Blackened your skin. Fried the soles of your shoes like you were walking across a hot griddle. You thought you had enough water on your back yet every time you ended up drinking your own urine through parched lips to stay alive. Then curling up in the pitch-black trunk of a super-heated sedan next to other rank-smelling people—you crushing them, them crushing you. Always feeling like you were going to die of suffocation or heatstroke. Some of the people crossing were little kids and young women. Rodrigo remembered the terror in their eyes, the way he felt like less of a man because he could do nothing to ease it.

It peeled off a layer of your humanity. Even after you showered and changed into clean clothes, the smell of desperation never left. It stayed with you as you traveled from Arizona to Colorado, an English-language book in your hand, hoping that no one would actually speak to you. You didn't have any money to buy food so you went a day and a half without. You didn't have enough English to ask where a bathroom was so you held it in as long as you could—twenty hours if necessary. You were so afraid. So afraid. Better to pee your pants than chance speaking and getting deported. Every white face felt threatening. Every uniform made your blood pressure soar.

By the time you arrived in a place like Lake Holly,

the sight of a police car made you duck between buildings, your heart kicking up in your chest like you'd swallowed a fistful of hot peppers. All to get a job— any job. You'd shovel shit with your bare hands for five dollars an hour if somebody showed you the money. This wasn't about making a fortune. This was about making it from one day to the next. It was lunacy. Sheer lunacy.

The police took his shoelaces when they put him in this cell. The laces were so old, they fell apart when the officer unthreaded them from his boots. They would have taken his belt but he didn't have one. When they took the laces, Rodrigo thought they were crazy. He had come this far—did they really think he would kill himself? But now, sitting in this cell for so many hours with no one to talk to, the unbearable loneliness and confusion of his life began to work its way into his marrow like a cancer.

They thought he had killed Maria Elena. That would not be a simple deportation. That meant prison—a long, long stretch in prison. He had done five months in federal prison the last time for buying a Social Security card from his employer. He had gone nearly insane from the noise and the confinement and the casual cruelty that made you always hold yourself in. He could not survive that again.

*Four paces one way, six paces the other.*

At this moment, he wished he had a rope or a belt or even those rotten shoelaces. After all, what good was he to his family in here? Señor Porter had promised he would only be in this cell twenty-four hours. But Rodrigo knew that worse things might await him.

He jumped when the metal door to the entranceway clanged open. The Spanish cop was standing there, freshly shaved and changed from yesterday. He had that shark look to his eyes. He showed more of his teeth than he needed to when he smiled. Rodrigo reflexively leaned his back against the cinderblock wall of the cell.

"Afternoon, Rodrigo," said the detective. "How's that lip you fell on yesterday?"

Rodrigo just stared at him. Porter had suggested to Rodrigo yesterday that perhaps he hadn't tripped in the woods. Perhaps he was assaulted by this detective. Rodrigo had tried to tell Porter the truth, but the señor held up a hand to silence him. Rodrigo saw right away that Porter couldn't tell him to lie, but he very much wanted Rodrigo to agree with his story. The truth didn't seem to matter to Señor Porter any more than it mattered to the detective. They were both playing him. He had no real friends here.

The detective pulled a chair in from the hallway and stuck it in front of his cell bars. Then he sat down.

"Thought we'd talk a little more."

"What about Señor Porter?" asked Rodrigo.

There was the slightest twitch to the detective's shoulder blades. Then he stood up and shrugged. "Okay, Rodrigo. You don't want to talk to me. That's your right. So we'll just do what we have to do without your cooperation." He got up to leave.

Rodrigo felt a panic thrumming in his chest. The detective seemed so confident. That could only mean they were going to arrest him either way.

"Wait," said Rodrigo. "I didn't kill her. Why do you think I killed her?"

The detective very calmly and slowly put the chair back in place, scraping the legs along the bare concrete floor, adjusting and readjusting it with annoying fastidiousness. He didn't speak until he was looking straight into Rodrigo's eyes.

"You lied to me, man. You told me you'd broken off the relationship with Maria soon after you arrived."

"I—I did." *What is "soon"? What does this man want?*

"When?"

"November, I think."

"You said October before."

"I did?" Rodrigo felt suddenly like he had the runs again. And now he couldn't use the toilet, not with this detective in the room. He felt so trapped—by his body and his circumstances.

"You never saw her again after that?"

Rodrigo blinked. No, he couldn't say that. That would be a lie. So he said nothing.

"Look, Rodrigo—you gotta tell me the truth. I just came from watching some film footage. A hunter rigged a video camera at the lake. It picked up everything—and I do mean *everything*—that went on there from October first until now. You're on it, man. You and Maria Elena. A lot. And I don't think your wife would like to see what I just saw."

Rodrigo slumped against the wall and closed his eyes. The detective had to be telling the truth. They were at the lake last fall. Where else could they go? They had no money, no means of transportation. He lived in a room with three other men. She was a live-in housekeeper with no privacy. He had to travel almost two miles on foot one way to see her. The reservoir was near where she was living. It was private and quiet and beautiful at night with the water reflecting the sky so perfectly, Rodrigo could hardly tell up from down. She brought fruit and tortillas and a blanket to lie on and he brought the beer. They stayed up by a grove of tall pine trees, far enough from the path so that no drunken teenagers could bother them.

Sometimes the pinesap would stick to their clothes. Sometimes the needles got lodged in their hair. But the smell beneath those towering evergreens was so fresh, so pure. Rodrigo thought there were few places on earth more beautiful to make love. When things were bad, he usually thought about home. But every now and then the image that came to his mind was of those moonlit nights at the lake. He remembered the soft crunch of deer hooves through the leaves, the whoosh of a fish breaking the surface of the water, the distant hoot of an owl.

And okay, sure, it was wrong. He loved his wife, Beatriz—his Triza. She was the mother of his three children. But he was human, wasn't he? He was lonely and when he and Maria Elena were together, she made him feel like a man again. Looking up, seeing those bright pinpricks of light scattered across the sky, feeling her hot breath on his chest, her delicate fingers wrapped inside his large callused hands, he felt so reassured. Almost like he was back in Esperanza.

"We were at the lake, yes." Rodrigo let the words out in one long expelled breath.

"In March?"

"Once, yes."

"What happened?"

Rodrigo lifted an eyebrow. What did this police detective think happened? He was a man, surely. Did Rodrigo need to go into details about such a private matter?

"You fought?" asked the detective.

"No. Never. We didn't talk much at all. I didn't kill her. I've told you that."

"Then why didn't you report her missing?"

"Because we had already broken it off. She was just—she was leaving. And I came to say good-bye."

"Leaving? For where?"

"She had lost her job. She was talking about going back to Guatemala."

"So Maria just *happened* to see you the same day she disappeared and you never contacted her again."

"I didn't know that was the day she disappeared." This was bad news. Very bad news. This detective would make a lot of this fact, Rodrigo knew.

"You've never seemed too upset about her being dead."

"What do you know about what I feel?" Rodrigo could not suppress the irritation in his voice. For a moment, he forgot himself, his circumstances. He felt only a heat rising inside of him at the casual presumptions this detective made in his nasal, swallowed Spanish. "You cross the border twice the way I have, you learn quickly that human life has very little value. You can only do so much and no more. I have a family. I have responsibilities. So I can do nothing." Just thinking about how long it had been since he'd heard his family's voices made Rodrigo's heart ache with longing. Then again, maybe it was better if they didn't know what was happening to him right now.

The detective tapped his pen on his notebook and stared at him. "We have you on video at the lake with Maria on the afternoon she disappeared in the very place her body was recovered. Her American employer says Maria told her she was going out with you that day. The employer is willing to testify to that in court."

Rodrigo felt something cold and thick congeal inside of him. "I didn't kill her," he repeated softly.

"Maria Elena was tied up and weighted down in the lake using the same sort of nylon rope a lot of the landscaping contractors use to tie up bushes. You've worked with a number of local landscapers, Rodrigo. You could have gotten your hands on that rope easily."

"I would never hurt anybody."

"Video doesn't lie, man. Why don't you just come clean? You loved her. You love your family. Do right by both of them. By your conscience. You didn't mean to do it. You're a good man, I can tell. You just didn't want her to come between you and your family, that's all."

Rodrigo couldn't breathe. It felt like someone was pouring cornmeal down his throat. Each breath just made the next one harder. This couldn't be happening. They would lock him away for twenty-five years on a murder charge. A state prison this time. Full of murderers and rapists and gang members. Big men. Blacks who hate Latinos. Latinos who hate immigrants. Guards who hate everybody. He had survived so much but he couldn't imagine surviving twenty-five years of that.

"If I tell you I killed her—if I confess—will they just deport me?"

"I don't know what they'll do, Rodrigo. But you stand a better chance of people being sympathetic if you tell the truth: you did it to protect your family."

Rodrigo closed his eyes and tried to think of what his friend Anibal would do. Wise, calm Anibal. He would tell Rodrigo to trust in God and be truthful. Always truthful. Rodrigo had messed up—no doubt about it. But not this way. Not like this.

He took as deep a breath as he could manage. It felt like a rubber band was wrapped around his chest. "I did not kill her, Detective," he said as evenly as his shaky voice would allow. "That is the truth. Am I going to go to prison?"

"I think you already know the answer to that one, Rodrigo." The detective's eyes got hard and shiny. Then he rose from the metal chair and folded it with a finality that made Rodrigo feel as if he were being folded up and disposed of the same way.

# Chapter 19

The hotel conference room was a sea of pink- and white-linen tablecloths and gold-rimmed china. The hundred and fifty or so faces—mostly white with a heavy representation of blondes, natural or otherwise— were the ones Adele expected at such an awards luncheon: directors of nonprofits, defense lawyers, university professors, journalists, and a few wealthy socialites who gave liberally to liberal causes.

The waiters and waitresses were typical, too. Many of them were immigrants—some Latino, some black. A good portion, Adele suspected, were working off fake papers at barely minimum wage. No one else seemed to notice the irony. They were honoring Adele for her work in bridging the gap between immigrants and Americans in her community. But any one of these waiters or waitresses could have told the audience firsthand just how wide the gap was these days. Twenty-five years ago, hard work and clean living could eventually secure an immigrant a green card and with it, the driver's license, education, and business opportunities that bought a toehold on the middle class. The people who came now stood no such chance. One raid, one infraction, one employer who looked at them the wrong way, and they were gone.

Adele was here this Tuesday afternoon to accept an award from the New York State Empowerment League for her work as executive director of La Casa. The award included a check for five thousand dollars—money the center sorely needed. Still, she felt a hollowness inside of her, as hollow as the clink of the empty wineglasses on the table, as the director of the Empowerment League, a dead ringer for Martha Stewart, walked up to the microphone.

*"Before Adele Figueroa started La Casa, Lake Holly was a place of fear and mistrust. A place where Latinos felt unwanted and unwelcome . . ."*

Was it really different now, Adele wondered? Matt Rowland, Brendan Delaney, and Eddie Giordano had already been released on bail for the brutal assault on Luis Guzman. Guzman, on the other hand, was still handcuffed to a bed at Lake Holly Hospital. As soon as he recovered enough, he was going to be arraigned for assault with a deadly weapon and transferred to the county jail. No matter that Guzman had no prior felonies. Or that he drew that pathetic pocketknife and exacted a superficial wound in self-defense.

*". . . Before La Casa, there was no dialogue with the police, no sense that Latinos and non-Latinos could come together as a community . . ."*

Some dialogue, thought Adele. The police had covered up the murder of that undocumented Latina at the lake until they could come up with another undocumented Latino to pin it on. The Guzman situation was even worse. The police took Guzman's fingerprints and fed them into the database while he was still in intensive care, which automatically alerted ICE that the local police had an undocumented alien in their custody. ICE faxed over an immigration detainer within twenty minutes of receiving the prints. Guzman was now guaranteed of being deported even if the DA's office eventually dropped the felony charges.

Adele was so deep in thought that she didn't realize it was her turn to speak until the audience rose to its feet and gave her a round of applause. She blushed, feeling embarrassed for her lack of attention. She grabbed her notes, dropped them on the floor, then bundled them together and carried them to the lectern in her arms like some magic trick gone awry. She'd had a good speech prepared—all about the symbiotic ways in which Latinos and Anglos helped each other and worked together to make Lake Holly a richer, more vibrant community. A few months ago, she believed it. Now she wasn't so sure. Still, she saw no choice but to give the audience the upbeat speech they had paid for. There was only so much truth people could stomach over coffee and crème brûlée.

She drove back to La Casa after the luncheon. She could feel the tension as soon as she walked through the door. The men were clustered in tight groups, their voices soft and strained the way they got after a raid. Nobody was using the computers to study English today. Even the pool players in back seemed to be doing more talking than playing. Enrique Sandoval was at her heel, his normal shyness gone, replaced by something closer to panic.

"Señora Adele—is it true what happened? That three white teenagers beat Luis Guzman last night and he is the one being charged? Everyone is talking about it here. Everyone."

Adele gave a quick glance around the room. She could feel the men watching her and pretending not to at the same time. Some began to gather around them. The playfulness she normally felt in them was gone, replaced by fear mixed with rage and frustration. A lot of them probably knew Luis. He was no poster boy, certainly. He drank too much and passed out sometimes in Michael Park. But he was not a violent drunk. If he was in a fight with three white teens, it was not because he started it.

"Yes, it's true," said Adele calmly. "Luis was in a fight last night with some teenagers." She changed "beaten" to "in a fight." She left out the inflammatory word, "white" and the three-against-one odds as well. Her voice was stiffer than usual. A school principal's voice. In these situations, she had to step back and maintain a cool distance. She could not run the center without it. "Both sides have been charged," she added. "The teenagers, for beating Luis. And Luis, for stabbing one of the teenagers with a knife."

"But the teenagers are free," Enrique countered. For a group of people who spoke little English, the men were amazingly well versed about what was happening in town.

Adele tried to give Enrique and the growing group of men around her a brief explanation of the American legal system with its notions of bail and presumptions of innocence.

"Then why can't Luis have the same thing?" Enrique asked. "He is in the hospital and everyone says he will go directly to jail after this."

"Because Luis has no papers, no permission to be in the United States, so he has to be detained. He may still be found innocent on the assault charges," Adele explained.

"So if he's found innocent, he will go free?"

"No," said Adele. "If he's found innocent, in all likelihood, he'll be deported. If he's found guilty, he'll be sent to an American jail."

"So he goes back to Guatemala if he's innocent and he stays here in the United States if he's guilty? That makes no sense."

*Welcome to United States immigration policy.* "I'm afraid that's the way it works, Enrique. I wish I could do something. I understand Scott Porter will be representing him so he'll have a good attorney at least."

Adele noticed Anibal standing off to her right side, running the thumb and forefinger of his good hand down his mustache. He kept his gaze respectfully down. She sensed he wanted to speak to her, but he understood she was busy. She turned to him and stood perfectly still until he realized with a hint of surprise and delight that he had her attention.

"Excuse me, Señora Adele," said Anibal with a slight bow of apology. "I just wanted to know what is happening with our friend Rodrigo."

"He hasn't been charged yet as far as I know," said Adele. "I guess we'll just have to wait and see what the police determine."

"He is a good man," Anibal said softly. "I am praying for him. Is there anything else my cousin and I can do?"

"There is nothing any of us can do, I'm afraid."

She moved past the crestfallen men. She hated seeing the disappointment in their dark eyes, the powerlessness they felt through all of it. They were smart and resourceful but they were no match for the law. She pushed Luis Guzman and Rodrigo Morales to the back of her mind and tried to concentrate on the things she could affect. She and Rafael needed to decide whether to repair or replace the microwave. She was expecting a shipment of donated toiletries from the Junior League that had yet to come in. The computer cable was on the fritz again. One of the alternative rental properties being suggested for La Casa needed a yes or no by today. Everybody had an urgent problem. Everyone needed her undivided attention.

But inside, she felt like she had failed them in some fundamental way. Her clients needed her protection and reassurance more than they needed any microwave or a shipment of toiletries. Maybe she couldn't change what was going to happen to Luis or Rodrigo, but she had a duty to make sure that the police knew they owed the Latino community an explanation.

She called Vega but he didn't answer his cell. Someone at the station told her he was out and they didn't know when he'd be back so she asked for Detective Greco instead. Greco sighed audibly when he realized it was Adele on the line.

"What? Did Ortiz finally decide to give me something I can use?"

"I'm not calling about Ortiz," said Adele. "I'm calling because the Latino community is in an uproar over what you're doing to Luis Guzman."

"He attacked a man with a knife, Adele. An Eagle Scout, he ain't."

"I know what you're doing and so do my clients: you want to get Guzman deported so he can't testify against three local football heroes, one of whom is the fire chief's son."

There was a pause. Adele sensed Greco was going to say something but checked himself. "You want my department to explain the finer points of police investigation to the Latino community? When the heat's off, I'd be happy to answer all your questions. But right now, I've got more important things to do than defend my tactics or my department. I don't tell you how to do your job, Adele. Don't tell me how to do mine."

"What about Rodrigo Morales? Are you going to charge him too?"

"At this point? It's a strong possibility. Vega's out talking to Maria's former employer to pin down a few particulars. If she comes through, yeah—we're gonna charge him."

"And you're sure he killed her?"

Again a pause. "What are you? My boss? I've got enough for probable cause. That's all I need. Porter knows it too."

"You're going to ruin his life if you're wrong."

"And I'll lose a lot of sleep over that, I can assure you." He hung up.

The harsh twang of the dial tone resonated through Adele's chest cavity. Here she was, a Harvard-educated lawyer, and she still felt fourteen around cops. Nothing could erase the memory of that long ago day with her father at the police station when he tried to report the theft of his business. She still burned with fury at the greedy neighbor and those contemptuous cops. But her greatest anger was reserved for herself, for the girl *she* had been—so meek that her voice never rose above a whisper when she translated her father's words. So cowardly, that when she left the station house, it was her father she silently raged against. For his broken English, his earnestness in the face of their mockery and his naïveté. She told herself that her father's inability to get justice that day was the reason his heart gave out two years later. But on those sleepless nights Adele lay alone in bed after the divorce, she wondered if the thing that really broke his heart was the look of shame that day on his daughter's face.

She had to prove to herself, if no one else, that she wasn't that cowardly little girl anymore. If Greco wouldn't listen to her, she'd make damn sure Vega did. Greco said Vega was interviewing Maria's former employer. That had to be Cindy Klein who lived over in The Farms. Adele had the address in her files.

She told Rafael and Kay she'd be gone for about an hour, then headed east out of town along Lake Holly Road. She rolled down the windows, hoping to wash away the shameful memories of her childhood. The skeletal branches of the trees caught the sun and held it like the tines of a fork. There was a golden strain to the light that hadn't been there even a few days ago. Everything seemed just a brushstroke more alive.

She typed Cindy Klein's address into her GPS and wound her way along the wide, immaculately groomed streets of The Farms until she was in front of what looked like a French castle on at least an acre of front lawn. A black Ford pickup was parked along the curb. It might have looked more out of place in the neighborhood except for the fact that there was a gardener's pickup parked in front of it with wooden slats on the sides and gas canisters and lawn mowers in back. In the distance, an older Latino man pushed a mower across

Cindy Klein's lawn while a lanky teenager took a Weedwacker to the edges of her Belgian-block driveway. The volume of noise brought to mind an airport runway.

A third Latino man, burly and stoop-shouldered, was fiddling with a piece of machinery in the back of the gardening truck. He lifted his gaze and smiled when he saw Adele. She got out of her car to greet him.

"Ay! My day is more pleasant for having seen you in it," the man shouted above the noise. To Adele, Jeronimo Cruz was a charmer. He'd crossed the border from Mexico about thirty years ago, worked his way up from a day laborer with a fourth-grade education to an American citizen who owned his own landscaping business. But several of her clients told her that Cruz nickel-and-dimed his workers, charging them for every mistake.

"How are you?" Adele asked.

He pulled out his wallet and flipped to a picture of an attractive young Latina in a bright blue graduation cap and gown. "My Ana Rosa. She just graduated with honors from SUNY Albany. She's been accepted to New York University Medical School."

"Congratulations!" said Adele.

Cruz beamed. "I tell her she must study hard. No work. Only make good grades. And she listens to me. Always she listens to her papi."

Adele went to ask what kind of doctor Ana Rosa wanted to become, but Cruz excused himself for a moment and stormed off across the lawn to the lanky teenager working the Weedwacker along the driveway. Adele watched Cruz gesturing angrily. The teenager froze beneath the onslaught, tense and coiled, then nodded without a word and went back to work. Cruz returned, shaking his head.

"Nobody knows how to do anything right anymore. I tell the kid: be careful with the stonework. You think he listens? I wouldn't even let him work for me except his father's a good worker and the kid needs money for college. What can I say?" Cruz shrugged.

*College?* Adele focused on the boy now. He was dressed like the other men—loose jeans smeared green with bits of fresh-cut grass, scuffed work boots, a frayed hoodie, and a faded baseball cap pulled low across his brow. But there was something about the way he carried himself that suggested a certain detachment from the work. The men Adele saw regularly at La Casa radiated hunger. Their eyes always roamed a room; their bodies seemed forever poised to pitch forward on some new quest—for work, for food, for survival. They wore their desperation like a second skin. It lingered in the set of their jaws, in the way their faces always seemed to pose the questions: "Can I make it? *Will* I make it?" This boy had none of that.

"Is that Kenny Cardenas?"

"Yes. His father, Cesar, is out there mowing the lawn," said Cruz. "Hector, my usual employee, cut his hand and Kenny was free today so I asked Cesar if his son wanted to pick up some extra cash. I should have just handed the kid a couple of bills. He's going to cost me more than he's worth."

"He's very smart," said Adele. "Our board just awarded him a scholarship."

"Cesar tells me he's smart," said Cruz. "All the time. But I can't see it. There's book smart. And then there's life smart. Some of these kids, they only got the first one."

Adele wondered which category Cruz put his daughter Ana Rosa into. Cesar Cardenas had the same ambitions for his child. He just crossed the border too late.

Cruz picked up a set of electric pruning shears and excused himself to do some work. Adele went back to her car and waited for Vega to come outside.

He emerged from a side entrance about ten minutes later. She watched him begin the long walk down the driveway, back to his truck. He took out his cell phone and punched in a number. While he was speaking, he caught sight of Kenny Cardenas and offered a brief nod. Kenny did the same, like they were both embarrassed to see each other. Clearly Vega knew him and clearly Kenny wished he didn't. Vega finished his cell call and noticed Adele for the first time walking toward him.

"I need to talk to you," she said.

He shook his head. "Not now. I'm under the gun."

"Guzman or Morales?"

"You know I can't talk about it."

She kept pace beside him. "My clients are going nuts, Jimmy. First you detain Rodrigo Morales without any real evidence—"

"Oh, we've got evidence now, believe me."

"What?"

"You'll know when he's charged." Vega stopped at the end of the driveway and looked at his watch. "I just spoke to Greco and asked him to start the booking process. He'll be arraigned in an hour. I've gotta go." He unlocked his truck and went to get in.

"How about Luis Guzman?"

Vega made a face. "Not my case." He opened the driver's side door of his truck.

"Don't hand me this, 'it's not my case' bullshit. You could do something about this if you wanted to—"

"Adele—"

"You could convince Greco to back off his little ploy of getting Guzman deported so that three white football players won't have to go to jail—"

"Adele!" he shouted over the noise of the mower and Weedwacker. "*I* was the one who told Greco to charge Guzman, okay?"

"*You?* How could you?"

He slapped the side of his truck. "Get in. I'm not having this conversation on the street."

She sat stiffly in the cab. The closed doors of the truck muted the roar of the gas-powered equipment. It did nothing to tamp down her fury.

"Is this your own vehicle?"

"Yeah."

"A pickup. It figures." She checked the rearview mirror.

"What?"

"I wanted to see if you have a gun rack."

"No gun rack. No deer antlers in my living room or collection of unusual beer cans in my garage. And I don't run a check of unpaid parking tickets on every person who pisses me off either. Though in your case, I might make an exception."

"Why did you tell Greco to charge Guzman?"

"Because otherwise Guzman will split the moment he leaves the hospital. Greco wants those teenagers to see justice as much as you do. He needs Guzman to make that happen."

"But you're punishing the victim."

"Who also happens to have been a drunk with a knife. Sooner or later, that scenario was gonna turn ugly."

The gardeners turned off their equipment and began packing up. The silence felt so unexpected at first that it seemed to have a weight of its own. Adele couldn't think straight while those engines were roaring. She wondered what it did to the men who operated them all day. She knew most of them wore some sort of ear protection. But even so.

Jeronimo Cruz and Cesar Cardenas were wrestling lawn mowers and equipment onto the truck. Kenny had a leg up on the bumper. He was trying to scrape a coating of fresh-cut grass and mud from the lower legs of his jeans. The men teased him for worrying about a little dirt. He looked embarrassed. He pulled his baseball cap down low and didn't wave good-bye as he climbed into the cab.

"I saw you nod to Kenny Cardenas earlier," said Adele. "Do you know him?"

"Yeah." Vega fiddled with his car keys.

"He cuts my grass," said Adele.

"He dates my daughter." It had the whispered angst of a confession.

"Really? You know he's—"

"Illegal. I know."

She rolled her eyes. "I was going to say, 'a really nice, smart kid.' And no one's illegal, only undocumented."

"Call it what you will. Without that precious paperwork, he's got no more hold on this town than Guzman or Morales." Vega checked his watch. "I've got to get back to the station."

"Can I at least tell my clients what you've told me about why the police charged Guzman?"

"Sure. But do me a favor? Don't say it came from me. Guzman's not my case. Greco might get sore."

"Deal."

She got out of his truck and into her car, intending to follow him back to town. But like all cops, he drove too fast, as if the laws of the road didn't apply to him. The sun was blinding at this hour. To her left, the lake reflected the light with the hard brilliance of liquid mercury. She cracked a window and felt the breeze on her face. It would be a long time, if ever, before Rodrigo and Luis felt such a breeze again.

She tried to keep up with Vega's truck but he took the bends at a much faster clip than she was used to. She would not want to be with him on a car chase. She sensed he'd actually enjoy it. She looked away for just a second to adjust her visor. Something large and gray scampered in front of Vega's pickup. A young buck. Antlers like two halves of a rib cage, eyes like a puppy. Adele could see its panic as Vega's truck bore down on it.

Vega swerved the wheel, missed the buck, and pulled back sharply into the bend of the road without even braking. But the animal seemed momentarily disoriented. It froze an instant in front of Adele's car. She could see the sharp in-and-out breaths along its sinewy torso, the whites of its eyes. She turned her wheel. There was a thud—not nearly as big a thud as Adele had expected. But still a jolt. A counter jolt. A jostling of plastic and metal that took milliseconds to fold and would take thousands of dollars to unfold. Adele pulled her car to the side of the road. The deer scampered off into the deep brush on the other side. There was a snap of dried twigs as the white tail rose up in the air and disappeared.

She wasn't hurt. Her air bag hadn't even deployed. Mostly, she was embarrassed. And annoyed. Vega shouldn't have been driving so fast. She shouldn't have been trying to keep up with him. She was competing with him even if she didn't want to admit it.

Vega's pickup did a one-eighty and screeched to a halt behind her car. He ran up to the driver's side. She opened her door.

"You okay?" he asked breathlessly.

"I'm fine. Just a little shaken up. You shouldn't drive so fast."

"I didn't have the accident."

"You could've."

He pulled out his radio and called for a patrol car and an ambulance.

"No ambulance," she insisted. "I'm fine."

"At least to check you out?"

"No!"

He relayed that they just needed an officer on the scene. Then he hung up and walked around to the front of her car to inspect the damage. "It's just a broken headlamp and a little hood compression. The cosmetic damage will set you back a grand perhaps. But you could probably drive the car forever with just a head-lamp replacement. Pop the hood, will ya?"

She did as instructed. He stuck his head inside and nosed around.

"What about that deer?" asked Adele.

"What about him?"

"You think he's okay?"

"If this is all the damage he did, he's not hurt, either." Vega closed the hood.

"You don't know that."

He shrugged. "It's a deer, Adele. We've got too freakin' many of them in New York anyway."

"Okay, fine. Go. They're waiting for you at Rodrigo's arraignment."

"Let 'em wait. I'm not leaving you here until an officer arrives."

"Then if you're staying, I want you to make sure that deer isn't bleeding to death in the bushes."

*"Puñeta, coño!"* he cursed. "Stay in your car." He reached across her and turned on her hazard lights. "I don't want you getting run over." Then he crossed the two-lane and stomped off into the bushes. They were about a quarter mile west of the main entrance to the reservoir. Even this time of year, the trees and bushes were dense. It was like looking through crossed fingers. She could see a sliver of the lake through the branches, the white of its surface so blinding, it sucked the color from everything around it. But that only made the woods less articulated, made the whole place feel like the entrance to a movie theater.

Adele waited, then waited some more. She had expected Vega to emerge almost immediately and assure her that the deer was gone. She wondered if the deer was more wounded than he'd led her to believe.

She powered down her window. "Jimmy?"

"Over here. Don't come any closer."

"Why? Bladder control problems?" she joked.

She heard his footsteps break free of the brush. He crossed the street, a grim look on his face.

"Is the deer dead?"

"The deer's long gone."

"Then what's the matter?"

He didn't answer. Instead, he pulled out his cell phone and hit a number on speed dial. "Greco? If you're there, man, pick up. It's Vega. I need to talk to you right away. Call me on my cell, ASAP."

He hung up and tried another number. "Where's Greco?" he demanded of the voice on the other end. He didn't even bother identifying himself. "Has he fingerprinted Morales yet?—*Shit!*—Has he sent the card out?—What do you mean, you don't know?—Yeah, I need him. Tell him to call Jimmy Vega on his cell right away. Tell him he can't even take a piss before he calls me. Got that?"

Adele went to speak but he motioned for her to stay quiet and dialed another number.

"Hey, Nick? Can you send a couple of our guys over to the reservoir in Lake Holly to do a workup ASAP?"

A reply.

"Are Joe and Dave working today?—Tell them it's an accident reconstruction, not a crime scene—Yeah, I'm sure—Tell them I need them to get here right away. There will be a Lake Holly cop on site." He got off the phone.

"What did you find in the bushes?" asked Adele.

"Let's just say I'm beginning to think Rodrigo Morales really didn't kill Maria."

# Chapter 20

Two uniformed police officers came down to Rodrigo Morales's cell. One had short blond hair. The other had a shaved head and a brown mustache that sat like a caterpillar across his upper lip. Rodrigo had never seen either of them before. Good news would have come with one police officer. Or maybe that Spanish detective. But two? In uniform? His breath fell away before they even yanked open the outer door of the cellblock.

"Stick your hands through the bars," the officer with the shaved head barked out in toneless Spanish. Rodrigo had a sense the officer knew only the Spanish commands he'd been taught. Rodrigo didn't even try to speak. He did what the officer asked of him and thrust out his hands. He showed no emotion. Inside, he was trembling like a child's wind-up toy. Thoughts spun through his brain so fast, he couldn't catch them long enough to understand their meaning. He caught the trivial ones. He needed to take a piss. He'd left his few meager belongings—his nonworking cell phone, a few changes of clothes, a razor, a little necklace for Juliza that someone had discarded in the trash—back in his room. He had ten dollars of emergency money sewn into the waistband of his jeans, the ones they would likely take from him as soon as he got to the county jail.

He missed the big thoughts, the ones that were too terrible to contemplate: What would happen to Triza and the children? How would they survive? Would he ever see them again?

The officer with the shaved head slapped a set of handcuffs around Rodrigo's wrists. "Back away from the door," he commanded. "Turn to face the wall."

Rodrigo obeyed. The blond cop shackled his ankles. Did they think he would try to escape? In these boots? He could barely walk. But he didn't protest. He stayed limp and compliant. There was no point in resisting. He was going to jail. That much he understood. There was a process, sure. There had been a process in Rhode Island two years ago when he got arrested. They assigned him a case number. They took a black-and-white headshot. They covered his fingertips with black ink that took forever to wear off and made him press down on a special card. They sent him before a judge with some man who claimed to be his lawyer but never spoke to him.

It was all for the *Norte Americanos'* benefit. Their sense of order and precision. Their charts and records and legal proceedings and case files. They had a million ways to count him and a million ways to tell him he didn't count. They might as well have thrown him into the back of a truck and driven off. The results would have been the same: jail-court-prison. It would be the same this time. Only the jail part might be longer and the prison part would be much, much longer.

The officers led him through the hallway, up a flight of stairs, and into a big room with a lot of partitions. The fat, white detective was waiting behind one of the partitions, chewing on some sort of red licorice candy. He looked at Rodrigo like he already wasn't there. A bag of garbage that needed to be dumped at the curb.

The officer with the shaved head pushed Rodrigo down into a chair. He said something to the detective and they all laughed. *Yaw-yaw-yaw.* That's what English sounded like to Rodrigo. Hard and angry, without any of the whispered rhythms of Spanish. No wonder Anglos couldn't dance, didn't even seem to particularly like music. Their whole language was devoid of it.

The two officers disappeared and the detective slipped on a pair of heavy, black-rimmed glasses and turned to his computer screen. He read off a series of questions in mangled Spanish: full name, aliases, birth date, place of birth, marital status, citizenship. Rodrigo answered in a soft, tight voice—so soft that twice the detective yelled at him to speak louder. He said it in English but Rodrigo got the gist.

The detective yawned a couple of times while he was typing and fished some more licorice out of the bag on his desk. He didn't offer anything to Rodrigo. Not that Rodrigo was the least bit hungry. It had been like this the last time he was arrested too. Every sensation left him. He ate the starchy bland food but never felt sated. He slept on a thin prison mattress but always felt exhausted.

He spent a total of two months in jail and five

months in federal prison, all of it in a shadow world of filth and noise and random cruelty that carved him out so completely that it took three weeks back in Esperanza before he could even speak about the experience to Triza. She held him like a baby the night he told her about the punches he took, the shanking he narrowly avoided. He cried in her arms while beyond their cement block walls, the guava trees rustled and the crickets and insects stood in mute witness. When he was in Esperanza, everything here had the flatness of a dream. Even now, his life here felt two-dimensional and devoid of texture, a netherworld that forever ensnared him between desire and memory, ambition and regret. God, how he wished he could talk to Triza just one more time, to hear her voice calling out to him in the humid night air.

The detective finished up and then escorted Rodrigo to a small room with a white wall. The detective motioned for Rodrigo to stand against the wall and look into the camera. He took a flash picture. Then he turned Rodrigo to the right and took another. The flash was bright. When Rodrigo closed his eyes, big black spots floated in front of them. The detective said something to him in English. Rodrigo shook his head. He didn't understand. The detective consulted his little postcard of Spanish words.

*"A-bo-ga-do?"* the detective grunted out, pronouncing every part of the word like he was ordering one off a menu. *"Su abogado?* Scott Porter? *Sí?"*

*"Sí,"* said Rodrigo. *"Puedo llamarlo?"*

The detective gave Rodrigo a confused look so he mimed making a phone call to his lawyer. It was hard to do in handcuffs but the detective understood. He shook his head and answered in English. "Not now. Later."

Rodrigo needed no translation. He didn't know what Porter could do anyway. Probably the señor would want him to lie and say the Spanish detective hit him. But what would that accomplish? It wouldn't get him out of being charged for Maria's murder. And if he lied about that, how could anyone believe he was telling the truth about anything else? No. He would not lie. He had sinned and he would ask God's forgiveness and Triza's, if he ever got the chance. But he would not compound one sin with another.

The detective brought him over to a small table and unlocked his handcuffs. Rodrigo's fingers were ice cold. His hands were shaking. He had quieted all the nerves in his body even though he was thrumming on the inside. But his hands refused to listen. They shook of their own volition.

The detective stared at Rodrigo's shaking hands and cursed. Rodrigo knew very few English words but he knew all the curses. He'd heard them often enough. On the table sat a white fingerprint card and a pad of ink. Rodrigo suspected it was more difficult to do prints on a shaking suspect.

The detective said something in English and mimed what he was going to do. Rodrigo nodded and surrendered his right hand. The detective pressed Rodrigo's thumb into the ink and then rolled it across a box on the card. He lifted the print, held it up to the light and cursed. He threw away the card and tried again, pressing down hard. Rodrigo felt the pressure on his nail bed. It hurt but he didn't know what to say or if, when he said it, the detective would understand or care.

It made no difference. The second print didn't work either. The detective opened the door to the room and called out to someone. The officer with the shaved head came in and tried. Both men were inking and pressing and cursing in equal measure. Rodrigo's hand felt like something that wasn't even part of him. Black at the tips. Wet and discolored. Shaking and cold. It was as if he could see himself from a very far distance in that room. His T-shirt, hoodie, and jeans, sour-smelling and crusted with blood that had turned brown and mud that had turned beige. His unshaven cheeks. His scabbed and swollen lip. His floppy boot. Rodrigo didn't recognize this man. Neither would anyone in Esperanza. Not his family. Not his friends. This was not Rodrigo Eliseo Morales-Aguirre. This was an imposter. A man who had misused Rodrigo's body, stolen his soul, taken all the best parts—his honor, his pride, his dignity— and sold them off for pennies somewhere between Mexico and Lake Holly for the price of a trip across the border and the chance to earn ten dollars an hour.

They were filling up the card now, the officer and the detective. Together, they'd found a way to get Rodrigo's prints by shaking out the hand first, getting the blood flowing. They were chatting and laughing on either side of him. Chatting and laughing like he was a cow they needed to brand before they sent him off to slaughter.

And the worst part of it was—Rodrigo saw himself the same way.

# Chapter 21

Jimmy Vega would have walked right past the few shards of broken glass. He would have walked by the cracked tree limb with the round three-inch depression that turned the bark concave and stringy like the inside of an underripe pumpkin. In a month, the woods would have leafed out too much to have ever found it. In a year, the limb would be too rotted, the glass too fragmented and scattered.

He found it only because he happened to look down and see something metallic. He'd assumed it was a bit of foil from a gum wrapper or the crushed remnants of a beer can. But it was a crucifix. Mud caked the carved depressions on Christ's tarnished body. Rust stains pitted the bird wings that dangled from each side of Christ's outstretched arms. The metal was already being reclaimed by the earth that had once delivered it up. But even with the damage, Vega recognized the crucifix as the one he'd seen around Maria's neck in the picture of her and her baby. He took a picture of it on his cell phone now to show Greco. Maria Elena had been in this spot, maybe even died in it, next to shards of broken glass and that odd round depression in a cracked tree stump.

"You think Maria was killed by a hit-and-run?" asked Adele while they were both sitting in his pickup, waiting for the police to show up.

"Don't know," Vega grunted, staring at the picture on his cell phone. The truth was, he'd stake his badge on it, but he didn't want to say that to Adele right now. He didn't want to say anything that could come back to bite him on a witness stand. It didn't mean he wasn't sure. Vega had spent too many years in uniform documenting car accidents not to recognize the telltale signs. He'd stood no more than ten feet from the side of Lake Holly Road, a winding two-lane that Adele herself had just had a collision on, albeit with a deer. There was no shoulder, no streetlights, and he already knew that Maria walked this way to meet up with Morales.

"If that's the case," said Adele. "Then Rodrigo is innocent."

"Maybe," said Vega. But there were no maybes about it in Vega's opinion. Morales didn't have a car. There was no way he could have killed Maria like this and no way he'd have stood by and let her die if someone else had. As Morales said himself, he and Maria had been through too much together.

"What are you going to do?" Adele asked him.

"If the fingerprints haven't gone through the system, we'll release Morales."

"And if Greco already put them through?"

Vega stared straight ahead at her reflection in the windshield. "It's not my fault, Adele. I couldn't have known."

"You mean he'll be deported?"

"As soon as ICE gets the prints, they'll run them

through their database and see that he's got a criminal record and a prior deportation order. They're bound to fax over an immigration detainer. I've seen it happen in under twenty minutes."

"Can't you call it back?"

Vega shook his head. "On what grounds? That he's not here illegally? He is. We caught him. For the wrong reasons, but he's been caught all the same. It's toothpaste from a tube, Adele. It only flows in one direction."

Two cars barreled along Lake Holly Road in quick succession, one in each direction, sucking the currents of air along with them. Each time Vega's body geared up for the police cruiser and each time he felt the tension of knowing it hadn't yet arrived. He couldn't leave the scene until a Lake Holly uniform showed up—first for Adele, and second, to secure the accident scene across the road until the specialists arrived. Not that time was really the issue here. If Morales's fingerprints had already been entered into the federal database, Vega could be at the station right now and it wouldn't matter.

"A man's whole future is at stake here," said Adele.

"Don't you think I know that?"

"So that's it? You're just going to shrug it off?"

"What do you want me to do?"

She turned her face away from him. "Nothing. You're good at that."

He tapped his fingers on the steering wheel to a rhythm only he could hear, a habit when he was nervous.

"My mother was murdered last year at her apartment in the Bronx," Vega said softly. "A botched robbery." His voice sounded oddly compacted, like it was traveling through snow. "I drove down as soon as I found out. Spoke to a detective on the scene. He barely acknowledged me. He kept forgetting my mother's name. While I was trying to get information from him, he took two cell calls about his girlfriend's birthday party. I'm a fellow officer, this was my mother he was talking about and he treated the whole thing like we were discussing a piece of broken furniture." Vega fought the choke in his voice. "So I know what it feels like to be on the other end, Adele. I'm not indifferent here. Just powerless."

She nodded. "I'm sorry about your mother." Then she placed her hand on top of his. It was a momentary gesture—she took the hand away quickly—but so unexpected that it undid something inside of Vega, shook loose all his thoughts, made them seem as petty as pocket change. It had been awhile since he'd felt this zero gravity sensation around a woman. He didn't think it was possible anymore.

Vega studied her reflection in the windshield. Her makeup was soft and blurry around the eyes and her lips had the pouty texture of a pillow just waiting for someone to press against it. He'd been fantasizing about those lips ever since he left the dance floor last night. He pictured himself pressing down on them now, running his hands along the curves of her thighs, cupping those full breasts to his chest—

—*Puñeta, coño!* Was he crazy? Bad enough that he was looking at a possible police brutality charge. Did he want to tack on sexual harassment as well?

A siren broke the spell. Vega was almost glad of it. He jumped out of his truck like it was on fire and drank in the cool air as he flagged down the cruiser. As soon as it pulled behind him, he ran over and tried to get the officer up to speed on the situation. Then he tried Greco's cell again. Still no answer. He tried the desk sergeant. He was handling another call.

"Go," Adele urged him as she stepped out of his truck. "I'll catch up with you at the station."

"Are you sure—?"

"—Go." He noticed a flush to her cheeks. He wondered if she'd read his thoughts in the truck. He hoped he hadn't embarrassed her. He felt pretty embarrassed himself right now. He ducked into his truck and pulled back on the road. He tried Greco again. Still no answer. He came around a blind curve and had to bear down on the brake. In front of him was a long line of traffic behind a payloader crawling along at fifteen miles per hour. The entire road was one long no-passing zone. Not that he could have passed anyway. There were three cars between him and the payloader. He didn't even have his light bar with him today.

He cursed and pounded the wheel. He was getting himself worked up—for what? Morales could always hop the border again—

—*If he had another five thousand dollars, which he most likely didn't.*

And then there was the risk. Every month, things got tighter. The fence became stronger, the U.S. patrols more numerous, the Mexican gangs more deadly. Vega had heard that the gangsters were forcing immigrants to mule drugs in order to cross these days. They were holding people hostage in safe houses without food or water, beating and torturing them until their families agreed to pay thousands more for their release. Twenty years ago, guys like Morales could fly from Guatemala to Mexico, hike across the California desert, hop a flight from L.A., and be in New York by dinnertime.

Now, they had to accomplish the whole journey on foot or smuggled in car trunks and tractor-trailers. The process took weeks, sometimes months. Hundreds died every year in the crossings.

Chances were, if Rodrigo Morales got deported, he'd never overcome all the odds a third time. Maybe Vega had found enough evidence to keep him from a long prison sentence. But he'd tinkered with the man's fate just enough to sentence him and his family to a lifetime of poverty—or worse, a fatal attempt at another crossing. Many people would say he was one more illegal in a country chock-full of them. But Vega's mother was one more homicide in a neighborhood chock-full of them. That sort of math is always a slippery slope. If one person doesn't matter, pretty soon nobody does.

Vega tried Greco's cell again. Still no answer. He was in sight of the station house now. He pulled into the parking lot, parked across two spots, and ran into the building. He was sweating like the police were going to deport him instead of Morales. He followed the sounds of Greco's voice to the detectives' bullpen. Greco was leaning back in his chair, a red Twizzler in his mouth while Tony Ross, a uniformed officer with a shaved head and brown mustache, told a dirty joke. Something about a hooker, a football coach, and two congressmen. Or maybe it wasn't a joke. Maybe it was just the latest newspaper headline. You could never tell these days. Ross and Greco looked at him like he'd interrupted a Papal benediction.

"Well—did you?" asked Vega breathlessly.

"Did I what?" asked Greco.

"Did you get my messages? About Morales?"

"About his fingerprints? Yeah." Greco yawned.

"Did you send them to the Feds already?"

Greco gave Tony Ross a pointed look, then shrugged. "What's the difference?"

"C'mon, Grec, don't dick around with me. Did you send them or not?"

"Jeez Vega, what's your problem? Morales isn't the president of some banana republic, you know. He's an illegal. A felon. One raid, one misdemeanor and he'll be gone anyway. Or is this about the fact that you've got the hots for Adele Figueroa?"

Vega felt as if the ambient temperature of the room had just been raised twenty degrees and someone was aiming a spotlight in his direction. He wanted to hit Louie Greco. He wanted to haul back and slam his bread-dough body across the partition. Knock the whole damn thing down. They'd have his badge for that. Maybe even his pension. But right now, it almost felt worth it to see the surprised look on Greco's fat face. Perhaps Adele had awakened some feeling inside of him, some sense of who he was and why it mattered. But that had no bearing on his actions here. He was doing this for reasons a man like Greco would never understand. There was the law. And then there was what's right. Most times, they were the same thing. But not always. Not always.

Greco went to fish a Twizzler out of a cellophane bag. Vega grabbed the bag and flung it across the room. It thudded against the copy machine. Red rods of dyed and processed sugar scattered on the floor like a child's set of pickup sticks. Greco reared back in his chair, his mouth open to somewhere between a curse and cry of shock. Vega rested his hands on the armrests of Greco's chair and leaned in close.

"Maria Elena was killed by a hit-and-run, man. A hit-and-run. Rodrigo Morales doesn't even own a god-damned bicycle. He's not our guy. I will stake my badge on it, which is probably what's gonna happen anyway once Porter gets a hold of me. Now, one more time, Grec—did you send off the prints to the Feds? Yes or no?"

"Okay, okay. Relax. Keep your shirt on, Vega. They're here. At the station. Took me and Tony freakin' forty-five minutes to get a decent set and you went and spoiled everything."

Vega straightened. Something inside of him un-clenched and took flight. He felt loose and limber the way he used to as a small boy on that first warm day of spring when he could shuck his jacket on the walk home from school and feel the sun on his bare arms. He had undone the damage. He had spared a man who would never know how close he'd come to losing everything. Or maybe he would know. Vega already sensed that Morales was not a stupid man. But in the end, it didn't matter. Jimmy Vega didn't do it for Morales. He did it for himself. As he'd told Bobby Rowland, you have to be able to look yourself in the mirror.

"Where's Morales?"

"Where do you think? Back in his holding cell." Greco gave a longing look to the Twizzlers scattered across the dusty floor. "I cancelled the arraignment and told the assistant district attorney assigned to the case to sit tight until I spoke to you. All I can say is: this better be good, Vega. 'Cause if you're wrong, I'm person-ally gonna nail your ass to the wall."

# Chapter 22

"Who the hell would be dumb enough to want to make an accident look like a homicide? 'Cause sure as shit, she didn't tie *herself* down in that lake."

Vega didn't know the answer to Greco's question. All he knew was that the evidence coming in from the county police's accident reconstruction team matched his gut intuition. The crucifix Vega photographed at the site perfectly matched the one around Maria's neck in their original photo. The glass by the roadside was from a broken car headlamp. Forensics would have to match the paint chips to a make and model of car and Dr. Gupta would have to see if they could uncover any microscopic bits of hair or skin from the depression in the tree but Vega felt confident they were looking at a hit-and-run.

He wanted to release Rodrigo Morales immediately but Greco felt they should wait until they could hand him over to Scott Porter when he showed up for the now-cancelled arraignment.

"Morales trips and falls or gets mugged between here

and home, and you *know* Porter's gonna be screaming we had something to do with it," Greco explained.

Vega saw his point. Besides, Morales had waited this long. An hour more or less wasn't going to make any difference.

They were sitting in Greco's cubicle poring over Maria's immigration records when Vega received a text message. He was hoping it was word from Verizon that they were faxing over her phone records. But it was Adele. He started to text her back when he caught Greco scrutinizing him over the tops of his glasses.

"A word of advice, amigo?"

Vega stopped texting and straightened. "You want us to be amigos, don't call me that."

"Fair enough." Greco nodded. "But my advice stands: you gotta do a better job of keeping your personal inclinations out of this case."

"I haven't done anything—"

"Ah"—Greco put up a hand to silence him—"You can feed that bullshit to Adele when she texts back— again—in five minutes." Greco nodded to Vega's phone. Vega bit his lip. Greco was a better cop than he gave him credit for. "Far as I'm concerned, on your own time you can drape yourself in Puerto Rican flags, dance a salsa, and petition to hand out green cards like they're lotto tickets for all I care. But here, you're a cop. We work together, that's gotta be your only allegiance. You get my drift?"

"I would never compromise an investigation."

"Never say never. It's a dangerous word." He sat back in his chair and folded his hands on top of his belly. "See, basically I like you, Vega, even if you go off half-cocked at times. Problem is, Adele does too. But she's got an agenda. And better legs."

"I'm not dating her, you know."

"Not yet."

Vega put his phone away. Adele would have to wait. He shot a glance at Greco's garbage can beneath his desk where the package of Twizzlers now resided. "Does this have anything to do with a certain projectile I launched from your desk earlier?"

"No. But you owe me two packages tomorrow, ya hump. Now do some work for a change instead of busting my balls." Greco tossed Vega Maria's immigration records. Full name: Maria Elena Jimena Santos-Alvarez. It showed just one arrest in a mass immigration raid at a food processing plant in Perkinsville, Iowa, eight years ago when she was twenty-two.

"I'm starting to think she snuck back in the country illegally at some point and had the kid," said Greco. "When ICE arrested her in Perkinsville, she told the agents she was unmarried and childless."

Vega read her file. It indicated that Maria was transported to Cedar Rapids after the arrest and charged with felony identity theft for having purchased a stolen Social Security card—the same crime that Morales was arrested for in Rhode Island six years later. Just as in Morales's case, the charge was plea-bargained down to a misdemeanor. She spent five months in a federal prison camp for women in Greenville, Illinois, before being deported back to Guatemala. Alone.

"There's no indication that she was deported along with any family members," said Greco. "I know some of these people, when they get arrested, they don't tell

ICE they got kids because they're afraid they'll get deported too. But that's 'cause they think they're gonna get to stay. This woman knows she's getting deported. I would think if she'd had any kids at that point, she'd want them with her."

Vega agreed. There was no record of Maria entering the United States before or since that time, but both Vega and Greco knew that immigrants often crossed the border in both directions illegally without getting caught. Odds were, she'd had the child in Guatemala or she'd made some subsequent trip to the United States in which she'd given birth.

"Least we know we're looking for a kid who's probably younger than eight," said Greco. "Question is: Where was she born? In the States? Or Guatemala?"

"We get the phone records, I'll call her mother," said Vega. "She can probably tell us a lot."

The desk sergeant buzzed Greco to let him know Scott Porter had arrived. Adele was also in the lobby.

"You fetch Morales," said Greco. "I'll handle Porter and Adele."

Rodrigo Morales was sitting on his bunk, elbows on his knees, his head between his hands. He looked up at the sound of the outer metal door opening. Instinctively, he got to his feet and backed against the wall of his cell. He wore his fear with the same hyper alertness as that deer Adele had just hit on Lake Holly Road. His eyes searched for sudden movements. His breathing seemed rough and shallow. He'd been in the same muddy, blood-smeared clothes for more than twenty-four hours. His face was shadowed in stubble. His fingers were black from fingerprint ink. The swelling on his lip had gone down, replaced by a brownish scab surrounded by varying pigments of purple. He looked like he needed a month's worth of sleep.

"Good news, man," said Vega. "You're cleared. Scott Porter's upstairs. We're just finishing up the paperwork and then you're free to leave."

"I—I am?" Morales's legs gave out and he sank down on the vinyl mattress pad covering the bunk. His eyes turned glassy. He pressed his blackened fingertips together and touched them to his forehead as if offering a prayer. His hands were shaking. Vega gave Morales a moment to collect himself before speaking.

"Her name was Santos, Rodrigo. Maria Elena Jimena Santos-Alvarez. She was thirty years old when she died. We still know nothing about her daughter."

Vega watched Morales's face, watched the knowledge spread across his features like watercolor on paper. He wasn't bluffing. He really didn't know her name.

"The case is still open, man," Vega told him. "So if you hear anything about what happened to Maria or you find someone who knows her daughter, you let us know, okay? We find out you didn't, it's going to be a different story."

"I understand."

Vega unlocked the cell door. It creaked as it swung open. The noise was jarring. It stopped your heart, made you feel for a moment the finality of a life lived inside such a space. Vega knew Morales felt it too. He shuffled out of it quickly as if it might have the power to suck him back. Vega unlocked the outer door. "You want Scott Porter to drive you home?"

"It's okay. I can walk."

Vega eyed the man's boots. Going without socks the other day had been agony. He couldn't imagine going without decent shoes.

He led Morales upstairs to the room where he'd been processed to give him back his personal effects. He didn't have many: a cheap watch with a scuffed dial face and a cracked leather band. A key on a knotted piece of string, presumably to the room he lived in. A dog-eared photograph of three dark-haired children in front of a tidy, one-story white cement block house with a clay-tile roof. A wallet woven of brightly patterned cloth with three singles in the billfold. He showed them to Morales.

"Is that all you had in there?" The original inventory receipt stated that the wallet contained three dollars but Vega didn't want Morales later claiming that the cops had lifted a roll of twenties from him.

"Yes. Three dollars." Vega wondered if the guy had any money at all. The only other personal items were a few coins totaling under fifty cents and a pair of shoelaces that looked as if they'd disintegrated when the officer took them out of his work boots. Morales strapped the watch back on his wrist. Then he took the wallet, key, and photograph.

"Your children?" asked Vega, pointing to the picture of the two girls with a boy in the middle. He guessed the older girl to be about twelve. She had her father's serious eyes.

Morales nodded. Vega waited for him to add something, but of course Morales wouldn't. A poor man may not have much, but he always has his story. It's his and his alone and he doesn't have to share it with anybody if he doesn't want to. Morales picked up the shoelaces and squatted down, patiently and methodically trying to relace the shredded nylon through the eyelets of his work boots. The ends of the laces were frayed and his hands were too shaky. Finally, he just stuffed the laces into his pocket and straightened.

"I will lace them later."

"How are you going to walk?"

"I can manage. Thank you."

"Maybe I can find some tape or string—" Vega offered. But Morales shook his head.

"It's okay. I just want to leave."

They found Greco, Porter, and Adele in the front lobby of the police station. Adele gave Vega a smile and Vega looked away. He felt like Greco noticed every glance between them. He hoped to hand Morales over and concentrate on the new direction of the investigation. But Porter had other ideas.

"I need a moment before my client is released to speak to him privately," said Porter.

Vega and Greco exchanged wary glances. Porter was going to try to convince Morales to assert police brutality. His charges would be much more credible now that the police had released him, just as Captain Waring had feared. Morales was probably pissed at all Vega and Greco had put him through. This would be his chance to exact some revenge and a little cash for his troubles.

Greco opened his arms like a maître d' welcoming his favorite patron. "C'mon, Scott. Let's be reasonable here. No harm done."

"I suspect my client feels quite differently."

Morales had no idea what the men were saying. Vega could read the panic in his eyes. He thought they were going to detain him again. Vega spoke quickly in Spanish.

"Your lawyer wants you to go back inside the station, Rodrigo."

"No, no, no!" said Morales.

Porter scowled at Vega and spoke in Spanish as well. "The police have already let you go, Rodrigo. They can't arrest you. They just don't want you to press charges against Detective Vega for what he did to you."

"Can we not have a UN summit here?" Greco demanded. "I'd like to be able to speak my own language in my own country and know what's going on."

Adele translated while Vega and Porter played tug of war in Spanish with Rodrigo in the middle.

Porter: "If the detective hit you—"

Vega: "It's a crime to lie, Rodrigo. You can go to jail—"

Porter to Vega: "Perjury works both ways, you know, *Detective.*"

Finally, Morales waved his hands in front of his face. "No! I don't want to press any charges. I just want to go home. Please." Morales looked over at Adele. "Señora Adele. Please can you take me home?" Clearly Morales had had enough of all of them, Porter included.

"Of course, Rodrigo."

Porter wasn't ready to give up so fast. "If you were mistreated in any way, Rodrigo. You don't have to be afraid to step forward. They can't send you to jail for that—"

"No," said Morales. He waved his hands vigorously in front of him as if his words were not enough to make them understand. "Thank you, Señor Porter, for your concern. But I tripped. I was not hit. That is the truth." Morales turned his bloodshot eyes to Vega. Vega gave the slightest nod to the man. A silent thank you. For one brief moment, each had held the other's fate in his hands. And it had gone well for both of them. So very often in Vega's experience, it doesn't.

"All right." Porter threw up his hands and sighed. "I'm done here." He seemed almost sorry that was the case. He left quickly, barely acknowledging any of them, including his former client. Adele and Morales headed out to the parking lot. Greco told Vega the cell phone records had just been faxed over from Verizon. They had a lot of work to do.

Vega looked through the heavy glass doors of the station house. It was dark now. Evening was here, but the sky remained a bright blue that would deepen soon. Already, lights glowed yellow behind curtains in the apartments on the other side of the station house. The phosphorus street lamps surrounding the parking lot made it feel like a stage, hushed and expectant before the opening curtain. He could see Morales walking beneath the too-bright lights, the way he had to shuffle his feet like they were still shackled, the way the open toe of his work boot kept tripping him up. Vega couldn't see the boot in the darkness but he could see the way the man compensated for it, the limp in his stride, the way he had to keep his head down, ever wary of stumbling.

"Catch up with you in a moment," Vega told Greco.

He pushed open the doors of the police station. He wasn't wearing a jacket and the night had grown cold. He jogged across the parking lot to Adele's car. Morales had just gotten in and she was about to do the same.

"Adele! Wait up."

She turned, her face unreadable under the harsh glare of lights.

"I—uh—just wanted to be sure you're okay." Now that he was standing in this lot, freezing, he felt mildly foolish.

"I called my insurance. The adjuster's coming to-morrow—"

"I mean—you know." He rattled some change in his pockets.

She went to say something and stopped herself. He had no idea what she was thinking. In the end, all she said was, "I'm glad things worked out tonight." She opened her car door.

"Wait." He pulled his wallet out of his back pocket, opened it, and fished out four twenty-dollar bills. He folded them and shoved them into her hand.

She frowned. "We already settled our bet."

"I realize that." He nodded to the car. "Buy him some new boots."

"What?"

"Work boots." Vega shoved his wallet back into his pocket and hunched his shoulders against the cold. "You should be able to get a halfway decent pair for eighty bucks."

"You—want to do this?"

Vega shrugged. "What the hell? The guy can't work in the ones he's got."

A slow smile crept across Adele's face. She tucked the money in her coat pocket. "I don't know what to say."

"Don't say anything. Not to anyone. Especially not to him. You got that? I mean it." He backed away. "If you tell anyone where you got the money from, I swear, I'll find a way to lock you both up."

"Thank you," she called out, but he had already turned away from her. He threw a quick hand of acknowledgment over his shoulder and jogged quickly back to the building.

In the detectives' bullpen, he found Greco at his desk, hunched over the Verizon records. Greco lifted his glasses when Vega came into view, a grim look on his face. The guy knew fifty ways to ruin a good mood.

"What?" asked Vega.

"We shouldn't have let him disappear so quickly."

"You found something? In the phone records?" Vega felt broadsided. His breath left his body. He'd looked at the evidence every which way and his gut and logic told him Rodrigo Morales couldn't have been involved in Maria's death. If he was, he'd never stay in Lake Holly. By tomorrow, he'd be in Georgia or Colorado or half a dozen places in between. In new boots, no less. Courtesy of Detective Vega. If Vega had made a mistake here, it was a big one.

"What did you find?" He was almost afraid to ask.

"Something you're not gonna believe."

Greco spread the Verizon records out on his desk. Maria's last three cell phone calls were all on Sunday, March eighth. To the same local number. The first two were short. The final call, at eight-twelve p.m., lasted almost fifteen minutes. *To Morales?* Vega couldn't recall his number offhand. He didn't need to. Greco took out his cell phone and dialed the digits on the computer printout. Then he handed his phone to Vega and sat back. Vega expected tinny mariachi music or one of those robotic voices asking him to leave a message—anything but what he got:

*This is Scott Porter. I can't take your call right now. Please leave a message.*

# Chapter 23

Vega leaned his arms on the puckered chain-link fence and drank in the sounds of the morning: the wind-chime chatter of children, the squeak of swings, the rumble of Hot Wheels tricycles tearing up the driveway of the Head Start preschool. He saw Linda Porter before she saw him. Her straw ponytail swinging as she scooped a girl off a slide. The milk white of her neck as she twirled a boy around like an airplane. She was a ballet of motion and purpose, beautiful to him for what she was and what she would never be—the prize he'd won and lost so many years ago.

She cupped a hand to her forehead to block out the sun and waved when she saw him. He lifted his arm halfway off the fence and let it drop again like it was made of lead. He wasn't happy about why he was here this morning or what he had to do. Right now, he wished he'd never set foot back in Lake Holly.

She walked over and gave him a kiss on the cheek. She was light and loose today, welcoming of his presence. But that just made what he had to do more difficult.

"I saw Rodrigo this morning at La Casa," she said.

"Yeah. We released him last night."

"Thank you."

"Don't thank me," said Vega. "If there was any chance he was involved in a crime, he'd be at the county lock-up right now."

It would have been easier all around if Morales had been guilty. Case solved. None of the uncomfortable loose ends that were plaguing him now. He'd spent a good part of yesterday evening trying without success to reach Maria Elena's mother in Guatemala using the number they'd found on Maria's Verizon printout. Each time he dialed, Vega geared himself up to deliver the news. And each time this uncomfortable Spanish robotic voice would ask him to leave a message. He didn't, of course. What was he going to say? *Hello, señora. Your daughter's dead. Her possessions are at a police station in a cardboard box?* This was a call that demanded a live voice on the other end.

"Things are looking up for Rodrigo in any case," said Linda. "Adele said somebody donated a brand new pair of work boots in his size this morning. So he's finally got a decent pair of shoes."

"Huh." Vega was glad Linda didn't know. He wanted to keep it that way. He looked over at the kids on the playground. He wished Joy was still that age. Back then, a lollipop and a kiss could solve all her problems. Now, he couldn't even guess what they were. "You, uh—working here all day today?"

"Just filling in," said Linda. "The head teacher had car trouble this morning. She's here now so I'm actually about to walk over to La Casa to do client intakes."

"Can I buy you a quick cup of coffee before you head over?"

She stiffened. "The last time we talked, an innocent man ended up behind bars. I'm not sure I want to go through that again."

"I'm not gonna ask you anything about your clients."

"Then what are you going to ask me about?"

"I can't talk to you?"

Vega read the reluctance in her pale eyes. He had a weakness for women with blue eyes, the way they promised something that was always out of reach, a lure trapped beneath the surface of a frozen lake. He could never reach her, not entirely, not even when they were together. That was part of the attraction. Part of the pain, too.

"He doesn't like you, you know," she said softly.

"So I've noticed. But that's okay. I don't like him, either."

"I can't go behind his back."

"I'm asking you for coffee, Linda. Not to go to bed with me."

A flush came to her cheeks and Vega felt for one brief moment like she wished he would. Damn, he wanted to. What was it Greco said about "never say never"?

"C'mon, Linda. It's just coffee. What do you say? My treat. I'll meet you out front."

"I can't stay long."

"Leave whenever you want." *You always do*, he thought.

He drove her to the Starbucks across from the train station in the center of town. He tried to come off as relaxed and casual, but inside, he felt like all his synapses were firing at once. He hated that everything he had to do today would undermine whatever feelings she had left for him.

He parked at a meter, didn't pay, and stuck his police ID on the windshield so he wouldn't get a ticket. Linda rolled her eyes.

"Cops always have an angle."

"This, from a defense attorney's wife?"

She stuck her tongue out at him playfully and he laughed. He forgot for a moment why they were here and when he remembered, it hit him all over again like a punch to the solar plexus. It made him feel the same way he sometimes did when he thought of a story or joke his mother would have liked and then remembered he couldn't tell her anymore.

Starbucks was bustling with women and toddlers and retirees with laptops. At the counter, Vega ordered an extra-large black coffee and refused to call it anything else, no matter how many times the server insisted it was a "venti." Linda ordered some complicated tea mixture that she made even more complicated by adding honey and soy milk and God-knew-what-else from the condiment bar. Then they settled into seats across from each other by a window. Linda loosened her ponytail and let her blond hair fall to her shoulders. Vega watched the spectacle with fascination and a certain embarrassment that after all these years, she could still hold his attention so completely. He suspected she knew it too. He tried to focus his mind elsewhere and pointed out the CVS that used to be Holtzman's Pharmacy.

"You used to work at Holtzman's, didn't you?" asked Linda.

"All through high school."

"Kids used to call him, 'the Nazi' behind his back."

"I remember," said Vega. When anyone thumbed the comic books, Holtzman would bark, "Buy it or stop reading it," in his thick German accent. If two prices were accidentally stuck to one item, he always charged the higher one. And he followed teenagers around the store with the grim countenance of an executioner, certain they were shoplifting. But in a curious way, Vega preferred the old German to the nervous native-born liberals in town, the ones who smiled too broadly in his presence, as if being Puerto Rican was like a fart in the room that might just go away if everyone pretended not to notice.

"You didn't invite me for coffee to discuss old times, did you, Jimmy?"

"No." Vega played with his napkin. "You and Scott— you get along okay?"

She gave him an expression halfway between amused and appalled. "We get along fine. Why are you asking?"

"He doesn't seem—you know—your type."

"You don't know him."

"Apparently, I didn't know you, either. Or rather—I didn't know you first."

She stirred her tea. If there was any surprise in her, it was only that he hadn't known before now.

"Jimmy," she said, leaning forward, a serious look in her eyes. "What is it you want?"

He balled up his napkin and stuffed it into his empty coffee cup. He couldn't muster any of the finesse he normally had as a detective. His default mode with her would always be seventeen. "I don't know how to ask this except to ask it," he sighed. "Has Scott ever fooled around?"

"What?" She reared back. "What kind of question is that?"

"A question you're better off answering with me than with half the Lake Holly PD looking on."

"I have no idea what you're talking about."

"We've identified the body at the lake as a thirty-year-old Guatemalan woman by the name of Maria Elena Santos and we have her cell phone records. She and Scott exchanged calls. Twelve of them between February first and March eighth. He said he didn't know her."

"He said he didn't *recognize* her. And why would he? She was probably a referral who consulted him over the phone."

"She called his private cell phone number, not his office."

"Scott gives his cell phone number to everyone. He's an immigration and criminal defense attorney, Jimmy, not a bank lawyer. You think he gets everyone's name, address, and driver's license photo before he speaks to them?"

"And you're sure of this?"

"Of course I'm sure."

Vega rested his elbow on the table, chin cupped in his palm, and looked at her without saying a word. He'd learned as a cop not to fill in the silences. People did a good job of filling those all on their own.

"You don't believe me," Linda said finally.

"I'd have sworn when I was married that my wife was faithful. And seven months after she left me, she and the man who became her second husband had full-term twins."

"I'm sorry," said Linda.

Vega shrugged. "That was five years ago. I've pretty much recovered. The point is, it happens a lot more than you think. And the last person to know is always the spouse."

"I'm not in denial. Scott would never do that to me, not after all we've been through. Three miscarriages. A bunch of infertility treatments. An adoption that fell through and broke both our hearts. Before Olivia came along, I swear, there were days I didn't want to get out of bed, days I wanted to kill myself. Scott lived through all of that. Loved me through all of that. I'd have probably died in Iowa if not for him."

*Iowa.* The word gave Vega the same dull ache at the back of his head as when he drank too much wine. *Iowa.* If he were pressed to name all fifty states, it would be one of the last that would come to mind. He pictured grain silos and church steeples. Cows and cornfields. Tractors and pickups. None of his imagery made room for Scott and Linda Porter. None of it for immigrants like Maria Elena Santos either.

"Where did you live in Iowa?"

"Cedar Rapids. That's where Scott's family is from."

"He didn't handle any immigration law there, did he?"

"Are you kidding? He was one of the lead defense attorneys in the Perkinsville case. You know—the one at that food processing plant where something like three hundred Guatemalans were deported?"

"Maria Elena Santos was arrested in that Perkinsville raid."

"So there's your reason for the calls," said Linda. "She knew his name or maybe had a friend who'd been his client. Why don't you just ask Scott? He'll tell you."

Not likely. The way Porter felt about him, he'd need a court order to find out what the guy ate for breakfast. But he didn't want Linda to think he had deliberately gone behind Porter's back so he said simply: "He's at Luis Guzman's arraignment today."

Linda's cell phone rang and she checked the number. "Olivia's elementary school," she apologized. "I need to take the call."

From the conversation on Linda's end, Vega gathered the child had taken a tumble at recess. Nothing catastrophic. Linda didn't look alarmed. She was off the phone in a matter of minutes.

"Is your daughter okay?"

"A scraped elbow from leaping off the jungle gym. Nothing a Band-Aid at the nurse's office can't cure. She's already back on the playground. Olivia's tough as nails—always has been. I never had her bravado or athletic ability. Neither does Scott."

"I guess it's a surprise package when you adopt," said Vega. "Did the agency ever tell you anything about her mother?"

"We didn't go through an agency," said Linda. "Olivia's birth mother was a client of Scott's."

"Scott had a client in Guatemala?"

"No, silly. Olivia wasn't born in Guatemala. She was born here. Her birth mother got arrested in the Perkinsville raid and asked Scott to take care of her baby. She didn't want the child going into foster care. Then she died in prison. It was so sad for her but so very lucky for us. Socorro had no family in the United States so we got to adopt her daughter."

"Her birth mother's name was Socorro? Socorro what?"

"Socorro Medina-Valdez. Olivia's middle name is Socorro, after her birth mother." A small crease settled in the middle of Linda's forehead. "Why does this interest you all of a sudden?"

"I'm just trying to find the connection between Maria and Scott. Maybe it was Socorro. Do you have any family contacts for Socorro? Siblings? Cousins?"

"No." A switch seemed to flick off inside of Linda. She drained her tea and rose from the table. "I have a lot of work to do, Jimmy. I really need to get back. If you want anything else, you'll have to ask Scott."

In the car, Linda was stiff and guarded. Vega tried for a breezy tone. There was so much more he needed to know and he didn't have a prayer of getting it from Porter.

"What a coincidence, huh?" he said. "You and Scott and Maria all lived in Iowa and all ended up a thousand miles away in Lake Holly."

"It's not a coincidence at all," said Linda. "We have dozens of clients at La Casa who all come from this one little area in Guatemala and all ended up in Lake Holly. They go where they have friends and family. For all I know, Scott has several ex-clients who were deported from Perkinsville and ended up here. They all try to come back to the United States, you know. Very few who get deported stay that way."

She had an answer for everything, like one of those Jehovah's Witnesses who show up at your door. She wouldn't—couldn't—believe there was anything unusual about a woman making twelve calls to her husband's cell phone and him never mentioning her to the police. Everyone has life stories they tell themselves whether they are true or not. Nobody knew that better than Vega.

It was only a mile or so to La Casa from the center of town, but the scenery transformed in stages, like a time-lapse photo. The frilly, gaudy Victorians full of restaurants and Realtors gradually disappeared, replaced by more modest businesses: secondhand stores, check-cashing services, Laundromats, and auto body shops. Vega watched a group of day laborers squatting on the stoop outside one of the Laundromats near La Casa. Linda waved and a few waved back.

For some reason Vega couldn't put his finger on, the wave irked him. Maybe it was the sense of playacting in all of it. Linda could move in and out of this world at will. Just as she had with him when they were teenagers. It was a game. A role that she was free to discard at any time. There was always a hint of dismissal in all their encounters. She was on the verge of dismissing him again, only this time he had more than personal pride at stake. He had a dead woman and her baby on his conscience. He had to do something. It would cost him whatever vestiges of feeling she still had for him but he didn't think he had a choice.

"So much for all this champion-of-the-oppressed bullshit," he muttered.

"Excuse me?"

"I thought you really cared about these people."

"I do."

"But only when it's convenient. Only when you

don't have to get your hands dirty. The moment something becomes a little unpleasant, you run away."

She exploded as he knew she would. "Who the hell do you think you are, coming in here making unfounded accusations against my husband? Against *me?* Because you're a cop? That gives you the right? What do you know about our lives and the work we do here?"

Vega nodded to the men at the Laundromat. "I know they call you *Horchata* behind your back."

Adele had told him that. They called Linda *Horchata* after a milk-colored rice shake popular in Latin America. They called Adele *Cajeta* after a Mexican caramel sauce. The nicknames were harmless, mostly just a way of distinguishing the women, a little inside joke among the men. But Vega knew it would bother Linda. He knew she probably spent all her time trying to be their friend when the truth was, they would always see her as an outsider, this wealthy milk-skinned American *rubia* who chose to spend her time in a place they wouldn't if they didn't have to.

"You can stomp off and tell me I'm full of shit about Scott," said Vega. "But a part of you is wondering—just a little—if maybe I'm not."

Vega turned onto the street and was greeted by the grind of hydraulic saws at the auto-body shop and the rumble of compactors at the dump. He pulled into the parking lot and cut the engine. The immigrants sitting and talking at a picnic table outside of La Casa barely seemed to notice the noise. It was part of their daily routine.

Linda sighed. She sounded beaten down. "I don't know what you want from me."

"Tell me about Socorro."

"I don't *know* anything. That's the truth. We picked Olivia up from a neighbor who was taking care of her after Socorro got arrested. Everything of Socorro's got trashed after the raid. Unless you have family to look after your stuff, that's pretty much what always happens, even here in Lake Holly. The landlords and neighbors steal everything of value and the rest gets thrown out." Linda kept her gaze on the dump at the end of the street as if she half-expected to find Socorro's things lying in a pile behind the chain link and razor wire.

"How did she die?"

"Cervical cancer, I believe. The prison doctors didn't see the signs. Or maybe they didn't want to see them. She was only thirty-eight." Linda spread her hands, a hint of frustration on her features, as if she sensed that down the line, she'd have to share this same thin biography with Olivia and it would be just as disappointing. "I wish I knew more, but I don't. That's the truth, Jimmy. And besides, I still don't see what any of this has to do with Maria Elena."

"Linda," Vega said, laying a warm hand over hers and looking at her evenly. "You're kidding yourself if you think Scott didn't know Maria. She wasn't just a voice on the phone."

"She probably just needed some legal advice."

"The last three calls Maria Elena ever made in her life were to Scott's personal cell phone number. *The last three.*"

Vega saw the knowledge move around beneath the muscles of Linda's face, trying to take up residence behind her pale blue eyes, in the press of her thinning lips, in the comma curve of her jaw. She was trying very hard to reconcile it with that book of stories she kept on her inner shelf. She removed her hand from Vega's and reached for the door handle.

"Obviously then," said Linda, "she needed that advice pretty badly."

# Chapter 24

Vega could practically dial the number by heart, he'd dialed it so many times. It had started to feel like a commonplace occurrence, like he was ordering concert tickets or pizza at a place that put him on hold a lot. He was prepared for the robotic voice again, not even really thinking about it, when he heard the click, the breath, the pause that told him a real live human being was on the other end of the line in a country he'd never been to, two thousand miles away from the cubicle in the Lake Holly police station where he was sitting.

Aguas Calientes, Guatemala.

He pictured jungles full of biting insects and exotic birds. Muddy villages full of toothless old people, barefoot children, and soldiers in camouflage. Hills canopied in green and roiling rivers the color of chocolate milk. He had no idea if his images were more Hollywood than *National Geographic*. The farthest south he'd ever traveled outside of Puerto Rico was to Cancún, Mexico, once, with a girlfriend after he and Wendy divorced. He got royally sick and had to spend most of the week in the bathroom. The girlfriend got a bad sunburn. They split up soon after that. Not a happy trip all around.

*"Alo?"* An older woman's voice came on the line, hoarse and tentative. Vega felt his limbs go slack.

*"Señora Santos?"* His own throat tightened. He was as nervous as an altar boy doing his first vespers service.

*"Sí."*

*"Señora Irma Alvarez-Santos?"* Just to be sure.

*"Sí."*

From his cubicle, Vega could hear phones ringing, the copy machine churning, cops discussing the upcoming NFL draft. He turned his back to the opening in the partition and stared at the dull beige fabric behind his computer. His body felt cold and numb. He tried to picture the woman. But all he could picture was his own mother in her gold-rimmed glasses, her thick iron-gray hair feathered short the way she had worn it most of her life. Her eyes would be curtained and reserved as they always were on first meetings. Her full lips would be parted slightly as if prepared to allow any news that was about to be delivered an avenue of ready escape.

"My name is James Vega," he said slowly in Spanish. "I am a police detective in New York, and I am afraid I am calling with some very bad news about your daughter, Maria Elena."

The woman said something Vega didn't understand. Her consonants were emphatic. Her voice sputtered and dipped with a staccato rhythm that sounded unlike any Spanish he'd ever heard. Vega knew his accent was different from Guatemalans. He knew the phone would exacerbate those differences, but he couldn't make out even one word of what she'd just said.

"Pardon, señora. My Spanish isn't that good. I don't understand."

She started to speak again. Vega still didn't understand. *Puñeta!* This was turning into a nightmare. He was going to have to ask Adele to find someone at La Casa who could translate for him. He was going to have to deliver the worst news anyone could get in the most impersonal way possible. At least that asshole cop who'd talked to him about his dead mother hadn't needed a translator.

"*No cuelgue, por favor,*" the woman said after a moment. *Don't hang up, please*. This, he understood. There was discussion in the background. Voices he couldn't make out speaking in a way he couldn't comprehend. He felt for a moment the way the immigrants at La Casa must feel every day of their lives.

"*Podría ayudarse?*" *May I help you?* The voice belonged to a young man. He had the reedy uncertain pitch of adolescence in his vocal cords. Vega took him to be about fifteen. "My grandmother speaks Q'eqchi'. Her Spanish isn't that good, especially on a phone."

Q'eqchi'. A Mayan Indian language native to Guatemala. No wonder Vega didn't understand a word. She might as well have been speaking Navajo.

Vega repeated who he was and asked the young man's name. The young man had no trouble understanding Vega's Spanish. He said his name was Oscar. A much darker thought suddenly cropped into Vega's head.

"Maria Elena—she's not your mother, is she?"

"No. My aunt. The sister of my mother. We have not

heard from her in more than a month. We did not know who to contact."

"I'm so sorry to tell you this, but she's dead."

Vega heard the old woman in the background, the panicked requests for information that were the same in any language. Oscar excused himself for a moment and spoke to the old woman. Vega heard her break into sobs. He remembered the day he learned of his own mother's death, the way his breath left him, the way he struggled for composure as he watched her body being carted out of her apartment, zipped up like a piece of oversized luggage at JFK Airport. That was bad. This was worse. Maria's body wasn't even human-looking anymore.

"My grandmother wants to know how she died," said Oscar, coming on the line again.

"The police aren't sure yet," said Vega. "She died in March, possibly from being hit by a car, but it's still under investigation. Her body was only recently discovered. We would be happy to put you in contact with the Guatemalan Consulate in New York to arrange for transport of her remains back to Aguas Calientes for burial."

Oscar tried to explain everything to his grandmother but Vega could hear the woman's rapid-fire questions shooting back at the boy, the anguish and panic in their tone. He felt for the grandmother. He felt for the boy, too. He was a kid and he was handling something that should only be handled by an adult.

"Do you have any other family who can be with your grandmother right now?"

"My mother will be here soon," said the young man. He was alone. Vega could tell he was overwhelmed.

"Would you prefer I call back when your mother is home?"

"No, no. I can manage. Thank you."

Vega hoped that was true. In his experience, nothing prepares you for death. It is inevitable, yet it always takes people by surprise. How can someone so unique in the world simply vanish? It still seemed inconceivable to Vega that his mother was really gone. No one told funnier jokes, made better *alcapurrias* or was a worse backseat driver. No one else would know his communion name—Emmanuel—or remember his first guitar or that crush he had on Rosalina Ramirez in the third grade. If scientists say energy can't be destroyed, where was the energy that was his mother? That was Maria Elena?

"My grandmother wants to bury my aunt in Aguas Calientes," said Oscar.

"I understand," said Vega. He asked Oscar for his grandmother's address and promised to pass along the information to the official at the Guatemalan Consulate who was in charge of repatriation of remains. *Repatriation of remains*—such a stilted term, thought Vega as he copied down the contact information. It sounded like a military objective. Worst of all, the poor families who pay a fortune to smuggle a loved one to the States often have to pay even more to bring their bodies back. Vega hoped the consulate had some sort of fund to help with the costs. He could only imagine how such a family might be ripped off in their moment of grief.

"Do you have any family in New York?" Vega asked Oscar. "Cousins, uncles—perhaps they could help facilitate the process?"

"Not in New York," said Oscar. "Only in Texas and Colorado." Vega asked for their names and phone numbers but already, he knew they couldn't help. They were too far away to act as the eyes and ears that the family needed so desperately right now. Oscar got the information from his grandmother and gave it to Vega anyway. Then he excused himself from the phone for a moment, had another exchange, and got back on the line.

"My grandmother wants to know if you've found Luz Maria."

"Luz Maria? Who's Luz Maria?"

"My cousin. My aunt Maria Elena's daughter."

"We found a picture of your aunt with a little baby among her things. Is this the Luz Maria you're talking about?"

"I don't know," said Oscar. "I never met her. She'd be about nine or ten now, I think. She was born in the United States in someplace with an *I* in it. Ohio? My aunt lived there when she first came to the United States many years ago."

"Iowa?"

Oscar said the name to his grandmother.

"Yes. Iowa. My aunt thought Luz Maria had died. When she found out she was alive, she came to New York to find her."

"Do you know where the child is?" asked Vega.

A pause and words he didn't understand. Now he knew how Greco felt.

"She lives in *Lago Sagrado?*"

*Lago Sagrado?* There was no Lake Sagrado, New York.

Oscar's grandmother said something sharp to the teenager.

"Where my aunt was living," said the boy. Then Vega understood. *Sagrado* meant "sacred" or "holy" in Spanish. Maria's mother had mistaken the name, "Lake Holly" for "Lake Holy." Maria Elena didn't come to Lake Holly because it was "safe," as Morales had thought. She came to find her daughter.

"Do you have an address for Luz Maria? The last name she goes by?"

"My grandmother doesn't know."

"Is she living with a relative? Her father perhaps?"

More conversation. "My grandmother doesn't think so. But she's not sure."

They were as clueless about Maria's daughter as Vega was. Still, Lake Holly wasn't that big. There couldn't be that many nine- or ten-year-old girls named Luz Maria in it. Vega would find her. He was sure he could find her. And maybe find the ex-boyfriend or ex-whatever who brought her here and check him out for the hit-and-run as well. The guy would have plenty of motive to get rid of a mother who comes all the way from Guatemala looking for her child. Maybe Linda was right: maybe Maria Elena did need to consult an attorney after all.

Oscar and his grandmother had more conversation back and forth. Vega could hear the plaintiveness in the old woman's voice.

"She wants to know if you will find her."

"I will certainly try," said Vega. He wished he could tell Irma Santos that finding Luz Maria and reuniting her with her grandmother were one and the same but they weren't. If Luz Maria was American-born and living with her biological father, there was nothing Vega could do about custody, visitation, or contact. The father could keep the grandmother out of Luz Maria's life and no court could intervene. Grandparents' rights never trump parents' rights even when they're Americans. A Guatemalan grandmother didn't stand a chance. On the other hand, if the guy was just a boyfriend who took a kid that wasn't his and ran, Vega had some leverage—especially if the guy was illegal.

Vega gave Oscar his cell number and told the teenager the family could call him anytime with questions. Normally, he didn't do this. But he could feel the helplessness of their situation. They deserved better than he'd gotten from that Bronx detective after his mother died. He would try to give it to them.

More chatter. He could hear something weak and spent in the old woman, as if she had already given up the fight.

"My grandmother says that my aunt worked for two years after she found out Luz Maria was alive to earn enough money to bring her home. She asks please, if you can make sure Luz Maria knows how much she loved her."

"I will make sure," said Vega. On the grave of his own mother, he would make sure.

# Chapter 25

Señora Linda offered Rodrigo a job cleaning out the rain gutters on her house. Rodrigo knew she didn't really need them cleaned. In all likelihood, they'd been cleaned in the fall and it was too early in the spring for much to have accumulated in between. Perhaps a few twigs and acorns and pine needles—that was about it.

She was doing it out of kindness, he knew. To put a little money in his pocket since it was almost three on a Wednesday afternoon and no jobs were likely to come into La Casa at this point. Anibal and Enrique had snagged a couple of days of yard work with Jeronimo Cruz, the old Mexican who always bragged about his daughter and shorted his employees. Even so, Rodrigo would have taken the work if he could have. He was never going to see the money Benito Silva owed him from clearing that land in Wickford and he sorely needed the cash.

At least he had sturdy work boots now. Really good ones—waterproof and everything. He pretended not to know where they came from even though he was sitting right in the car when that Spanish detective handed

Señora Adele some money and five minutes later, she asked his shoe size. Rodrigo understood. Everyone has a role to play. They had respected his dignity. He would not embarrass either of them for their decency.

Rodrigo felt shy and awkward as he followed Señora Linda to her big blue minivan. He saw her at the center all the time but he'd never actually spoken to her. The *Norte Americanos* at La Casa—even those who spoke very good Spanish—all made him slightly nervous. He couldn't say why. They were always gracious and generous. He supposed it was the otherness of them. Their pink skin and light hair. Their tall, long-limbed bodies. Their instant familiarity. Rodrigo couldn't get used to the North American way of treating everyone like they were your cousins. Enrique loved it. But Rodrigo preferred the respectful dividing lines that separated men from women, adults from children, bosses from employees. At least you knew where you stood. In the United States, he was never quite sure how to behave, always fearful of offending.

Señora Linda unlocked her minivan and Rodrigo climbed into the front passenger seat.

"Did you have lunch?" she asked.

"Yes, thank you," he lied. He did not want her to think she had to feed him. He would eat tonight after he got off work.

She pulled onto the road and tried hard to engage Rodrigo in conversation. She asked what town he came from, whether he was married, how many children he had, whether he'd known Enrique and Anibal growing up. Her Spanish was excellent, with all the soft sing-song rhythms of Guatemala in the accent. Rodrigo wished he could speak English even a little the way she spoke Spanish. He wanted to learn but he couldn't admit to anyone what was holding him back. He hadn't been able to afford to go to school in Guatemala until he was fourteen and though he did eventually learn to read and write, it was always an effort. He feared if he tried to learn English, his attempts would come off as embarrassingly crude. Someone might make fun of him.

She drove past the reservoir. Rodrigo turned his face to the window and stared through the thatch of trees at the ribbons of light on the water.

"That's where they found Maria Elena," she said.

"I believe so. Yes."

"It's so sad that she died."

"Yes, it is." Since that Spanish detective first told Rodrigo about her death, he'd had no moment to absorb the loss. But now that everything was behind him, he allowed himself the sorrow he could not afford before. Perhaps one day, he would take some rose petals to the lake and say an Ave Maria for her. He could float the petals on the water the way people in Esperanza do when someone dies. Unless that would get him into trouble. Maybe it wasn't permissible here. *Norte Americanos* had rules for everything. Half the time, he never understood what he was doing wrong even when he was doing it.

Señora Linda finger-combed some stray blond hairs that had fallen out of her ponytail. He had never seen her in makeup or anything fancier than jeans—another thing that was very different about Anglos to him. She could have been quite striking but she made no effort to showcase it.

"Rodrigo? Did you know Maria Elena well?"

"I think so, yes."

"Did she ever mention a woman by the name of So-corro? Socorro Medina-Valdez?"

"Not to me, no."

"Did she ever mention having worked years ago in Perkinsville, Iowa?"

Rodrigo kneaded his new baseball cap, a present from Anibal and Enrique. The words BEAR STEARNS were embossed across the front. It sounded like a cartoon character but Anibal said it was the name of a bank that went out of business. "We didn't talk about such things, señora. I knew she had been to the United States be-fore, but we did not really talk about it."

"Did she ever mention Scott? My husband? Perhaps he had been her lawyer at some point?"

Rodrigo could not hide his astonishment at the con-versation. He had answered every question the police and Porter had asked him. He could not see why he had to answer any more. But he did not want to offend her. She seemed almost panicked about getting an answer. He was only sorry he didn't have the ones she seemed to want.

"I do not think Maria would have needed a lawyer in Lake Holly, señora."

Señora Linda nodded. She seemed sadder and qui-eter after that. Rodrigo wished he understood why. It was one of the things he missed most about Esperanza. There, he knew everyone's family, everyone's history. He knew that the Garcias drank too much and beat their women; that Anibal's family, the Roldans, were very religious. He knew the Pavon and Asturias fami-lies had had an argument over the sale of some chick-ens years ago and hadn't spoken to one another since. He knew Enrique's sister Sucely had had a baby with one of the Asturias boys but was distantly related to the Pavons so neither family was speaking to her.

And this didn't even begin to take in the immediate families. Rodrigo was one of seven siblings, Triza, one of nine, so there were brothers, sisters, nieces, nephews, and cousins with gossip of their own. He knew all of it and kept up with it through Triza when he could afford to call. It was the landscape of his life. But here in Lake Holly, he knew almost no one, understood nothing. He often felt like a colorblind man in a room full of reds and greens. He could not read the subtleties because everything looked the same.

Señora Linda turned onto a long, winding street and then drove up a steep driveway through the woods. When Rodrigo looked out his window, there was no shoulder to the driveway and the woods fell away from him at a steep angle. It was like riding one of those brightly painted chicken buses in Guatemala, the ones with no suspension and only two speeds: fast and crash. No wonder his people were religious. You did a lot of praying in a chicken bus.

At the top of the climb, the land leveled out to an enormous house with a front porch, big windows, and a giant play structure out back. Rodrigo had worked on the landscapes of many big houses, but he had never actually met any of the owners. He couldn't believe that this very sweet and unassuming woman would be the mistress of such a grand place.

Señora Linda powered open the door to one of the bays in the garage and parked. Rodrigo got out of the car and put on his baseball cap.

"Can I get you some coffee? A sandwich?" she asked him.

"No, thank you," he said. He hoped she couldn't hear the growl of his stomach. "I will need a ladder. If you can tell me where one is, please."

She took him to a gardening shed in the back of the property and showed him where everything was. Then she excused herself to fetch her daughter off the school bus.

He started on the gutters surrounding the garage first. He was right about there being very little to clear out. He scooped out some acorns and small twigs, a few spiked seedpods and pine needles. But basically, the hardest part of the job was winching the aluminum ladder up and down and setting it at a proper angle to the house.

He worked quickly, starting at the back of the house using a small brush to whisk the leaves and twigs from the gutters. He could not see over the roof. It was only when he moved to the side of the house where the roof didn't obstruct him that he was able to get his first glimpse west toward town. He saw a sight that filled him with awe: the entire town, spread out like one of those model railroad sets they sometimes put up in store windows here during the Christmas holidays. There was a fuzzy green cast to the land, like mold on a peach. Spring was here, even if he couldn't see it up close yet. Through the gray tufts of trees, Rodrigo counted half a dozen ponds—all of them a surprise. They sparkled like earrings half-hidden beneath a woman's long hair. A train lurched into the station and a hawk circled above the granite spires of that old Catholic church the Anglos went to.

He could see it all, could see how small and con-nected everything really was. He could not tell where one neighborhood ended and another began. The lonely peal of the train whistle floated toward him, crisp and clear as an Indian flute player on the square in Esperanza. But the siren that accompanied an ambulance speeding through town failed to rise above a mewl. Perhaps this was how God saw the world, thought Rodrigo. Men carving boundaries that didn't exist, offering prayers too faint to hear, much less answer.

He hummed softly while he worked. A tune Triza had taught him. A child's song about an owl in the forest. He liked the feel of the notes in his chest, the way they muted the loneliness and boredom. He stopped humming once Señora Linda reappeared in the driveway. He was shy about others hearing him.

A girl hopped out of the backseat, her long, black hair pulled tightly into two shiny braids, a backpack with pink and white flowers slung over one shoulder. Rodrigo had forgotten that the Porters' daughter was adopted. He felt a small pang of longing looking at the child. She reminded him of his Juliza at that age. She disappeared inside with Señora Linda but reemerged about ten minutes later with a tray and called up to him. He still felt astounded when he heard Guatemalan children speaking like *Norte Americanos.*

He told her he was sorry, but he didn't speak English.

"My mother asked me to bring you cookies and coffee," she said in American-accented Spanish. He was surprised at her fluency.

"Oh. Many thanks." He climbed down the ladder and took the tray from the girl with a shy bow of his head. The cookies were chocolate chip. Fresh from the oven. The coffee was hot and strong with plenty of sugar the way he liked it.

The girl stared at him. "What happened to your lip?"

She was a forward child. Children in Guatemala would never stare at an adult or ask such a question. He touched the back of his hand self-consciously to the scab.

"I fell." His lip looked like a piece of chorizo sausage had gotten plastered to the lower portion. But it didn't hurt anymore. It would heal in time.

"I fell once on the handlebars of my bike. I had to get three stitches."

"That must have hurt."

"I didn't cry. Daddy says I'm brave."

Señora Linda came out and said something to the girl in English. She scampered off without a good-bye.

"Many thanks for the coffee and cookies," said Rodrigo. He stacked his empty plate and cup neatly on the patio table and went to climb back up the ladder. Señora Linda stayed on the patio, bobbing on the tips of her toes like a schoolgirl. Rodrigo didn't know her age—in his experience, Anglos always looked and acted younger than they were—but he sensed she was older than he was. He let go of the sides of the ladder and faced her.

"Yes, señora?"

"Do you know anything about toilet tanks?"

"Your toilet isn't working?"

"It's working. But the handle is broken. My husband bought a new one but he never installed it. I was wondering if while you're here, you could do the job."

"I would be happy to."

"Thank you."

By the time Rodrigo was finished cleaning out the gutters, the sun was on the far horizon. He put the ladder, gloves, and tools away and knocked on Señora Linda's back door. A dog barked inside. Rodrigo hoped it was friendly.

When she opened the door, her eyes were red-rimmed and puffy. The dog paced nervously at her feet.

"Señora?" He removed his cap and shoved it into the back pocket of his jeans. "Is this a bad time?"

"No, Rodrigo. No. I'm fine." She ushered him into the kitchen. He made a point of wiping his new boots on the doormat. "It's the toilet in the master bathroom that needs fixing. Come upstairs, I'll show you."

The master bedroom had a bed almost as big as the room Rodrigo shared with three other men. There was an enormous flat-screen television on the wall opposite the bed. Señora Linda walked over to a dresser in front of the television and handed a plastic carton on top to Rodrigo.

"I have no idea how to do this, and I'm pretty sure my husband doesn't either." She forced a smile. He could see her heart was heavy with some sort of sadness that had happened while he was outside cleaning her gutters. He wished he could help her but he knew that was impossible. She was the boss. He was the employee. There was a divide here that they both had to respect. She was trying hard to keep up appearances. So would he.

"I think the directions are in English and Spanish," she said, "so you shouldn't have a problem."

Rodrigo looked down at the small black print, a

whole dense paragraph of it. It would have taken him an hour to get through all of that, but he didn't tell her that. He'd always been good with his hands. He could figure out a simple plumbing job without directions.

"Call me if you need anything," she said and went back downstairs.

The dog stayed behind. She seemed to like Rodrigo and Rodrigo was glad of the company. He pushed open the door to the bathroom. A small gasp escaped his lips. He was glad Señora Linda wasn't around to hear it. He would have felt embarrassed to gawk in her presence.

The room was like something out of a palace. It was tiled in soft green-and-white marble. There were two sinks with shiny gold swan-neck fixtures, a toilet, a shower stall behind frosted glass, and an oval-shaped bathtub set in a dark wood frame that looked big enough for a small party. It was in front of a bay window that overlooked the woods in back.

Rodrigo ran a hand along the cool beveled rim of the bathtub. He wondered what it would feel like to soak in such a thing, to be enveloped in a caress of warm water like a baby in its mother's womb, to gaze out such a window on your own private paradise. Growing up, his family didn't even have an outhouse until he was ten. He remembered having to make his way to the river at night, how difficult it was to see. How terrifying. He was always afraid of stepping on a snake. He was afraid *La Llorona,* the spirit who drowned her children, would pull him into the water. It was a proud moment for him when he was able to build his wife and children a house with a real flushing toilet. It made him feel like a millionaire. But this? This

was something he could not have conceived of if someone hadn't shown it to him. He wished he had a picture
of it for Triza.

Enough of this foolishness. Time to work, as Anibal
would say. Rodrigo opened the top of the toilet tank
and depressed the handle. He saw right away what the
problem was—the lift wire on the handle had sediment
deposits on it. If it were up to him, he'd have removed
the lift wire and handle, cleaned it all down with vine-
gar and a touch of mineral oil, and then tweaked it until
it worked perfectly. But he knew from experience that
when *Norte Americanos* want something replaced, they
want it replaced. Not fixed or reconditioned. Replaced.

The dog went into the master bedroom and came
back into the bathroom a minute later with a pair of
brown men's moccasin-style slippers—Porter's slippers
from the looks of them. Rodrigo laughed and murmured to the dog in Spanish.

"No slippers, dog. What I really need is a pair of
scissors." There was thick plastic packaging on the toilet repair kit that Rodrigo would never be able to open
without scissors.

He checked the medicine cabinet and could only
find a tiny nail scissor. He didn't want to go rummag-
ing around. Señora Linda might get the wrong idea so
he walked into the upstairs hallway to find her. The dog
followed. He heard her voice downstairs on the phone.
She was speaking English. She sounded upset.

"Do you need my mother?" asked the girl in Spanish. She was sitting on her pink-canopied bed on the
other side of a beaded curtain that separated her bedroom from the hallway.

"I need scissors if you have them, please." Rodrigo held up the plastic carton so she could see his dilemma.

The girl put down her electronic game and pushed herself off her bed. She opened a drawer of her desk and tossed aside broken pencils and erasers. Rodrigo waited on the other side of the beaded curtain. The floor of her bedroom was covered in a fluffy white carpet that looked as if no one ever walked on it. Her walls were plastered with posters of a dark-haired Anglo boy who smiled like a girl. He was probably a musician or movie actor the girl liked. Rodrigo suspected Juliza had such crushes also. He wished he were around his own children to know such things.

"I can't find my scissors. I think my dad borrowed them."

"It's okay," said Rodrigo. "I will wait until your mother can help me."

"She's going to take a while," said the girl with a roll of her eyes. "She's been on the phone since I got home."

"Everything okay?" *What sort of rudeness was that?* He had no business asking a child about her parents. No business at all.

The girl shrugged. She had no wariness of strangers. Rodrigo wondered if that was her nature or because she was adopted. "I think she's having a fight with my dad."

"I'm sorry," said Rodrigo. *Ay, caray!* He shouldn't be hearing this!

"It's okay," said the girl. "They don't usually fight. They'll probably make up by dinner." She shoved all the pencils and erasers back in her drawer and slammed it shut. "I'll find you some scissors. We usually have a pair in my dad's office downstairs."

Rodrigo followed the girl downstairs to a room off the kitchen with certificates in black frames on the wall and several large bookcases crammed with gold-bound books. He suspected it was Porter's home office. It all looked very official and important. Rodrigo wasn't sure he should even be in here.

Señora Linda was in the kitchen talking on the phone. The little girl perked up at something she heard her mother say. She called out a question to her but Señora Linda motioned for her to be quiet and turned away from them. Rodrigo hung back by the doorway of Porter's office and kept his eyes on the floor.

"I think we're going on a plane trip," the girl told Rodrigo. "My mom's talking to my dad about it now. I think it's supposed to be a surprise."

Unless you're getting deported, Rodrigo was under the impression that plane trips were supposed to be fun. But nothing in Señora Linda's demeanor suggested fun to Rodrigo. She paced the floor. Her voice rose and fell in tight little bursts that, even without knowing the language, sounded panicked and angry.

The girl rummaged through the center drawer of the desk until she found a pair of scissors. She handed them to Rodrigo.

"Many thanks," he said, looking down. He did not feel comfortable looking at the girl as openly as she looked at him. All he wanted at this moment was to open the packaging, remove the guts of the old fixture, and replace it with this new one. It would be an easy job. He could already see that. Ten or fifteen minutes at most with the right tools. He felt bad that Señora Linda would have to drive him back to town. She was obviously busy right now. He'd offer to walk but it was a long hike on a narrow road and it would soon be getting dark.

The girl shoved the desk drawer closed. The motion dislodged a folder of papers that was lying on the edge of the desk. It tumbled to the floor, spilling the contents across the rug. Rodrigo bent to pick the papers up and put them back in the folder. He did not mean to read them. In most cases, he couldn't have if he'd tried. But it was the layout of the page that was so familiar. Shapes and patterns were things he seldom forgot, probably because he'd spent so many preliterate years as a boy depending on his visual memory to tell him things printed words could not.

He recognized the form as the same one Señora Linda had wanted him to fill out when he first came to La Casa. Señora Linda had called it an "intake sheet"— whatever that meant. Rodrigo had refused. Politely, but firmly. Too personal. Too much information he'd rather not have on file. Maria was with him when he refused. For some reason, she agreed. He would never have remembered that except he saw the name now, printed in block letters that were easy enough for even him to decipher: *Maria Elena Vasquez*. She had not given Señora Linda her real name either. Rodrigo was sad that in death he knew more about her than in life.

He was standing in Porter's office with the form in hand when he suddenly became aware of the jingle of dog tags behind him and the absence of echoing voices. Señora Linda was off the phone and both she and the dog had walked into the room.

"What are you doing with that?" she demanded in

Spanish. The harshness of her voice surprised him. He'd never heard her speak like that before. He couldn't imagine what he'd done that was so terrible. He put the form down on the desk. He didn't even bother to stuff it back in the folder.

"It dropped on the floor, señora. I picked it up. I came to get scissors. To cut open the packaging." He held up both for her to see. He felt likc asking if she wanted to frisk him. He'd never seen her look so angry. It made him feel angry too. He wasn't stealing or snooping where he didn't belong. How could she think such a thing?

"How long will it take you to fix the toilet?"

She was impatient, too. He'd never seen someone's mood change so quickly.

"Fifteen minutes perhaps, señora. I may need a *llave inglesa.*"

She frowned. "What is a *llave inglesa?*"

Rodrigo supposed she wasn't used to using Spanish words for tools. He tried to explain and mime at the same time. "It's to tighten bolts. It adjusts—"

"A crescent wrench," she said in English.

Rodrigo tried the words on his tongue. "Cre-set rech." Señora Linda turned to her daughter and said something in English and the daughter left the room.

"Olivia will bring one up to you. When you're done, I'll call you a cab, okay? I can't drive anywhere tonight but I'll give you a hundred dollars and you can pay the cab from that and keep the rest. The cab shouldn't come to more than eight or nine dollars."

"That is very generous of you, señora. Thank you. I'm sorry if I've done anything to offend."

"It's not you, Rodrigo." She let out a deep sigh. "This isn't a good night. I hope you understand."

He didn't. But there was a lot he didn't understand these days.

"Señora—I just want you to know: I would never read anything I'm not supposed to." Would never. Could never. At least not without a great deal of effort. But the second part he kept to himself. Everyone has parts they keep hidden. He was only sorry he'd found his way into one of hers tonight.

# Chapter 26

There were no nine-year-old Luz Marias in all of Lake Holly. Or ten-year-old Luz Marias. Or eleven-year-old ones, for that matter. None in any of the surrounding towns either. Vega and Greco checked all the schools—public, private, and parochial—and came to the conclusion that Luz Maria wasn't Luz Maria anymore and probably hadn't been for quite some time.

Greco fished a Twizzler out of his bag and shoved it into the corner of his mouth. Vega had bought him two king-sized bags as penance for yesterday and Greco was nearly through the second one. A "two-bag" day, he called it. With good reason. They were looking for a nine-year-old Guatemalan girl who lived in Lake Holly without her biological mother. A nine-year-old girl who was born in Iowa. A nine-year-old girl whose parents would have the know-how and smarts to cheat an illegal alien out of her own child. They had only one candidate.

"We make a mistake here, Vega, it's a whole universe worse than anything we could have done with Morales. We've got to be sure."

"Sure means DNA."

"DNA requires a court order," said Greco. "So does unsealing Olivia Porter's adoption records. Both take time. Plus, we gotta talk to the bastard. I mean, what if Porter's the dad? He's got a right to the kid then. We have to be careful what we're accusing him of."

"She doesn't look a bit like that slimy worm."

"All my kids look like me and none of 'em like my wife. What's that tell ya?"

"That they got unlucky?"

"Smart ass."

Greco had a point, though. They had to be sure— damn sure—that they knew what Porter was guilty of before they spoke to him. That meant a long, exhausting search of public records. That meant both of them working an all-nighter at the computer.

*Puñeta, coño! Not tonight.*

Vega's cell phone rang. Wendy. She only ever wanted to talk when he didn't. Story of their marriage.

"So, we'll be done with dinner in like, fifteen minutes," she said. He could hear sizzling and chopping sounds in the background. They were still at the hibachi place.

"I'm going to be tied up tonight, unfortunately. I can't get away."

"What do you mean, you can't get away? You *asked* for this."

"I know. I'm sorry. I want to talk. I really do," said Vega. "But things changed on this end."

"You couldn't call?"

He could've. He should've. He kept thinking he'd be able to get away.

"My God, Jimmy—you asked me to rearrange my *whole* schedule for this—Joy's *whole* schedule—"

"How about tomorrow?"

"Alan's working late. I have no one to leave the boys with."

"I'll come over to your house."

"You will not."

"Wendy, please. It's important."

"What's the 'it' referring to, Jimmy? Your work? Or our daughter?"

"Both."

"When you decide which of them is your priority, let me know. This is why Joy's in therapy." She hung up.

Vega ran his palms roughly down the sides of his face and fought the urge to drop everything and walk out of the station. Joy was the only thing that mattered to him when you came right down to it. But walking out under these circumstances would be tantamount to going AWOL under fire. He had to stay. He had to hope that whatever was going on with his daughter could wait just a little bit longer. He caught Greco looking at him. "Women problems?"

"Not now, Grec." Vega put his phone away and continued scrolling down a list of Iowa birth records. Greco's gaze remained fixed. He drummed his fingers on the armrests of his chair.

"We're going to have to interview Porter about all this at some point."

"Yeah, I know."

"Gonna be fun having the two of you in the same room again."

Vega looked up from his computer and said nothing.

"Something between you and Porter that I don't know about?"

Vega went back to the computer screen. "Linda," he mumbled.

"Huh?"

"I guess this isn't the best time to tell you, but Linda and I—we were sort of more than friends in high school."

"More than friends." Greco rolled the words around on his tongue. "Is that like confessing 'impure thoughts' to the priest when you're fifteen and what you really mean is you jacked off a dozen times between breakfast and lunch?"

"Something like that."

"Jesus H. Christ, Vega!" Greco threw a balled up piece of paper at him. "You couldn't tell me before now?"

"It was personal."

"Ain't nothing personal between partners when you work a case."

"I didn't think it would matter."

"What is it with you and women? Is it that Latin-lover shit?"

"What women?" Vega pushed back in his chair and massaged his eyes. "I'm divorced, Grec. That was my ex yelling at me on the phone. I was with Linda when I was seventeen years old."

"Those first loves can stay with you." Greco got a wistful look. At that moment, he reminded Vega of some kindly Italian grandfather in his vegetable garden. Then again, Don Corleone was an Italian grandfather with a vegetable garden and he had people hole-punched for a living.

"Can you handle this, Vega? If it turns out that Linda Porter's involved? Can you do your job without letting your personal feelings get in the way?"

"I guess I'm gonna have to."

"If you think at any moment you can't, you gotta speak up. You drop the ball because you got all nostalgic on me, I won't be sympathetic."

"Understood."

They managed to dig up Olivia Porter's birth records online. Like most adoptees, her birth certificate had been amended so it showed only that her full name was Olivia Socorro Porter, that she was born in Perkinsville, Iowa, nine years ago and that her parents were Scott and Linda Porter. Any proof to the contrary would be in her pre-adoption records and those would have been sealed at the time of her adoption seven years ago.

They did the same online search for Luz Maria Santos in Iowa. Nothing came up. Not in birth records or on the Social Security database. But all that did was confirm what they had already suspected: Luz Maria Santos wasn't Luz Maria Santos anymore. It didn't necessarily mean she was Olivia Porter.

Vega and Greco tried a different tack, focusing instead on Olivia's purported mother, Socorro Medina-Valdez. They ran her name through the ICE database. What Linda had told Vega seemed to check out. Federal records showed that Socorro Medina-Valdez was a Guatemalan who had been arrested in the raid on the Perkinsville food processing plant eight years ago, just like Maria. She'd been represented by the law firm Shanahan & Pierce in Cedar Rapids—the firm that employed Scott Porter—just like Maria. She'd served her sentence at the same federal prison camp for women in Greenville, Illinois. Maria was released after five months. Socorro died three weeks before her release. Cause of death: complications from cervical cancer.

So far, so good. Scott Porter had a reasonable connection to both women. Both women had a reasonable connection to each other. There was just one problem. Greco didn't notice it, but Vega, the accounting major, did.

"Socorro was forty-eight when she died, not thirty-eight."

"You sure?"

"Do the math."

Greco grabbed the file, mumbling his little "carry the ones" as he subtracted her birth year from the calendar year of her death and saw that Vega was correct.

"Sounds a bit long in the tooth for the mother of a two-year-old," Greco agreed. "Then again, it could be a misprint. Immigration files aren't exactly accurate when it comes to personal information."

"Has to be a misprint," said Vega. "Otherwise, we're talking about Porter tampering with birth certificates, death certificates—a lot of paperwork that's not easy to fake."

"I used to think that, too," said Greco. "Until I met our Mexican Michelangelo last year."

"A forger?"

"An *artiste*. Right here in Lake Holly." Greco leaned back in his chair and rested his hands on his belly—his favorite stance when he was talking war stories. For a small-town cop, he had quite a few.

"Guy was minting New York State driver's licenses for illegals. I mean, primo quality. *I* couldn't tell the difference. He was wholesaling them to this local building inspector who was retailing them to illegals for two grand a pop. If we hadn't caught the guy red-handed, I doubt the licenses would've been questioned."

"You think Porter found a guy like that in *Iowa?*"

"No less likely than finding one here," said Greco. "These people's lives are all about missing paperwork so they get real good, real fast at finding ways around it. Same time we collared that Mexican? I had this guy in town—a Salvadoran illegal who wanted to bring his thirteen-year-old daughter to Lake Holly but didn't want her—you know—going the overland route? He was afraid she might get raped. So he found a couple in El Salvador who were legal U.S. residents, paid a guy down there to forge his daughter's passport so she was listed as their kid, and brought her over. Cost him like two grand for the paperwork and another five to pay off the couple. But the girl's trip to the States was a piece of cake."

"And this father just uh—told you all this?"

Greco got a wicked smile. "Actually, the father was about to become another satisfied customer of our paper-hanging Picasso. He hadn't actually *bought* the driver's license yet so we had a little leeway. Guy spilled his guts about how his thirteen-year-old would be here in Lake Holly by herself if we got him deported—not even allowed to go back with him on account of the fact that her passport now listed her as somebody else's kid. So I let him off with a warning."

Vega raised an eyebrow at Greco. "*You?* Let an illegal alien go?"

"Must've been my hemorrhoids acting up."

"Or the fact that you had thirteen-year-old daughters once too."

"How do you think I got the hemorrhoids?" Greco gave a throaty chuckle. "My point is, if Porter had wanted a document forged, he could have gotten it. Judges just make sure your paperwork's in order. They're not about to check the individual documents that closely, especially when it comes from a colleague."

"Okay," said Vega. "Maybe Scott could've gotten good forgeries to cover his tracks. But I can't believe Linda would go along with something like that."

"So you think because you took a few rolls in the hay with her when you were teenagers, that you know what a grown woman will do when she's desperate to have a baby? Read the papers, Vega. Women walk out of hospitals all the time with newborns under their arms who don't belong to them. That maternal urge is strong, don't kid yourself."

"Strong enough to kill?"

"That's what we need to find out." Greco frowned at the paperwork scattered across his desk. "Wish we had somebody who knew these women and could tell us what their story was. But we're talking eight years ago now. That's like centuries in an illegal immigrant community."

Greco was right. People would have moved away, gotten deported, changed jobs, addresses—even names. The lives of the poor are always in flux. Nowhere was that more true than in a community full of people who could never legally put down roots. But there were some constants. Vega had only to think back on his old neighborhood in the Bronx to know what at least one of those constants was.

"Go to Google," said Vega. "Type in *Catholic Churches, Perkinsville, Iowa.*"

Greco pushed his glasses up the bridge of his nose and typed in the words. One church came up: Saint Theresa's. Vega copied down the telephone number.

"A lot of Guatemalans aren't Catholic, you know," said Greco. "They're evangelical Protestants."

"I'm gonna start with the Catholics and pray that Maria Elena was a better one than I ever was," said Vega. " 'Cause there's no way a good Catholic wouldn't have had her baby baptized soon after she was born. Which means somewhere in Saint Theresa's there'd be a baptismal record with Luz Maria's name on it and her date of birth. If it's a match to Olivia's, that's one more piece of rope to tie around Porter's neck."

# Chapter 27

Scott Porter had missed the monthly board of directors meeting at La Casa. Adele called his home, his office, his cell—even Linda's cell—but no one picked up. In five years of being on the board, he'd never missed a meeting that Adele could recall. This was a big one to miss. Adele had presented several options to the other four board members about where La Casa might need to relocate in the event their lease couldn't be renewed.

It was almost nine in the evening when the meeting wrapped up with nothing decided. The truth was, none of the options was good. The proposed locations were either too far from town for the immigrants to travel to, or they lacked enough parking for would-be employers and volunteers, or there was too much opposition from the immediate community. The board needed to agree on some backup property soon. Any location was better than no location. But they could hardly be expected to make such a serious decision without their chairman present.

When Adele still didn't get an answer on any of Porter's or Linda's phones after the meeting, she decided to pay a visit to their house. She'd worked with both of the Porters almost since their arrival in Lake Holly seven years ago. Their families shared so much in common. Their daughters went to the same elementary school and were only a year apart in age. Both girls played AYSO soccer and belonged to Girl Scout troops. The families regularly bumped into each other at school events and in the supermarket. Yet Adele could count on one hand the number of times she'd been to their home, and in every instance, Adele's title and position were the reason she'd been invited at all.

She was always slightly uncomfortable being around the Porters socially, always aware in unspoken ways of the chasm between her life experiences and theirs. Despite their activism on behalf of Latino immigrants, they had a surprisingly monochromatic, all-American group of friends. The men played golf with Porter at the country club. The women were in a tennis league with Linda. In the summers, the Porters and their friends visited each other at their homes on Cape Cod and in the Hamptons. In the winters, they made yearly pilgrimages to Disney World and the Caribbean. Everyone knew how to ski and sail. Their kids went to each other's bar and bat mitzvahs and sweet sixteens. They had seen all the latest Broadway shows and toured the major cities in Europe.

Being around the Porters outside of La Casa felt a lot like being at Harvard all over again. They and their friends were pleasant and gracious. But there was always a forced cheer about them in her presence, always a sense that the real social interaction had gone on before Adele entered the room and would pick up again after she left. She was not one of them, and in little ways—from a comparison of notes on a new French restaurant in Manhattan to the best slopes in Vermont— that distinction was always reinforced.

Adele didn't much care for driving Lake Holly Road at night, especially since her recent encounter with a deer. She took the turns slowly. She used her brights whenever possible. She could see how easy it would have been for someone to accidentally run over Maria. There were no streetlights outside of town, no shoulders on the road. The curves were hairpin. Objects seemed to drop into her field of vision without warning like one of those fun-house rides.

The Porters' driveway was no better. She drove slowly up the steep incline, half-expecting to smash into Porter or Linda traveling the other way. But the woods on either side of the house remained still and velvety with only a thumbnail of moonlight to guide the way. At the top, the land leveled out and Adele felt her heart unclench. The outside lights were on. The garage doors were open. Porter's black Acura was in one bay of the garage, Linda's light blue minivan, in the other. The rear of the minivan was open and Porter was stuffing what looked like suitcases and cartons inside. He was dressed in gray sweats and white sneakers. Adele's headlights caught the gold rims of his glasses when he turned. The reflection on the lens obscured his eyes but the rest of his face did not seem happy to see her.

Adele pulled to the far corner of his driveway across from the garage and near the redwood play gym. Porter walked up to her car as soon as she got out. She could smell liquor on his breath. She couldn't recall ever seeing him drunk before, not even at parties. If anything, he always looked like he could have used a drink.

"Get out of here, Adele. This doesn't concern you." His thinning blond hair was tousled. There was a wild look to his eyes. "I mean it. Go home."

"What's wrong? Are you going somewhere?" He had no business driving in his condition.

"Not me. Just Linda and Olivia."

The door from the house to the garage opened and Linda stepped out with Olivia in hand, their golden retriever on a leash. Linda was dressed in jeans and a shapeless oversized sweater. Her hair was pulled back into a haphazard ponytail. It looked stringy and unwashed and plastered to her face at the edges as if she'd just splashed cold water on herself. Olivia was wearing pajamas with cupcakes all over them. She had a pink-and-blue stuffed cow under one arm. She looked like she'd just woken up from a deep sleep. The dog encircled their legs, nearly tripping Linda with the leash.

Linda hesitated when she saw Adele standing there. She gave her husband a searching look and Porter nodded. The interchange surprised Adele. She had assumed the Porters had been fighting, assumed Linda was maybe spending the night at her parents' or something. That's why Scott had been drinking. That's why she was leaving with their daughter and the dog. But the look between them was a shared one. They had agreed to this, whatever it was, however painful it was. Linda helped her daughter into the rear seat of the minivan and belted her in. The dog climbed in after the child. Then Linda went around to the driver's side and opened her door.

"Let her get down the driveway first," said Porter. "Then you can leave."

"I don't understand," Adele said softly. "You missed a board meeting. I was worried about you."

"Believe me, that's the least of my troubles—or yours."

Linda paused for a moment before she got into the car and faced her husband across the floodlit blacktop of their driveway. Something passed between them, something so intimate that Adele felt she had to look away. Porter cleared his throat as if to speak—or cry— she wasn't sure which. He did neither, instead giving his wife a slight nod of the head. She stepped into the car and started the engine. Her headlamps reflected back the contents of their garage: bicycles, sleds, Hula-Hoops. The plyboard from a long-ago puppet theater. A Dora-the-Explorer scooter Olivia had probably outgrown three years ago. Linda reversed out of the garage and did a three-point turn before shifting into drive. Then, without looking back, she started down the hill. The sound of the engine floated up to them, dying by inches as the minivan pushed aside the stillness of the night.

Porter turned away from Adele and pulled off his glasses. He ran the back of his sweatshirt sleeve across his eyes.

"Are you okay?" Adele didn't know what else to say. She shouldn't have barged in like this. "If there's anything I can do—"

"I didn't do it," he said thickly. "I should tell you that now before you hear anything to the contrary." His voice was slurred slightly from alcohol and nasal from crying.

"What are you talking about?"

"The police are going to say I killed Maria. Because

of Olivia. They're going to take me down and the whole damn center with me. But I didn't kill her. That's the truth."

Adele fell back against her car, as disoriented as a child playing pin-the-tail. She'd thought she'd interrupted a domestic dispute. She was blindsided by the gravity of what she was hearing. "What are you saying, Scott? Are you saying what I think you're saying?"

"I'm saying that I gave Olivia a better life than Maria ever could have. Two parents. A beautiful home. A good education. Love. What could Maria give?"

"You don't mean . . . ?" Adele felt sick to her stomach. "Please don't tell me you *stole* an undocumented woman's baby."

"Olivia was eighteen months old when Maria got out of prison," said Porter. "By that point, she'd spent almost half her life with us. *Half her life.* Maria would have taken her back to a dirt-floor shack in Guatemala. What I did—that's not stealing. That's rescuing."

"But if Olivia was her child—"

"She was the product of a rape, Adele."

"Maria told you that?"

"She didn't have to. She got pregnant on the journey from Guatemala to Iowa. That shit doesn't happen by choice. You know that. We've both heard enough clients' stories. Imagine going through life knowing your father raped your mother. Knowing that's the sole reason for your existence. And Olivia would have known—or guessed it—or other kids would have told her. Don't kid yourself. She would have been an outcast. This was the life I saved her from."

"And Linda? She knew about what you'd done?"

Scott leaned against Adele's car. He put his hands on

his thighs and bent over. He looked like he might throw up. "She does now," he said thickly.

"Is that why she left you?"

"She didn't leave. I ordered her to go. I don't want her and Olivia involved in this. My choices. My mistakes."

"But Olivia *is* involved," said Adele. "She's another woman's child."

Porter straightened. "That woman was a stranger to her. *We're* her mom and dad—no one else. This is the only life she knows."

Adele's head was pounding. She tried to imagine how she was going to explain this—to La Casa's benefactors, to her clients, to the Lake Holly immigrant community. Scott Porter had earned a reputation for empowering people who were powerless, giving a voice to the voiceless. Yet all the good he'd done seemed to pale before this great evil. He had stolen a poor, defenseless woman's baby—and maybe, just maybe—he'd done something far worse. She stood in front of him, her rage as strong as if someone had plucked Sophia from her own arms, her muscles aching as if they bore the strain.

"You bastard!" Adele slapped him. She had never done anything like that before—not even during the darkest days of her marriage. Her fury startled both of them. Porter's face turned bright red where she'd hit him, like a bad sunburn. He covered it with his hand.

"How dare you stand there and feed me this bullshit about how you *saved* Olivia, how you gave her a better life. You wanted to give her a better life? You could have mailed Maria a check every month to care for her daughter. You could have offered to bring the child to the United States when she was eighteen and pay for her education. This has nothing to do with any charitable impulse, Scott. You didn't save Olivia for her sake. You saved her for your own! Because you and Linda wanted a baby. Because everything people like you want, you get. You didn't care who you hurt or whose life you destroyed. It was all about you—your needs, your desires. Don't play the hero, Scott. There are no heroes here."

Porter sank down on the curb of the driveway and put his head in his hands. The fight had left him. The fight had left them both. "Maybe you're right," he said softly. "Maybe the love wasn't so much for Olivia. But it wasn't for me, either. It was for Linda. She'd been through so much trying to have a baby, then trying to adopt one. I knew she'd die if I took Olivia away from her. Olivia was ten months old when Maria asked me to find someone to care for her while she was detained. By the time Maria was ready to be deported, we *were* Olivia's family. I didn't create the circumstances."

"No, but you exploited them. You made a judge believe the child's mother had given her up for adoption when she hadn't. They'll disbar you for that. They'll send you to prison."

Porter shook his head. "I never filed any false paperwork with the courts. As far as the court was concerned, Maria had had no contact with her daughter for over a year. That's the legal definition of abandonment, Adele. I used our daughter's real birth certificate, her real everything for the adoption. Did I lie to my wife? Yes. I had a dead client with no baby and a live one with a baby and I switched them as far as Linda was concerned. She'd have never agreed to the adoption otherwise. But did I lie to the court? No."

"Maria would have contacted Olivia if she could have and you know it, Scott. You let her go back to Guatemala thinking her baby was dead, didn't you?" She read her hunch in Porter's eyes, the way they slid away from her, the way he covered his red cheek as if he expected Adele to hit him again. "I'll bet her name wasn't even Olivia, was it?"

"It was Luz Maria Santos," Porter said evenly. "Like I said, I've got nothing to hide."

"Nothing to hide? You lied to a judge and to the birth mother—not to mention your wife."

"You can theorize, Adele. But you can't prove a damn thing and neither can anyone else." Adele watched him trying on different excuses in his head, reframing the facts to fit the image he wanted to portray. Once a criminal defense attorney, always a criminal defense attorney.

"Are you asking if what I did was moral? No. Are you asking if what I did was legal? Yes. I'm an American citizen. Luz Maria Santos was an American citizen. Her undocumented birth mother had been deported by that point and, as far as the courts were concerned, she'd had no contact with the child for over a year. The adoption will not be nullified. I told Maria the same thing on several occasions."

"And then killed her when she threatened to ruin your career."

"No. I didn't. We talked back and forth. She came to see me. She wanted to see Olivia but I said no. It would be too confusing for her. I offered Maria money. She got offended and left and I didn't hear from her after that. I didn't know what had happened until that cop, Vega, showed me her photograph. The police will charge me with obstruction of justice for withholding information in a criminal investigation. Depending on the judge, I'll probably do some jail time and maybe get disbarred. But Olivia will have Linda and Linda will have Olivia. Nothing will ever change that."

"Then why did you send them away?"

"Because the cops will try to separate Olivia from Linda until the paperwork gets sorted out. Maybe put her in foster care, I don't know. This way, by the time the cops find them, they'll see there's nothing anyone can do. She's ours and she'll stay ours."

"What about when Olivia gets older and starts asking a lot of questions or wants to search for her birth mother? How's she going to feel when she learns the truth?"

"Who says she has to know? You think all these Chinese adopted kids know where they come from? You think a few of them aren't better off *not* knowing? The truth's overrated, Adele. You're a lawyer. You should know that."

Adele's voice trembled. She couldn't remember ever being so angry. "This is different, Scott. Olivia had a mother who loved her. She had a name. A history. That's all a poor person has—their history. And you stole it."

"Correction: I rewrote it. Luz Maria Santos had a past. Olivia Porter has a *future.*"

Adele heard a squeal of car tires turning onto Porter's road. The vehicle was traveling fast in their direction, slicing the air with an urgency that was hard to miss.

"I stood the cops up too this evening," said Porter. "I

had a feeling they wouldn't take it well." He tried for a light touch but his voice came off as shaky. He pushed himself to his feet. "For what it's worth, I never meant to hurt anybody. I didn't expect it to come to this."

"This will close down the community center," said Adele. Red and blue flashers slit open the darkness, aborting any sense of normalcy left between them. Adele's heart beat faster as if she were the one getting arrested.

"Consider my resignation, effective immediately."

"A lot of good that will do."

"Adele." Porter gave up any show of bravado and kept his eyes on the driveway. They could hear the police cruiser making its way up the hill, jewel-colored lights bouncing off tree trunks like in a pinball game. Porter looked scared, dismantled, as if some piece of him were already missing. He kept his arms plastered to his sides. He knew enough about the police to make sure he made no sudden moves. "La Casa was never about me or the other board members. It was always about you. You can keep that place alive. I know you can."

Adele faced the cruiser's headlamps and shielded her eyes from their brightness. She felt as Maria Elena must have felt on the night she walked along Lake Holly Road, a whole world of hurt, anger, and frustration on her shoulders. She must have noted the glare as the car barreled toward her or perhaps lit her up from behind, the push of displaced air that heralded the onslaught. There had to be a fraction of a second before impact when life cruelly presented its irony: she was about to die two thousand miles from home in search of a daughter who was less than a mile away—a daughter who would never know who she was.

# Chapter 28

"Look, Scott," Vega said, straddling a chair backward. "We've put an AMBER Alert out on Olivia. You have to know we're going to find her and Linda." He and Greco were in the same interrogation room with Porter that Morales had sat in forty-eight hours ago. Only Porter was no Morales. He'd spent his whole career pleading with clients not to open their mouths to the police without a lawyer present. He spoke offhandedly only once to Vega and Greco and that was to deny he'd killed Maria.

"All you can charge me with—all you'll *ever* be able to charge me with—is obstruction of justice."

It pained Vega and Greco to admit for the moment that he was right. They would have preferred to hold off making any sort of arrest until they could have built up a murder case against him. But when Porter stood them up this evening, they were forced to arrest him on a lesser charge rather than run the risk that he and his family might flee. Still, Vega wasn't willing to back off just yet.

"You had motive up the ying-yang, Scott. You were

the last person to speak to Maria. She died near your house."

"Yeah? Well, whatever you think you've got in the way of evidence, it's not going to match up to me. I know you're gonna try hard—you especially, Vega." Porter pointed a finger at him. "You'd love to see me take the hit for this, wouldn't you?"

Vega saw Greco frowning at him. He pushed himself off the back of the chair and said nothing.

"You think I don't know?" Porter glared at him. "About you and my wife?"

"That was in high school, Scott. Not now. She and I never—"

"I see the way you look at her. I'm not blind, Vega. You want me? Get me. But if you care about Linda the way you seem to, leave her alone."

Vega and Greco were hoping their subpoenas would produce a paper trail of forgery and deceit. But as far as the state of Iowa was concerned, Olivia's adoption was textbook legal. Her unsealed adoption records correctly identified her as Luz Maria Santos, the child of Maria Elena Santos. Scott and Linda were Luz Maria's lawfully designated foster parents before they filed for adoption. Her mother was alleged to have abandoned the child because she'd had no contact with her for over a year after her arrest. The only person who could have testified that Porter had lied or misrepresented that abandonment was Maria, and she was dead.

Porter had covered his tracks well in everything. Vega and Greco got the lab reports back from the accident investigation and they too were disappointing. The paint chips recovered at the scene could be matched to any black Acura model in a five-year production range—

good news, since Porter owned a black Acura RL. The problem was, his car was in pristine condition and they had no insurance claims of any damage to his vehicle in the past six months. They still needed to check directly with auto-body repair shops, however. Porter could have paid for the repairs in cash.

An assistant district attorney showed up at Lake Holly town court and Porter was arraigned on obstruction of justice. He agreed to surrender his passport in exchange for being released on bail. The alerts were out for Linda and Olivia. There was little more either of the detectives could do this evening. They'd get a fresh start in the morning.

Vega walked out to his pickup in the parking lot. It was past eleven p.m.—too late to call Wendy and Joy and try to work things out. His mind was drifting, asking questions that had no answers, a habit he had when he was exhausted. He imagined what would have happened if Maria had lived. Would she have gone to court to get custody of Olivia and take her back to Guatemala? Was that even desirable anymore? Olivia was an upper-middle-class American girl now. English was her primary language. Taylor Swift and Justin Bieber were her cultural references. She texted. She tweeted. She wouldn't know how to survive in a world where iPads, iPhones, and Instagram didn't exist, not to mention indoor plumbing, higher education, and twenty-first-century medical care. Scott Porter had done a terrible thing, but there was no way now to undo it— not without traumatizing that girl for the rest of her life. The mold was set. The cement had hardened. Olivia Porter was not Maria's any longer.

Sometimes when Vega looked at Joy, he felt a little

bit of that same sense of loss. He could locate parts of himself in his daughter: her talent for math, her fiery temper, the way her skin bronzed easily in the sun. But the culture that had spawned him was as foreign to her as a Spanish-language soap opera.

Maybe it was necessary, this shedding of the old ways with each generation. He had abandoned so much of what defined his mother: her religious faith, her kinship ties, her attachment to their old neighborhood in the Bronx. But lately, he'd begun to wonder if he'd abandoned too much. He felt like there was a box inside of him that had been locked away for so long, he'd forgotten where he'd put the key. There were things he treasured in that box: the sultry music of his childhood, the playfulness and sensuality of his culture. He longed to open himself up to these things again, to find comfort and acceptance in who he was rather than in what others wanted him to be.

He backed his truck out of the parking lot and tried to clear his mind for the forty-five-minute drive north to his house. At the first stoplight, his cell phone rang. *Adele*. He pulled over to the curb and took the call.

"I'm beat, Adele—can it wait 'til tomorrow?"

"She wants to know if you've spoken to the family."

*"What?"*

"She called me, Jimmy." Adele's voice was soft and husky. "She wants to know if Maria has family."

That woke him up. "Linda called you? When?"

"A little while ago."

"From where?"

"I don't know."

"What's her number?" If he had the number, he could triangulate the call and bring her in.

"Can you stop being a cop for just a moment and listen? She wants to do what's best for Olivia."

"Then she needs to turn herself in."

"She wants to. She's just afraid the police will take Olivia away and put her into foster care."

"I can't guarantee that won't happen."

"But Linda's innocent, Jimmy. Scott told me she didn't know about any of this before this evening."

"Just because Porter says it doesn't make it true."

"I would think you of all people would care what happens to her."

He did care. He would always care. But this wasn't ultimately about Linda. It was about Olivia. His duty was to the child. He had failed Desiree Soto. He did not want to fail Olivia Porter.

"Linda's got to hand Olivia over, Adele. I'll do my best if she's innocent. But we need the child returned safely. Give me her number and I'll call her."

"No."

"*No?* You're telling a police officer *no?*"

"Why are you being such a hard-ass?"

"Why are you letting Linda turn you into an accessory after the fact?"

"Because like it or not, I'm involved. 214 Pine Road. That's my address. Linda will be here in about an hour to surrender to you. Come alone. And don't you dare turn this into some sort of SWAT operation. My eight-year-old is asleep upstairs." Adele hung up.

# Chapter 29

Adele's house was a small, blue, wood-frame Victorian on a street of similar-looking houses set apart from each other by the width of their driveways. It was a house that looked comfortably lived in. The driveway dipped and buckled like the surface of a home-baked cake. The garage behind the house had moss growing on the roof. A basket of pink flowers hung from a well-worn porch, along with several wind chimes, one made of forks and spoons and pieces of broken pottery that appeared to have been strung together by a child.

There were no parking spots on the street so Vega parked in the driveway behind Adele's Prius and lumbered up the front steps. His boots sounded hollow on the planks. The carpenter in him wondered if the boards beneath were beginning to rot. He peeked in the living-room window to see if there was anything he should be aware of before he rang her doorbell. Lights glowed behind gauzy curtains but he saw nothing else so he rang and waited.

Adele opened the door with a broom in her hand.

"You normally clean house at this hour?"

"I'm not cleaning." Her eyes scoured the floor. "Oh my God!" She flattened herself against the door. "He's in the living room. He's going to go upstairs if I don't stop him. My daughter's upstairs!"

"Who?" Vega pushed past her and snapped back the restraining hood on his holster. He automatically shifted his weight to a crouch. It took him a minute to place the shadows and contours of the living room. Someone had pulled the sofa away from the wall and stacked a pile of books helter-skelter on a coffee table. But otherwise, Vega saw nothing out of place, no sign of a struggle, no movement.

"Who's in the house?"

"A mouse."

"A *mouse?*" He took his hand off his holster and straightened. "That's what all this hysteria's about? A little mouse?"

"He's a big mouse." She squinted into her living room. "There he goes!"

A flash of dark gray scuttled from beneath the sofa to an umbrella stand. It was the size of a child's fist. Adele ducked behind Vega like she thought it was going to attack her.

Vega laughed. "You can't be frightened of a little mouse. A fencing champ like you? You could probably impale the sucker if you wanted to."

"Foil fencing's a sport, Jimmy. Not a form of rodent control."

"You got a trap? I'll bait it for you."

Something pained crossed her features. "I don't know. Maybe in the garage?" Vega wondered if this was her first year alone since the divorce. If there were any mousetraps at all, it was probably because her ex-husband had bought them when he was still her husband, when this house was part of a bigger dream and not just a remnant of its failures.

"Come on," he said gently. "Let's go see if we can find one."


They crossed the driveway to the garage and went inside. One of the bays was completely filled with lawn mowers, leaf blowers, hedge trimmers, and canisters of gasoline.

"Is this a second career you've got going here? Moonlighting as a landscape contractor?"

"The equipment's not mine," said Adele. "It belongs to Cesar Cardenas. He's trying to start his own landscaping business to help pay for Kenny's college. I let him use one bay of my garage in exchange for him and Kenny doing my yard work."

Vega started pawing through boxes on a shelf. "Are you such a soft touch with all your clients?"

"Once an immigrant's daughter, always an immigrant's daughter, I suppose."

In the boxes, Vega found half-empty cans of paint thinner, rusted wrenches, and old tennis balls. He wondered how much of this had been her ex's. At least he and Wendy had been able to make a fresh start after their divorce.

"Here we go." Vega held up an unopened package of three wooden mousetraps. They'd been stashed in a box between cans of Raid. "You got peanut butter?"

"I thought you're supposed to use cheese."

"Trust me, peanut butter gets them every time."

In the kitchen, Adele found a jar of peanut butter.

Vega began smearing it on the bait portion of one of the traps. He looked at his watch. Fifteen minutes had passed. No sign of Linda.

"What time did she tell you she'd be here?"

"She said it would take her about an hour."

Vega retracted the catch on the first trap. Then he slid it between the refrigerator and stove. "How about you call her and ask how much progress she's made?"

"She said she'll be here," Adele told him stiffly.

Vega fumed silently. Since when did suspects dictate the terms of their surrender? When Adele went upstairs to check on her daughter, Vega walked over to a row of hooks by the back door. On one of the hooks, he found Adele's shoulder bag and located her cell phone. The last call she'd received was at ten fifty-five this evening. *Caller unknown* read the display. *Linda?* There were no other calls after six-thirty p.m. He copied down the number and tossed the bag back on the hook. Then he walked out to the driveway, called Greco, and gave him the cell number to see if he could triangulate the call. When he walked back in, Adele was holding her bag open and glaring at him. He must have forgotten to do up the zipper. He probably didn't hang up the bag exactly the same way, either. Women were such sticklers for details.

"Did you just get Linda's number off my cell?"

"C'mon, Adele. It's not like I stole anything."

"Only my trust."

He walked over to the counter and began baiting the second trap. He could feel her eyes burning a hole in his back.

"I'm not the bad guy here." But all of a sudden, he wasn't so sure. It had never occurred to Vega until that moment how much of her life she'd invested in La Casa. It had probably cost her everything: a high-paying career, her personal life, most likely, her marriage. And tonight, it was all in ruins.

He began to set the spring on the second trap. "Look, it's gonna be okay—"

He lifted his hand too quickly. *Snap!* The spring closed on the tip of his left middle finger. Vega flung the trap to the floor and tore through a stream of Spanish invectives. The noise must have scared the mouse because a flash of dark fur suddenly darted across the vinyl tiles.

Adele yelped and stepped back against Vega. Instinctively, he wrapped his good hand around her.

"It's okay," he murmured. "You're gonna be okay."

They stayed that way, neither relinquishing the moment. Then she turned to him and reached for his hurt hand. A purple welt was already beginning to form across the nail bed.

"Serves me right, huh?" asked Vega.

"I didn't say that."

"But you thought it."

"Maybe a little."

Her mascara had smeared, giving her eyes a smoky look. Vega could see the glassy sheen in them, the uncertainty that this night had brought her. He lifted her chin and looked at her squarely. She was so small in stocking feet. Almost like a child.

"Listen to me, Adele. The center isn't going to go under. Not if you don't let it. I saw those people the other night, how much they need you. They believe in you." He swallowed. "*I* believe in you."

He brought his lips down on hers. He'd been fantasizing about the moment so much that the mere press of her flesh, the warm exhale of her breath, brought goose bumps to his skin. She leaned in to welcome him, her fingernails running in tandem down his back. He forgot about the pain in his finger and allowed his hands to drift down the seams of her jeans, to feel the way they hugged her curves like a second skin. She stilled a nervousness inside of him, a note that had been reverberating off-pitch for far too long. It was like they were back on that dance floor again. Only now the music came from within and they didn't need any accompaniment at all.

He flicked off the kitchen light. The room plunged into darkness with only the blue glow of numbers on the stove to guide them.

"Come." She took his hand, her fingertips soft as rose petals, and led him to the living room. The floorboards creaked beneath his feet. Upstairs he could hear the heartbeat drip of a water faucet and the ticking of a clock.

His eyes gradually adjusted to the hint of streetlight seeping in through the gauzy curtains. Adele lit a candle on the fireplace mantel. It flickered across her features. She was such a beautiful woman, her body a generous roadmap of peaks and valleys all waiting to be explored. Vega pulled her close and snaked an arm around her backside. He gently untucked her shirt from her jeans. His body thrummed with anticipation as he brushed her silky black hair away from her neck and ran his lips down its contours. Her muscles quickened beneath the firm assurance of his fingertips. It was crazy, this hunger that had come over both of them. Linda could be at the front door at any moment. Adele's daughter was upstairs. But all that did was make everything feel more urgent.

And then a snap came from the kitchen, sharp as a firecracker. Adele jumped out of his embrace.

"Oh my God."

Vega wasn't sure if the exclamation referred to the mouse or to him. He dropped his hands and stepped back. He felt light-headed and dizzy, certain that if Adele blew out the candle this minute, he'd see white arcs of current flowing between their bodies. They stared at each other for a long moment, neither saying anything. Finally, Vega spoke.

"Maybe I should get rid of the mouse." His voice felt foreign and stilted, like he was trying out a new language. He walked into the kitchen and switched on the light. Its brightness jarred his senses.

The mouse was spread across the snapped trap, its tail dangling over the end like some rubber toy. Adele walked up behind him. She covered her eyes when he fished the trap from its hiding spot.

"Oh, the poor thing."

"Now you're feeling sorry for it?"

"I can't help it. I feel bad."

"That's a liberal for you." Vega rolled his eyes. "You want someone else to make the nasty stuff disappear, then you act all guilt-ridden when it's accomplished."

"Don't turn a mouse into politics, Jimmy." They were back on solid ground again. It felt reassuring.

It felt disappointing.

"Do you have a garbage bag?" he asked her.

"Can't you just—I don't know—bury it? I don't want it in my garbage for a whole week. It will freak me out."

He let out a long, slow exhale. "I'll get one of Cesar's shovels from the garage."

Vega dug a shallow grave right behind the garage, thankful to have a physical outlet for his energies. When he was done, he covered the spot with a smooth fieldstone just in case Adele wanted to point out the grave to Sophia. Joy had always been sentimental about animals that way. Vega had buried more than a few squirrels in his time.

He returned Cesar's shovel to the garage. He was trying to rehang it on its proper hook when he accidentally hit a cardboard carton on the shelf above. The carton tumbled to the floor. Out spilled a rusty penknife and a plastic bag full of muddy rags and pieces of nylon landscaping rope. Vega started tossing the contents back into the carton. Then he noticed a faint green line running through the center of the rope.

He opened the plastic bag and examined the contents more closely. There was something hasty and haphazard about this stuff that didn't match the rest of Cesar Cardenas's neat and orderly arrangement of equipment. The way the rope had been cut into fraying bits and pieces, the way the blade of the penknife had been allowed to develop rust, the balled-up rags caked with mud. No. On closer inspection, they weren't rags at all. They were a T-shirt and jeans. And the mud—it wasn't just mud. Vega could distinguish that reddish-brown tinge from mud.

Something like distant thunder began a low, steady rumble through his chest cavity. Vega shoved the clothes and rope back into the plastic bag and returned the carton to the shelf as if simply restoring things to their original place could halt the unease he was feeling. None of the items was out of the ordinary. Mud, grease, blood—it came with the territory whenever you worked around tools. Vega's unease came, not from the items themselves, but from the careless way they'd been stashed. Which made Vega wonder: Did these things belong to Cesar? They couldn't be Adele's since she seemed to have no idea what she did and didn't have in here.

That left only one other person who could have put those things in that box. His father probably wouldn't have noticed. Neither would Adele.

Vega's cell phone rang, interrupting his thoughts. Greco.

"We found them."

"Linda and Olivia?"

"Yeah."

Vega heard the sound of a siren in the background. "Something wrong?"

"They're hurt, man. I'm out on Route 170 now. Bobby Rowland's kid was driving the other way and slammed into their minivan."

*Dios mío.* "How bad is it?"

A pause. Vega felt his heart drop to his shoes.

"I think you'd better get over here right away."

# Chapter 30

There are almost no straight roads in the counties north of New York City. Everything curves and kinks, wandering beside streambeds, cutting paths between hills that blot out the sun too early in winter. Even the highways look like they were drawn onto the landscape by a cartographer with Tourette's. It doesn't take much to become an accident statistic here. A patch of slick pavement, a deer in the headlights, a truck in low gear on a bend and it's over.

Vega didn't handle accidents anymore. Before he became a detective, however, he'd probably done hundreds. They always caught him by surprise. The sudden alteration of the landscape. The stark before and after of the lives involved. They weren't like homicides, which usually had some buildup to them, or other sorts of accidents where an ounce of common sense might have made all the difference. No. Car accidents had the hand of God about them. The way they shredded any sense of power or control people thought they exerted over their lives.

The local police had blocked off part of Route 170

to civilian traffic. Vega saw the flares and emergency lights first, the way they made a spectacle of the darkness. At the checkpoint, he powered down his window and flashed his badge. Beyond, he could see the smashed remains of car carcasses sandwiched between police cruisers and fire trucks. The ambulances were gone but not the van from the medical examiner's office. Vega's chest tightened. Somebody was dead. He tried to get his emotions under control enough to ask the cop at the checkpoint who.

"The nineteen-year-old driver of the red Mazda hatchback."

"Bobby Rowland's son? Matt?"

"Yeah," said the cop, nodding grimly. "He was DOA by the time the first unit arrived." Vega felt the breath leave his lungs. Rowland had already lost one son. It seemed inconceivable he'd lose the other.

Vega drove slowly past the accident and parked farther east before heading back on foot. Torn metal and pebbled glass littered the asphalt. Rowland was sitting in his fire department SUV with Greco, who was taking down his statement. Every part of Rowland seemed to sag from the weight of what was happening. His shoulders melted into his chest. His jowls hung slack. His head looked too heavy for his neck. Every now and then, he would let it rest on the steering wheel of his car. His body would start to quake and Greco would wordlessly lay a patient hand on his back until he could straighten and begin again. Vega wanted to go over to his old friend but he knew this wasn't a condolence call. It was a police investigation. The accident was on a local road, not a highway. He had no jurisdiction here.

He made sure to steer clear of the officers taking measurements and photographs at the scene, of the volunteer firefighters with their grim faces. Vega could see that the red Mazda hatchback that Matt Rowland had been driving had taken the brunt of the collision. It was smaller and lighter than the minivan Linda had been driving and it looked as if Linda had had the quick instincts to turn away from the oncoming car and perhaps spare Olivia the worst of the crash. Matt may have been too impaired to react.

Vega studied the car now. The front end had folded like a child's paper fan. The back windshield was shattered and bloody. Vega suspected Matt hadn't been wearing a seatbelt. The seat had been pushed all the way back to make room for the teenager's large frame but the belt was still in the retracted position. The car's white airbag hung limp and deflated over the steering wheel like someone's just-washed underwear.

Vega stared at the seat, at the way it had been pushed all the way back. Of course it would be. Matt Rowland was a big guy like his father. Well over six feet. Well over two hundred pounds. Every time Joy used to borrow Vega's black Acura TSX, she pushed the seat close to the steering wheel to accommodate her tiny size. And every time Vega reclaimed it, he'd had to step into it like he was squeezing himself into a child's preschool chair and adjust it so he could exhale.

Something shrill and atonal rose above the white noise in Vega's brain. He felt edgy all of a sudden thinking about his totaled car in that auto-body lot. He'd only concentrated on the crumpled fenders and crazed glass when he saw it. He'd only felt the gratitude of knowing his daughter had not been inside when the damage occurred. It hadn't even occurred to him to look at the position of the driver's seat until Tim Anderson mentioned it. But now he understood.

The tow truck driver hadn't pushed the seat back.

The accident hadn't pushed the seat back.

Someone tall had done it before he drove the car, the car that Joy was supposed to be driving herself that Sunday night in March on her way back from studying with friends. Sunday night, March eighth, eleven-thirty p.m. was the time Joy totaled Vega's black Acura TSX on the Metro-North railroad tracks. Sunday night, March eighth, eight-twelve p.m. was the last call from Maria Santos's cell phone.

All this time, Vega had been racking his brains to figure out why someone would turn a car accident into something far worse. And now he understood. Only two scared teenagers could make such a stupid, reckless, life-altering decision. Bobby Rowland wasn't the only parent who could be blindsided by a child.

"Toughest accident I've been to in a long time," said Greco, coming up behind Vega. "The autopsy will have to confirm it, but it's likely Matt Rowland was DWI. Too bad our guys didn't catch him before this happened."

"Yeah." Vega could barely choke out the word. He felt like someone had stuffed a rag down his throat. He was suffocating on the inside, drowning in his own world of hurt and denial. "Any news from the hospital?" he managed to ask.

"One of our guys notified Porter," said Greco. "He's at the hospital now. Olivia's doing well. Just a few scrapes. As for Linda? No news is good news at this point." Greco put a hand on Vega's shoulder. He'd assumed the look of despair on Vega's face was over Linda.

"She could still pull through, man. I've seen it happen. One minute, you're thinking, that's it, it's over. And a couple of weeks later, they're up and about like nothing happened."

Vega wasn't sure whether Greco believed that or wanted to believe that. The longer he'd worked with the man, the more Vega had come to realize that Greco was like a lot of cops. He really did have that fairy-tale notion of good and evil. Sometimes, there is no good and evil. Sometimes, there are just moments when a millisecond of indiscretion meets up with a micrometer of misjudgment.

Joy could have called him when it happened. Okay, he was at work that night. But she could have gotten through. Why the hell hadn't she called him?

*Because she knows I wouldn't have been all that broken up if Kenny got deported over this, that's why. She knows I don't want her seeing him.*

It was entirely possible no one else would ever put the pieces together. His Acura had long since been turned into scrap metal. Even if the car had survived, the damage after the train collision was so extensive; there'd be no way to separate it from the damage to the car from the fatal hit-and-run. There was likely to be DNA on that carton of rope and clothing in Adele's garage. But that box could sit there for years and no one would think to look inside. There were no eyewitnesses. Forensics had only one fingerprint on that hate letter that didn't show up in any database and probably never would so long as Joy and Kenny never got arrested. The car paint would prove that Maria had been hit by a black Acura similar to Vega's. But it wouldn't conclusively prove that that was the car that hit her.

Vega could choose to say nothing. It would be so easy to go that route, to let Kenny and Joy move on with their lives. They both still had a chance to have bright futures ahead of them. Nothing could bring Maria back. Joy was already racked by nightmares and guilt. Kenny too, from what Vega had observed and what Cardenas had said at the *quinceañera*. Forcing them to come forward might push his daughter over the edge entirely. She would hate him forever. So would Wendy. So would Adele who was so desperately pulling for Kenny and his family.

One of the volunteer firefighters agreed to drive Bobby Rowland and his SUV home. They didn't want him on the roads tonight. They didn't want him to have to deliver this news to his wife alone. Vega and Greco watched him get into the passenger's seat of his SUV. The big man wiped an arm across his face and fought back tears.

"I feel bad for Bobby," Greco said softly. "I'd never say it to him, but Jesus, what did he expect? He let Matt go on too long that way. You can't cover for your kids like that. They gotta take responsibility for their actions. Didn't he understand that it was only going to get worse?"

Vega felt like his thoughts were being ripped out of his head and thrown under a white-hot spotlight. He turned on Greco. "Who the fuck made you judge and jury?"

"Relax, man. I'm just saying—"

"Do you have any idea what sort of pain he had to be

in? You know how hard a decision like that is? He loved his kid, Grec. You're a cop. You're a father. You know what jail does to people. It kills their souls. How many people you ever met were better after they went in? Do you really think that was gonna save his boy?"

"Would've saved him tonight and two innocents besides," said Greco. "Would've let him know there's right and wrong and what's expected of him."

"Oh, and doing right automatically gets you brownie points in this world. C'mon man. Look around. Matt Rowland's dead. But his two pals, Delaney and Giordano, are probably gonna walk for Guzman's beating and the other crimes as well now that he's gone. Porter's gonna get away with stealing Maria's baby because he legally covered his tracks. Where's the life-is-fair clause in any of that?"

"I didn't say life is fair, Vega. I said there's right and wrong. Just because it doesn't work perfectly doesn't make it any less true."

"You can't really believe that."

Greco put a hand on Vega's shoulder and gave him a long, searching look before he spoke. "Yes, I do," he said softly. "That's why I became a cop. Look inside, man. You do, too."

# Chapter 31

The high school was spread out long and low, like pieces of a jigsaw puzzle waiting to be assembled. The design had won awards when it was built in 1957, but now, it had a dated feel with its oddly angled windows and chrome supports that looked vaguely space-age to Vega. A convoy of yellow school buses idled out front. Vega waited with them, drinking in the diesel fumes from their engines, craning his neck for Joy. He felt like a convict being sent upstate, watching from the mesh windows of a corrections van as the free world floated by. Nothing would ever feel the same again.

Teenagers pushed out of the front doors, their chatter like birdsong to the basso profundo of the buses. They all looked so young. He couldn't believe he'd ever been their age. There were girls on cell phones, walking in pairs and groups, Siamese-attached as always, backpacks slung over their shoulders. There were boys in track shorts and T-shirts, their hair uncombed, their sneakers so big they looked like clown shoes.

He sat in his pickup and waited. He'd texted Joy an

hour earlier and asked her to meet him after school. *I KNOW ABOUT MAR 8*, he wrote. *WE NEED TO TALK.*

*OK. IM SORRY DAD* she'd texted back.

Never had four words had to cover so much ground.

He'd spent the last fourteen sleepless hours tracking down every lead and every piece of evidence he could find, hoping to locate something to convince himself that Kenny and Joy weren't behind Maria's death. He visited Tim Anderson at Metro-North and pored over the evidence photos and police report of Joy's car accident. He reread the report from his own agency reconstructing the accident that killed Maria. He scanned the forensics findings on the paint chips and the medical examiner's conclusions from Maria's autopsy. Everything pointed to Kenny and Joy, right down to Maria's rib fractures that Dr. Gupta had originally said might have come from a bad attempt at CPR. Kenny and Joy would have tried to save Maria's life—Vega was sure of it. They weren't cold-blooded killers. They were kids who had made a tragic mistake.

He told no one what he was doing. Not Greco, who was phoning him nearly hourly with updates on Linda's and Olivia's improving conditions. Not Captain Waring, who kept pressuring Vega to track down more evidence on Porter. Not even Wendy. If he told, there was no going back. And he was scared, more scared than he'd ever been in his life. Maria had been dead a month. The case was public and high profile. Hell, with Matt Rowland dead, Giordano and Delaney had a much better chance of walking for all the shit they'd pulled than Joy and Kenny did. He could not count on leniency here.

The school buses were loaded up and heading out. A

few stragglers wandered the sidewalk, scanning their text messages or rolling back and forth on their skateboards. Joy was nowhere in sight. She'd stood him up. A part of him was no longer surprised.

*My daughter is a liar.*

*My daughter is an accomplice to manslaughter.*

Such simple statements, so hard to come to grips with. There was so much failure in those words, so much feeling that he was to blame. He was on unfamiliar turf, a tourist in a country he'd never expected to visit. He wasn't prepared. How do you prepare for such a thing? He felt like someone had switched time zones on him. He was queasy. His reflexes felt sluggish. A dull headache took up residence in the back of his head. This girl he was supposed to meet today wasn't the Joy he knew, not the girl who used to cry over dead squirrels and goldfishes.

His phone rang.

"Daddy?" Her voice sounded husky and choked. She rarely called him Daddy anymore.

"Hey." He tried for a light tone but the words wouldn't flow. "I'm in the school parking lot. Where are you?"

"I cut class and left early."

A month ago, such a transgression would have been unthinkable. Now, Vega couldn't even process it with all the other things on his mind. "We need to talk."

Silence. Then a wave of confession, her words all jumbled together: "It was an accident, Daddy, I swear. We never meant it to happen. It's all my fault. Kenny didn't want to do any of it. I talked him into it. I came up with the idea. Everything—"

"Joy." Vega cut her off. He couldn't do this over a phone. Besides, she was panicking. Panicky people say and do stupid things. Cops bank on that. Fathers don't. "We'll assign blame another time. Right now, you need to tell me where you are."

Her voice got small and tight, like she was trying to shoehorn it into a much younger child's body. "Please don't be angry with me."

"I'm not angry." Anger would have been easy. This was—he didn't know except to say that when people talk about a broken heart, he understood now that it wasn't a metaphor. There really was such a pain in the chest. His heart felt like it had been cleaved in two. "Are you home?"

"I can't go home anymore."

"Don't talk nonsense. Are you with Kenny?"

"No." That eerie silence again. Wherever she was, it was outdoors and not near any major roads or parking lots. He heard the caw of a crow and little else except a slight breathlessness on her end. Wherever she was, she was on the move and it was requiring all her energy. Then she seemed to stop in her tracks. She was panting.

"It's amazing up here. Everything feels so far away."

"Where are you?" He willed himself to stay calm but already he felt the warning sirens going off in his body. They had the sharpness of microphone feedback.

"She must have mattered very much to you," said Joy.

"Who? Your mother?"

"No. When you were seventeen and you just—you closed your eyes and did it. I know what you were feeling, Dad—like no one could ever matter as much again."

*Puñeta, coño! She's up on Bud Point! She's going to jump!* He could feel the adrenaline punch in every one of those words. A cold sweat broke across his skin. His breathing turned rapid and shallow. Better that he had not survived that jump at all than to endure this. He had used up the good luck for both of them. There would be no more.

"No, *Chispita!* Please, stay where you are. I'll come get you. We can work this out—"

"I love you, Daddy. Please tell everyone I'm sorry."

The disconnect felt like a gunshot. Vega redialed frantically, like some radio-show contestant hoping to be caller number twenty-five. The phone went straight to her voice mail.

He fumbled for his light bar and threw it on the dashboard. Red and blue lights pulsed along the windshield of his truck as he gunned his engine out of the parking lot. He cursed his stupidity for having texted her earlier today. He should have waited until she got home from school and confronted her in person. What would an hour have cost anyone? His own need for answers had pushed her over the edge.

He thought about calling Greco for backup or Wendy to try to intervene. But he dismissed both ideas at once. Joy may have already jumped. He did not want her mother seeing that, nor did he want his grief on display for the entire Lake Holly PD. If she hadn't yet jumped, then the carnival that would surely follow would embarrass them both and force the situation out of his hands. No, this was something he needed to do alone.

He turned onto Lake Holly Road and accelerated into the bends, whipping past cars on the narrow stretch of roadway. He was close enough to feel the stream of air as he passed. Horns blared. Drivers gestured. Vega barely noticed. He felt like there was a fist wrapped around his heart, a rubber band cinching his lungs. He gripped the steering wheel so tightly his fingers tingled with pins and needles.

He was not a praying man but he prayed now. He cut deals with God like he was back undercover, setting up a score. He'd be a more attentive father. He'd tone down his temper. He'd trade twenty years of his life. No, thirty. *Hell, take me now.*

He took the turns too fast, felt the pull of his tires as they kept a bare grip on the road. Up ahead, he saw the reservoir's small gravel parking lot and swerved in. Yellow crime-scene tape still fluttered from several tree trunks. There were no other cars in the lot. If Joy was here, she must have walked—left school early and just *walked*. He cut the engine and tried her phone again. There was no reply.

Already, the sun was taking leave of the woods as Vega hiked the muddy footpath to the lake. He sensed the approach of night in the shadows beneath moss-covered rocks and decaying limbs. The air was growing colder, wetter. He could feel the dampness like a dishrag in his lungs as he tried to catch his breath. The forecast called for rain this evening.

"Joy!" He called hoarsely through the crosshatch of bare limbs. There was no answer, no movement save for a solitary red-tailed hawk that hovered like a kite overhead.

He had a stitch in his side by the time he reached the shore. His eyes skimmed the water, looking and not wanting to look at the same time. The lake still held the promise of late afternoon, its surface striated with ribbons of shadow and light. Three ducks rode the ribbons, leaving an arc of incandescent ripples in their wake. He squinted up the dark granite face of Bud Point. Atop was a cluster of overgrown barberry bushes, their sinewy brown branches as tangled as fishing lure this time of year. Stuffed in the middle was something fuzzy. Something the color of Pepto-Bismol.

It didn't move.

Vega's limbs went slack. He forgot how to swallow. He could think of only one reason why Joy's jacket would be stuffed in those bushes: because she didn't need it anymore, no matter how cold it got.

His leg muscles registered the loss first. They gave out completely. He sank to his knees in the gritty mud along the bank. His lungs forgot how to take in air. He could only gulp at the humidness like a drowning man.

"Joy!" he wailed hoarsely, his daughter's name a mockery of his pain. He couldn't imagine ever getting up again.

Then the jacket moved.

"Dad?"

Vega squinted at the granite face, certain he was hallucinating. A thumb-sized figure emerged from the bushes and stepped closer to the edge of the cliff, the jacket wrapped tightly around her, her arms hugging herself against the cold. The waning sun lit her up in profile, giving her baby face more shade and shadow than he was used to. It was as if she had aged ten years on that cliff. Maybe she had. Maybe they both had.

Vega pushed himself to his feet and tried to brush the mud from his hands and pants. He wiped the sleeve of his jacket across his eyes and fought to collect himself.

"Come down, *Chispita*." His voice sounded unfamiliar, even to his own ears, like a car that hadn't been started in awhile.

Joy took a small step forward.

"No!" he shouted. "For God's sake, no! I just want to talk to you."

"There's nothing to talk about."

"There's *everything* to talk about."

"I e-mailed you a letter, Dad. It's all there. My confession. Everything."

"I didn't get the e-mail."

"I just sent it."

Vega fumbled with his phone. His hands were shaking. The new e-mail came up on his screen. He gambled instead on a lie. "I didn't get it, Joy. Let me come up. Maybe I'll get it in a few minutes." Now was his only chance. Now, while she was undecided. To reach her, he would have to circle the edge of the lake and climb up to the point. He would have to lose visual contact with her. Anything could happen. He needed a distraction.

"I want you to do me a favor, Joy, okay? One favor?" he called out, willing his voice to sound firm and confident. He'd had only the most rudimentary training as a hostage negotiator. But he knew one basic: keep a person talking. If you can keep communication going, you've got a chance.

"You always sang that Pink song really well—you know the one? 'Perfect'?" he asked. "Can you sing it to me now?" She had a lovely voice, a breathy alto just like Pink's.

"I can't."

"Yes, you can. Come on. Curse words and everything. I don't care." He began the song himself: "Took a wrong turn, once or twice—" He was a good singer normally, but his throat had constricted from panic and adrenaline. He sounded like a saw cutting wood.

And then he heard her, those raw, earthy notes that formed little more than a tiny vibrato in her chest. But it was the most beautiful thing he'd ever heard. She was singing. She was alive—and she would stay that way as long as the notes kept pushing out of her.

He doubled his step, picking his way over tree limbs and pushing past branches that snapped like broken bones in his wake. He climbed toward her voice. It's what kept his legs moving when he thought they'd give out, when the rocks got too slippery or cut up his hands until the knuckles began to bleed.

The light was fading. He hadn't climbed Bud Point since he was seventeen, a lifetime ago. He'd forgotten how steep it was, how dense the vegetation was, even now in early spring. He felt hemmed in and claustrophobic, surrounded by thick, remorseless timber that walled him off and left him directionless, like a small child in a sea of legs. He could barely hear Joy's voice for the hard pulls of breath he was taking.

And then the singing stopped.

"Joy?" He was just below the summit. He could hear nothing but the distant backwash of cars speeding along Lake Holly Road and the vague yawn of a jet engine coursing through the sky. He hoisted himself up the final rock and pushed past a thicket of barberry bushes, thorns digging into his bloody hands. That's when he saw her, shivering in that ridiculously gaudy pink jacket like some hip-hop diva.

She was standing on an overhang of granite no

wider than a picnic bench, kicking at small pebbles. He hoped to God she wasn't fantasizing that one of them was her. He couldn't believe he'd ever gone over that ledge. He felt like Alice in Wonderland. Every dimension seemed different to him on the other side of that looking glass.

She seemed to register his presence as if waking up from a very deep sleep. She turned to face him. Her lips were blue. He longed to wrap his Windbreaker around her but he sensed any sudden move might spook her, so he stood very still.

"Come to me, *Chispita.*"

"I'm scared."

"I know you're scared," he panted, trying to catch his breath. "But I'm here now. Come."

She tucked her fingers under her armpits to keep them warm but she didn't move. "It's my fault, Daddy. All of it. I talked Kenny into doing it—"

"He was driving, Joy. It wasn't all your fault." Vega unzipped his jacket and shrugged it off. His shirt was damp with sweat. He fought off a shiver. "Here." He held it out to her. "Take this." He hoped the promise of warmth would coax her from the ledge. She didn't move. A shadow crossed her features.

"They'll deport him, Dad. You know they will. That's why we did what we did."

"Were you drunk?"

"We were at a party. I'd had two rum and Cokes— I'm sorry. I know it was wrong but everybody was doing it. Kenny had just gotten off work so I gave him the keys. You always told me never to drink and drive. I thought it was the safest choice."

"Are you saying . . ." Vega let the arm holding his

jacket fall to his side. He couldn't believe what he was hearing. "Kenny was sober?"

"He only had a Sprite. Honest."

Vega closed his eyes and cursed softly. He felt weak with the realization: this didn't have to happen. None of this had to happen.

"I don't see what difference that would have made," said Joy. "Kenny's an unlicensed driver. He's in this country illegally and he killed somebody. Look what happened to that other immigrant in February, Dad! The cops would have torn Kenny to pieces. The whole town would have turned against him."

"Not if he was sober!" Vega slapped a hand to his forehead. He couldn't hold back his frustration any longer—at Joy, at Kenny, at a schizophrenic system of justice that turned two scared teenagers into felons. "He's an honors student with a clean record. He's lived in this town since he was ten years old. You could have called me. I'd have gotten him a lawyer. Or Adele Figueroa would've. We'd have made sure it never left town court, that the whole case got adjudicated before ICE ever got their claws into him. And you?" He blew out a long stream of breath and tried to keep his emotions under control. "You were in the clear."

"Can't you do that now?" She brushed her dark bangs out of her face and suddenly, all the worldliness seemed to disappear the way it did when she drifted off to sleep. There was hope in her dark eyes. For the first time in weeks, there was hope.

Vega wanted to rail against her immaturity, her naïveté. There was no way he could turn back the clock and undo what had happened. And yet he couldn't tell her this. Hope was her lifeline back from the edge of that cliff. He couldn't sever it, no matter how childish or unrealistic it was. He couldn't lie to her either. So he simply held out his jacket again.

"Please come here and put this on, Joy. I will do anything you want me to do. Just please stop this foolishness."

She took a step toward him. Then another. Then she ran into his arms like she was five again. He hugged her so tightly she let out a whimper.

"I'm sorry," she whispered. "I've made a mess of everything."

"You're okay. That's all that matters." He slipped the jacket on her and zipped it up. This time, she didn't protest. Then he wrapped his arms around her, feeling the warmth of her breath on his chest, drinking in the smell of her, something halfway between vanilla and bubble gum.

They stood like that a long time watching the sun dip below the gray hillsides of trees. The lake, so welcoming earlier, had a blackness to it now, a cold and unforgiving depth. Streamers of clouds threaded the sky. Vega laced his fingers in Joy's and wordlessly guided her down the bluff and back toward the parking lot. It would have been so easy just to drive her home without mentioning any of this again. But Jimmy Vega was a cop through and through, just as Louie Greco had said. He couldn't go against what he knew was right. He wished he were still enough of a Catholic to believe in salvation from such things. Even so, he had to try.

In the truck, he pulled out his phone and brought her e-mail up on the screen. Then he pushed "delete" without reading it.

"I want the truth from your lips, *Chispita*. Not this."

"But you already know."

"I need to hear it from you."

Joy stared out the side window. She tugged on her fingers inside his oversized jacket, a habit she'd had since she was little when she was nervous.

"Kenny didn't mean to kill her. It was dark and the road was narrow—"

"Was he texting?"

"No." Her breath fogged up the side window. She traced a finger across the condensation. "Maybe he was changing stations on the radio," she admitted. "But we tried to save her, Dad. We performed CPR and everything. She was already dead. And then it just snowballed, I guess. Kenny got hysterical. He said the immigration authorities would send him back to Mexico, maybe send his whole family, on account of how angry people already were about what happened to that woman and her little girl."

Vega didn't have the heart to tell Joy that no police agency could have summarily deported the entire Cardenas family for an infraction only Kenny had committed. He didn't want to compound her misery.

"I just thought if we could make her—you know—sort of—disappear," said Joy. "Maybe all the problems would too."

In halting words that trailed off and sometimes died in her chest, Joy spilled out the story of how she and Kenny dragged Maria's body into the bushes to hide it, then drove to Kenny's house and picked up some of his father's landscaping rope, then drove back to the lake, tied rope around Maria's limbs, and weighted each rope with a stone.

Joy didn't know that her father had already seen the muddy, blood-spattered T-shirt, jeans, and rope in Adele's garage. Vega wanted her to *choose* to come forward, not to feel trapped into doing so. And besides, the clothing and ropes would convict Kenny but the letter would convict Joy. Even before she admitted to writing it, Vega had the sense that she was the one doing all the planning, the one clever enough and calm enough to realize that if the police ever found the body, they might trace it back to a collision—unless they found that hate note in her discarded handbag. And it was Joy who understood that they needed to put Vega's car on the tracks so that the damage from the train would obscure any damage from the hit and run. By the time they'd accomplished all of this, a couple of hours had gone by and Joy was sober enough to pass the Breathalyzer when the police showed up. Also, her nervous demeanor would have made perfect sense considering the condition of Vega's car.

Vega tried to ask the questions he would ask in any police interrogation. He tried to divorce himself from the fact that this was his daughter. But he couldn't escape a taste of something bitter and metallic at the back of his throat. This couldn't be the girl who used to beg him to check for monsters under her bed. When did she stop believing in monsters? When did she become one?

"Joy—do you understand how serious this crime is? Kenny killed a woman and that's terrible enough. But then you treated her death like she was some sort of broken cookie jar you could sweep under a rug."

Joy buried her face in her hands. "I didn't want this to ruin his life."

"So you sacrificed yours?"

A quiet came over both of them after that. It was the quiet after an explosion when everything that could have happened has happened already. Vega rested his hand on top of hers and gave it a squeeze.

"That's why you and Kenny need to turn yourselves in."

"Can't you just—not tell what you know?"

Vega shook his head. "I'm a police officer, Joy. I can't turn my back on the law, on everything I believe in. And neither can you. It's what's eating you alive. And it will keep eating you alive until you and Kenny own up to it."

"What will happen to us?"

Vega let out a long breath of air. There was despair in the exhale, and frustration too. Things didn't have to be this way. "I don't know. I don't want to give you false promises because it's not up to me. It's up to a judge and the DA's office. But it's always better if you turn yourself in rather than let the police come after you."

"But this time, you're saying, they might deport Kenny."

"Again, I don't know. I can't say." He could not bring himself to tell her that Kenny's chances of getting deported were infinitely higher for not having come forward after the accident.

"Then I'll tell the police I was driving. It's what I wrote in my e-mail. No one can prove otherwise."

"Do you understand what you're suggesting? You're talking about lying to the police in a criminal investigation. And for what? For a boy who is here illegally? A boy who could get deported no matter what you do?"

"But I love him."

"Does he love you?"

"Yes."

"Then he'd never ask you to lie for him. Or throw yourself off a cliff for him or any of those things you seem to think are love. You are seventeen years old, *Chispita*. You still have your whole life ahead of you. Don't throw it away like this."

On the drive back, Joy cried silently in the truck. When Vega reached for her, she shrank from his touch. She unzipped his jacket and flung it at him. "I don't want this anymore." The pull on the zipper grazed his cheek. He welcomed the sting. At least it allowed him to feel something besides this unbearable numbness.

The lights blazed inside the white-columned house when Vega pulled into the driveway. Wendy was home. "Do you want me to come in and speak to your mother?"

"No. I'll tell her."

Vega had a sudden panicked thought. "She doesn't know, does she?"

"No," said Joy. "Why? Do you want to arrest her, too?"

"I don't want to arrest anybody. I just want to know what you're going to tell her."

"That you're going to arrest me if I don't turn myself in. And Kenny, too."

"I'm not going to arrest you. I'm going to resign from the investigation and help you through this."

She opened the door of the truck and stepped out. The bright lights on the driveway framed a halo around her raven hair. She was so young. So beautiful. It hurt to look at her, hurt to know he was scraping the shiny silver plating off her life, asking her to summon whatever steel she had beneath. Then again, judging from what she'd confessed tonight, she had a fair amount of steel in her already—more than he would have guessed.

Vega leaned over. "Joy, listen to me. Your life went into the water along with Maria's that night in March. You can keep pretending that that's not true. Or you can face what you've done, try to make amends, and get back to living. I can't do that for you. You have to do it for yourself. But you don't have to do it alone. I'll help you through whatever's in store."

"And what about Kenny?"

Vega had no answer.

"I thought not." She slammed the car door and walked across the driveway. Vega waited for her to look back, but she didn't. He heard the side door shut. There was a finality to it, an echo that he wondered if he would identify as regret one day, years from now, when he thought back on this moment, when he asked himself whether he'd done the right thing and heard only that echo in reply.

# Chapter 32

Four days later, Jimmy Vega stood in an airless court-room and watched Joy and Kenny, both pale and shaky, stand before a judge and admit in tiny voices the totality of their crimes. Cesar Cardenas wailed when Kenny pleaded guilty to driving the car that killed Maria Elena Santos and concealing the accident. Vega had never heard a noise so anguished—like the bark of a sea lion. He himself had managed only a little better at the sound of Joy's own guilty pleas, biting hard on the inside of his cheek to keep from losing it completely as the counts against both teenagers were read.

Both the lawyers and the families agreed that the relationship between Joy and Kenny had to end for each to be adequately represented. Kenny's family yanked him out of Lake Holly High and enrolled him in the county vocational school for his final few months before the June court date; Wendy got Joy into a small private girls' school in Connecticut. Vega supposed he had known all along that this would happen. But he had never spelled it out to Joy. And for this reason, she felt angry and deceived. She blamed her father for the breakup and punished him by refusing all contact. He had saved her, perhaps. But to do it, he'd had to lose her. He sent her her grandmother's pearl earrings that he'd promised her, hoping that this small gift might heal the divide. She never responded.

At night, he woke up in a cold sweat, trembling at the thought that Joy might go to prison. That was certainly more possible than college at this point. Amherst had withdrawn its offer of admission to Joy as Binghamton had to Kenny. Their lives were on hold until June.

Vega resigned from the investigation and, with Captain Waring's blessing, buried himself in paperwork following up leads on other detectives' cases. He didn't return phone calls. Not from friends. Not from Greco. Not even from Adele. After Joy and Kenny turned themselves in, Vega had had to confess to Greco about the box of Kenny's bloody clothes and ropes in Adele's garage. If Adele hadn't hated him enough for destroying Kenny before this, she surely did after the police got a search warrant and tore apart her garage.

Greco tried to stay in touch. He cornered Vega on the phone to give him updates on Porter's trial as well as those of Rowland's pals, Delaney and Giordano. He filled him in on Linda's condition; she was walking again, albeit on crutches. Olivia, all healed up, was back at school. But that didn't change the fact that he and Greco were playing for opposing teams now—Greco working to prosecute Joy, Vega trying to defend her and neither of them allowed to discuss it. So he listened politely and offered the requisite yeses and nos until Greco got off the phone. He was relieved when the calls stopped after a couple of weeks.

Then one day at work, about four weeks after Joy's arraignment, a county detective dropped a large manila envelope on Vega's desk.

"A woman just left this with the desk sergeant for you."

Vega opened the envelope and tipped out a black cotton shirt—the *guayabera* he'd worn to Gabby Martinez's *quinceañera*—along with a note:

La Casa is moving. I'm cleaning things out.
Thought perhaps you might want this.
Toss it if you don't—Adele.

Vega wasn't surprised at the cold tone of the note. He'd never apologized for what happened to her garage. He should have. He'd been so caught up in his own pain; he'd never considered anyone else's.

"Is she still here?"

The other detective shrugged. "Don't know. I think she was headed back to her car."

Vega sprinted down the cement-block corridor and out to the visitors' lot. He caught sight of Adele scanning the last row of cars for her Prius. A faint spring breeze fanned the asphalt and billowed the sleeves of her red silk blouse. *Red.* He wondered if she'd chosen that color on purpose.

"Hey Adele, wait up!" He gave her his best cop voice. Lots of confidence. He wished he felt it right now.

She turned and lifted her dark sunglasses as he trotted over. The hesitation in her eyes made him stop short. He knew he looked terrible. His tie was badly knotted. He'd cut himself shaving this morning. He was at work before he noticed he was wearing one black sock and one blue.

"Thanks for the shirt," he said breathlessly. "Listen, I'm sorry about that search warrant. But honest, I had no choice—"

"I'm aware of that," said Adele. "You're a police officer. You had knowledge of a crime. I could not expect you to remain silent about evidence you'd uncovered." She was using her courtroom voice: cool and logical. He'd have almost preferred her to be mad at him. It made her feel a million miles away.

"So—you're not sore at me then?"

She let out a long exhale. "Let it go, Jimmy." He'd hurt her. He could see it in her eyes and lips, the way the muscles refused to yield to him as they once had so easily. He didn't want to leave things this way.

"Look, Adele," he said, running a hand nervously through his hair. He needed a haircut. Then again, who was likely to notice these days? His life consisted of desk duty and sleep and neither required an audience. "I didn't call because you deserve better than I can give you right now."

She tossed off a laugh. "How come men only say that when they're trying to get *out* of a relationship? Have you ever heard some sixty-year-old with a thirty-year-old bride say, 'She deserved better'?"

"You got a point," he said, smiling sadly. He tried to change the subject. "You wrote that La Casa is moving. Did you find a new property to lease?"

"Property is too kind a word." She pulled a snapshot out of her shoulder bag and handed it to Vega. "Welcome to the new headquarters of La Casa."

The photograph showed a one-story concrete-block

warehouse that abutted the railroad tracks at the north end of town. Graffiti covered two of the outer walls. Fast-food wrappers and cigarette butts moldered in the weeds. The front path was littered with broken bottles that sparkled liked chipped ice.

"You're taking over the old fish wholesaler's?" Vega couldn't hide his shock. "That place hasn't been used in like—"

"Six years, I know. It's going to need a ton of work inside and out but we've got no choice."

"You lost your lease on the other building?"

Adele nodded. "So I've had to clean out the center, get rid of everything we don't need. The band member who wore that shirt I gave you took a job in New Jersey and isn't coming back. I figured perhaps you could use it."

"Don't think I'll be invited to any *quinceañeras* any-time soon." He hated the way that came out—whiny and self-pitying. He decided to back off before he made a complete idiot of himself. "I'm waiting on a phone call for a case," he lied. "It was good to see you, Adele." He started to walk away.

"You didn't fail her the way you think you did."

He turned. "Who?"

"Your daughter."

"You don't know my daughter."

"I know she went to the Bronx last week to visit your mother's grave."

"What?" He walked up to her. "Who told you that?"

"Father Delgado. At Saint Raymond's in the Bronx. He's an old friend of mine. He knew your mother, I be-lieve."

Vega gave Adele a quizzical look. She shrugged.

"It's not every day he meets a girl from Lake Holly wandering around his neighborhood in Ugg boots and Guess jeans looking for her grandmother's grave and the building she used to live in. He was bound to call."

"*Joy?* Wandering around *the Bronx?*" He was surprised his daughter could even find her way to her *abuelita's* old neighborhood. She must have remembered more about those childhood visits than he'd realized.

"Anyway," said Adele, fishing through her bag for her keys. "I thought you should know." She opened her car door.

"Wait." He put a hand on the sleeve of her blouse. The warmth of her body traveled like a current through his own. "I'll never wear that shirt—"

"Then give it away—"

"I was gonna say—" He took a deep breath. "I'll never wear that shirt unless I can wear it with you."

He tucked a hand under her chin and lifted it so that their eyes met. "So," he said, "it's your call. Want to give it a try? I'm good for mouse-catching if nothing else."

She grinned. "I think I can find better uses for your talents."

# Chapter 33

Autumn was a tease in New York. Sun-baked and vine-ripened. Tented in a canopy of red and gold. All summer, the land had been a chorus of green. Now suddenly each tree and bush wanted a solo and every note could be heard.

In Lake Holly, nearly every doorstep groaned with the weight of a pumpkin. The shop windows were decorated with witches and ghosts and skeins of fake spider webs. There were baskets of mums and purplish cabbage plants by the train station. Not that Jimmy Vega spent much time strolling Lake Holly these days. When he wasn't working in the southern part of the county or at his own house, he was at Adele's. Helping her, he believed. Hiding, some might say. In the summer, he replaced the rotting floorboards on her front porch. In September, he rehung a couple of her doors. He was only good these days with things he could hold in his hands: a hammer, a saw, his guitar, at night, her forgiving flesh. He made love to her with an urgency he hadn't felt in years, as if only by feeling the heat and sweat of her body could he prove he was still alive.

There were things Adele didn't understand about him. But this one she seemed to: he needed to escape what he could not control.

The court date, originally set for June, ended up being pushed back until July. During a record heat wave, Vega sat in the back of the courtroom, sweating through his suit jacket the same way he had before a judge all those years ago. So steeled was he to accept the bad news, that he almost missed the good. Joy's lawyer had been able to bargain the charges against her down to a misdemeanor. She was given a one-year suspended sentence, six months community service, and three years probation.

He had expected her to forgive him when it was over. Even if Amherst was out, she could still enroll in the local two-year college, complete her community service, and figure out what her future held from there. But for Joy, it was never about what happened to her. It was about Kenny and for Kenny, the U.S. legal system was an entirely different animal.

Adele found the boy a good attorney who took the case pro bono and managed to convince the judge to give Kenny a three-year suspended sentence—lenient by all accounts. The problem—always the problem— was his immigration status. Jail or not, Kenny Cardenas had still been convicted of a felony, which automatically triggered an ICE hold. As soon as the case was over, he was remanded into federal custody and deported back to Mexico. The last Vega had heard from Adele, Kenny had moved in with his grandparents in a rural mountain village in Guerrero where he knew almost no one and couldn't find work beyond the level of a field hand.

Joy blamed her father, and Vega, unable to bear even one more shred of guilt, retreated. He stopped calling, stopped even trying to make contact with her. Instead, he kept his hands busy, kept his mind blank, and accepted the seasons as they rolled into one another, hoping to find comfort in the passage of time.

One Friday afternoon in early October, Vega went to the hardware store on the highway to buy a few new roofing shingles to replace some missing ones on Adele's garage. He could have bought them down at Bobby Rowland's store but Vega couldn't bring himself to face his old friend since Matt's death. He did a lot of avoiding these days.

By the time he returned, Adele was already home from work. Her Prius was parked in the driveway and another car was parked behind it, a fat-ass white Buick that looked like a roll of toilet paper on wheels. It took up Vega's space on the driveway and forced him to park across the street and walk back over with his package of roofing shingles. The white Buick wasn't the sort of car anyone he knew would drive. But he knew whom it belonged to the moment the driver's door opened and he heard Frankie Valli and the Four Seasons crooning, "Oh, What a Night." He knew only one person who would listen to a bunch of over-the-hill Italians singing about the one time they got lucky over half a century ago.

Louie Greco hitched up his pants as he stepped out of his white Buick. He fetched a red licorice stick out of a bag in his pocket, shoved it into the side of his mouth, and walked up to Vega. He eyed the package of roofing shingles in Vega's hands.

"I think she'll let you stick around whether or not you fix her roof, you know."

"Keeps me busy."

Greco offered up a knowing smile. "I'll just bet she does." Vega hadn't spoken to the man since those few awkward calls soon after he resigned from the investigation. He had to admit he was glad to see him. They hadn't started out as friends, but somewhere along the line Greco had grown on Vega, like an old jacket you don't care about until you discover it's missing.

Vega put the package of shingles down on the edge of the driveway and shook Greco's hand. His hair was thinner, his waist thicker. Vega wondered if the case had taken a toll on him as well. "How are you doing?"

"Just passed my thirtieth anniversary with the department."

"Congratulations."

Greco made a sound like an engine on low throttle. "Way I see it, if I'd killed the bastards instead of working for them, I'd be out on parole by now, a free man. Free health coverage all those years, too."

"Yeah, but look at all the fun you'd have missed."

"Thrill a minute. Which reminds me . . ." Greco pulled a sealed plastic bag out of his pants pocket and held it out to Vega. "Here. Got a present for you. From your people at the county crime lab. They released this evidence a couple of days ago to the Lake Holly PD to return to its rightful owner. I thought perhaps you could do a good deed with it, earn your Eagle Scout badge or something."

Vega took the bag from Greco's hands. He recognized the silver cross with the tarnished bird-wing *milagros* dangling from each side. He frowned. "Why are you giving Maria's cross to me? She's already buried in Guatemala and I'm not in touch with her mother anymore."

"I know," said Greco. "But the old lady's in Lake Holly for a couple of weeks with that grandson you spoke to."

"They are?"

Greco nodded. "They're staying with Linda Porter. She got a special visa for them to meet Olivia. It can't make up for nine and a half years. But hey, it's a start."

If Vega had thought he'd had it tough these past six months, it was nothing compared to Linda. Scott was in prison, disbarred and sentenced to twenty-two months for obstruction of justice. He'd never be able to work as a lawyer or with the immigrant community again. And then there was the accident, which had left Linda with a permanent limp. Yet the few times Vega had seen her around town, she'd seemed surprisingly upbeat. The whole tragedy had opened up a part of her daughter's past that had been hidden until now. Instead of fearing this connection, Linda seemed to embrace it. Vega wondered how very different things would have been had Porter simply told his wife the truth when Maria first came to see him. Perhaps they could have found common ground. It was too late now to ever know.

"Why don't you give the cross to Maria's mother yourself?" asked Vega.

Greco took a bite of his licorice and chewed slowly. "Thought it would be better if it came from you and Kenny and Joy."

"Hey, news flash, Grec: Kenny's in Mexico and Joy and I aren't speaking."

"News flash, yourself: Kenny's in Lake Holly. Got back about a week ago."

"*What?* Legally?"

"He wasn't legal the first time. Now he's a felon with a three-year suspended sentence hanging over his head. What? You think he hopped the red-eye to JFK?"

No, and the realization filled Vega with guilt. He slumped against the side of Greco's Buick. Kenny Cardenas, barely eighteen years of age, had made a nightmare journey through the blistering desert. He'd crammed his body inside some coffinlike compartment in a sweltering trailer. He'd run and hidden from men with guns and flak vests who saw him as little more than dung to be scraped off the soles of their boots. Kenny's journey couldn't have been all that different from the ones Rodrigo Morales, Maria Elena Santos, and countless others before them had made. The boy might have started out as an innocent when he first turned himself in to the Lake Holly police. But if detention and deportation hadn't stripped away that thin veneer of boyhood, crossing the border surely did.

"You're not going to arrest him, are you?"

"Nobody officially *told* the PD he's in Lake Holly. So—kid keeps his nose clean, who's to say we know he's here?"

Vega gave him a surprised look. Greco touched his chest. "I'm not the hard-ass you think I am. Our guys have better things to do than to hassle the kid. But ultimately, Lake Holly's too small for him to stick around in and not get noticed. He's here until his family can scrape together enough money to ship him off to some other part of the country where he can make a fresh start. Not college or a green card or anything like that, of course. He's probably fucked up forever any chance of being legal. But maybe—I don't know—he can build some sort of life for himself."

"Not the life he'd had in mind."

"Hey, how many of us *ever* get the life we'd had in mind?" Greco clapped a meaty paw on Vega's shoulder. "You didn't do this to him, man. That's what I kept trying to tell you back in April but you didn't want to hear it. We'd have caught up with him and your daughter sooner or later."

"Just like you caught up with Brendan Delaney and Eddie Giordano?"

Greco gave Vega a pained look. "You heard about that, huh?" In August, a clerical error at the county jail caused the charges against Luis Guzman to be dropped. ICE deported Guzman back to Guatemala before Lake Holly could hold him as a witness. Without Guzman to testify, the DA's office was forced to drop the case. Delaney and Giordano walked on all charges.

Greco sighed. "If it's any consolation, Maria was higher profile. And Porter wasn't good for it. We'd have kept searching until something clicked."

Vega looked down at the cross in the plastic bag, still encrusted with dirt just the way he'd found it that afternoon by the side of Lake Holly Road. "I don't know what you think I'm supposed to do here. My daughter's not going to listen to anything I have to say. She hates me."

"Huh. Shows what you know." Greco trudged up Adele's front porch steps, and banged on her door. The figure that opened it made Vega's breath stop in his chest. She peeked around the side of Greco and blinked the way she used to as a toddler when she'd just woken up from a long nap.

"Dad?"

She looked different somehow. Less girlish. Her cheekbones were more defined. Her bangs had grown out and she'd started wearing her hair in a loose side ponytail that trailed like blackstrap molasses down her shoulder.

Vega walked to the bottom of the porch stairs and stopped.

"Hey." His voice caught. He could feel the uncertainty in his pitch. He was still clutching the plastic bag with the crucifix. He held it the way he used to hold carnival bags filled with goldfish that he won for Joy. He was holding something fragile and precious, something he knew he had to keep alive between them.

She walked across the porch and down the front steps until they were face to face. She was dressed in one of his old police sweatshirts that rode halfway down her thighs. He'd had so many conversations in his head with her these past six months that now that she was in front of him, he couldn't think of a single thing to say.

He swallowed hard. "I've missed you."

He opened his arms and she fell into them with the force of gravity. Something warm and carbonated burbled in his chest, a sensation he recognized as hope. He hadn't lost her. Whatever else, he hadn't lost her.

"I've missed you, too," she whispered in a voice that brought to mind the girl he used to dab witch hazel on doorknobs for. "I want to try to make things better. With you. With Maria's family tonight."

"Are you sure you're ready for that?"

"No. But I don't think I'll ever be ready for such a thing."

Greco lumbered down the porch steps. "If it's all set, I'm outta here." He patted Vega on the arm. "You want some advice?"

"I think I'm gonna get it anyway."

"We don't get a lot of chances in our line of work to put the pieces back together. You got one now. With your daughter. With these people. Take it."

Greco opened his car door and regarded Vega over the hood. "Don't be a stranger. At least, not any stranger than you already are." He got back in his car and pulled out of the driveway, trailing doo-wop and exhaust.

Vega watched him go, his arms around his daughter. Then he brushed back a loose strand of her hair and noticed for the first time the delicate pearl earrings she was wearing.

"Are those Abuelita's?"

"Yes," said Joy. "I wear them all the time. It makes me feel like she's with me."

"She is, *Chispita.*" He laced a hand in hers and led her up the stairs. "She's with us both."

Rodrigo Morales bought a dozen pink roses from the Asian grocery store across from the train station in Lake Holly. Tiny buds with some sort of feathery green ferns around the stems. They cost him twelve dollars plus tax and the owner of the store never smiled at him once while he was counting out his money. They were both immigrants to this country. Sometimes he wondered why immigrants didn't treat each other better.

Still, he liked the soft, velvety feel of the rose petals between his fingers, the way they reminded him of the touch of Maria's skin, of those nights at the lake when they reached out for something comforting and familiar in the darkness and found each other. He had thought it was lust that had driven him into her arms. But he recognized the sensation as closer to longing. He was here and he wanted to be in Esperanza. He wanted to hear Triza's whippoorwill voice drifting from an open window. He wanted Stephany on his shoulders and Juliza and Lorenzo walking beside him, talking his ears off. He wanted to taste the dust in the square, the ripe mangoes in the marketplace, the salty sweat on his wife's skin after they made love.

Soon, he told himself. He had worked hard this season—seven days a week most weeks. His hands were so callused that when he tried to sew a loose button on his shirt, he could not feel the needle between his fingers. He was working regularly for one landscaping contractor but he also did some work for another man who paved driveways and built stone walls. Both of the contractors were Latin Americans and while they worked him hard, they were fair. He had paid back the cost of coming here, kept food on his family's table, and provided money for his children to go to school. He had saved up enough in rent to survive the winter. Another year or two or maybe three and there would be enough to return home. He hoped he wasn't lying to himself. He'd met men on his first journey to Lake Holly five years ago who told him they were headed back home for good after the season. On his return journey, they were still here, still vowing to leave.

He had wanted to do this trip to the lake by himself,

but that was impossible. The reservoir was too far to hike to after work. He was too tired. Most days, he worked too late to consider such a journey. It would have been pitch black by the time he arrived. Besides, knowing what he knew now, he felt it only fitting that Olivia accompany him. So one day, when it was too wet to work outside and Señora Linda had hired him for some small projects around her house, he asked if she might consider driving him and Olivia to the reservoir some late afternoon to say a prayer for Maria.

He was nervous making such a request. Neither of them had ever spoken about what had happened, though it was an open secret that Porter was in prison and Olivia was Maria's child. Many of the immigrants Rodrigo knew spoke against the Porters in private. Neither of the Porters had anything to do with La Casa anymore. Still, Rodrigo felt for Señora Linda. He knew she had suffered, both physically and emotionally. He knew she loved Olivia and that she had brought Maria's mother and nephew all the way from Guatemala to visit. In the end, Maria wasn't dead for anything Señora Linda or her husband did anyway. It was an accident—an accident that Cesar Cardenas's boy would probably be paying for for the rest of his life.

And so one day in late October when work was cancelled because of bad weather and the rain had finally let up, Rodrigo bought his roses and he and Olivia and Señora Linda headed over to the reservoir. They were quiet in the car. Olivia was listening to her iTouch. She had asked to hold the roses and Rodrigo urged her to be careful of the thorns.

Rodrigo looked out the car window at the scenery passing by. For all the work he did on people's yards, he seldom took the time to appreciate the landscape. He saw leaves as something that needed to be blown or raked or bagged. He saw branches and tree limbs as appendages that needed cutting. A stretch of green was something to weed or mow. Now, looking out the window, he found himself captivated by the colors and textures before him. The deep scarlet of a Japanese maple. The billowy bright yellow of a tulip tree against the dark gray sky. The feathery defiance of a grove of spruces that would remain green all winter.

He knew the names of trees and plants here now. He felt an affinity for them. This would never be his home. The *Norte Americanos* would never let it be, nor could it be, really. But he felt some measure of ownership all the same. He could point to stairways and stone walls and patios he'd helped build, driveways he'd resurfaced, bushes and trees he'd planted that would grow in stature long after he was gone. He had staked a claim, however small, on this patch of New York. It was not home, no. But it was not entirely foreign anymore, either.

"You must think Scott and I are terrible people," Señora Linda said after a long spell of silence. Her voice was so unexpected, Rodrigo jumped.

"I don't think that."

"But Maria must have."

"I don't know what she thought. She never told me. She would have been very sad, yes. But you are doing what you can now."

"Her death touched so many lives."

"I think," said Rodrigo, "she would have preferred to think her life touched so many lives."

"Her life, yes," Señora Linda agreed.

At the lake, Olivia scampered ahead with the roses

while Rodrigo clutched Señora Linda's elbow and gently guided her across the slick leaves and dropped acorns that rolled like marbles beneath her unsteady feet. Since the accident, she'd needed a cane to walk. He suspected she might always need one from now on.

"I'm sorry," she apologized, her gait awkward and slow.

"You are doing fine."

"I wish things were the way they used to be."

"I find," he said slowly, trying to put his thoughts into words, "it is better to look for beauty in the way things are." So much of Rodrigo's life he'd had to hold with open arms. He'd learned not to hold on to anything too tightly—especially, the past.

At the edge of the lake, Rodrigo, Señora Linda, and Olivia pulled the pink petals off the roses until they each had two fistfuls. They floated them on the water while Rodrigo said an Ave Maria softly in Spanish. Olivia blew her petals like little sailboats. Some gathered in a pocket along the shoreline but others drifted on the tin-colored surface until they had scattered far and wide, until the waning light showed only their cupped outlines bobbing across the water.

Olivia stood in front of Señora Linda and rested her head in the crook of her arm until a deep chill settled down over them and the trees lost their definition in the fading light. The little girl played with her earlobes. Rodrigo suddenly remembered Maria doing that. And he thought with a smile that Maria had staked her claim on this land too.

"We should go," said Rodrigo. "The child is cold."

They walked more slowly now, even Olivia. Above,

a flock of gray-white birds called out across the milky sky. Maybe they were headed south, to a place half-remembered and half-envisioned, a place where warm winds would welcome them and hold them in their embrace. Rodrigo hoped they would find their way. He hoped in time, they would all find their way.

# Acknowledgments

This book grew out of a desire to tell the stories of real people who live their lives with courage and dignity as undocumented immigrants. I am forever grateful to the men and women who shared their experiences with me: Adolfo, Amanda, Ana, Carmen, Enrique N., Enrique P., Gabriela Monroy, Gonzalo Cruz, Higinio, Maria Luisa, Marlla Sanchez, Minerva, J. Nelson Arboleda, Ovidio, and Raul. I have been moved to tears by their accounts of harrowing journeys, desperate partings, and unwavering determination in the face of incredible odds. I hope this book does justice to their stories.

I am grateful to Professor Louise Yelin and the Purchase College Writers Center for their fellowship grant that enabled me to start this project; to John Gitlitz, professor of Political Science and Latin American Studies at Purchase, for his careful read of my manuscript; and to Ileana Savvides who helped with all my early interviews as both translator and editor.

My deepest thanks to Graciela Heymann, executive director of the Westchester Hispanic Coalition who provided help and support on so many fronts. I couldn't have done this project without her.

On the legal/medical front, I am very grateful to Westchester County Medical Examiner Dr. Kunjlata Ashar for her forensic expertise and attorney Theodora Saal for sharing her understanding of the legal issues facing the undocumented. I would also like to thank

380     *Suzanne Chazin*

Westchester County Police Department detectives Captain Christopher Calabrese and Lt. James Palanzo for their help on county police matters and Detective Sgt. James Wilson of the New Castle Police Department for insights at the local policing level.

I'm grateful to my agent, Stephany Evans, for her unwavering support on this project—and for dragging me into twenty-first-century technology! Thanks also to Rosemary Ahern for her keen eye in helping to shape this story early. And a special thank you to my editor at Kensington, Michaela Hamilton, for seeing the book's potential and to her assistant, Norma Perez-Hernandez, for advocating early for it.

My thanks most of all to the people who give me encouragement when I need it most: my husband, Thomas Dunne; my children, Kevin and Erica; and Bill Hayes, Sol Chazin, Gene West, and Janis Pomerantz who have been there over the long, long haul.

Don't miss the next Jimmy Vega novel

by Suzanne Chazin

A BLOSSOM OF BRIGHT LIGHT

Coming from Kensington Publishing Corp. in 2015

Keep reading to enjoy a teaser excerpt . . .

# Chapter 1

There are decisions you make in life without realizing you are making them. They don't even seem like decisions at all until you're suddenly bounding along, breathless as a husky in the snow, farther and farther from some elusive fork in the road where it all could have been different.

Had he seen the fork or even had an inkling it was there, Jimmy Vega could have saved so many things that night. His relationship. His conscience. A life. Had he thought with his head instead of points considerably farther south, he would have chosen far differently. It would have changed everything—because it wouldn't have changed anything at all.

It was a Saturday evening in late October, a time when the trees flame with color and the leaf peepers form conga lines on the highways heading north from New York City. There was talk of a dusting of snow in the forecast. Lights flicked on early from windows decorated with carved pumpkins and paper ghosts cut by children itching for Halloween.

Normally Vega would have clocked in at work by

now, but he'd switched tours with Teddy Dolan so Dolan could take his kids to their adoption agency's fall dinner tomorrow. Normally Vega's girlfriend of five months, Adele Figueroa, would be fetching her nine-year-old daughter from gymnastics, but Sophia's best friend had begged the girl to sleep over. As a result, a rare and beautiful thing opened up on their calendars: a whole fourteen hours to spend together. Alone.

They knew how they were going to spend it, too. A log in Adele's fireplace. Chinese takeout. Coronas and limes. Marc Anthony and Shakira on the stereo. The evening stretched out before them like a vast blue ocean waiting to be explored.

One minute, Adele was sitting with Vega in her funky, adobe-colored dining room, holding a fortune cookie playfully out of his reach, breaking off bits of it and rolling them around oh-so-suggestively on her tongue. The next, her phone was ringing in the kitchen, harsh and insistent. It was eight p.m. They'd been together just over an hour.

*"Puñeta!"* Vega slumped in his chair, the air suddenly gone out of him. He always fell into the Puerto Rican street vernacular of his youth when he got frustrated.

Adele rose and shot him a warning look. "It could be Sophia, you know." Vega had to remind himself that they were on different sides of the parenting divide. Vega's daughter, Joy, was eighteen, a freshman at the community college. He'd have fallen off his chair if she'd called him on a Saturday night.

It wasn't Sophia. It was Rafael, the evening manager at La Casa, the Latino community center Adele had founded ten years ago and given up a promising law career to keep afloat. Not to mention her waste of a Harvard degree.

Vega could hear Rafael's panicked, rapid-fire Spanish through the receiver. Something about Jazmin, his six-year-old daughter. It sounded like she'd gotten hurt.

"Oh my goodness," said Adele. "Do you think the thumb is broken? Can she move it?"

Vega already had an idea where this conversation was headed. He blocked the doorway of the kitchen and waved furiously at her like she was standing on a cliff, about to jump.

"You're not covering Rafael's shift tonight, Adele. Tell him to close the center early if he has to take Jazmin to the emergency room."

Adele ducked under Vega's arms and walked back into the dining room. The table was littered with half-empty takeout cartons and palm-sized packages of soy sauce. Two brightly painted Mexican candlesticks sat among the ruins, their tapered candles still glowing with promise. She leaned over and blew them out. Ribbons of smoke curled from their snuffed wicks. Just like Vega's evening—up in smoke.

She spoke into the phone. "Did you try Luis? Is he available to take the shift?"

More panicked words from Rafael. Adele turned her back. "Of course you have to go. Can he speak to me tomorrow?" Vega had a sense this wasn't just about Jazmin anymore.

"Close the center," he said again.

Adele ignored him. "So is Zambo there now?"

*Zambo.* That was all Vega needed to hear.

"Oh no. No way, Adele. You're not going in for that drunk." All the cops and social workers in the area had

Zambo stories, and as a county detective, Vega had heard every one. Zambo wasn't his real name. Vega didn't even know his real name. Everyone just called him Zambo, short for *patizambo*—"bowlegged"—in Spanish. He was a homeless alcoholic from someplace in Central America with a penchant for religious delusions and a long string of petty misdemeanors that never quite rose to the level of deportable offenses. Vega was betting he'd just walked into La Casa with some new claim that God had personally singled him out for something other than an extra case of communion wine.

More chatter from Rafael.

"Zambo says he just saw Jesus." Adele listened, then corrected herself. "The baby Jesus. In the arms of the Virgin Mary. In the woods behind La Casa."

"*Coño!*" Vega cursed loudly enough for Rafael to hear. "Every time that mutt gets a couple of drinks in him, he thinks God's sending him an Instagram." Some of the local cops took bets on where Zambo would have a religious delusion next. Once he claimed the Virgin Mary spoke to him from behind the Slurpee dispenser at the Subway on Main Street. Another time, he saw Her at the laundromat over on Sunset. He considered the Mobil gas station owned by two turbaned Sikhs to be sacred property because he saw the head of Jesus in an oil stain there.

Oddly, Zambo never seemed to see Jesus or Mary in church. Then again, Vega had spent years as an altar boy, and he'd never had anything that would qualify as a religious experience in church either.

"Tell him to lay off the extrastrength lagers," Vega called out.

Adele's mouth went slack. She slid a glance in Vega's direction. He expected annoyance. He was behaving like a child. If she chewed him out later, he'd take his lumps without complaint. But what he saw instead stopped him cold. Not anger. Or frustration. Or any emotion with a shred of heat in it. No. There was something more tepid and sad in the watery set of her big, chestnut-colored eyes, the slight downturn in her full lips, the slow exhale from her chest. This was disappointment. And it sliced right through him because he understood that this was not the first time lately she'd given him that look. It had been building. Somewhere in the dim recesses of his subconscious, he knew that. But he hadn't realized it fully until now.

Nothing had been said, of course. It was telegraphed in her shortened embraces, the way she no longer sent little "thinking of you" texts, or returned his with only *x*s or smiley faces at the bottom. Sometimes he'd catch her lost in thought. He'd tense and wait, but the words never came. People brought their troubles to Adele. Adele brought her troubles to no one—sadly, not even to him. Maybe because he was the source.

She cradled the phone to her ear and grabbed some plates off the dining table. Then she walked the stack past Vega into the kitchen and dumped them into her deep, cast-iron sink. Vega grabbed the cups and bowls and followed. Adele had a dishwasher, but the sink was so big, she and Vega always did their dishes by hand. Vega loved the routine. It reminded him of when he was a little boy in the Bronx, watching his mother and grandmother in the kitchen. Just thinking about his mother brought an ache to his heart. She'd been gone eighteen months now, murdered in a botched robbery in the Bronx. The police had yet to arrest a suspect. Every month, he called the station house for an update on the case, and every month, the only thing that changed was the name of the detective in charge.

"So I take it Zambo wants to show me the spot behind La Casa where he had his vision," Adele said to Rafael over the clatter.

La Casa was only a five-minute drive from Adele's house. Taking her there was no trouble at all. But Adele wouldn't walk behind the center and come right back. She'd chat with clients and restock the copier and clean out the refrigerator and answer the half dozen emails that seemed to come in every hour at that place. And she'd be there until midnight. She might as well have kept her promising Wall Street law career for all the hours she put into that place.

Vega came up behind her and wrapped his arms around her waist. He pressed himself into her body and breathed in the scent of her—vanilla and limes and something entirely her own. He massaged the muscles on either side of her spine, then brushed her silky black hair away from her neck and ran his lips down the contours. She shivered in response. He wanted more than anything to make love to her in front of the fireplace tonight. He wanted to buy sweet rolls and strawberries in the morning and dip them in whipped cream that they'd lick off each other's lips.

He wanted her to look at him like she used to.

"Don't go, Nena," he whispered. He was the only man she'd ever let call her "baby" in Spanish. "Tonight belongs to us."

She closed her eyes and exhaled a prayer over the phone that was disguised as a question.

"You think this is just another one of his hallucinations?" she asked Rafael.

Vega wanted to tell Rafael to do what he should have done in the first place and kick Zambo out. The mutt was probably only at La Casa because it was cold out tonight. Too cold to make trouble and chance having the Lake Holly police pick him up and dump him in neighboring Wickford like they always did when he got on their nerves.

"You can talk to Zambo tomorrow," Vega whispered into her neck, his breath hot and moist on her skin.

Vega untucked Adele's blouse from her jeans and snaked a hand inside, letting his fingers tease at the elastic of her underwear. Her body grew sweaty and liquid to the touch. There was a catch in her breathing, a moment when he had her, really had her, the way he used to. He could sense the wave breaking over her. Soon she would be bobbing in the current, her thoughts pulled out with the tide. He could feel them receding in the foam, a mere blip on the horizon. In an hour, they would lie in the afterglow of their lovemaking and forget they had ever harbored any other thoughts.

*Going . . . going . . .*

She pushed his hand away.

"Fine." Vega raised his arms in a gesture of surrender. "Some drunk means more to you than I do." He stomped to the door.

"Rafael? Can you hold for just one moment? One moment, I promise." Adele put the phone down and followed Vega to the front hallway. "Jimmy, please. Something's wrong."

"No kidding."

"No, I mean with what Rafael's telling me. Zambo's never said anything quite so specific before. He called the woman he saw in the woods 'the Lady of Sorrows,' like the Catholic church in town."

"It's just another term for the Virgin Mary, Adele."

"I know that. But this doesn't sound like one of his usual rants. I feel like I should check it out."

"How 'bout what I feel? That place has got you on a chain, Nena. Every time somebody over there needs you, you go running back. I'm tired of it."

Vega grabbed his jacket from the coat tree. It was a bluff. He wasn't leaving. Not really. He'd drive her over to La Casa and sit in a corner, hunched and sulky, checking his email and playing games on his iPhone until she was ready to leave. He knew when they'd started dating last May that her life wasn't her own. He'd tried hard to be happy with whatever part she gave him. God, he'd tried. But he was a man, after all. And he wanted her. Just this once, couldn't *he* be the focus of her attentions?

Adele blinked at him. There was no disappointment for once in her gaze. Only longing. She walked over to the table and picked up the phone.

"Listen, Rafael? I—can't come in tonight. I'm sorry—I just can't. Close down the center. Tell Zambo I'll speak to him another time. I hope Jazmin's thumb isn't broken. I'll call you tomorrow, okay?"

Vega tossed his jacket back on the coat tree and scooped up Adele the moment she clicked off the call. He could barely contain his excitement as he buried his head in her chest and felt the pleasing give of her flesh. He was seventeen again, awash with the thrill of a woman's body. Awash with the thrill of Adele. "You won't regret it, Nena," he breathed into her hair, his voice husky with yearning.

Never in his life had he been more wrong.